T0277760

BLUES IN THE BLOOD

SEAGULL
BOOKS
•
CELEBRATING
40 YEARS

THE FRENCH LIST

Julien Delmaire

BLUES IN THE BLOOD

Translated by
TERESA LAVENDER FAGAN

LONDON NEW YORK CALCUTTA

PAP
TAGORE
www.bibliofrance.in

This work is published with the support of the Publication
Assistance Programmes of the Institut français

Seagull Books, 2023

First published in French as *Delta Blues* by Julien Delmaire
© Éditions Grasset & Fasquelle, 2021

First published in English translation by Seagull Books, 2023
English translation © Teresa Lavender Fagan, 2023

ISBN 978 1 80309 246 1

British Library Cataloguing-in-Publication Data
A catalogue record for this book is available from the British Library

Typeset at Seagull Books, Calcutta, India
Printed and bound in the USA by Integrated Books International

For Martine Boutang
For Nicolas Repac

In memory of Michel Le Bris

"That sound, the driving sound, always makes me see a black cat, face brilliant and sweating in the sunlight which pours down on his face, pacing, prancing, up a long, high hill."

JAMES BALDWIN
Just above My Head

"The poor people fight during the day to survive. And at night the same land is inhabited only by gods, devils, men transformed into beasts."

DANY LAFERRIÈRE
Pays sans chapeau

Contents

Translator's Note

This is an extraordinary book. The author, Julien Delmaire, an Afropean novelist, poet and spoken word artist, living in France, captures the essence of the poor Black experience in the rural south of the United States from the 1930s through World War II—in the Delta region of Mississippi, the birth-place of the blues, the unique musical expression of that experience.

When I first encountered the book as a potential trans-lation project, I jumped on the opportunity. Its title in French—*Delta Blues*—was immediately enticing. Having grown up on the South Side of Chicago in the 1970s, a semi-regular patron of the famous blues clubs the Checkerboard Lounge (the original on 43rd Street) and Theresa's Lounge, the blues have always been in my life. Buddy Guy, Junior Wells, and the countless others who performed in those tiny venues became my touchstones. To be able to share Julien Delmaire's book with an English-language audience seemed almost pre-ordained!

Blues in the Blood is a rich combination of fiction and his-torical events from the period, written in a blend of poetic, mystical, and often stark prose. There is humor as well as horror, compassion and harsh realism. Whites and Blacks are seen in three dimensions, neither race entirely sinners or saints. The author brings his characters to life, gives breath and heat to the Delta and to those who lived—and died—there. And the reader, beyond simply learning how the blues emerged from this region of pain and endurance, how it is a blend of African/slave/Christian/pagan sounds, is immersed in, infused with the Delta's aura.

Before beginning, I urge readers to listen to the music of the blues artists who appear in the book: Charley Patton, Son House, Willie Brown, Robert Johnson, Ma Rainey, and others. Look at images of these incomparable artists from the American past. And share your discoveries. The blues and its origins must never be forgotten.

TERESA LAVENDER FAGAN
Chicago, 2023

Main Characters
in Order of Appearance

LEGBA: Voodoo divinity, master of metamorphosis.

STEVE: baker's assistant, married to Betty.

BETTY: young laundress, married to Steve. Sapphira's niece.

SAPPHIRA: old sorceress and healer, Betty's aunt.

ANDREW WALLACE: rich mulatto, unrecognized bastard son of Edward Longhorn.

THEODORE MITCHELL: old, doomed Black man, electrocuted by memory.

BOBBY: Robert Johnson (1911–1938), mythical bluesman.

PEARL: young laundress, wounded but brave.

AUGUSTUS LLOYD: Baptist pastor.

DORA: singer and prostitute, mother of Joshua.

JOSHUA: called "Josh," son of Dora, adopted by Steve and Betty.

JOE HIVES: former dockworker, saloon owner.

SERGEANT ELIAS: one-eyed pianist, World War I veteran.

MISS ROSETTA BROWN: former slave, fervent Christian.

WILLIE BROWN: famous bluesman (1900–1952).

SON HOUSE: famous bluesman (1902–1988).

JAMES CONRAD: pensive landowner, district head of the Ku Klux Klan.

RICHARD THOMPSON: mayor.

AARON AND RACHEL POSNER: Jewish immigrants from Germany.

ABRAHAM: called "Abe," prisoner.

JASPER AND WADE MULLIGAN: bootleggers.

CHESTER BURNETT: aka Howlin' Wolf (1910–1976), famous bluesman.

HARRY BRADFORD: sheriff.

ANTHONY MADDEN: sheriff's deputy.

EDWARD LONGHORN: landowner, unacknowledged father of Andrew Wallace.

DOROTHY: daughter of Betty and an unknown father, adopted by Steve.

I

"Would you kill a man dead?
Yes, I will!"

CHARLEY PATTON
A Spoonful Blues

Mississippi, May 1932

Despite the avalanche of light, the knife refused to shine. A gloved hand held the handle firmly. The blade rested on a forearm, cut the radial artery, destroying nerves and tendons. No blood, O sweet Lord, not one drop.

The hand stops. The metal moves regretfully away from the flesh.

His face hidden in the shadows, he contemplates his wounded forearm and his fingers travel over the damage.

What is this gigantic body? To which kingdom does it belong? Is it dead? But why would a cadaver continue to torture itself?

A block of granite next to a ditch. He bends over and picks it up. A copperhead moccasin, furious at being uncovered, turns its angular head toward him. The crack of a whip, a sudden leap—the snake plants its fangs into the wounded arm. The animal doesn't let go when the gloved hand crushes its spine; it moves for a moment, then dangles limply, a hideous strap of scales. The knife is used again, cuts through the neck. The steel has its reward, red liquid.

He dips the blade in the dust, rubs it against the sole of his boot and puts it into its sheath. He rolls the remains of the reptile around his arm. Picks up the snake's head and attaches it to his belt.

He stares at the sun. His ashy hair falls to his shoulders, as wide as railroad ties. Is he really a man? His face reveals nothing.

The wind is dying, hoarse and dusty. He walks through a field sown with grain. The forest is getting nearer. His body is drawn to that kingdom of cool darkness. He leaves the rye field behind, continues to an oak grove into which he vanishes. The name of this creature who has just disappeared behind the trees is Legba.

Twisted branches of oblivion. A shimmer of gold flowed over the bark. Legba wasn't really sleeping, his head resting on a stump, his mind wandering. He was maddeningly thirsty. He had to lean on a tree to stand up. He remembered his mutilated arm. He untied the scaly tourniquet, dropped the reptile's remains onto a pile of dead leaves. Once again, he had overcome his pain.

Pinecones crackled under his feet. He walked through the trees, a forest pierced intermittently by rays of sun. His face was waxy, his hands brushed the junipers, the thorn bushes; sometimes his fingers squeezed a berry, releasing its acidic juice. Intermittently he would crouch down, scratch the ground in quest of tiny traces of life, then stand up again.

The cry of a bird of prey. The bird remained invisible. Through the vines Legba saw a path marked with rocks placed at regular intervals, following it he reached a clearing. The grass was a sickly yellow, it hadn't seen rain for many months. The light stunned him, he staggered and went back under the protection of the trees.

A creek wandered through the woods. He bent down and the metallic-tasting water washed through him. The forest closed up—the great plant night, dark, disturbing. The path he had followed, he was sure, plunged into the deepest depths of anguish.

A cellar. A lightbulb casts shadows. Steve plunges his arms into the kneader, working the sticky dough, his back stretched to its limits. A paradoxical power emanates from his scrawny body. His torso, black and naked, is covered with flour, his biceps hard as rocks. Bits of yeast stick onto him. A lamp recasts his effort onto the plaster of the walls.

It is his second batch, it must be close to nine in the morning. It was three-thirty when he went down the stairs of the bakehouse. Steve shapes the dough into two-pound loaves; without weighing, he can tell their weight to within a few ounces. He sticks the tip of his knife into the loaves, then puts them into the oven using a scorched-edged paddle.

A wonderful smell fills the room. Steve breathes in deeply. The warm scent takes him to Betty. His sleeping beauty is still under the covers, completely wrapped up in her dreams. He left her in the thick of the night, after dozing for a few hours. The lightbulb blinks, its light stutters. In the air Steve's hands trace the curves of an ideal body. He abandons himself, eyes closed, carried away by the floating image of the woman he loves. He imagines Betty possessing the light. His eyes half-open, the smell of her hair fills the room: ripe wheat, nutmeg, too. It is for Betty that Steve works so hard, toils in the blazing heat, carries heavy sacks of flour, and scrubs the kneader—to keep her far away from hunger, from shame, so that she will continue to smile and sing until the end of time. Sunday, he'll take the bus to Clarksdale to buy her the most extravagant of gifts. For two years he has been saving every nickel, every penny.

Steve takes the loaves of bread, crusty and golden, out of the oven. He takes a drink from a jug of water, puts thirty or so still-burning loaves into a basket, and goes back upstairs. The lightbulb dies just as he closes the door.

Betty places her hand on the sheet. The mattress has kept the imprint of another body. Steve's image immediately appears. Her beloved Black man. She can't remember the caresses of the night before, what might have distinguished that coupling from thousands of others, so many moments of loving abandonment. Pleasure always took her so high, so far . . .

Betty gets up, convinced that this day will not be upset by any disappointments—static beings, humans and spirits alike, will prove as dependable as the floor under her feet. She opens the shutters and greets the light. Oh, Jesus, you know that life provides nothing more and this morning Betty gives thanks to you just by breathing.

She walks to the edge of the well at the back of the yard. Her eyelids fight against the sharp light. In a few moments her washerwoman's arms will easily bring up the heavy sloshing bucket. The water will spill forth! . . . And Betty will begin to sing.

Her skin cleansed with soap, wearing a crisp cotton dress, Betty sets off to attack the dusty road. A heavy basket of laundry rests on her hip, a linen scarf protects her hair. On the road that leads to the laundry, accompanied by the cackling of chickens and the laughter of children squabbling over vegetable peelings, Betty's voice, heard above the coughing of an old Plymouth and the creaking of a horse cart, rises up in rhythmic harmony with her supple, brown legs, the sun a brilliant impresario. A blues tune teases her lips:

> *My daddy come home this mornin', drunk as he*
> *could be*
> *He used to stay out late, now he don't come home at all*
> *I know there's another mule been kicking in my*
> *stable . . .*

My, how Betty can sing! Her voice can handle everything, from solemn church hymns to growling roadhouse tunes, but she does not convey tragedy, she always bets on life. When she sings "Go down Moses," you would swear that Moses has just left the Sunday dinner table. Pastor Lloyd wouldn't mind a bit more gravity, he sometimes reins Betty in during choir practice, but how can you rein in joy?

> *. . . If you don't like my ocean, don't fish in my sea*
> *Stay out of my valley, let my mountain be*
> *I ain't had no loving since God knows when . . .*

Betty lingers on the bass notes, slows the tempo, and Ma Rainey's song begins to sound like a true spiritual. Betty's voice reaches the tops of the poplars, her shoes float on the waves of dirt. She sees the weathervane on the roof of the Abbot farm. The farmer is standing in the middle of the pig pen; he's pumping water, and a cloudy flow runs into the trough. The sweltering pigs dip their snouts into the murky water. Nahum Abbot turns to Betty. He is huge, wears coarse denim overalls, his skin so dark it looks burned. The farmer's voice is drowned by the grunting of the pigs.

Betty is getting closer to town. She hears the babbling of the river behind the bulrushes standing up arid and pale along its banks. The river is flowing, praise God, but already the streams, which in this season are usually the breeding ground for crayfish, are drier than the heart of a pagan. Betty reaches the fork separating the two roads that lead to town and chooses the longer path to avoid the shanty town, its hovels, its violence. The sheet-metal roofs reflect a painful light, the heat cracks the planks of the shacks whose foundations still show the marks of the most recent river flood. In town, the main street looks like an overwhelmed anthill, black, industrious insects scurrying in the dust. Betty goes by the apothecary with its caduceus painted on the front. On the drugstore's display shelves, sweets are beginning to melt. The shopkeeper is drowsing outside on a rocking chair, his face sagging like chewing gum. A bit farther, the Jenkins grocery store, one of the rare shops with a refrigerator, has attracted a crowd hoping to buy cold sodas.

Betty sings an improvised hymn. The crowd greets the young woman who walks up humming. Over here, hats are tipped, over there, hands are waved, smiles are so wide dentures seem about to fall out. Ah, the street and its disguised carrion smile! Because these folks, truth be told, don't really like Betty. But nobody would dare insult her to her face, because nobody forgets that she's the niece of Sapphira, the old fetish priestess of the forest. Sapphira, whose ears are more delicate than the petal of a poppy and who, with a simple incantation, while rolling a few cowry shells in the dark, can suffocate you in your sleep, smother you with your own mucus, and plug up your ass for eternity. And if it isn't your anus that the witch seals up with her spells, it will be that of your mule, and your plow will be pulled by a sickly beast. Betty must be something of a witch herself, the folks say silently, her blood must be tainted by magic. But until they can find enough courage to burn them, they leave witches and their families alone. Truth be told, in the here below, it's better to be feared than liked.

At the corner of Pine Street, Betty's song is interrupted. A dozen or so curious people have gathered in front of the garage owned by Andrew Wallace, a rich mulatto, who also owns the laundry, the barber shop, and most of the stores on main street. A gurgling of pipes and a sticky cloud come out of the building. Betty gets closer and sees the beast that is groaning out of all its valves; a Ford pick-up, with muddy hubcaps, whose wheels are wallowing in motor oil. Around the hood, wide open and still emitting smoke, three mechanics are toiling, their undershirts covered in grease. Suddenly, one of the mechanics stands up straight, screaming; a splash of hot oil is dripping from his forehead, his co-workers hold him up and help him sit down on a barrel of fuel. Alerted by his screaming, Andrew Wallace, freshly shaved, comes out of the barbershop next to the garage. His face, a beautiful shade of copper, his thin lips and his delicate nose all wrinkle in a single movement. Aware that this type of scene is bad publicity for him, Wallace cuts through the small group of onlookers and lowers the metal door, depriving the curious of a welcome morning distraction.

Theodore, an old Negro who looks like a battered sphinx, is sitting in front of the Boyd shoe shop. His face is blacker than a tire, his hair and beard seem sprinkled with chalk, his eyes shine like polished spurs. Theodore's eyes focus on a figure approaching with a wicker basket balanced on her hip. Her dress isn't an obstacle for the eyes of the old satyr who assesses the curves, the hills and the valleys. Theodore scratches his beard: he knows this woman, she's the daughter of Joyce, the laundress, Sapphira's niece. Damn, the gal has really grown! Theodore is old enough to have known Sapphira when she still had enough charm to attract the attention of half the men in town. He had even been her lover, well, let's say her companion. That was a long time ago, before back-alley spells, potions and smoke turned her into a grey and lonely she-wolf. Yep, that witch was really a nice piece back then, and her niece has some of that wild beauty . . .

The young woman walks in front of him, her eyes focused on the end of the street. Theodore now breathes her in and feels his cock harden in his raggedy pants.

"How come ya smell so good, gal? Y'all got a flowerbed in yo basket, or you fall head first in a barrel o' happiness?"

Betty turns around. She smiles at the old man, to be polite, because old people are rare in these parts and a Negro doesn't often get to see snow settle in his hair, but also because the compliment was well fashioned and the words that came out of the old man's mouth sounded something like a song.

"Oh, it just laundry I takin' to wash. It ain't my basket smell so good, just the spring the good Lord done sent us to put balm in our hearts."

Theodore hesitates before responding, fearing his true voice, dirty and overflowing like a bar ashtray, would be revealed.

"C'ain't give the good Lord all the credit, sweet gal! He ain't the one walkin' in front o' me wearin' that dress and showin' them legs! Shor enuf the Lord wouldn't be havin' this effect on me . . ."

Betty feels as naked as Susanna in the pages of the Bible. She stops smiling, pulls at the bottom of her dress and says in a scolding voice: "Old man, I needs to go to work . . . I bids you good day."

Betty walks away quickly. She doesn't feel like singing anymore. She can feel the old man's eyes on her back, and hopes the steam in the laundry will wash away the filth she feels on her skin.

On a rickety bed, a young man was sleeping naked, his face buried in the pillow. The room's stucco walls were a dubious white. Above the bedside table, a glass-covered frame protected an engraved portrait of that courageous Abraham Lincoln; next to a window stood a walnut-stained solid-oak dressing table, the only apparent luxury item in this sad bedroom.

A fly alighted on the man's back, lingered on his round, hairless buttocks, then moved lightly to his crotch. The fly probably would have had the indecency to continue further, if a decisive hand hadn't squashed it. The man who got up grumbling was Robert Johnson, called Bobby by the few people who spoke to him. He wasn't yet twenty. He was tall and thin, sculpted from the finest ebony. Even after a night of debauchery, his face remained pure and beguiling. Bobby stood up, his legs wobbled for a moment, then agreed to walk. On the dressing table was a flask of whiskey; he brought it to his lips and took a long swig. The explosion in his empty stomach brought him to his senses. He looked at his reflection in the tilting mirror, stuck out his chest, hefted his member vainly and allowed himself another swig. His suit trousers and a shirt had been abandoned at the foot of the bed. Bobby frowned: his honor as a dandy was at risk. He sat down on the bed and began to dress.

The bedroom door opened with a creak. The smell of strong coffee. A woman walked in, her round face smiling. She was carrying a platter bearing a steaming porcelain cup, some cornbread and biscuits. She must have been around forty, her arms copper-brown and plump, through her robe some well-endowed shapes could be seen. She was exactly the type of woman the local guys called "Mama."

"Y'all ain't gonna leave on an empty stomach, is ya?"

The voice was honeyed, slightly husky from smoking. Bobby drank his coffee in one gulp. He bit into the cornbread, a bit overcooked. Mama sat on the bed and began nibbling on his earlobe while her hand fondled his groin.

"I ain't even washed," Bobby protested, his mouth full.

"Me, neitha . . ."

He let himself fall back. A warm tongue began licking the crumbs in the corners of his mouth. The dressing gown fluttered down and joined the shirt on the floor.

Silent and concentrated, Bobby labored with the precision of a metronome. Mama bellowed loud enough to knock down the walls of Jericho, swearing more than a heretic at the stake: "Bobby, son of a ho of Sain John! . . . Oh, my man, yo' dog's tail makes my pussy drool! My angel baby, I want yo cum . . . I want it to the day I die! Oh, I loves you, you lil piece o shit! Oh, Bobby, you hurtin' me, hurtin'! . . ."

Abraham Lincoln in his glass-front frame would have probably averted his eyes from the spectacle of these two Negroes who were perhaps a bit too emancipated. The church bell rang noon, and Bobby marked each ring with a violent thrust.

15

Mama was lying on her side snoring. Bobby chewed on a biscuit. The rank smell of coupling bodies and stale cigarettes didn't bother him at all. Mama turned over on her back, moaning in her dream. Bobby picked up his scattered clothes and quietly left the room. The bathroom was flooded in wonderful light. On a chair was the jacket of a tweed suit, perfectly folded. From the bathtub's copper faucet emerged a drop of liquid more precious than amber. For Bobby, running water was a miracle. Outside, the river was evaporating, the ground counted its cracks, but water still found a way to rise up to him. Bobby turned on the faucet and let the cool gift trickle down from his neck to his feet.

A face like his isn't deserved, it isn't earned, it is Mother Nature's lottery, that's all . . . Bobby smoothed his eyebrows with the tip of his finger, patted his cheeks warmed by the razor, and adjusted the collar of his shirt. Through the window he could hear the muffled sounds of the street. Despite the horrible heat that awaited him, he put on his jacket. In the bedroom, Mama was still sleeping. Bobby leaned over her purse lying in the middle of the room. He rifled through her wallet and took two dollars. The night had been long, his back confirmed that. He took another quarter as compensation for the impromptu noon servicing.

The dragon's steaming breath filled the vast space. The vats drooled a lye-filled foam that ran down to the dirt floor and onto the bare feet of the laundresses. In the boiler, the coal glowed red, the heat rose up in a spiral to the sheet-metal ceiling. Acidic fumaroles, mirages, condensation. Hell, it is said, has a thousand entrances, but the laundry had only one door. At the back of the building. Closed.

Dozens of irons are lined up on a trestle table. A teenaged girl, lean and spindly, approaches the boiler, collects some of the incandescent coke using a steel scoop then fills the reservoirs of the irons the women use on the sheets piled up in a corner of the room.

No one speaks. The dragon is breathing.

Climbing up onto a platform, Betty takes a spindle which she turns around in a vat where a greyish water is stagnating. She battles with a mass of soggy laundry, slapping it against the sides of the vat before pushing it down deeper. She is breathing a bit heavily, a toxic puff of vapor irritates her lungs, she is getting nauseous. She contracts her chest, commands her muscles to make an additional effort, and the nausea is transformed into a wave of sweat. Betty returns to battle.

A woman with salt-and-pepper hair and wrinkled cheeks was watching her, a red-hot iron in her hand. Constance Reed was the oldest worker in the laundry. She had been toiling in this netherworld of smoke and water for almost thirty years. Seeing Betty struggling with her stick, the veteran felt her heart contract. She was both proud and sad to see Betty a part of this suffering team where Joyce, her mother, had already sacrificed her vitality and her health. Joyce had been more than a co-worker to Constance, she had been a true friend. They had been hired the same year, when the laundry belonged to a White man from Greenwood. Together, the two young girls had watched the hours, the days, the centuries go by. Joyce had died from a bad fever and Constance, stricken with grief, had left the laundry. For fifteen years she had been the nanny for the children of the Conrad family, an old line of plantation owners in the county. Then the children grew up and Constance returned to toil at the laundry. The veteran remembered Betty perfectly, the little girl with an unruly mop of hair, running around the laundry; the girl would meet her mother after school and would cool the steamy laundry with her laughter. Today, a married woman, Betty always stood in front of the vat, her hands strong, a song on her lips. Andrew Wallace, the new owner, had hired her at a lower salary and, not content simply to exploit her, harassed her worse than a goat.

The lanky teenager, who has temporarily abandoned the boiler, pours large pails of fresh water into the rinse vat, almost dislocating her shoulder with each bucket. Betty approaches her and passes her hand over the girl's hair, sticky with soap. How old is this girl? Not much more than fifteen. She's as skinny as a rail, but her forearms are as muscular as those of a brakeman. The girl raises eyes to Betty in which nothing can be read, not even pain.

It's noon. The women don't hear the ringing of the church bell on top of the hill; it's the hollow in their bellies that resounds with the precision of a clock. It's noon. The break. The blessing of a breath of fresh air for those suffocating in the laundry. The workers inspect their hands, tally the new stigmata superimposed on old ones; in a bucket of warm water, they rub their palms together to dissolve the incrusted lye. In a line they go through the door, drawn into the light.

The girl was the last to go out. She still had to smooth the carpet of ashes in the boiler and line up the irons on the trestle tables. Constance and Betty helped her.

"Cherry, gal," said the veteran, "I gots three lovely ears o corn fo lunch and a quart o milk, an I shure Betty ain't come empty-handed."

For a moment the girl's eyes seemed less dull.

"Oh, I ain't got much," said Betty. "I made a punkin pie, like at Thanksgivin, and some hardboil eggs."

The girl's name was Cherry. She must have been born in May or June, but looked more like a shriveled pit than a juicy fruit. The three exited the building, leaving the dragon to stew on its anger.

Bobby pats his jacket pocket. When he takes it out the Hohner harmonica glints in the harsh sunlight. Bobby improvises an upbeat tune, a hearty blues that harmonizes with the rhythm of his steps. His lips navigate the steel, his breath teases out notes, exalts or strangles them. In front of the Frazier bakery the aroma of warm bread tempts him, but Bobby doesn't care about hunger, that noisy busybody. He's keeping the dollars in his pocket to get away from this shitty burg, uglier than a chamber pot, as fast as possible.

Pastor Augustus Lloyd, a holy colossus, his black face as greasy as suet, his goatee that of an Oriental wiseman, his silver cross on his jacket lapel, is walking toward Bobby. The pastor gloriously ignores the bluesman; with his nose in the air, he pretends to be reflecting on an essential theological question. In response, the harmonica blares out a burst of sound, the music as salacious as intercourse. Bobby shimmies, ups the drama, moving his pelvis and stomping in the dust. Pastor Lloyd passes by him and leaves behind the sound of damned souls.

On the banks of the river, in the shade of a sycamore tree, the women have taken out their meals and are having lunch. The sun up above is a brute full of ill-will and arrogance.

"It like a husban who hit you when he get out o bed," says Pearl. "White folk thinks we others don't feel it, cause of our black coverin, but I sweah no nigga be suited to that sun and . . ."

Pearl doesn't finish what she was saying and bites into a slice of pumpkin pie: "Hey, Betty, yo cookin' be real tasty, how you make that?" Pearl smiles. Her round face, jet black, her straight white teeth make her look almost like a society woman, but her teasing voice is that of the people. "I's guessin' it be witchcraft." she adds, winking at Alice, who's sitting next to her, a tall, slender young woman with skin' the color of caramel. Betty doesn't respond to the allusion. Pearl is an incorrigible gossip who talks nonstop. She peels a hardboiled egg and holds it out to young Cherry. The girl gobbles down the egg in one bite, under Constance's tender gaze.

"Whoa, gal, if ya gone swallow mens like that, y'all gone choke yoself!" says Alice.

"Swallowin' good, but you c'aint use y'all's teeth on it," adds Pearl with an obscene grin.

"Cherry be too young to hear y'alls nastiness!" scolds Constance.

"Go on now, talkin' bout mens make me hongry," Pearl responds. "By the by, Betty, I seen yo husban yest'day comin' out o the bak'ry. He were streaked wit flour, lookin' like a zebra!"

Betty fights back the electricity traveling through her bones. In her mind she sees herself wringing the neck of this bad-mouthing Negress.

"Anyways, y'all ain't the worst off," says Pearl to calm things down. "Least y'all gots you a man who come home evr'y night and don't wander off to visit them hos down to the bad part o town."

The church bell rings again. Alice and Pearl let their grins fall onto the dry grass. Their muscles are already preparing to suffer. They stand up, turn their eyes to the front of the laundry, that impatient tormentor. Cherry waves goodbye to Constance and Betty who stay in the shade of the sycamore tree. The three figures walk away, their shapes fading in the vast shimmering of the sun.

"Lord, it shor be good not to work in the afternoons no mo," Constance sighs. "Mist Wallace, he be lookin' out fo my ol years."

"Hey, auntie, who be lil Cherry's kin?"

"Oh, she Kate's niece."

"Kate Adams, the blacksmith's wife? So she Eugene's cousin?"

"Or his half-sister, don't rightly know."

Betty was stricken again by the sudden absence. She tried not to let it show, stood up and kissed the old woman's forehead with the tenderness of a daughter. With her basket of clean laundry on her hip, she walked along the river, going past the metal bridge that shone like the barrel of a Winchester.

Images came together in her mind. Eugene's name, which no one had spoken for ages, began to resonate in her. Betty struggled to reassemble his features, his wonderful smile which turned his face into a never-ending party. She had often encountered Eugene, playing with his tops, lost in his thoughts, glowing with a secret joy. The young boy worked with his father in the family's smithy behind the old sawmill. He had never gone to school, his only teachers were embers and steel. He assisted his father in forging barrel hoops, wagon axles, and the machetes which hard-working Negroes wore in their belts to clear underbrush. Though the blacksmith was tall and strong, a worthy servant of Ogun, the incandescent voodoo god, his son Eugene was frail and delicate, his high voice that of a girl's. He was often teased for that. Eugene was sweet, but his skin, accustomed to the sparks of the fire and paternal beatings, didn't fear pain. He had no friends and asked no one for sympathy. The boy spent his free time whittling toys out of wood with his penknife; his eyes followed the spinning of the tops and his spirit soared far from the marasmus of the town.

Little Eugene had disappeared a few months before the river flooded. His father, convinced that he had deserted the smithy out of laziness, cursed him, but Kate, his mother, never stopped looking for him, everywhere, in the surrounding forests, on the riverbanks, persuaded that something terrible had happened to him. In the beginning, a few good souls had assisted her in her search. Betty and Steve had shouted Eugene's name deep into the woods, with no luck. Then the

Mississippi had broken through its dams, the flood had surged and everyone counted their own dead, wrapped their own wounds. On the plain, the memory of the young boy faded into the silt of oblivion.

Betty walked down Oak Street. Eugene's smiling face continued to haunt her from that no man's land where the missing survive. The heat was reaching its apex, the voices around her were crackling. With her head lowered, she didn't see Pastor Lloyd who was walking up to greet her. "Betty, my child, aren't you going to greet your pastor?"

Betty raised her head and her field of vision was blocked by the mass of Reverend Lloyd, his wide chest, his shining black face. The little silver cross on his jacket caught the light.

"Beg your pardon, Rev'rend, I was lost in my thoughts."

"Heedless woman, listen to me now!"

The pastor was smiling but his voice was serious and harsh. "I'm joking, my daughter, there is nothing heedless about you, you're a hard-working wife and a good Christian woman. But you know I can't resist the pleasure of quoting good ol' Isaiah."

The big body in black was oppressive, and Betty instinctively stepped back. The pastor sensed her unease but didn't move.

"I can't be present tomorrow for choir practice," he said. "You're going to have to see to everything, dear child. I needn't remind you that in two weeks' time the mayor himself will be with us at services. We mustn't leave anything to chance, you understand."

Betty nodded. Ever since Pastor Lloyd had learned that the mayor, Richard Thompson, intended to visit their church, his orders had become increasingly urgent. He insisted on absolute control of the smallest details of the service.

"Don't you worry, Rev'rend," said Betty, eager to cut the conversation short. "And please take care in this cursed sun."

"Thank you, child, but the turpitudes of nature do not concern me." The pastor's face crinkled, his lips drew up from his teeth. "I will leave you now, my child."

Betty watched the man of God as he walked up the street. From the back as from the front, he looked more like a lumber-jack than a preacher. In fact, his father and grandfather had wielded axes in the forests of Alabama, and the pastor never missed a chance to remind his flock from high on his pulpit that the Lord Jesus Christ had revealed Himself to him while he was carrying enormous oak logs.

"I know the weight of the cross," he said, "and I can affirm that it is light for those who abandon themselves to the will of God."

Betty wondered why she felt so uneasy in his presence. She had known Reverend Lloyd since she began to walk and nothing in what he did or said had ever disturbed her. When she was a teenager he had often scolded her, sometimes even threatened her with fire and brimstone, but that was all part of his ministry. Today, the authority of his voice seemed to be hiding something and his entire demeanor seemed suspicious to her. Betty was ashamed to think that, she blamed it on being tired, the heat, then more charitable thoughts returned. Pastor Lloyd had been a widower for years, his wife had passed fol-lowing a terrible illness, and since then a cloud of perpetual sadness veiled his face. Betty was relieved to have again found the deep and indiscriminate compassion that was her true nature.

She stopped at the corner of Oak Street and Ashton Alley, in front of the Frazier bakery where Steve worked. She knew her husband didn't like her to buy bread from Jerry, his boss, his so-called "uncle," who had never even offered him a muffin. Such stinginess outraged her man to the depths of his being. He had made Betty promise that she would never buy a single crumb from that miserly Jerry. Betty had kept her word and every week made a long detour to a bakery on Yazoo Avenue, bringing home a tasteless loaf of bread which Steve praised outrageously. "The bread o justice," he said, "don't need to be well baked or well kneaded!" How proud he was, the Negro she adored, oh yes! He could endure a lot and swallow his troubles, but his indignation remained alive, stuck in his jaws like an abscess.

A boy was playing with some pebbles on the red dirt. Betty called to the boy who turned his little ingrate face to her. His eyes squinted, his round forehead and jutting brow made him look like a wild boar.

"Can y'all fetch me some bread, boy?" said Betty, holding out a coin. "Y'all can buy yoself a candy with the change."

The boy looked at the coin in the palm of her hand.

"Don' want no candy, I rather keep the money."

His voice was as serious as an adult's.

"That fine," said Betty. "I needs a two-poun loaf, not too cooked. I'll wait for y'all here."

The boy was getting ready to run off with the coin but thought twice.

"Y'all the witch's daughter, ain't ya, m'am?"

"Her niece," Betty answered, frowning.

"Ah . . . how much yo' bread cost? How much gone be left fo me?"

"You'll see. Go on, now, skedaddle!"

Betty looks at the loaf of bread and sees that the boy couldn't resist biting into it. Why didn't he buy something to eat with the change? He was probably going to keep the coin in his pocket like a talisman, a lucky charm. Hope is the sustenance of the poor.

Betty goes back up Pine Street. The sun's reflections on the dairy's sheet-metal roof blind her, she heads into a narrow street and goes back to the road leading to the shanty town. After the old Western Union office, she passes in front of the decrepit hotel, at the intersection of Alma and Hancock, which the debauched of the neighborhood call the Post Office Saloon. A cemetery of cigarette butts in the dirt, nasty smells, unidentifiable puddles. Betty hates this neighborhood and the creatures that wander around in it. She zigzags between the detritus, her basket against her hip, holding her bread. She's met the saloon's owner, Joe Hives, a former roustabout, a distant friend of her mother, but she has never gone through the doors of this place out of which every night emerge the raucous chords of the blues and the shouting of depraved women.

A young woman in a negligee takes a few steps on the saloon's porch. Betty stops walking. She thinks she recognizes Dora. Dorothy Payne. The young woman stretches and yawns. She looks like she hasn't slept much. Her arms, light brown, are covered in dark spots. It is indeed Dora. She is beautiful and always has been. Dora lights a cigarette, coughs even before she has taken a puff. She crushes the butt with her bare foot and goes back inside. Dora the proud, the untamed.

It's been more than three years since Betty and Dora have run into each other. The last time was just before the great flood. They had met by chance, near the bandstand in front of city hall. Dora was holding the hand of her son, a little boy of four or five. What was the boy's name? Jeremy? No, Joshua. The two women had exchanged a few words, not enough to dissipate the tension and do away with the resentment. Then Dora had gone off to Tennessee or maybe Georgia, Betty couldn't remember. Recently she had learned from her co-workers' gossip that Dora had come back to town and was singing in the evenings at the saloon. Betty hadn't paid much attention, especially not to the slander that suggested Dora rounded out the ends of the month by turning tricks in a room upstairs.

A boy of around eight is standing in a doorway next to the saloon/hotel. His hair is uncombed, he is wearing pants that are too big, and a shirt open on his chest. It's Joshua. The boy's gaze is focused on the loaf of bread in her hand.

"Y'all want a piece?" Betty asks, as naturally as she can. The boy doesn't dare answer, but his face has already given him away. Betty breaks off a piece of bread and holds it out in front of her as if to attract a sparrow.

The boy walks up, takes it, and bites into the crust.

"Y'all remember me, Josh?"

The boy stops chewing and shakes his head.

"I'm yo mama's frien. Last time I seen y'all, ya weren't no taller than a chair."

The child stares at Betty suspiciously: "First off, Mama ain't got no friens . . . She just got me."

Betty puts her hand on the child's warm head. He doesn't try to move away, accepts her caress.

"Who tole y'all you can touch mah boy?! Leave 'em be right now, you bitch!"

Dora flies down the porch steps, her hands held out as if to strangle the air.

"Dora, it me, Betty, I . . . "

"I knows who you is! Y'all thinks I gonna let you play the big lady with my boy? Y'all thinks I don feed him, that it?!"

Dora slaps the boy. He doesn't cry and goes into the hotel, his chin high. Betty is torn. She isn't afraid of Dora, at least not physically. She remembers the fights they had as children, when the two friends pulled each other's hair, before making up and singing together. Betty always emerged victorious from those childhood battles. But in this instant, she knows that no reconciliation is possible. If she's afraid, it is of the definitive loss of someone to whom she has been attached beyond time. The ghost of affection.

"Yo boy be good-lookin, Dora . . . I's the one give him the bread, he ain't askt fo nothin. I aughtn't . . . "

Dora puts her hands on her hips, ready for a scene, hoping for one, even: "Y'all still the same, ain't ya Betty? Jealous and takin' advantage! Y'all ain't been able to have no kid, so you comes take other peoples'!"

Betty shuts herself up in silence. She walks away slowly, waves goodbye to Dora, a wave that is returned only by the shadow of her hand on the dusty ground.

The boy had kept the coin in his hand for safekeeping. It was better than putting it in his hole-filled pocket. In the bakery it had been hard to resist the heady smell of bread and muffins, but he had stayed strong. He walked along, his feet bare, the dirt trickling between his toes and the sun making his round forehead shine. He crossed a small section of Alma Street and ended up in the twists and turns of the shanty town. He lived even further, in the so-called jungle, among the huts made of cardboard boxes and mud, the miserable enclave where he had grown up and where everyone knew him. He walked quickly in front of Humility's shack. The woman, still young but already worn out from having a baby every year, was washing rags in a tub. Humility grabbed him as we went by.

"Pats, you no-good nigga, where you runnin' from with the devil's pitchfork on yo ass? If you done stole somethin' you best tell me. I shur nuf gonna beat you to the bone, but it gone feel like a love pat next to what the others gone do ifn they catch y'all. You know, chile?"

Pats shook his head.

"I ain't stole nuthin, Hum', I swear on the cross and the blood. I gone so fast cause I wanna play some music."

Humility sighed and returned to her washing, wringing the laundry with stupefying strength. Pats disappeared behind a cabin that was a bit less delipidated than the others. Where

Humility and her five kids lived. It wasn't exactly his home, even if he often slept there and ate the best meals of his life. Humility wasn't his mother, not even his aunt, just a soul spared of meanness and selfishness who took care of him and made sure he didn't die of hunger or cold. As for the rest, if he were bitten by a snake or drowned in a surging river, like Humility's daughter a few years earlier, it wouldn't be her fault. There was a countless number of such orphans in the county, who were looked after through the kindness of women. Even before they were teenagers, they would depart to try their luck on the roads; most became itinerant farm workers—day workers for the luckiest—many landed in prison, the rest ended up as wandering hobos. Ever since he had heard a mouth harp twanging in the wind, Pats knew he would become a musician.

A metal wire taken from around a broom was nailed to the cabin wall, stretched three inches from the floorboards. A piece of wood from a hazelnut tree notched with a pocket knife served as the upper nut; below, the bridge was a small, flat stone, the frets simple marks drawn with chalk. This poor man's instrument, the locals called it a diddley bow, was the obligatory first step for budding bluesmen, even Son House, Pats' idol, had bloodied his fingertips on rough strings before being able to afford his first guitar.

The boy adjusted the tension of the metal string by moving the stone. He played low on the string, which emitted a hollow, scratching sound, a sort of E note. He held the penny between his thumb and index finger, rubbed it on the steel and created a raspy glissando. He used the coin as a pick, and played the string, tackling different notes using his left hand, like a double bass player. His foot marked the beat, his hips moving slowly; his senses attuned to a hypnotic groove, a dirty, deep alley beat, emerging from his heart. Good Lord, how that little coin played! Pats alternated between slides and picking and repeated the sequence, adding words to the music. He sang in a deep voice much older than his age, like an old war-torn veteran, his voice gravelly, broken by alcohol and bad luck. Pats already knew quite a bit about bad luck, being a sickly-looking orphan. The song on his lips didn't have a refrain, nor a precise meaning, it spoke of disappointed love, of decline and of bread that is stolen from your mouth. Humility appeared at the corner of the neighboring shack and stopped to listen, a yam in one hand and a knife in the other. Maybe it was true that this boy had a gift, maybe a destiny.

In any case, his voice told the truth, his sadness wasn't fake. He existed in the heart of the blues, and even the Evil One couldn't have driven them away. Humility smiled and went back to peeling her potatoes.

Pats kept playing until the tips of his fingers were red and sore. He wiped his forehead and put the coin back in the middle of his palm. His head started to buzz, his legs to wobble. He was hungry. There was always a more or less deep hollow in his belly, true, but this time it was serious. To ease his stomach, he drank the brackish water at the bottom of a jar, then looked underneath the cabin porch. He took out a fishing rod made of cane. He had chosen a supple and solid stalk, the hook a safety pin he had stolen from the grocer. With this rod he had already pulled from the river fish weighing more than three pounds. It was the right season for bluegills, greens, carp, or catfish, they proliferated near the river banks and didn't pay much attention. Pats unearthed a metal box from a corner of the cabin; inside, a brownish mud where fat, slimy worms were writhing. Pats put the box in his pocket, the rod on his shoulder, and walked away from the shacks.

The Delta is woven with voices lying in ambush, with enflamed syllables and cries. Here all is music and everything resonates: jars, washboards, cardboard boxes, tubs, floors, sheet iron, empty bellies and prideful chests. Here song is born out of a wound and is returned to the birds, without misunderstanding or pretending. A child makes a coin pluck against steel, the echo of metal climbs up the wall, fills the drain pipe and rises into the weakened oxygen. Now, the shack is a point in the middle of orange-tinted fields, of the pale squares of cotton and islands of green. The humming in the distance becomes mechanical—it's the Dixie Flyer working its pistons at full steam, unless it's the Green Diamond, its heavy cars filled with clandestine young vagabonds en route north, maybe the Cannonball transporting mail, rare love letters and eviction notices. Screeching wafting through, train cars in grey spasms. When the din has faded away, a few seconds before the night shudders and the lamp shimmers, there is silence. A strange, dangerous silence, unhinged like a laugh, a laugh unsheathed from the throat of a Negro, from the belly of the earth. That laugh is the Delta triumphant. Laugh, yes, laugh, pick up from the dust the fragments of our voices, kick the clocks' asses, laugh, even if tomorrow will be worse, even if dreams are destroyed and destiny shoots us like rabbits. Laugh, laugh, laugh! . . .

His belly was deflating fast. Pats stopped for a few minutes and leaned against the trunk of a pecan tree. The forest around him rang with the chirping of kinglets and warblers. He only had a few hundred yards to go before reaching the banks of the river. He kept going, expending only the breath he needed. A branch cracked behind him; he didn't turn around. The animal was probably better fed than he was, he hadn't brought his slingshot and didn't have the strength to pursue a wounded animal in the underbrush. He walked along the river; the banks were covered with cordgrass, the long, green leaves bordered in gold brushed his head. Pats stopped in front of a dead river arm that had formed a sort of bog, framed by two maple trees, their branches filtering the light. He heard a characteristic roiling, the song of the drumfish in the season of love. Pats knew that his fishing pole was crafted to pull in bullheads, possibly small zander, but wouldn't hold up in a lengthy battle with a "freshwater drum." He took a worm out of the metal box and impaled it on the hook. He cast his line and stood motionless, waiting for the jerking in the water. Soon bubbles appeared on the surface; Pats felt his elbow and wrist tremble, he put the coin in the metal box and held the rod with both hands. He had snared a big one, for sure. A force born of the mud was confronting him in a struggle whose outcome could only be the suffocation of one or the other. He saw a smooth, shimmering shape appear among the cattails and water lilies. The line was stretched to its limits, the rod bent in half—he would have to act fast before the hook came off. Pats arched his back; hunger had dried his organs, his head vibrated and his blood thrummed in his chest. He breathed in and held his breath, his two hands gripping the rod. He saw the creature, hideous and dripping, dirty scales and twitching whiskers. He maneuvered the fish a few millimeters from the surface, hoping it would tire. He glanced quickly around him for a rock to finish it off, but couldn't see anything. He would have to use his rod as a spear, or his fists. He realized the metal box had disappeared. A shivering among the vines continued along his spine. The blow he received on the back of his head knocked him out but didn't kill him. The rod fell onto the banks of the river and was pulled down into the depths of the water.

A greedy shadow leaned over the boy's motionless body. Hands seized his head and struck it repeatedly, the sound dull, on the ground. What the shadow then did would neither be seen nor told. The boy's naked body was bound. The shadow dragged it to the edge of the river. Pats didn't sink. The shadow joined him and forced the black water into Pats' open mouth.

The blacksmith's hammer, the whinnying of horses driven crazy by the burning furnace, the squealing of a sickle against a grindstone, at another time would have brought a song to her lips, carrying her to the threshold of her house. No song in her today. A few bitter notes and tears, which she would have gladly allowed to flow, but which are stagnating deep inside her and slowing her down. A sharecropper takes off his hat and greets her like a good Christian. Betty walks by him without even nodding. In a small town it isn't very wise to ignore a greeting like that. Sooner or later she would have to pay.

Presly Barnes, the barber, has escaped the damp heat of his shop and is working outside. Andrew Wallace, the mulatto, is sitting in a chair, Presly brushing his chin with white froth. Wallace notices Betty who is approaching like a sleepwalker, her eyes focused on her feet. He grabs the barber's wrist and stops the razor a few millimeters from his cheeks. "Nice little piece, ain't she? . . . I do believe I prefer that one when she's sad."

The barber turns his gaze to the street, blinking his eyes.

"Shure nuf she nice to look at, Mist Wallace. That no-account husban o hers be mighty lucky."

At the mention of the husband, the mulatto's face darkens. Wallace snaps his fingers and offers his neck up to the blade.

Betty walks up an asphalt path masked by red dust. A path of pine trees, a grove of hickories, the rushing of the river. The sound of a motor coming from the other side, the squealing of animals going to slaughter; an odor of stolen lives floats in the air.

Betty goes through the wooden gate that opens onto a little yard, passes in front of the well, climbs the front steps. She closes the door. Her thoughts are all jumbled. Images and faces are superimposed, blending inside her head. Unsettled, moving faces—those of Eugene, Joshua, Dora . . . Finally, Steve's face, black and smooth, where misfortune is never etched and which, in Betty's presence, expresses only immense gratitude. Steve who will soon be home and who under no circumstances must find her in this state, fighting back tears.

Betty thinks about her man, about the first time she saw him, skinny and slouching on the church pew. She remembers the boy of that time, torn from his town in the hills, the only escapee—or almost—from a horrible epidemic. One of his uncles had brought him in a wagon and had essentially sold him to the baker, Jerry Frazier. Scarcely ten years old, Steve was already working, exploited, and paid next to nothing. He slept on a pallet in the bakehouse, and on Sunday went to church wearing his patched-together shoes. On the podium, Betty sang, glowed, reflected a bit of the divine glory. She felt a tenderness for that boy who was incapable of deciphering the Bible, but who felt the Word in the fibers of his soul. Hers was a diffuse feeling which slowly, year after year, grew into a tender love. At first Steve refused her attentions, fearing she wanted to humiliate him. She had to tame him, reassure him. Betty swept aside the sarcastic remarks of her friends, of Dora and the others, shrugged off the advice of her aunt Sapphira, shouldered the stinging remarks of Pastor Lloyd, who saw Steve only as an uneducated little nigger. For Betty, pity had always been a precondition for affection. She was attracted to Steve the way she had been drawn to Jesus.

Betty began to hum. She heard the gate creak. She got up, ready to greet the man she had chosen.

*

A taut night. The scent of rawhide. Between the sheets, jerking, shivering, secret calculations. Betty expulses the creatures born of the tensions of the day. Lying on his back, Steve senses his abandonment. She's the one who leads the dance, kisses him, sets him on fire. Betty rises up, sinks down, reaches inner eruption through forcible entry. She pours out, he floods her, he gives in, she collapses. In the darkness, her voice whispers, then is silent. Betty falls asleep. Steve gets up, drinks a glass of water, and lies down on the old sofa in the sitting room. In a few hours, at dawn, he will board the bus and will return with his arms holding a wonderful present.

The forest is behind him. Deep and unfathomable. Legba adjusts to the darkness as he would a necessary companion. A sound makes him stop: the fluttering of wings, a large sonorous specter. Flies. A few steps farther and he finds them, swarming in a compact mass: flies with dark bellies, short, sharp wings; some with yellow-striped thoraxes like wasps; the largest, as round as marbles, earthy bodies, whose elytra seem too frail to sustain flight, and finally, the female warriors with greenish armor, which cause beasts so much suffering and which humans suspect of peddling the worst poisons. Flies of shit, meat, blood . . .

The swarm stops. He holds out his right hand, the one wearing a leather glove. The flies now in submission pass between his fingers in a docile flow. A smile grows on his face. He seems younger. He is no longer alone. He lowers his hand: the squadron moves and guides him to a wide ravine, its edges covered in thistles and sumac. The pit is filled with animal carcasses and scrap metal—all the trash the town doesn't want to see, the everyday garbage that is thrown out, piles up, stinks, and accuses. Popular legends, the truth of the conquered, say that in olden times, women came in the middle of the night to throw dead babies into this ravine, those aborted without baptism, those whom the women, themselves, had sometimes suffocated so not to deliver them up to chains.

The flies alight on the surrounding bushes, covering them in a velvety magma. He plunges his hand into the detritus. He clears, scatters greasy papers, pieces of crockery, finally reaches the ground. His hand becomes harder, like a hoe, the *daba* of the ancestors. A pale object emerges from a layer of humus and twigs. A bone. The remnant of a person. He leans over, his movements are careful, almost gentle. He unearths a secret.

Crouching, Legba has lost all sense of time. He stands up, immediately the black cloud settles on the skeleton at his feet. He uncovers absolute nudity. The bones are white, stripped by the flies, maggots and pinworms. Next to the skeleton, the remains of a leather belt and a wooden top, eaten by the humidity. He picks up the object. In his head, a sudden vision, unbearable. A trampled, annihilated childhood. He puts the top in his pants pocket. The boy or girl lying here didn't see anything coming, face down on the ground, pants lowered. A terrible end. But all is not finished, the skeleton hasn't completed its great transhumance.

He goes along the ravine looking for a tool he can use. He picks up a piece of flint. What comes out of his mouth, prayer or groan, cannot be heard, only the sound of the stone resounds in the chasm. He straddles the skeleton and pounds, a great drum of war, without warning or truce. The dust flies up, the death shavings dance before his eyes. The sun descends, his arm stops. Around him, a whitish carpet. He drops the flint whose sharpened edges could slit the throat of any victim. Now is not the time for murder, but for compassion. He takes a little leather pouch from his pocket, sifts ashes into his palm. Using the tips of his fingers, following a secret ritual, he fills the pouch with the death dust, then sweeps his feet over the ground, erasing any trace.

Evil escapes. The moon casts its light over the threshold of a twisted world. Fear dominates. Hinges begin to creak, and the accursed barn opens. Evil crawls on the gravel, laughs at the pain. Stained with fish eggs, its mouth gaping, tongue dry, its depths ooze an icy seed. A shutter bangs. It isn't the wind. Evil is watching you, polluting your dreams and waiting for you to surrender.

Evil loves this land, its forests, its swamps where dawn is aborted, where death comes to drink. Evil creeps in between the layers and the realms. Since the defeat of ancient tribes, looting in semi-darkness, piles of scalps, badly sealed mass graves; since the first columns of slaves, human beasts of burden, blind raping, suffocated Negroes draining the swamps: Evil is the leaven of this land, its silt, its substance. It is neither White nor Black. It is at home here. Behind the dams. Beyond danger. Evil struck yesterday, today, it is dozing like a well-fed monster. It will take only a shout for it to awaken and strike.

In the darkness, impossible to distinguish his muscles from branches, his hair from leaves. Roots crack and a tree falls; Legba drags it, hefts it onto his shoulder, to a clearing where lupines and thistles thrive. A fire illuminates the space. He places his burden on the flames and the green wood is absorbed by the fire. Legba doesn't step back. He is in front of the fire like a son in front of his father—silent and full of admiration.

*

A lit candle placed in a saucer where a pool of wax is stagnating. Above the flame, a portrait of the Black Madonna of Guadalupe. The elderly Sapphira was panting, her shoulders shaking with short tremors, her light sleep accompanied by a dream which would cause most of the living to suffocate with terror. Her cheeks were flaccid, her eyelashes embellished with ash. Her eyes opened. Gradually she distinguished the outlines of the shadow and sat up on her pallet. Sapphira watched the dripping wax. A shiver ran through her. A macabre kiss. She turned around. No sound. No clue on the wooden walls covered in batik cloths and tanned furs. She inspected the cabin, trying to find a place where only an animal could have hidden— in the tight corners, behind the few pieces of furniture, under the straw mats covering the earthen floor. The candle illuminated the remains of foxes, rickety shelves where clay pots and fearsome Guinea statuettes were piled up.

A suspicious scratching under the porch. The old woman stomped her foot three times and the sound stopped. The night was full of evil spirits against whom she was unarmed. She didn't possess the spells to ward off the spirits; she knew how to summon them if necessary but avoided getting involved with invisible mysteries. She didn't know the ritual chants, the true names of the magical entities holding up the universe. Her intimate pantheon was a jumble, a residual mass of knowledge eroded by time and exile. She indiscriminately invoked Papa Legba and Eshu, Dada Segbo and Olorun. When she abandoned herself to a trance and a spirit from the land of before approached her, she found the archaic hymns and dedicated formulas but was incapable of remembering them when she returned to her senses. Sapphira was more of a healer than a *mambo*; she put to good use her knowledge of plants and the seasons to treat women with menstrual pain and during childbirth, to cast the evil eye out of homes, protect harvests and watch over the birthing of calves. She had her place in the community, a precarious and exposed place. The slightest error in dosing could lead to her end. She was like the Southern Devil Scorpion, discreet but present, both feared and detested.

*

The moon reigned over the black vault. The embers were docile at his feet. He sat cross-legged and opened the leather pouch; he threw handfuls of the bone powder into the middle of the red heart—the fire devoured the offering in a geyser of flames. From his belt he removed the mummified head of the snake. A stench of corruption, of poisoned fermentation. Legba placed the reptile's head on the embers; for a second the snake appeared to have come back to life, its fangs emerged for a final strike, then the rotten skin was consumed by the flames. He took the wooden top out of his pocket, rolled it around in his large palm and gave it to the fire.

His benumbed body leaned toward the ground. Not fearing the sparks flying up, he began to doze off, hoping to awaken thousands of miles away, in a very ancient time or an indeterminate future. Before the crackling of the fire, it was as if he were in a mother's womb—confident and invulnerable.

*

Sapphira is shivering. Over her nightgown she wraps a blanket with Indian motifs, a relic from her grandmother who was born among the Chickasaw tribe. Holding the candle, she goes through the door that has never had a lock. No lock will protect you from the spirits. The circle of the moon is shaded in rust, its light creating substance around it—shadow flowers, secret coverings, the earth's wrinkles. The old woman crosses the little clearing where her cabin is standing. To the east she sees the town, a few lights, will-o-the-wisps; in the distance, the smokestacks of the foundry on the Banks road. Reaching the edge of the woods, she realizes her eyes are of no help to her. She blows out the candle. Her eyelids closed, she questions the space around her, her worn flesh filtering the mystery. A beating of wings, the hooting of a hunter whose patience has just been rewarded. A gust of wind against her back. An invisible fugitive. Don't turn around, don't breathe. Remain still.

The old woman opens her eyes. A fabulous column of fire, orange and blue, climbs up to the moon before evaporating, a final flash behind the tall trees.

Sapphira turns back. Inside the cabin, she breathes better. She relights the candle. She takes an immaculate cloth out of a chest and unfolds it on the ground. Her hands dig around in a pouch, tossing strange objects onto the cloth: tortoise shells, seashells, a clump of hair, a pack of mint chewing gum, a thimble. Her hands move around the objects, arrange them into seemingly random patterns. Her forehead is dripping. Her jaws clenched, her lips speak in a language she has never learned, a drowned language, which takes on water from every direction. Abruptly her heart stops and the message appears before her. Evil is there, spreading, winding its way into the town, striking indiscriminately. When her heart begins beating again, the old woman kneels down offering praise to the sovereign forces that have deemed it good to keep her alive.

Their feathers covered in red dirt, the chickens peck with the tips of their beaks, their jet-black eyes watching a cloud through the fence. The sound of a harmonica carried by the echoes coming from the town. The birds don't react to this distant music, except for the youngest, a rebel. The dirt blends into her red feathers, her feet tap the rhythm, trace a strange score in the dirt.

A figure enters the enclosure. The red hen presses against the fence and sees the figure merge with her fellow chickens. One by one, the birds are picked up and put into a wooden crate. Their heads stick out of the bars, their feeble eyes beg in vain. The red one, driven by the energy of despair, flies up and almost manages to escape the enclosure. A pitiless hand grabs her by her wings.

"Stop makin' me sweat, you li'l ho!"

A wagon pulled by a mule is moving on a dirt path in the middle of plots of green corn. The sun is beating down joyfully. In a cage in the back of the wagon the chickens are lying on top of each other.

"Oh thank you, Lord! Thank you fo this sun what burns us and reminds us of the hell we gone know if we stray from You!"

Emerging from a row of corn, scarcely taller than a child, Miss Rosetta Brown, an old woman in her Sunday clothes, crosses the path without paying the slightest attention to the wagon bearing down on her. Miss Brown cries out, her arms raised: "Thank you, Jesus, for this sun! . . . Oh, You spoil us! Oh, You burn us like You should! . . . Blessed, blessed art Thou!"

The wagon swerves and rocks, the cage in the back breaks open. The red hen leaps out of the wagon and escapes among the stalks of corn.

The Greyhound bus was rolling along on an interminable straight road; the sun made the corrugated shell shimmer, the exhaust pipe coughed out noxious smoke. The windshield, covered with mosquito cadavers and traces of antediluvian rain, revealed almost nothing of the landscape. An abominable heat reigned in the interior. In the front of the bus, the driver, a potbellied mulatto, wiped his shiny forehead every five minutes. A fan with metallic blades was turning, emitting its weak cool air onto the first rows, those reserved for Whites. There wasn't one White person on the bus, and the Blacks were crammed into the seats in the back, so close together that the merest snore, the most innocent fart were experienced like an assault.

Steve had his eye on a box sitting on the seat next to him. Those at the far back of the bus, farmers returning home from the market in Lula or Stovall, thought he was somebody, a rich businessman, in any case, a nigger who hadn't lost his job and deserved a minimum of breathing space. The Greyhound made a stop at the Clayton exit. Several passengers got out, a greater number got in. A tall man, his face deep black, a guitar case under his arm, sat next to Steve who had to put his box on his lap. The bus took off again.

"I's gettin' off after Evansville, what 'bout y'all?"

Steve remained silent to show he had no desire to chat, even less to be friendly. The musician continued:

"What 'bout y'all? Where you gettin' off?"

"At the last stop . . . I stays in the nice part o town," Steve finally spat out.

"It just the opposite fo me, I's goin' to the rough part o town. Goin' to see a lil gal I ain't seen fo mo than a year. I's hopin' she remember me . . . any case, she sho ain't forgot my slide trombone!"

Steve sighed, rested his cheek against the window and dozed off. He woke up when the Greyhound made another stop. Dusk was coloring the landscape with purple ink. His hands immediately sought the box. It was still there, his neighbor, too, smiling and cheerful.

"A lil snooze, that do ya good, right? Don' you worry, I been keepin' my eye on yo stuff."

A lady got on and sat in the first row, taking advantage of the breeze from the fan. She was wearing an elegant dress, though somewhat out of fashion. Her face was white, with a sprinkling of freckles, but her full lips and her wide, flat nose were indeed those of an African woman. The driver looked at her, seemed uncertain. The lady gestured for him to drive off. A woman at the back of the bus, squeezed for hours by her neighbor, spoke loud enough to be heard by everyone: "Who she think she foolin', that un?! . . . She gone come back heah with the rest o us, and stop her mannerin'!"

An old woman, a scarf over her head, her gums purple and bare, chimed in with a vulgarity from the depths of the ages: "Hey, ugly gal, you 'bout as black as my ass, so why you puttin' y'all's up front?!"

Outraged, the lady in the first row stood up and in a haughty tone asserted her status as a White woman; she unfolded her family tree back five generations, revealing Scottish, Welsh, and even French ancestors, swearing on her great god that not a single darkie had sullied her noble lineage.

"Yeah, yo granny shorely been ridden by one o our boys and ain't tell y'all!," shouted the old toothless woman.

The driver had to stop the bus and intervene so they wouldn't come to blows. In the end, the Negress from Scotland demanded to be let off to finish her journey on foot.

The moon was round, the cotton plants sprinkled with silver. The bus pulled into the shanty town, passing the dairy and the tall walls of the steelworks.

"This where I gets out!"

Steve shook the hand his neighbor held out.

"My name Willie. Willie Brown, yassir . . . Tonight, I be playin' a gig in a lil place on Alma Street. If the spirit move you . . . "

Steve nodded and watched with relief as the musician got off the bus.

*

Right after he walked through the front door, Steve hid the box behind the closet curtain. He was greeted by the warm smell of a roasting chicken and by Betty who wrapped her arms around his neck. She didn't press for details of his day: she was all attention and pure trust. Steve sunk into a chair and immediately a vise of anxiety gripped his throat. His life was too happy. How much longer would his incredible wife continue to dispense her grace upon him, a poor fellow without prospects? Still, the box he had hidden in the closet reassured him a bit. Tonight he would be worthy of her . . .

While Betty was pouring the coffee, Steve snuck to the closet, took out the box and put it on the table. Betty's reaction was exactly what he had hoped for. Lord, her eyes! . . . Lord, her hands which began to tremble when she discovered amidst the nest of packing paper protecting it a magnificent radio: the latest model Crosley, with a solid mahogany case, a needle dial and Bakelite knobs to change stations. Steve watched his wife rearrange the side table and place the radio on it. She took the cord, unrolled it, instinctively looking for an electrical outlet somewhere at the bottom of the wall. Betty seemed distraught: "Honey . . . How we gone listen to the radio without 'lectricity?"

The simple question hit Steve like a punch to his gut.

"I . . . We gone find a solution," he stammered. "The mayor promise we gone have 'lectricity fo Christmas . . . I gone go see him and tell him to begin the work, now, right away."

Betty clung to him, ran her fingers through his hair. Yes, he would go see the mayor, yes, the work would begin before winter, and they would spend next Christmas in the sweet crackling of Hertzian waves . . . Betty was barely pretending, she believed her man capable of moving heaven and earth. Using whispers and caresses she managed to restore a weak smile to his face, and kissed him full on the mouth.

The train lights illuminated him with a supernatural glow. Pastor Augustus Lloyd turned onto Main Street, his satchel in his hand. The train journey had not dispelled the tangled mass of absurd things people had said, the sycophancy and hypocritical confessions that had assaulted him all day long. The small Baptist community in Walls had only a few dozen members, but its ranks included the most unbearable battalion of old gossips and doddering fools in the county. He still remembered that woman, with her hair done up in the shape of a pear, who told him about her transportation problems and her bunions and whose every complaint was accompanied by: "Lord Jesus, I so bloated! Lord, take pity on my warts!" How annoying, what baseness! These not-very-compassionate thoughts made Augustus Lloyd veer off his usual route. From out of the shacks scattered randomly along the road there emerged raucous voices and sounds of people eating. Pagan music sounded above the metal roofs. At the end of a narrow alley, he saw a couple copulating like animals; the woman's buttocks were propped up on a barrel and her partner was pounding her relentlessly, his pants bunched up at his ankles. The pastor turned his eyes away without knowing where to look: the entire quarter attracted vice like a spider's web.

Augustus Lloyd found himself in a dilemma he would have been happy to avoid. Should he condemn unequivocally or attempt to save if only one soul from this inhabited sewer?

Should these strayed and drunken beasts be accounted for like profit and loss? Wasn't it his place to raise up his black-skinned broken-hearted brothers and sisters? The pastor felt like a coward. Having ignored Evil, allowed it to extend its grasp into the bowels of the town, he found he was incapable of confronting it and its innumerable tentacles.

A small crowd had gathered in front of the entrance to the Post Office Saloon. A harsh light escaped from the swinging doors. The pastor walked up cautiously. The crowd merged into a single laughing mass. It was still early, it wasn't yet time for drawn knives or damning blasphemy. A tall fellow holding a guitar case passed him on the right, tapped him on the shoulder as if he were a drinking buddy and said: "Holy shit! Man, there be some frou-frou in the air tonight!"

Augustus Lloyd summoned all his moral superiority so his response would need no words. Willie Brown perceived the scorn conveyed by that silence; he called upon the reflexes that had enabled him to survive in the worst juke joints in the Deep South, and his fist clenched, ready to strike. "My man, all I wants is to have some laughs an enjoy myself, you hears me?!"

The pastor humbly nodded his head. Willie Brown made do with this sign of respect and climbed the stairs onto the porch. The sound of a badly tuned piano could be heard coming out of the brightly lighted room. Willie Brown and the crowd disappeared into the saloon. Augustus was alone in front. He waited, his stomach in a knot. A woman's voice rose up, as satisfying as a cigarette after making love. The voice melted over the pastor, caressing him, undressing him, confusing him. Augustus Lloyd turned and began walking on the lighted road that led to the nice part of town and respectability.

Welcome to the Post Office Saloon, brother! Welcome to Hell, Purgatory, and Paradise. The former relay station hotel for businessmen, once quite elegant, now exudes only a vague impression of luxury, but don't be fooled by the chandeliers or the height of the ceiling; the prosperous times are in the distant past and the clientele has changed dramatically. Admire this tableau if you would: superb losers clustered together like beans in sauce, always only a hair's breadth from a fight, those pirate faces that don't even dare look at themselves in a mirror. Take a good look at those hands, black and worn—hands of cotton pickers, farmers, loggers, high rollers, hands covered with rings or naked from want. Nowhere will you find such a concentration of the damned. On Saturday night, here, the dead are resurrected. And it's the same in Vicksburg, Jackson, Eden, and Yazoo City: every weekend the Delta reconnects with its truth, the one that is there, at the bottom of the bottle that empties before your eyes, in that raggedy guitar exuding its vibratos, in the bodice of that mother who remembers she has her own special truth and tenderness to sell.

Willie Brown is leaning on the bar. It's already been fifteen minutes since he ordered his bourbon. Next to him a drunk is snoring, his head on his arms, a full glass of amber liquid sitting next to his ear. Willie puts a dime in the man's pocket, takes the glass and raises it to his mouth. The smuggled booze must be mighty strong. Willie Brown looks around the smoky room. In the back, near the toilets, someone is playing cards, Coon Can; it's no use explaining the rules, those at the table change them depending on their level of drunkenness and their moods. Underneath the stairs, others prefer to play Texas hold 'em, with a small local variation. The players have their own bottle placed next to the chips, a switchblade or a Derringer at the ready in an inside jacket pocket. Not one of these tough men hasn't spent at least two years in the Parchman penitentiary. They are the worst sorts of scum: gamblers in debt to their eyeballs, pox-ridden bookmakers, brutal and sneaky pimps. The whores stand a safe distance from the tables, trying to decipher their pimp's game, anticipating either caresses or a beating.

Willie Brown jerks upright, a particularly horrible wrong note makes him turn around. He had scarcely noticed the background music, covered by the din of voices. On a small stage, an older fellow, his back hunched over, is pounding out a wild boogie-woogie on a dying Trayser piano. The pianist is Elias Coleman. Sargent Elias. A veteran of the Great War in Europe, demobilized over fifteen years ago. The medals he earned in the trenches of France are pinned onto his jacket. Elias reached the rank of non-commissioned officer, but left an eye on the battlefield; a glass marble stuck in his eye socket gives his gaze a strange fixed look.

The owner here is Joe. Joe Hives. At first, with his jowls, his silky eyebrows, and his little Cab Calloway mustache, he seems benign, but that's deceiving; he's a first-rate bad-ass-nigga. You just have to see the big veins of his buffalo's neck swell when he gets angry, and you immediately freeze in your tracks. Joe sweated blood and tears for thirty years as a roust-about on the Greenville docks; with his savings he bought the former hotel for a song. He manages the place with an iron hand, he is a waiter, cook, and mainly bouncer—oh man, when he picks up a keg of whiskey and throws it outside, it's a spectacle to behold! His little business does pretty well, but given the city taxes, the protection money he pays the sheriff and the fear of every night seeing his bar become a crime scene, you can't say Joe has an easy life. Tonight, the tension can be felt, no time to wipe glasses, too bad for the finicky. Joe glances at the Elgin watch on his wrist. He picks up a hammer and begins to pound on a bell at the end of the bar, managing to impose a bit of calm.

"And now, I want y'all to welcome our house singer, Miss Dora Payne, born in Robinsonville and famous as far as Texas!"

The splendid Dora, her face made up, comes down the main staircase. She is wearing a ruffled Mexican dress. The drunk next to Willie Brown emerges out of his coma: "There she be, you fuckers! There be Dora Payne! She have a voice o gold, an I ain't gotta mention her ass!"

More pounding on the bell. Silence.

Hundreds of eyes follow the diva to the stage. Sargent Elias suspends his hands above the keys. Dora begins her performance with an Ida Cox classic. Her version of "Wild Women Don't Have the Blues" is raw, uncompromising. A rough song for a rough-hewn audience.

When my man starts kickin' I let him find another home
I get full of good liquor, walk the streets all night . . .

Dora doesn't have the virtuosity of the "Uncrowned Queen," she struggles with the high notes and articulates badly. Her voice isn't that seductive. The pianist plays a bear cat crawl, stresses the low notes to punctuate the song and doesn't do too badly. The applause she receives doesn't seem to affect Dora. "This next number fo my lil boy Josh . . . " she says before launching into Bessie Smith's lament, "Nobody Knows You When You're Down and Out." Elias knows instinctively that he can't add anything to such a flood of sadness, so he puts his hands in his lap and lets a tear fall onto his veteran's cheek.

> . . . Then I began to fall so low,
> Lost all my good friends, I did not have nowhere to go.
> I get my hands on a dollar again,
> I'm gonna hang on to it till that eagle grins.
> 'Cause no, no, nobody knows you
> When you're down and out.
> In your pocket, not one penny,
> And as for friends, you don't have any.

Bobby enters the room just as Dora's voice is reaching a crescendo. The shockwave erases his usual smile. The applause is brief and self-conscious, everyone tries to find a reason for hope in the bottom of his glass. The owner mutters a few words to Dora who gets down from the stage. At the corner of the bar Willie Brown says to her: "You be the blues, gal, you and nobody else." Dora smiles vaguely and goes upstairs. At the poker table the pimps eye Bobby suspiciously. The young man is dressed like them, a real "Jellybean": polished shoes, silk tie, starched shirt. His brutal little cherub mouth goes well with his assumed profession, but the pimps can't figure out who he is. He could be "Harpoon" Mike from Greenwood, or Harry "The Rooster" Jones who might have abandoned his fiefdom in Memphis. Bobby makes his way to the bar and starts chatting with a heavily made-up woman.

"Hey, look there, that dude be talkin' up yo Suzy?" says an angry male voice.

"Jus let him try, I gone rip out his guts and stuff'm with gravel, Harpoon Mike or not . . . "

The bourbon Willie Brown ordered finally arrives. He picks up his guitar case, climbs onto the stage, and places his glass on the piano. "Sargent," he says to the pianist, "you deserve yoself a lil break." Elias, flattered that someone has remembered his rank, sips from his glass, wiping his forehead. Willie takes his Washburn out of its case, puts the strap over his shoulder and starts playing a piece by his mentor, Charley Patton.

> . . . *You can shake it, you can break it,*
> *You can hang it on the wall*
> *. . . throw it out the window, catch it 'fore it falls*
> *My jelly, my roll, sweet mama, don't let it fall!*

The room begins to dance: Lindy-hop, Hootchy-kootchy, Cake-walk, jitterbug—good Lord, it's really shaking! Bobby tries his luck. He blows into his harmonica with all his strength and reaches perfection at the bridge before the refrain. Willie gives him an approving wink and the young man joins him on stage.

> *You can shake it, you can break it,*
> *You can hang it on the wall*

Throw it out the window, catch it 'fore it fall
My jelly, my roll, sweet mama, don't let it fall

Joe Hives hammers on the bell like a crazy man and pushes recalcitrant revelers to the door. Willie Brown and Bobby enjoy their success, toasting with some Bulleit whiskey from the owner's personal stash, a drink from before prohibition, distilled following the rules of the art.

"Y'all gots some talent fo blowin, boy," says Willie Brown, discretely pocketing the bill the bar owner had slid into his hand and which he doesn't intend to share.

"Thank ya, pops. I plays some guitar, too . . . "

"Next Sat'day, we playin' a gig at Fat Sam's down to Woolfolk. My ole frien Son House gone be there. If y'all wants, come on by with yo harp."

"Mist House gone be there? I sho nuf gone come!"

"Y'all know Son, boy?"

"Yassir. When y'all see im, tell im Little Robert say hey."

Dora comes back down into the room, followed by a well-dressed Black man who looks around the room nervously. The boss has the john leave by the back door.

"Boss, y'all gots a drop o brandy left for the gal who made my heart cry dry?" Willie asks.

"Dry hearts, I done known a fair number," says Dora, "and I don't thinks y'all be one o those . . . "

Dora sits down next to the bluesman, puts her arm around his neck, and looks Bobby up and down condescendingly.

"Boy, it bout time y'all go home, yo mama gone worry."

Bobby clenches his teeth, angrily stamps out his cigarette and goes straight to the door.

"I do believe you done made him mad," says Willie.

"Shit, he a youngin, he gone get over it."

*

Whenever he got up on stage, Willie Brown had trouble sleeping afterwards. Next to him Dora was scarcely breathing, the sheet just barely covering her body was slowly emerging from the darkness. Willie lit yet another cigarette and allowed the music in his head to die down.

Several knocks on the door. A kid's voice. Willie shook Dora who twisted on the mattress like a woman possessed, refusing to let go of her dream. More, increasingly loud knocks.

"Mama, Mama! . . . Get up, please . . . "

Dora got out of bed, her hair tumbling around her. Willie heard a slap in the darkness. Dora came back and collapsed onto the mattress and immediately fell back asleep. Willie Brown got dressed and went into the hallway; a boy was there, bare feet and chest, leaning on the staircase banister.

The bluesman went up to him and the boy moved away.

"Don't be fraid . . . I's uncle Willie, yo mama's frien."

"Mama asleep again, ain't she?"

"Yeah. Heah, I found a pack o chewin' gum in my pocket. It cola flavor, y'all like that?"

The boy nodded and took the chewing gum. Willie Brown watched him walk down the hallway, the wooden floorboards creaking timidly under his light weight.

The rye and the wheat were awaiting the sickles. Turnips had shrunk under the ground, the young millet shoots, too puny to defend themselves, endured the assault of the hot waves of air; a few harmless clouds floated in the blue expanse. It seemed the rain would never again be seen on the land, or only to drown it, beat it down with thunder and deluge. Trust between men and the heavens had been broken. What crimes had those men committed, which terrible forces had they mocked to be promised only a desert or a flood?

Willie Brown had hitchhiked at the edge of town and been dropped at the intersection of Star Landing and Blythe Road. To orient himself in the middle of the fields, he had only the vague directions of a girl of the night, her eyes encircled with kohl, whom he had loved until dawn. A poor compass. Before collapsing on her pallet, the girl—he couldn't remember her name, but Lord, how she sang, and fucked her heart out—had pointed out the road that went to Lake Cormorant. He just had to follow the train tracks. "To the east," said the girl, "where the sun rise up." But the sun came up everywhere, covered everything. Willie Brown picked a direction and started walking, heading toward a dried-up stream whose bed wandered like a dead artery over the plain.

Son House was steering the tractor, opening his eyes wide to make out the end of the row. The sun was full on his face, the smoke of his pipe mixed with the bitter cloud that came out of the exhaust pipe standing in front of him like a miniature smokestack. When he got to the end of the row, he bit on the end of the pipe between his teeth and negotiated the turn. The tractor endured the heat without complaining. It was a good old Waterloo Boy, the body a bright green, yellow wheels, the kerosene tank attached to the motor. From time to time Son House turned around in his seat to make sure the big steel harrow was still in place. The earth was in mourning, crumbling and black, he felt deep compassion for it. Son House wasn't thinking in terms of yield, working a plot of land that wasn't his and for which he was only a humble sharecropper. In his head there grew the specter of famine. He remembered that cursed year, a long time ago, when the boll weevil, that rotten eater of cotton plants, had destroyed crops. Along with his parents and young brothers and sisters he had been forced to chew on bark and eat bread like clay to satisfy his hunger. Son House didn't want to succumb to the vision of his own kids brought down by poverty, but as an old Negro of the land, he remained lucid: if rain didn't come before the end of the month, no one would escape unharmed.

The tractor made a slow U-turn and now the sun was at his back. At the end of the field a figure was approaching, gesticulating, struck full on by the sunlight. Son House shifted into a higher gear, a roar came out of the machine's pipes. The figure was less than thirty feet away, a guitar case under his arm, stomping along on the clumps of dirt, his clothes covered with dust. Son House smiled through the smoke. That damned

Willie Brown was going to have to get his nice suit dusted and his shoes polished.

As soon as he climbed up on the tractor, Willie Brown was overwhelmed by an irrepressible desire to start singing. His ass balancing precariously on the half of the seat he was sharing with his buddy, he took out his Washburn and started singing above the rumbling of the motor:

> Fella, down in the country, it almost make you cry
> Fella, down in the country, it almost make you cry
> Women and children flaggin' freight trains for rides
> And it may bring sorrow, Lord, it may bring tears
> It may bring sorrow, Lord, and it may bring tears
> Oh, Lord, oh, Lord, let me see your brand new year.

Son House, without taking his eyes off his row, listened to that heartfelt blues which Willie Brown's raspy voice rendered even more plaintive.

"That ain't one o y'all's."

"No," said Willie, "it a gift from 'Papa' Charley, he tole me he write it fo yose truly."

"Yeah, I recognize his sound," said Son House, tapping his extinguished pipe against the side of the tractor. "Hole the wheel while I fills my pipe."

"I ain't never drove this sort a machine."

"Jus keep her straight. It easier than playin' banjo, believe you me."

Willie Brown held the wheel firmly while his friend took out some strings of brown tobacco which he stuffed into his pipe.

"By the by, you got any news of the ol man?" asked Son House. "Seem he not doin' so good down to the Dockery plantation, a guy from Indianola tole me a while back."

"I don't rightly know," Willie answered. "Last time I seen Charley was up to Grafton to record his record with you, then Louise."

Willie Brown didn't feel like conjuring up the sparkling ghosts of his youth, when he used to make the rounds of the barrel houses, the scandalous dives, with Charley Patton, from north to south, east to west, from Clarksdale to Lorman, from Gravel Springs to Vicksburg, never stopping, breathing only the music and the steam rising off bodies. Willie Brown had lied to his friend. Yes, he had seen Charley Patton, less than a year ago, near Itta Bena. The idol of his teen years, the man of five hundred songs, the bane of jealous husbands, Charley, who could go for three days without sleeping and who mumbled the blues even in his sleep, Willie Brown had seen him, slumped in a rocking chair, starving and depleted, his tail between his legs and his pride in his socks. It was as if he had discovered Christ dead drunk, wallowing in a puddle of piss. The worst thing he had ever seen.

The tractor was reaching the end of the row. Son House took back the wheel and gave his friend a smile in which one could read regret for not having written about the legend sitting next to him, for having traded his guitar for a Bible, then for a shovel. Willie Brown tuned his guitar and stared at the horizon shimmering in the light: "This heah 'Down the Dirt Road Blues' be so sad it gone shorly bring us some rain."

I'm goin' away to a world unknown
I'm goin' away to world unknown

I'm worried now, but I won't be worried long
I feel like choppin', chips flyin' everywhere . . .

Son House was lulled by the chant. Sadness and the sun smoothed his peaceful, Abyssinian face. The two friends sang the refrain together:

. . . Every day seem like murder here . . .
Can't go down any dirt road by myself . . .
Can't go down any dirt road by myself . . .
I don't carry me, gonna carry me someone else . . .

James Conrad scanned the white tide over his land that extended as far as the eye could see. The cotton was begging and the treacherous light seemed to feed on its suffering. The corollas, which should have been green at this point in the spring, were brown and brittle; the buds, which had become bracts, released their first creamy white petals whose tips were speckled pink.

James Conrad kneaded a flower between his thumb and index finger hoping to see a hint of moisture. He picked up a clump of dirt, broke it and let it fall between his fingers. His brown mustache and hair stood out from his skin, discolored by decades of working outside. His blue eyes probed nature's secret intent. His partner, Jonathan Barrel, short and rotund, had found some relief in the shadow of Conrad's body. Jonathan Barrel in turn squeezed a flower whose texture seemed completely normal to him. He knew nothing of the whims of the land; he was in charge of selling, watching prices, drawing up lines and columns of accounts, much more concrete in his mind than the dusty rows that dirtied his shoes, something he usually tried to avoid. Jonathan Barrel didn't dare interrupt the musings of his partner, whose motionless contemplation was fascinating—he looked like a scarecrow, with his dirty jeans, his shirtsleeves rolled up and his Texan cowboy hat. James Conrad pulled off a head of cotton and turned around. Not a word. The tension in his jaw spoke for him.

"Not very good, eh . . . " said Jonathan Barrel.

"Not very good?! The coffee you served me this morning wasn't very good, but this, what's happenin, it's . . . "

James Conrad threw down the flower and stomped on it like he was killing a destructive insect.

"Listen heah, James, they must be a solution, and maybe sevral, you just gotta explain to me . . . "

Conrad's hands started to tremble, a wave of anger went through him, a sterile anger that he couldn't pass on to anyone. "I see only two solutions. We either advance the harvest a month, but we'll have shit cotton and we'll be crushed by the harvests in Georgia and Alabama. Or we gotta pray the rain falls by Monday, and not too hard and not for too long, else it'll all rot right heah."

Jonathan Barrel translated his partner's raw data into accounting projections. Selling second-rate cotton at a low price was not an option; any profit would scarcely cover the costs of production and the plantation's reputation for excellence would suffer for several seasons. So they would have to bet on rain, entrust the future to the vagaries of the climate, await deliverance from the heavens. Nothing plannable about it: a biblical fuck-up, the brimstone of an alcoholic preacher.

Neither James Conrad nor his partner believed in divine providence, and even if he was looking at a pile of ashes it wouldn't have occurred to him to pray. But he believed in the land, and to think that it could betray him, allow his life's work to burn under the sun or rot on the ground, made him almost hate it. He stared again at the dazzling immensity of the fields. He remembered that day on the road to Flanders, when he and his company had pursued the Germans in the middle of bombarded expanses. In the winter he had seen wheat fields change into sticky swamps; he had heard the lowing of dying cows that no one had come to milk. One morning, against the orders of his captain, James had knelt down and relieved an animal, getting liters of milk from it. The only charitable act he had accomplished in those pitiless times. Even more than the dead, more than the dying wails of his brothers in arms and his enemies, it was those abandoned acres of grain and those martyred animals which for the young soldier had symbolized the atrocity of war. Since then, he had stuffed any notion of transcendence into the pocket of his coat and never thought of it again.

James Conrad kept scanning the sky. In his mind, Flanders and the Delta shared the same desolation. Jonathan Barrel put his hand on his partner's shoulder, felt his muscles stiffen and saw his teeth bared like a dog getting ready to bite. "Sorry James, but we gotta go see the corn and other crops, too."

The two men made their way through the rows of cotton back to a Buick, its wheels filthy, the windshield covered in dust. James Conrad started the engine and lit a cigarette. In the back Jonathan Barrel consulted his accounting books.

"We got no choice," he said, "we gonna have to put off a few families and hire more day workers, at least till next season."

"Puttin' someone off right now, that's the same as makin' them bums, there's no work anywhere," replied James.

"I know, but sharecroppers cost a lot, and their vegetable gardens are land not bein' used."

James Conrad lit another cigarette with the glowing end of the one he had just finished.

"By the by," added Barrel, lowering his voice as if someone might hear him, "seems there was a cross ceremony last night in the forest?"

"What the hell is this bullshit?"

"That's all the niggers are talkin' about. They say you could see the fire as far as town."

"Listen, son, if there is a cross burnin' anywhere in this county, I'm the first to know, got that? It was probly some hoodoo witchcraft to summon the rain."

"Well, now, that wouldn't be a bad idea." concluded Barrel, going back to his books.

Two friends, connected by music, continued along a path surrounded by an ocean of cotton plants. Son House had taken Willie Brown's guitar. Looking at the sky he sang an ersatz gospel tune. His middle finger and his thumb, reinforced by calluses, gripped the strings, ready for blistering picking, while his palm struck the beat on the wood. Without swagger, Son House played the blues like someone pulling weeds.

> *Yes, I'm gonna get me religion*
> *I'm gonna join the Baptist Church*
> *Yes, I'm gonna get me religion*
> *I'm gonna join the Baptist Church*
> *You know I wanna be a Baptist preacher*
> *Just so I won't have to work*
>   . . .
> *You know I wish I had a heaven of my own*

Willie Brown was indeed in heaven. Every time his travels through the country took him away from the Delta for too long, he felt the need to get back to Son House, who had never deserted his origins.

"Yo guitar tell the truth," said Son House, turning the pegs. "You kin tell it done lived."

"Damn, good thang it dont talk! It seen me in some unglorious situations, believe you me."

"A real guitar keep secrets."

A Buick drove up the path and stopped alongside the two men. James Conrad tossed his cigarette butt into the dust and stared at Willie Brown.

"Who's he?"

"He my ol frien, Willie Brown from Clarksdale. He gone spend a few days heah. He a legit guy, Mist Conrad, yessuh."

"I don't know any legit bluesmen. You done weedin' the field?"

"I done raked mo than half and I gone finish up tomorrow, seein' as it not gone rain anytime soon."

James Conrad put his arm through the open car window and punched the car's body.

"Tomorrow? You kiddin' me?! You will finish before this evenin' and if your pal helps you out he shouldn't expect to be paid, is that clear?"

Son House hid the anger that was coursing down his back.

"I asked if that is clear?"

"Yessuh! It be done fore nightfall."

James Conrad muttered "lazy" just loud enough to be heard, and the Buick took off in a cloud of dust. Willie Brown picked up the cigarette butt. He spat out smoke and looked at his friend: "I gone help ya, man, don't you worry. Two of us gone finish fore the sun go down."

Son House didn't answer. He guessed that the humiliation of the day, once again, would feed the inspiration of the night. Oh Lord, tonight the blues would live up to his fatigue and his rage.

There is so little room here to love, so little space to hug without harming. Kids grow up too quickly, girls watch their bellies swell before they figure out the mysteries of childhood. Hunger forces them and poverty backs them into a corner. Blood leads to blood.

Steve watches Betty get out of bed the way one watches the corolla of an omen open up. Betty gets dressed in front of the window. She turns around before going out the door. She is smiling. She says only what she needs to, without moving her lips: I'll be back, you know, and I will still love you. I will return and we will continue the course of our days, our distractions, we will celebrate our three-month anniversary, we will leave our imprint on the wind. Steve allows Betty to go through the door. There is enough hope in her wake for him to survive.

Betty loves Steve, and Steve exists only for her. This love defies the laws of gravity, the laws of Jim Crow, the cawing of power, the teasing and the goodbyes. That love exists like a cross in the darkness, a phosphorescent gun loaded to the muzzle with innocence and risk. One day, Steve knows, a child will be born. A chubby, wailing, wrinkled baby; that child will prolong their love, perfect it, make it shine like oil on the leather of a saddle. Their love will survive and between gullies and swamps will create the outlines of a new delta.

A door slams shut, startling Steve. Through the window he sees Betty walking across the yard. He asks the light to escort her, the oxygen to embrace her, and God, whom he never found outside of her arms, to make him worthy of such a miracle.

A path covered with gravel; a forged iron fence; a building made of bricks, sheet metal, iron, without windows or transparency; a canal whose water often flows red.

On the other side of the canal, leaning on a wooden fence, a wad of tobacco in his cheek, Sargent Elias Coleman is traveling back in time. He was fourteen, maybe fifteen, when he was hired at the slaughterhouse, which at the time was a simple shed through which the wind blew. The teenager's task was to lead the animals to the blade, after securing their horns and hooves. With a shovel and pail, he cleaned out the cement vats filled with entrails—on "the killing floor." There were three of them working there. There was that guy, a convict, a regular at Camp Lambert; he was the one who disemboweled the animals and hung the carcasses from the iron hooks in the backroom. Naked to the waist, he danced with the bloodless cadavers, whistling old prison tunes. Then there was the man with the blade. The killer. Elias had never learned his name. He was as skinny as a bag of bones, with a harelip and eyelids that were purple from lack of sleep. He started drinking at dawn, his hands shook constantly, except when he took hold of the knife; then his hand became as steady as that of a seamstress, his eyes plunged into those of the bound animal in front of him, and the victim understood there was no more hope for escape; the blade came out, the steel passed under the animal's throat, the blood spurted all around, and the man stared at the beast with a look of intense pity. Elias had found his master. Without a word, imitating his movements and stance, the young man learned how to sharpen the knife, channel the terror of the condemned. When his teacher died, brought down by cirrhosis, Elias became the head sacrificer. For years he had loved his profession, that artisanal way of taking a life. But the business grew, was modernized, investors bought machines, manual at first, then electric, and every day there were more and more animals. Elias killed on an assembly line. The blood flowed into endless pipes that disgorged into the canal.

Then came the tragedy. A trivial story, really, almost an anecdote in this land of pure violence. Elias had a fiancée, Rose Grant, a girl who radiated sweetness and good humor. Rose worked at the laundry, she washed away the stains of the city and he came home at dusk covered in unspeakable filth. Rose was a believer and had convinced Elias to go to church with her; after services, the young lovers went on long walks, holding hands, becoming drunk on pollen and promises. Rose was a virgin and Elias had respected her virtue. He worked hard at the slaughterhouse, hoping to save enough money to marry her in a righteous ceremony. One Sunday, Rose didn't come to their meeting spot on the banks of the river. The day before, her boss, a White man from Greenwood, had kept her after work and had raped her on a pile of laundry, afterwards putting a wrinkled bill into the pocket of her skirt. Rose had dared report it to the sheriff. The owner of the laundry claimed that Rose was a slut and everyone had believed him. Rose left town, without saying goodbye to her fiancé. Rumors had it that she had become a nun in Illinois, others suggested that she had drowned herself out of shame, in the belly of Old Father Mississippi.

Young Elias became consumed by a hunger for vengeance that he couldn't satisfy. He sabotaged his work, willingly made his victims suffer, slit their throats only halfway, spitting on their shuddering meat. He imagined he was bleeding out one of those White bastards: the owner of the laundry, his son, his daughter, his wife, the sheriff, the mayor . . . Reality surrendered, a door locked on him, and hatred became the sole backdrop to his life. One evening the young man saw on the wall of a juke joint a flyer announcing recruitment. He enlisted in the army. In Europe he was allowed to kill as many Whites as he could find, he even earned medals for it. Elias became a war dog, a sweeper of trenches. When he returned home, his medals pinned on his jacket, his hatred was still intact. It took years of wandering, of aimless travels in freight cars, nights spent outdoors, for Elias to be able to articulate something other than shameful resentment.

A truck moves along the path leading to the slaughterhouse, pathetic bleating coming out from inside. Two guys get out of the cab, one is carrying a long metal poker. The animals descend the truck's ramp, in a line of desolation: ewes with dry teats, lame lambs, wounds on their legs. The man sticks the sheep with his poker and the wooly column goes through the gate. Elias stands up, spits out a long jet of tobacco. He feels no pity for those that are going to die, nor does he feel solidarity with the executioners. He realizes that he spent the best years of his life between those blind, stained walls. Elias thinks of Rose, the love of his youth, his only love. Maybe he should have gone looking for her, followed the rumors, gone to Chicago, dredged the bottom of the river to find her body and mourn her in his arms. Instead, he had drunk and gambled away his last penny. The price of spilt blood.

Elias walks along the canal edged with milkweed and purple loosestrife. He brushes a Cape impatiens and the flower leaves a cloud of seeds at his feet. Elias gnaws on the bars of his mental cage, blind to all beauty. He has enough in his pocket to get drunk at the saloon this evening, enough tobacco to blacken his gums and enough courage—or cowardice—to keep on going.

It is difficult to pinpoint the fateful moment that caused you to veer off toward where you never should have set foot. You just turn the corner at Pine Street, walk by the armory, the square, the bandstand, and already, looking at the buggies, you can see the pink, chubby flesh of a few babies, which a black hand is fanning with the energy of a windmill. The first Whites you meet are still in diapers, they are babbling and whining. The ebony faces that lean over them are familiar to them, perched above their baskets since the day they were born, smiling at their whims and scolding them with a kindness preserved in scruples. Unlike the Mason–Dixon line, the border that separates the Black town from the small White enclave is not just geographic, it is primarily found in the hesitation of gestures and the discomfiture of bodies.

Steve approaches the square edged with willow and lime trees. He has never dared go through the entrance to wander on the paths, out of fear of sitting on a bench not assigned to him. He stops to check his shoelaces, meets the gaze of a nanny with black, plump cheeks who is offering water to the open lips of a baby. The nanny looks at him warily; a strange sense of guilt assails him and Steve walks more quickly, being careful to stay on the sunny side of the street. Here, even the sidewalks have their rules. The houses are several floors high, their foundations show no trace of floods. A peaceful White crowd is moving along the pavement. Steve clutches his bag against his side and becomes humbler than a rotisserie chicken. At the end of the street, beyond the equestrian statue of General Lee, the man who for most of the people here, Blacks and Whites alike, remains the true hero of the nation, the city hall rises up, with its majestic flight of stairs, its ancient columns and its solid wood door. *By Valor and Arms.* The Mississippi motto, engraved on the marble above the entrance, makes him bow his head. Steve enters the great lobby as one of the defeated.

A huge chandelier with electric bulbs illuminates the main staircase. The floor is tiled, the ceilings decorated with stucco motifs. Steve is in the holy of holies, the epicenter of power. He is paralyzed with fear, but the promise he made to Betty forces him to continue. He has come to demand electricity. He remembers the speech the mayor, Richard Thompson, gave during his last electoral campaign. Steve was too young, too poor, and too swarthy to have been able to vote, but he had attended the meeting, opposite the steelworks. He had heard Richard Thompson promise a crowd of folks with coal-black faces, putting his hand on his heart, that every home would soon have a bulb hanging from the ceiling. Five years later, Steve has decided he should make good on his promise.

At the top of the stairs, he is suddenly parched with thirst. He sees a drinking fountain with paper cups. Steve takes a cup. "Hey, young man, c'aint you read?!" Steve turns around. A fifty-something woman, black as the bottom of a cauldron, little teacher glasses on her nose, talks to him as she would an illiterate pupil: "That there the White folks fountain, boy. I works here, and I seen peoples taken out in handcuffs fo less than that."

"Where we others drink?"

The woman points to a service staircase.

"Over there, but they ain't changed the water fo weeks, you liable to get sick. You best go to the privy on the second flo. But fo the love o heaven, boy, read the signs!"

Second floor. Steve can't read, but like all Negroes in the South, he recognizes a few words: WHITES ONLY and its counterpart: NO COLORED ALLOWED. The door to the colored men's room is locked. A piece of paper which he is unable to decipher is taped on the wood. At the end of the corridor Steve sees two pale faces coming out of the toilets reserved for them. A terrible dilemma. Should he get a drink from the sink of White men or Black women? Going through the White women's door would be signing his death warrant, but colored women wouldn't be accommodating either, and the idea of being hit with an umbrella keeps him undecided. Finally, he goes on tiptoe into the colored women's bathroom, rushes to the sink and drinks enough to swell his stomach.

For over an hour Steve wanders around the hallways, before collapsing on a bench at the end of a badly lit corridor. Three Black men in workers' clothes are sitting on the bench. Steve turns to the man next to him.

"This where you see the mayor?"

"This where you wait, boy, that all I knows," says the man lethargically.

Steve waits so zealously that his eyelids close. When they open again he is the only one on the bench. Steve stands up feeling he has been swindled. He grabs his bag violently and runs down the big staircase. On the landing, a stocky man wearing an expensive-looking three-piece suit is talking to a policeman. Steve recognizes the mayor, Richard Thompson. He goes down a few more steps and stands in front of him: "Mist Thompson, I begs yo pardon, but I shorely must speak to y'all."

The policeman, with red hair and the face of a disgruntled Irishman, already has his hand on his nightstick. In the blink of an eye the mayor judges the social category of the man standing in front of him: a Black man with an ironed shirt and polished shoes is a potential voter. He signals to the policeman to let the darky speak. Steve takes a deep breath and launches into a long tirade in which he reveals the extent of his grievances. The mayor listens without reacting.

"Come now, boy," Thompson finally says, "Rome wasn't built in a day, not even in ten years. You will have electricity soon, my third term will be decisive, I promise you." Richard Thompson holds his hand out to Steve. The policeman next to him can't contain a grimace of disgust. Steve shakes the mayor's hand and detects in the pressure that it is holding a suspended threat.

"What is your name, boy?"

"Steve, Mist Mayor, Steve Young."

"Very good, Steve," says the mayor, wiping his hand on the back of his pants, "I'm going to make you my emissary, my messenger if you prefer. It'll be up to you to spread the good word to all the honest colored folks."

Steve passed through the lobby in a daze. He was probably one of the only Blacks in the town whose hand Richard Thompson had deigned to shake; he was thinking only of going back home to tell Betty the news. The Irish cop caught up to him right before the exit and grabbed his arm, squeezing his bicep painfully: "Listen up, coon, if ya don't know to stay in yer place, sure it is I will teach ya!"

On the landing, the mayor, expressionless, observed the scene. The policeman formed a V-shape with his index and middle fingers and put it in front of his eyes: "I'm watching ya, Steve-the-nigger, don't ya ever forget."

The streets were filled with shadows, moving and unconnected. In whichever direction Steve looked, he saw only distress. He could have been in the shanty town, among the Negro masses who piled up along the banks of the canal, except the wretches around him had changed carnal envelopes. Those he saw along the sidewalk couldn't reasonably be called Whites: their skin hesitated between gray and yellow, some were almost green, old stumps covered in moss. They were lined up in single file in front of an empty shed where last-chance soup was being served. Castaways of the Depression, factory workers without a factory, ranchers without cattle, evicted tenants, bankrupt shopkeepers, mothers in search of diapers and food for children with absent smiles. All were lethargic, with tattered shoes, disheveled hair, and unkempt beards of broken prophets. And above all, their eyes, shining with almost cannibalistic hatred.

A boy, barefoot and wearing rags, got out of line and threatened Steve with a stone. The boy obviously had nothing to lose and life didn't have much left to offer him. Lower than the dirt, poorer than a nigger, that's what he was, what they all were. The stone hit Steve on the shoulder; he winced and continued walking. A sharp pain in his lower back forced him to turn around. Several men and a few women had joined the boy and were looking for projectiles in the dirt. The stone throwers came closer and Steve stood petrified where he was. He foresaw his death, a biblical death, that of adulterers and blasphemers.

Then a man opened a shop door and started running in Steve's direction. He was short, his hair slicked back, wearing a business suit. The man held out both arms to Steve as if to embrace him: "My dear friend, you are early!" he said with a strange accent. "Your suit will be ready only tomorrow . . . but this doesn't matter, come inside, please, don't make me beg."

The man locked the door of his shop behind them. Through the window Steve saw the horde armed with stones standing in front of the entrance.

"I beg you, do not look at them, it will only excite them more."

The room contained a wonderful array of polished wood cabinets. Suits and dresses, of impeccable cut, were hanging on hangers. On a cast-iron counter, rolls of fabric, a pair of silver-toned scissors and ribbons of all colors. There was an odor of wax and furniture polish. The man held out a slender hand with smooth nails: "I have not introduced myself, I am Aaron Posner, tailor and alterations of all kinds. I also provide sewing supplies," he said, gesturing to a cabinet containing hundreds of nooks filled with spools of thread, buttons, and skeins of yarn.

"My name Steve Young, and I thanks y'all for openin' yo door to me, Mist Posner."

"If you please, call me Aaron."

"Aaron? I believes I knows him . . . Ain't he the one whose rod were filled with rose buds?"

"Exactly!" said the tailor with a big smile. "But I do believe that they were almond blossoms. I see that you are an avid reader of the Bible."

"Not really," said Steve. "I just 'member the pastor said that one time, when I were a boy. Are you a Jew?"

"Indeed I am. And, this will make you laugh, but just this morning when I woke up I still believed in God!"

The tailor looked out the shop window at the street.

"Good, they are gone. I can hear them from here cursing the alliance between niggers and yids."

It was getting dark in the shop. The two incandescent bulbs on the ceiling were off.

"Y'all don't turn on the lights?"

"No, forgive me," said Posner. "It is Shabbat. All that I am allowed to do this evening is to save the life of a man. In a way, one might say that you have been in luck. But wait . . . "

Aaron went into the back of the shop and returned with a candle which he placed on the counter. He took a box of matches out of his pocket and held it out to Steve.

"You can light it, unless you, too, are an Israelite . . . "

A soft glow lighted the counter.

"*Zal es zeyn likht*," said the tailor. "Tell me, Steve, may I ask what brought you to such a rough place? Of course, you may very well ask me the same question."

Intimidated by the tailor's refined English, Steve struggled to describe his plight as plainly as possible. He told him of his meeting with the mayor, his promise to provide electricity. The tailor seemed upset. He went behind the counter and took out a cotton shirt.

"You know, Richard Thompson is one of my customers. This shirt is for him. I don't know if I should repeat this to you, but the other evening he told me in a joking manner that

Blacks don't need bulbs for illumination, and that an oil lamp was already too modern for them. I hope I have not shattered your illusions on this matter."

Steve wanted to protest. He sought an argument to defend the mayor, but what the tailor said had the terrible sound of truth.

"I will be frank with you," continued Posner, "Personally, I believe that Richard Thompson belongs to the past. For next year's election there is a candidate, let's say unofficial, a man of color, a certain Andrew Wallace. Do you know him?"

"Andrew Wallace, the half-colored, him that owns all the shops down to the main street?"

"That is him. It so happens that he is planning very soon to hold a public meeting in Mr. Barnes' barber shop. Wallace is an ambitious man and he has the means for his ambitions. My wife and I plan to attend that meeting."

Aaron Posner looked a final time at the sidewalk out the window.

"You can go now if you wish, they are gone. Poor people, one must pity them. But first, one must fear them."

Steve shook the tailor's hand warmly and blew out the candle as requested.

As he was cautiously walking up the street, he saw lying in the dirt the stones intended for his lynching; going past the Salvation Army building, he heard the gloomy sound of spoons scraping bowls, slurping and the clamoring of the famished. A hundred mouths were eager to eat today, not knowing if there would be a tomorrow.

Children aren't monsters. If they imagine the worst and sometimes carry it out, cruelty in them is related to dreams. Their wickedness is uncalculated, and that makes them fearsome creatures, even more so than werewolves, zombies, or headless ghosts.

It is impossible to count such children—black heads, hard heads and rough heels. They have strange names, as flashy as nicknames: Buck, Mooky, Ada, Dood, Crunch . . . One might think they were named in a dying breath or through the clacking of a tongue and that their poor mothers, before dying, had just barely had the strength to utter an onomatopoeia that would follow them the rest of their lives. They are raucous, these brats, they run from one sidewalk to another and the main street, though quite straight, appears winding under their wild trajectories. They are heated milk, life on Earth.

"Fin'ly, I gots her, that bitch!" shouts Buck, the tallest and strongest of the gang. Buck has grabbed a chicken and is holding it firmly by the neck. It is a red and rebellious hen that had developed a taste for freedom. The bird emits sharp squawks, beats its wings, its eyes bulging. Buck dispenses slaps and kicks to keep away the other kids who are intent on getting their share of the booty.

"C'mon Buck, hey, we gone share, a wing for ev'ryone," begs little Ada.

"It only got two wings, ya ijit! Y'all get nothin, it fo my mama birt'day!"

"Yo mama be daid, dirty liar!" spits Mooky, Buck's rival.

Buck and Mooky roll around on the ground. The red hen takes advantage of the confusion and flies a few meters away. Joshua is standing at a distance. He's been chewing a cola-flavored chewing gum for hours; the flavor is gone, but the hunger that was gnawing at him has disappeared. The hen comes up to him. The child kneels down, holds his arms out wide to it: "Here, chickie . . . "

Buck sounds the alarm: "Hey, Josh be stealin' our chickin!" Joshua is caught. Joshua is beaten. He doesn't give in. He knows he'll have to account for every welt to his mother. Buck pulls on the chicken's wing like a madman, Joshua stands firm; the animal is pulled between two equal forces, its feet moving in the air; a wing comes off with a terrible crack, and blood spurts out in a jet.

"Ain't nobody gonna get this bitch, it be cursed anyhow," says Buck as a eulogy.

"Y'all be murderers, y'all be worse than White folks!" Joshua cries out.

"Y'all ain't hongry, that the truth!" says Mooky. "Yo mama be rich cause she sell her jelly roll to ev'rone!"

Constance Reed appears and breaks the gang's circle. Her hand strikes out at random, harsh and sonorous slaps, which no kid dares try to avoid. "Ain't y'all ashamed?! Specially you, Buck? If yo po mama done seen y'all from up above!"

Buck receives a major slap. Deep inside his head he suddenly has the impression he's a child like any other with a mother who punishes him and sets him straight. The gang scatters into the adjacent streets.

A yellow dog emerges from its hiding place beneath a porch. The dog is so pitiful that no one bothers to throw a stone at it. It sniffs the cadaver, bites into it, and carries its meal into its refuge, sheltered from humans and the light.

Dreams don't pardon, they are the shroud in which everyone is buried; in that teeming solitude, no one has a name, and thoughts are tracings stripped away by fear.

Bobby lingers in indecision. The images in his head are ugly, slowed by alcohol. Lying on the ground, pale bars of light above are cast on him like the bars of a cage. His thoughts are gum chewed to the point of disgust; nasty odors reach his nostrils. He's unable to sit up, his head knocks against boards. Beyond his legs, the night. Lights appear, then fade away. The animals are there. The phantom army. Bobby creeps on his back. The dark battalion leads the assault; the animals run between his legs, attack the leather of his shoes. Bobby crawls, his head thrown back, his neck stiff. A hairy creature with claws leaps onto his chest, he sends it flying with the back of his hand. Reach the light. Quickly. Bobby kicks wildly, he hears the varmints squealing angrily under the boards.

He sits up, breathes the burning air. Reflexively, he thanks the Almighty, then immediately regrets his praise. He bends over his shoes. A few scratches and teeth marks. He brushes off his jacket, his pants. He doesn't know through which witchcraft he has always been able to keep himself from the common filth. While his drinking companions soiled themselves at the first opportunity, he always remained impeccable. Bobby recognizes where he is: he slept under the porch of the former haberdashery, in a narrow street behind the saloon. He can't remember how he got there. He often woke up, hungover, in the bed of some unknown woman, or on damp grass, or in a freight car in the depot, but never before under a building inhabited by rats. He touches his slightly painful left cheekbone. He must have been in a fight and the state of his stomach indicates he drank beyond all reason. The causes and effects don't matter—he is alive and his youth can withstand anything. He breathes out into the palm of his hand, his breath is nasty. He needs to take a good bath. He'll have to knock on Mama's door. He will probably receive some chastisement, a typical domestic scene. It will be the last one. The gigolo era has come to an end. "Little" Robert Johnson crosses the town like a prince of the blood.

. . . Baruch atah Adonai, Eloheinu melech ha-olam
Asher kid'shanu b'mitzvotav
V'tzivanu l'hadlik neir shel Shabbat.

The candle flames were dancing, two figures bent over, then sat up following the haunting rhythm of the glow. A woman's hands brushed the flames and crossed against her chest. Her hair was covered by a linen shawl, the flames colored her smooth, pale cheeks. Rachel Posner addressed the Creator of the world first, the blessing of the candles was reserved for her, as ever. Aaron, sitting next to her, still rocking his body, began to sing. A single voice with countless echoes: "Go, my beloved . . . " This song which had been sung for millennia through meridians and history, as moving among the porphyry columns as under the blackened beams of a hovel, this song of kings and peddlers, of megalopolises and ghettos, everywhere announced the coming of the fiancée of Shabbat.

Aaron was wearing a large talith with braided fringes. His voice was an even warmer garment. He turned toward his wife who held out a Bible, one that resembled an incunable, the cover darkened by the years. Aaron opened it carefully, approached the flame, and began reading Psalm 95, with a voice as careful as that of a young boy on the day of his bar mitzva:

Lechu neranena Le'Adonai, nariah le'tsur yesh'einu,
Nekadma panav be'toda . . .

Aaron stumbled on a word and paused. For nothing in the world did he want to betray the meaning or distort the music. Rachel assisted him, leaned over his shoulder, and quietly continued:

. . . bezmirot nariah lo, Ki El gadol Adonai
u'melech gadol al kol Elohim . . .

The couple sang the psalm, side by side, like two travelers supporting each other in the middle of a hostile forest. The candles burned until the end of the reading, then there was darkness. Aaron and Rachel went into another room where large candles awaited them. Aaron removed his talith and folded it, Rachel did the same with her shawl. They didn't speak for some time and returned to the language of before, before they had crossed the ocean.

"They burn well . . . It's been over four hours since you lit them," said Rachel.

"They come from Jenkins' grocery. He told me that Pastor Lloyd also likes them. We pray to the same God, with the same lighting."

Rachel smiled, then her face became sad again: "Do you remember the candles in the Semper synagogue? They would burn through the night. We should have brought some with us."

"Yes, but we would have had to rent an ocean liner just for us."

The tailor guessed that his wife's thoughts were traveling in the opposite direction of their exodus, returning to the banks of the Elbe. He caressed her cheek and said in English:

"You are thinking of Myriam and Karl, are you not?"

Rachel nodded and replied in German:

"Why don't they join us?"

"Myriam is finishing medical school, it's long, you know. And Karl's paintings are just beginning to sell."

"Until the time when they will burn his paintings and expel Myriam from the university."

"Then they will come," said Aaron, calmly. "It won't be too late."

He put his lips on his wife's forehead and teased her: "Luckily you were there earlier to help me read. You would have made a great rabbi, if you had had a bit more beard."

Rachel leaned her head on her husband's chest.

"And you would have made a wonderful hazzan, with your beautiful voice. But you prefer to wear out your eyes putting thread through tiny holes."

Aaron and Rachel stayed with their arms wrapped around each other, halfway between Europe and America, their origins and the future. They left the room. The candles continued their silent praises, printing on the wall a kabbala of drop shadows.

The moon came off of its pedestal. Legba rubbed his eyes, the veil disappeared and he could see the black sky. He stretched and walked, without fatigue, soaking up the landscapes slowly emerging out of the light. The plain, inseminated with purple and mauve, as fertile as an Egyptian valley, electricity poles leaning over, the buzzing of mosquitoes stuffed with the blood of livestock colonized the space, confirmed that he had not left the Delta.

The sky was now a solid blue. He walked along some abandoned train tracks covered with wild chicory, euphorbia and dried peonies. Rails heated like pincers cracked the earth. Miles disappeared under his legs. He left the tracks and went to the road. A convoy went by, a slow saraband under the sun. An entire people projected onto the road. He stopped to watch the fifteen or so wagons—axles wobbling, torn tarpaulins, hoops twisted. Seeing him, a mother made the sign of the cross and hugged her children to her breast. The man driving the wagon brought his stick down onto the back of a mule that seemed to feel nothing. They had left in the deceptive cool of the dawn, and now they were roasting. For weeks they had prayed to Jesus and his escort of saints for a storm to come. Given the silence of the angels, they had turned to the ancestors: the *orishas* and the spirits of Dahomey hadn't responded, either. So, seeing the horror of scarcity looming, anticipating being put off the farm they worked, they had harnessed the first nag they could find, paid for with the crinkled dollars earned over a lifetime. Now they were drifting, some westward, to the ocean with raging waves and mythical orange groves, others to the everlasting smokestacks in the North. Aunt Hagar's children, the offspring of Ham, who had endured it all, continued to pay for the ancient curse. They had committed the crime of being born naked, of being born Black, and of believing in the infallible clock of the seasons; and now they were leaving, in search of new certainties. Been here and gone . . .

Legba watched the drifting caravan fade away. His chest was heavy with suppressed sobs. It must be noon. The burning heat was everywhere. Surrounded by the ocean of flowering cotton plants, he walked in the direction of Lake Cormorant. He was returning to the place where he had fallen asleep the day before. Why had he been assigned such a long journey? Deep down, he didn't mind. He knew he was just a cog in the machine, a jumping board for the great dive.

Legba passed through several crossroads, finding at the foot of trees talismans of cloth and sculpted wood. He was the one they were invoking, imploring. An uprooted maple tree, the trunk devoured by termites, barred access to a track. He could see between the tendrils of the roots a tiny bark doll dressed in a piece of red fabric. An ill child somewhere and her bark-rag double. A mother's last resort. He grasped the effigy in his hand. He could see a little girl, convulsed with fever, wrapped in sheets soaked in sweat. He immediately knew that the vision belonged to the past. The little girl had been resting underground for months. He put the doll into his pocket. Once again, he had arrived too late.

Dried-out irrigation canals streaked the plain with dusty rivulets. Cotton fields spread out like a fragrant continent; tangy scents blended with the chemical stench of lead and arsenic that the earth belched out in invisible wafts. Cotton plants spread out, millions of heads covered with soft filaments—deposits of snow in the open sky, snow that never melts. Legba advanced in the middle of the drifts, guided by a force greater than he. Suddenly, he stopped. At the precise place where his steps had taken him, beneath the strata of time, lay a pit, dug by groaning, ragged breathing.

. . . Black hands grasping pickaxes, hands that cleared and filled, legs chained together, stifled voices, caged destinies . . . Around the ditch diggers, foremen watching every movement of the shovels, rifles at the ready, whips in hand . . . Dig, nigger, dig the grave of your fallen brother . . . Scorpions bite your feet, mosquitoes from the swamps have drunk your beautiful red blood . . . You are dead and your brothers in exhaustion dig your last stanza . . . Here, at the crossing of rhymes, along the Natchez Trace, the Indians' sacred path, the cursed path of slaves, this is where your song line ends . . .

Legba observed the multitude of plants on the surface, the echoes of the martyrs underground.

"Hands up, shithead!"

The voice behind him was virile, but trembled slightly.

"Now, turn yourself round and if you try anything, I swear I'll take y'all down!"

Legba raised his arms and turned around, pivoting on his heels. A man was aiming a Springfield rifle at him. His blue eyes were glowing with rage. Another man, a few meters behind the first, had his hand on the butt of his revolver. He was fat, his jowls shining with sweat. Legba immediately knew that he wouldn't dare shoot. But the one threatening him with a rifle had already killed, more than once.

"Damn bastard, what you doin' on my land?!" James Conrad's voice reeked of fear. Never had he been so afraid, even in the trenches on the front lines. The colossus in front of him hid a large part of the sky. His face was terrifying: a mixture of genes and races. He wasn't armed, apart from a hunting knife on his belt. Given the short distance that separated them, his finger would have just had to touch the trigger and a bullet would have dug a tunnel in the middle of the man's chest. The rifle became too heavy for his arms and James Conrad lowered the barrel to the ground. The colossus walked by him, plunging his eyes into those of Jonathan Barrel, and returned to the road.

James Conrad gasped for air. Jonathan Barrel went up to him, a wet streak staining his pants.

"Shitfire, James, why didn't y'all shoot?"

II

"Love, oh love, oh careless love
Trusted you now, it's too late."

BESSIE SMITH
"Careless Love"

The Parchman state penitentiary in Sunflower County looks like a large plantation: acres and acres of cotton fields, more acres of dense forests; only the main entrance, with its watch-towers and gatehouses, sets it apart from a prosperous farm. The waning light, the hint of honeysuckle and slurry, Negroes bending over brown clumps of earth, the subjects of the same photos, sepia and misleading, as those taken anywhere else in the Delta. The photos are resilient, the prisoners, too. Those who come out of it alive will tell you that Parchman is unique in its cruelty and desolation. It is the domain of the devil. The great American gulag. One does not escape from Parchman.

I'm choppin' in the bottom wid a hundred years,
Tree fall on me, I don bit mo care . . .

The hoes struck in rhythm, the curved blades penetrated the earth, the chanting swelled, echoing in the crisp early-morning air. The song leader was indistinguishable among the thirty or so men lined up in front of the furrow, all wearing striped shirts and pants. The leader launched his tune and the chorus picked it up, with tiny breaks in tone, like a Negro brass band whose sound was heard beyond the barbed wire fences, unfolding over the free land.

. . . I ain't been to Georgia, but I been told
Women in Georgia got the sweet jelly roll . . .

The row of prisoners advanced meter by meter, their worn boots stomping in rhythm. The column was made up of a mixture of heights and crimes: assassins were alongside pickpockets, gambling cheats, and tramps arrested for vagrancy. Their gazes avoided the morning's bright light and concentrated on breaking up the earth.

O Rosie,
O lawd gal.
Stick to the promise that you made me,
Wasn gonna marry till I go free . . .

The guards in beige uniforms, rifles against their chests, watched the slow transhumance of the convicts. Their clairvoyant eyes hunted down any potential disturbance: the unbroken one who leaves the row, the slacker who is saving his strength. Despite the apparent distaste they showed for the singing—which they put up with all day long and surprised themselves by whistling the songs in the evening in front of their plate of fricot—the hacks were willingly rocked by that virile, heady chanting, feeling a paradoxical alliance between the singing Negroes and themselves, the guardians of silence and order.

The sun reaches its apotheosis. Shirts are soaked. Abraham is thirsty, he laps up the sweat that flows down to his lips. He could ask for a drink from the jug the guards put in the shade of a tree, but to ask for something is to stand out from the herd and take a risk. Spasms seize his muscles, his heart labors to move his blood. He thinks about his father, Old Doug, who came to visit him the day before. His worried face and his eyes overflowing with love. Abe knows that his father is spending all his money on gasoline driving his ancient Terraplane to come visit him, and that one day he won't have enough to fill the tank. And yet, Old Doug shows up every month, faithful to his promise, without judging this son whom justice has already condemned and whom he still sees as the naughty boy he had been before the event. The father's forgiveness intensifies the son's guilt and sometimes Abe would prefer that Doug forget him and erase him from his life.

Abraham brings his arm down like a machine. The earth . . . the earth . . . black clumps of dirt. On his right a tall guy is going full force, he has a wild ball of hair and smallpox scars on his forehead. His name is Cooper, Abe knows him a bit, they were in the infirmary together, the year before, during the typhoid epidemic. He's not a friend—you don't have friends in the devil's house, just allies or enemies. The man next to him is an ally and Abraham moves to the rhythm of his arm. In fact, something is wrong: Cooper has lost the rhythm, he strikes out of sync with the group and has stopped singing. Wanting his ally's silence not to be noticed, Abe digs deep inside and lends his voice:

> . . . *I seen little Rosie in my midnight dreams.*
> *Midnight dreams, Lord, my midnight dreams.*

Cooper glances quickly at the guards behind him. They're drinking coffee from a thermos. When noon approaches, the screws often relax, their stomachs growl and their eyes struggle to focus. Cooper senses his pulse accelerating. He calculates the distance between the row he is working and the woods that stretch out before him. A few hundred yards before the first rows of trees, another half-mile to the impenetrable forest. He's been dreaming of it for five years, day and night. Five years he's been dreaming of the glorious one; not of Rosie in the song, the true one, escape . . . He turns around again. The screws are even more relaxed. An obese guard, with drooping, blotchy cheeks, is urinating against a tree while the others sip their coffee. It's now . . . Cooper plants his hoe with a blow and leaves it sticking out of the earth. He takes a step forward, and that mere step has something fateful in it. It's now! If the song continues, that means the other prisoners support him and he has only to follow his line of escape. If the song stops . . .

"What the fuck you doin, Coop?! You crazy, man, come back heah!"

Abraham doesn't move a muscle. Terrified, he watches Coop move away from the column and start running toward the woods.

> *. . . I'm going to Memphis when I get parole,*
> *Stand on the levee, hear the big boats blow.*

The singing fades away, and Cooper starts zig-zagging, anticipating the bullets that will soon whistle next to his ears like a squadron of wasps.

> *. . . You go to Memphis, don't you hang around.*
> *Police catch you, you'll be jailhouse bound.*

Cooper trips on a tree root, gets back up; he can already smell the damp humus, the violent scent of sage. Once under the protection of the trees, he'll continue to trudge, until he reaches the border of the prison property, he'll go over the barbed wire fences and even if he ends up flayed like a piece of meat, he'll reach the other side.

The obese guard picks up the Winchester he had set down against the tree. His movements are slow, weary. He puts the rifle stock in the hollow of his shoulder and squints his left eye. The figure getting close to the forest is at the distance he likes—something like the deer he shot last month. He holds his breath. The chorus stops singing. All eyes, those of the guards, those of the prisoners, are riveted on the shape that is leaping to the edge of the woods. A gunshot, sharp like a branch breaking. The figure collapses and doesn't get up.

The guard lowers the gun barrel. "You theah, and you over theah, go get 'em fo me and bring 'em back! And if y'all try any shenanigans, I'll be ver, ver happy."

The two designated prisoners leave the column and run quickly toward the forest. The other guards surround the group, their faces tight, their rifles at the ready. A screw picks up Cooper's hoe and turns to Abraham:

"He was standin' next to y'all, right? . . . So why dint you sound the alarm?!"

"I were workin, suh, I sweah I were lookin' at mah feets, then mah ho . . . "

"Is you foolin' with me, snow ball?! . . . You woulda laughed real hard, eh, if that bastard had got away?"

Abe doesn't speak. He tries to burrow his eyes into the ground.

"Get back to work, all o y'all!"

Hands seize handles, muscles tense and metal strikes earth. Only the dull sound of the implements can be heard. The song is buried. No one escapes Parchman.

The mule was suffering, and Steve didn't have the heart to whip it. He half-heartedly brought his switch down between the animal's ears and it continued on to a boxelder tree at the edge of the road. Behind in the wagon were piles of large burlap sacks of flour that Steve had just picked up from the mill on Prichard Road. He was as tired as the mule. In the branches, the birds chirped weary songs. A sharp sound broke through the leafy branches. It wasn't the song of a bird he knew. Steve got down from the wagon and walked around the tree. He had thought he recognized the whistling of a fife, and the past unfolded over him like acid rain. He again saw the bands of flutes and drums at nightfall, the lascivious and unbridled dances, the smiles on the faces of the Negroes of the hills. He remembered his uncle Gussie pounding on the big crate, and Napoleon, "Nap," producing fabulous harmonies from a simple piece of hollow cane.

Steve instinctively turned to the east, toward the valleys of his childhood. He was born in Senatobia, but had lived the first ten years of his life in Free Springs: the fields of corn, the red clay, and the spectacle of sunsets on the bald hillocks, cracked by erosion, which the locals called mountains. Steve again sees the murky figures that fade like charcoal: that of his mother, those of his brothers, sisters, cousins. He recalls that spring, dark and hot, when he had followed his uncle's band for several weeks through Marshall and Benton counties. At each stop there were improvised musical picnics that went on until the first stars appeared. Steve was in charge of the meals: open the beer, start the fire for the barbecue, and sell sandwiches. While the band played, he passed the hat. At night, around the fire, he stood guard with his uncle's old rifle and stretched out the skin of the drums above the fire. For the boy of that time, it was almost happiness, those deceptive parentheses that surrounded the nastiness of life.

When he got back from the tour, Steve had discovered the hamlet bloodless and silent. His entire family had been wiped out by the flu epidemic and hastily buried at the bottom of a pit out of fear of contagion. For awhile he had lived with his uncle Gussie, but Steve felt like dead weight, since he couldn't play or dance, and his scrawny body kept him far from the fields. One evening, Gussie had his nephew get into the back of a wagon. They went across desolate saddlebacks covered with heather and broom, dry and rocky valleys, then reached Tate County, on the edge of the Delta. They continued to an unnamed town and Gussie let him out in front of a bakery. Steve went into the cellar and lay down on the pallet that Jerry Frazier, the bakery owner, had pointed to. He filled his belly with leftover rolls, said a random prayer, and fell asleep.

Steve had never seen his uncle again, and had never gone back to the hills. Not only because he didn't have the time, but also because he would not have been able to find his family's graves. Elsewhere, perhaps, the story of his childhood might have induced floods of tears, but here in the Delta, among the orphans and survivors, no one would have dreamt of feeling sorry for him, except, of course, Betty, whose compassion infused him with dignity.

Steve got back in the wagon and started whistling a jaunty marching band tune—"When the Saints Go Marching In." The road's shoulder was filled with invasive plants: imperials with pale down, tufts of bluestem furry, tridents with bloody spikes . . . "Lord, how I want to be in that number . . . " A peacock emerged from a clump of grass and fanned out its feathers as the wagon passed by, the ocelli sparkling like divinatory eyes. The animal trotted along and started cackling furiously . . . "Oh, when the Saints go marching in . . . "

Built in the center of a clearing, surrounded by stately trees, Sapphira's cabin doesn't have true foundations and remains standing only through the will of the gods. Ogun watches over the walls of straw and clay, and Shango, his brother, holds up the thatch roof. During the great river flood, the spirits had come together and the shack had been spared from the surging water.

Sapphira and Betty were sitting on a bench made of logs in the shadow of an overhang. They were sewing on a thick cloth spread out over their laps, a patchwork quilt which the old folks called "boutis" and which young girls had given the vulgar name of "scrap quilt." Side by side on the bench, the women worked in unison—supple wrists, pursed lips, holding their breath. From time to time, Sapphira looked over at her niece, admiring her dexterity. Sapphira had taught her to sew when Betty came to live in her cabin after Sapphira's younger sister Joyce had died. The pupil had become better than the teacher, Betty had grown up and Sapphira had aged—unless the opposite were true.

"I needs a lil pick-me-up, gal," said Sapphira, "you, too, I's guessin."

The old woman went into the cabin and returned with two steaming cups filled with a dark liquid on which a few greenish leaves were floating. She held a cup out to her niece.

Betty was suspicious of her aunt's brews; their effect was often slow, but when she went to bed, she would begin to sweat, her pulse would race, she couldn't sleep and had to relieve herself several times during the night. Sapphira hadn't wanted to pass on her occult knowledge to Betty, her recipes for poisons and antidotes; Betty could recognize most of the plants Sapphira used, sometimes helped her pick them, but no more than that.

"Why ain't you drinkin? It better when it boilin," said Sapphira, who gargled with the liquid before letting it flow down her throat. "You thinks I gonna poison y'all? That I be a no-account witch?"

Betty didn't have a choice. She drank and felt the mysterious substances take effect on her entrails. Sapphira had prepared a fertility brew made with mugwort, mullein "white bouillon," and lemon balm. Her niece, married for close to five years, had still not gotten pregnant. Sapphira cleared her throat and nonchalantly said:

"Tell me, gal, you an yo man, y'all enjoy yoselves? And not jus once a month, cause all those doctors calc'lations ain't never been proved."

Betty stopped sewing. She looked at her aunt who was drinking her brew in little sips. The old woman had spoken in a neutral and slow tone, the same voice that had soothed Betty so often when she was a child.

"Yes, Steve and me loves each other and shows it as often as we can," answered Betty with a smile.

Sapphira's dark eyes locked onto those of her niece: "I hopes he not playin' the heathen and don't water the sheets instead of yo drum."

Betty held back a burst of laughter: "No, auntie, he do ever'thin' he suppose to, and he no heathen, fo sho."

Sapphira frowned and picked up her needle. She wasn't really concentrating and the thread missed the eye: "So, maybe you ain't the problem, maybe it be him."

Betty was stunned. She was used to Sapphira raining a storm of reproaches on her husband, criticizing his scrawniness, his being unable to read, his clumsiness, but her aunt had never dared attack his virility.

"Why you say that?!" said Betty in a wounded voice. "Why you hate him so much?"

Sapphira put down the needle and thread and placed her withered hand on her niece's shoulder: "I don hate yo man, even if it true he ain't to my likin. I jus sayin' that sometime it be the mens got a worry an not the womens."

"Listen, if y'all want to know, Steve be a real bull and waters me real good . . . ifn I ain't with chile yet it cause the Good Lord be waitin' fo the right time."

Sapphira decided it best not to say anything more. She picked up her sewing and managed to pass the thread through the eye of the needle.

To the west, the laundry smokestacks emitted fumaroles shaved into ashy filaments by the rays of the sun. A squadron of rock pigeons flew over the clearing. The song of the plovers was blended with the chirping of the crickets under the grass. Betty raised her head from her work and found her aunt had fallen asleep; her mouth, with sparse yellow teeth, was wide open. Betty took advantage to pour the rest of her brew onto the ground. She continued to sew for a moment, then she heard someone walking on the path leading from the woods to the clearing. A woman approached wearing an elegant dress and leather pumps. She was holding a parasol in her left hand, the other waving to disperse a swarm of mosquitos. She must have been around thirty, tall and slender, her skin the color of gingerbread. The woman stopped, visibly upset by the presence of a witness. It was rare that Betty encountered her aunt's clients, as most consultations took place at dusk or in the middle of the night.

Betty shook Sapphira gently. The old woman got up and gestured to the woman to follow her inside the cabin. A half-hour later, the woman came back down the front steps and disappeared behind a briar patch.

Sapphira noticed the cup of brew at Betty's feet. "It not fo the ground that I make that mix'tur." The old woman didn't want to sew anymore. She wouldn't have admitted it for anything in the world, but her vision was declining and she had fallen prey to a continuous nervous trembling.

"You see, chile, the world be in big trouble, oh yas."

Sapphira hesitated. Betty was a fervent Christian, always in the front row of the church and still under the influence of Reverend Lloyd. Sapphira didn't dare tell her that she had just concocted an abortive potion for her client, preferring to remain vague.

"The woman who just gone, well, lets jus say she don want no mo chilren . . . Now I tells her that it were nature and we c'aint do nothin' bout it . . . Still, I wonder why poor folks who gots nuthin' but air in they bellies have youngins at the drop of a hat, when the rich folks wants to cut short ev'ry thrust."

Betty's hand was suspended over the quilt. She was fuming. She wasn't unaware of either the criminal assistance her aunt had just provided that woman, nor of the painful allusion to her own situation. She refused to raise her voice, but couldn't take anymore. She looked sadly at the tips of her shoes and tears rose in her eyes. Sapphira took her in her arms. Her finger traced the contours of the young face, Betty immediately became the little girl whom Sapphira swore she would take care of until her dying breath.

"I jus an ol' crone full o' suspicion," she said. "An I jus might be jealous, too. Deep down I do believe I jus might want yo Steve fo myself."

Betty dried her tears. Her anger had faded away.

The afternoon passed between light chitchat and everyday matters. The colorful quilt was almost done. Betty folded it carefully and put it under her arm to take it home and complete it in the glow of a lamp.

Hugging her niece in front of her door, Sapphira asked: "Hey, gal, did y'all see some time ago a fire comin' from the forest? The flames bout touched the moon."

"No, auntie, I ain't seen nothin' . . . I musta been in bed wit Steve and we was real busy," said Betty with a mischievous smile. "What you think that fire were?"

"Was shorly some White folks burnin' one o' they cursed crosses . . . The heat bother they nerves worse than us other folks."

The straw broom raised more dust than it collected. Sam Patterson, the proprietor of the place, was working up a sweat, the folds of his large belly shook to the rhythm of his sweeping. Fat Sam's juke joint was a dive constructed of rickety wood, polished by filth. On the plank walls, ads for Coca-Cola and Canada Dry ginger ale, as well as a portrait of Christ, his tunic open to a heart of flames, and people indeed wondered what he was doing in such a hole.

Fat Sam set down the broom and decided his meager housekeeping was enough for the evening's rout. Bluesmen weren't very finicky about hygiene, and the audience even less so. The real concern for everyone was alcohol. The Mulligan brothers had still not arrived with the casks of whiskey he had ordered, and the keg of beer he had tapped at the beginning of the week was almost empty. If the two bootleggers didn't show up with their precious booze, he might as well cancel the performance. An evening of blues without hooch was like a baptism without water: unimaginable.

Sam dawdled behind the bar, wiped a few beer steins with a dubious rag. He assessed the two regulars at the bar. An albino Negro, his skin creamy and spotted with red pimples, didn't take his eyes off his copy of the *Meridian Star*; talismans hung from his neck, alligator teeth and rooster feathers. At the end of the bar, a drunk was sleeping, his head resting on his forearms, a half-empty stein of beer in front of him. Sam dipped a container into a barrel and filled it to the brim with a yellowish liquid that looked like donkey piss. He slammed the stein down in front of the albino who raised his head from his newspaper.

"What yo rag tell y'all this mornin, Sidney?"

The albino assumed a theatrical air:

"Tell the truth, boss, nothin' good . . . Men are scoundrels and women irredeemable hussies."

"That be God's own truth."

"I's a good Christian," Sidney continued, "I's quick to pardon, but I do believe it'd be best to go straight to the apocalypse."

The albino took a sip of his drink. Through the joint's open door came the rumbling of a diesel motor.

"They fin'ally here, them som'bitches!" Fat Sam moved to the door, followed by the albino. A small truck whose bed was covered with a tarp had stopped in front of the door. The Mulligan brothers got out of the cab. The eldest, Jasper, was tall and lean, a wide forehead, crooked nose, and square jaw; he was wearing a fedora with a peacock feather. Wade, shorter and plumper, was wearing a suit as white as the dress of a virgin; on his feet, a pair of polished brogues shone in the light.

Fat Sam shook the brothers' hands.

"Boys, I were beginnin' to be'lieve y'all had forgotten me."

"We got a schedule, that's all," Jasper replied dryly. "The ice wagon'll be here directly."

Sam and the albino began to unload the barrels of whiskey, sweating like overfilled sponges. The two bootleggers, smoking cigarettes, watched them, with the vague scorn of parvenus in their eyes.

. . . Be not rash with thy mouth, and let not thine heart
be hasty to utter any thing before God: for God is in
heaven, and thou upon earth: therefore let thy words
be few.

Ecclesiastes 5:2

Pastor Augustus Lloyd's elbows were resting on the table, his damp fingers made impressions on the bottom of the pages; he had the disagreeable sensation that he was soiling the Good Book. Anxiety rose in him, along with a feeling of guilt. He had sinned through pride, delaying the moment he would write his sermon, indulging in an over-confidence in his inspiration and experience. He had slept badly, the heat had stifled his appetite, and he had made do with a few slices of fruit at noon.

There is a severe evil which I have seen under the sun:
Riches kept for their owner to his hurt.

Ecclesiastes 5:13

Augustus Lloyd closed the Bible, walked to the sink and drank a glass of tepid water. If even Ecclesiastes, the son of David, king of Jerusalem, abandoned him, tomorrow's service would surely be a fiasco. Yet, how many times had he delved into these chapters for the righteous fodder for his sermons? But Ecclesiastes had a disadvantage: it constantly referred to the sun, and it was perhaps inappropriate to overwhelm his congregation with that burning star under which nothing new ever occurred. At tomorrow's church service the mayor and his wife would be in the front row, the sermon had to be subdued, nicely boring, almost like a Catholic mass, like the one he had attended one day in Birmingham. During choir practice the reverend had stressed to young Betty that everything should unfold with calm level-headedness. The young woman had had the children rehearse innocent hymns, those that didn't allude to the Promised Land, the exodus, or the enslavement of the Israelites.

Ever since he had been invested as spiritual leader of the community twenty years earlier, Augustus Lloyd had gradually managed to eliminate any disruptive elements in the congregation as well as all types of holy rollers. Oh, yes, he had suppressed those gnawers of psalms who brayed in the aisles of the church as if they were still harnessed to the back of a mule, those old foul-mouthed deacons, with their ceremonial tunics embroidered with gold thread and their superior looks. The pastor's conquest responded to the highest moral exigency: he had to banish Africa and its stench from the House of God, nip in the bud any idolatrous practices. He had quite logically begun with the "Amen Corner," to the right of the pulpit, where overexcited church ladies and troublesome deacons assembled. During the service, the old spirituals, remnants from the plantations, and rustic hollers had been replaced by the hymns of the good Dr. Watts, and the tambourines had been put back in the cupboard, making way for a brand-new Mason & Hamelin organ. Inspired by his idol Booker T. Washington, whose famous Atlanta speech he never tired of rereading, Augustus Lloyd was convinced that in the face of the terrible deficiencies with which almighty God had stricken the South, the Black race had to show humility and, rather than dreaming of mirages of egalitarianism, do the honorable thing and purge itself of the savagery that disfigured its countenance. From atop the pulpit, Augustus Lloyd had always preached that they should turn the other cheek, calling upon his flock to render unto the sheriff what was the sheriff's, and unto the rich planters their due. In the face of iniquity, of being spit upon, and even of lynchings, he had recommended patience and compassion, beseeching his colored brethren to pardon their persecutors. Throughout his ministry, Pastor Lloyd had celebrated a pale-faced and docile God.

Augustus went into his sitting room. A pain in his knee forced him to limp a few feet. On a shelf, next to a clock whose tick-tocking got on his nerves, a glass-front frame protected the photo of his dead wife, Fannie, a bored-looking mulatto woman with a tight bun. Fannie had died nine years earlier, the victim of a terrible flu: "The same strain as the one that took down millions of men and women after the Great War in Europe," Doctor Howard had diagnosed. Of his wife Augustus remembered only interminable complaining, interspersed with bitter reproaches.

Light flowed in through the curtains. Augustus opened the window and heard the sounds of the town. He turned around and bumped against a side table. In a stoneware vase a bouquet of magnolias was dying. Next to the vase, another photo, unframed. A sepia print, blurry and overexposed. On the banks of a river, among the reeds, some twenty children, girls and boys, posed in white outfits, immaculate dresses and shirts. In the photo, Augustus was recognizable by his height and his goatee. His arm was around the shoulder of a girl with a rebellious smile, her hair in thin braids. Dora wasn't yet twelve but already stole the spotlight. Next to her Betty seemed almost erased, despite the purity of her features. Looking at Dora's face made him uncomfortable. He turned the photo over. A song rose up from the street. The voices of two men responded to each other in a call out full of vigor and spirit:

> ... *Woe, Lord, Berta, Berta, woe Lord gal*
> *Be my wife, Berta, and I'll be yo man*
> *Everyday Sunday dolla' in yo' hand* ...

Pastor Lloyd stuck his head out the window. A wagon was parked on the street, surrounded by a noisy crowd. On the wagon bed large blocks of ice were piled up. Two young men, shirtless and muscular, were singing while they worked; one cut off big pieces of ice with a saw, then the other picked them up with large tongs and put them in the containers the crowd held out to him. Augustus knew these fellows vaguely: alcohol traffickers, working for the Mulligan brothers, bad seeds whom he would never see on the pews of his church. And yet the quality of their voices imbued them with undeniable grace. They resembled two black angels bearing snow. The pastor buttoned his shirt and left the room.

Sitting on a straw bottom chair, the reverend was sipping a contraband beer, his eyes riveted on the bulb hanging from the ceiling. The pain in his joints had eased with his slight inebriation. He drank his beer in one swallow and put the glass down on the table a bit too vigorously—a foamy drop splattered onto the cover of the Good Book.

Augustus Lloyd opened the drawer of the kitchen table, took out a school notebook and reread his notes from the sermon he had given the Sunday before Christmas. Matthew 3:13. Jesus's baptism. Something solid, something familiar, nothing more reliable, more understandable: a hint of prophesy, the background sound of a river and a white dove to top it all off. The reverend regained his smile and allowed himself to be carried by the sweet current of words.

Betty looks at the radio sitting on the low table. She kneels down, turns the buttons looking for an imaginary station. She starts singing, softly, then more loudly:

> *Love, oh love, oh careless love*
> *In your clutches of desire*
> *You've made me break a many true vow*
> *Then you set my very soul on fire*

A magnificent band unfolds in her chest. When she stops singing, it seems she can hear the applause of an invisible audience. Betty bows to the ghosts in attendance. For a moment, she had seen herself as a singer. She had seen herself as Dora. Bessie Smith's ballad hadn't risen to her lips by chance; "Careless Love" was the girls' favorite song. Oh, Dora, Dora, what happened? How could two hearts that beat as one, loving the same colors, dreading the same darkness, today avoid each other and even hate each other?

The past is suffocating her. Betty has trouble breathing, she almost falls, the ground is beckoning. She sits down on a chair, and instead of trying to overcome the spell, chooses to be overcome by it, like she does with everything that overflows in her: music, pity, joy . . .

Betty had always admired Dora. Before becoming almost her sister, she had been her rival. On the stage of the church, the two girls elbowed each other, trying to attract the favor of

Pastor Lloyd and the old deacons of the congregation. The day the pastor had picked Dora to lead the choir, Betty had sobbed from disappointment. Then, choking down her resentment, she had decided to join her. Dora took Betty under her wing and led her far from her habitual haunts. The two girls roamed from ravines to backwoods trails, climbing over fences, ignoring the rutted ground; on their way back, they would pass in front of Sam Patterson's juke joint to listen through the walls to the itinerant bluesmen, their wild guitar chords and their gritty songs. One day, Betty saw a poster stuck up on the wall of a shop. The Rabbit Foot Minstrels, who were traveling through the Delta, were performing a few dozen miles away for one evening only.

The girls dared. They hitchhiked and were let off in front of a large tent erected alongside the road. Despite all of Dora's ruses and pleading, they weren't allowed in, but they could peek through the tent's flaps and hear the holy trinity of the blues: Ma Rainey "The Mother," Ida Cox "The Queen," and a young Bessie Smith, "The Empress." That unpaid-for concert, in the light of Coleman lanterns, was an explosion, a deflowering, for the two friends.

When Dora's mother died, Pastor Lloyd became a substitute uncle for her. He invited the young girl to have dinner in the evening, even tried to teach her to read from his old Bible. But the blues had Dora in their grip, changing her voice and her behavior. This didn't escape the reverend's notice, and he expelled her from the choir and banned her from church. Dora, proud Dora, took that affront with contempt and began to spill her venom in the wake of the man of God. One morning, the young woman left town to try her luck in Memphis, on the other side of the river. She told only Betty, making her promise to keep her secret. The secret had been kept. Dora had left and Betty saw her again only years later, accompanied by a boy of around eight, a little Black boy with sad eyes. Joshua.

Dusk settles outside the window. Motionless on a chair, Betty doesn't notice the sky changing. Steve would be home soon. She hasn't begun the meal, the very thought of eating makes her sick. Random humming comes out of her mouth, a rustling of notes, the sound of moving leaves. Betty identifies the type of song that is moving in her: it is the gospel song she is to sing tomorrow in church. She has known this hymn forever and the energy of her childhood helps her stand up.

*

Steve turns onto King Street, an ice pail in his hand. The sun has suddenly fallen over the field like an old Negro full of whiskey. Steve walks faster. Maybe Betty will agree to put aside her principles and drink a beer with him. In any case, she will be there. With just a word she will avenge his day and sweep away his fatigue. Steve had still not dared tell her about his encounter with the Jewish tailor or of Andrew Wallace's meeting at the barbershop, which he planned to attend. He was thinking about Aaron Posner: what a strange man, what a strange accent . . . No one had ever shown him such respect. When he was in his shop, Steve had even forgotten he was talking to a White man.

Steve went through the gate to his house and walked up to the well. A crawfish net was nailed to the edge. He spread

125

apart the netting, slipped the bottles into the net, and lowered it into the bottom of the well. Through the front door he heard Betty singing.

*

Thin strands of mist streaked the moon. Huge gallinippers buzzed and flew around him—they were thirsty, too. Steve bent over the edge of the well, gripped the rope and pulled the net up. He took a bottle whose label had fallen off and removed the cap with the handle of a spoon. Really tasty, that beer, nothing like the swill they served in the local dives. He finished the bottle, allowed himself a second. His brain was freed of his routine and his thoughts became airborne. The night displayed its stolen jewels that no fence would dare sell. Steve went into the house and joined Betty in the bedroom. She was sleeping, her regular breathing punctuating the darkness. He couldn't see her. He breathed her in and knew she was naked.

The problem with Negroes on a Saturday night is that they can't stop moving. The music possesses them, you watch them being consumed from the inside, and you're in the cargo hold, the boiler room, you stoke the fire, you are blackened, your hand is stiff on the guitar neck, your mouth hurts from singing—there's no microphone here, fella, did you think you're at Carnegie Hall?! You're going to have to bellow, my man, salivate, rise over the din of voices and the pounding of heels on the floor. And you can't sing just anything, either, because the worst is that these folks are listening to you, their ears are alert. If you say "right," they're going to turn right, if you say "up," you know they're going to take off, if you sing a dirty verse, they're going to rub up against each other every time! Sometimes, they turn towards you—that's it, they've got it! They've figured out you've been talking about them, about their shitty lives, rather about the shit that covers their lives; they are moved, they lap up your words, some hold back tears, you hold them by the throat. You're these fine folks' hero, but be careful, if you wander off, if you lose control of the helm, they won't forgive you . . . A blues singer in this type of port, has a major responsibility. You watch over dozens of souls, you help them cross reefs of emotion, and you have to embellish them, scrub them from inside. You're the guarantor of the beauty of the race, my man! When you've played three hours straight, with just a little break to take a piss and wet your whistle, then you'll have earned the respect of these folks, and when you run into them on the street, they'll tip their caps as if you were the mayor himself! No wonder the pastors, the holy-roller preachers, the hairy, furry holier-than-thous, can't get rid of you: you are their only rivals in the here-below.

Willie Brown, up on the little stage, was watching the crowd of dancers. Leaning over on his chair, Son House was struggling with a borrowed Martin guitar whose wobbly neck looked like it was going to give out any minute. Son House beat the rhythm with his hand, a true lumberjack shuffle; Willie Brown played some deep-felt riffs, slipping in some blues notes by using a pick. When Son House wanted a smoke, he glanced at his partner who brought a cigarette from his pocket, lit it, and stuck it in Son's mouth, without skipping a beat. The two musicians had been keeping the audience breathless for three full hours and those crazy revelers were still not satisfied. Behind his counter, Fat Sam wondered if the floor was going to survive the pounding. Son House started playing one of his own compositions, a "low down" blues number, both rough-hewn and catchy:

> *You just bear this in mind, a true friend is hard to find . . .*

On the dance floor, in the mass of bodies, a young fellow dominated. He didn't need to elbow anyone, and he best not step on your feet. The guy's name was Chester Burnett, he was so massive that he could have stopped a bull with one hand and beaten the ass of a grizzly with the other. A safety perimeter had been improvised in the middle of the floor to avoid the gesticulations of the colossus.

"Beat on it, my nigga! Beat on it! Show 'em what you got in yo gut!" bellowed Willie Brown.

Chester Burnett, galvanized by the encouragement, puffed out his chest and let out a roar that made the shack tremble on its foundations. Son House broke his E string. God damn! Imagine a fox smoked out of his burrow emerging with his tail on fire, a 200-pound bitch giving birth to triplets in the moonlight, a runaway slave who taunts his pursuers from atop a mountain, and you'll have a vague idea of the intensity of the moment!

"My man, you a wolf, a fuckin' howlin' wolf!" said Son House. "Too bad fo the angels who wings you just plucked!"

Chester seemed to enjoy the compliment. From then on he would be Howlin' Wolf—with such a nickname, it was a sure bet he wasn't done plucking the feathers of angels.

Fat Sam rushed onto the dance floor and shouted that the bar would stay open during the break. On the stage, Son House was rubbing his sore wrist. "This here guitar ain't worth a rabbit's fart. Y'all got a spare string?"

Willie Brown shook his head no, he rifled in his jacket pocket and took out a little hollow steel cylinder which he held out to his partner: "Jus play us some bottleneck."

Son House slipped his pinky into the cylinder, and moved it over three frets—the slide produced a wonderful whining sound.

"If only ol' Charley could hear that!" said Willie Brown. "Sometime he play with a knife on his Stella, say that make the young girls' nipples go hard!"

Pearl had already gotten drunk the night before in another dive bar, but she had decided to party again this evening. She went up to the stage carrying two steins of beer. Pearl held out the drinks to the musicians with the irresistible smile of a drunk young woman: "Compliments of the boss, he say y'all can drink as much as you want."

"As much as we want . . . Hmm, well, gotta taste it first." said Son House. He took a big swig and spat out an oat seed. Willie Brown just dipped his lips into the brew. "Well, it ain't too nasty, but you tell Sam we'd rather have us some good whiskey."

Bobby came through the bar's front door, his shoulders straight, his head high. He had been standing outside the building, not missing a note of the music, waiting for the right moment to try his luck. He made his way through the crowd and accidentally bumped into Pearl. She was getting ready to curse him out but stopped when she saw his face, the face of a rare bird. Bobby wasn't there to mess around, he walked by the shameless young woman and stood in front of Son House and Willie Brown.

"Hey, this here the young fella I were tellin' you bout," said Willie Brown, "the famous harmonica player!"

"Hey boy, it's been awhile," said Son House. "If y'all wanna play sumpin' with us, ya gets all the beer y'all can drink."

Bobby acted as humbly as he could. "You know, Mist House, I plays guitar, too, and it seem I do alright. If y'all will let me play one or two tunes durin' the break, that'd be mighty kind of y'all."

Son House and Willie Brown observed the boy in front of them feigning humility, not able to hide the ambition that was devouring him. The two musicians hesitated—it wasn't so much that they feared the whippersnapper would steal the spotlight, but they knew their audience: a roadhouse, close to midnight, alongside Route 61, was clearly not a place to make a debut. Bobby pleaded his case, made up some triumphs, sold-out concerts throughout Mississippi. Son House, tired of hearing Bobby sing his own praises, finally put down his guitar and joined Willie Brown outside.

It was still warm, the pine trees exhaled their resin into the depths of the night. Son House was enjoying puffing on his pipe and Willie Brown indulged in another cigarette. The two musicians were quiet, recharging their batteries before the next assault. Suddenly, through the open door, a voice rose up, raspy enough to rip off your balls. The kid had started to play, and holy shit, he was off to a bad start! The guitar hadn't been tuned, there was no rhythm, and the voice cracked even before the chorus. From outside it was bad enough, but in the room, it must have been real torture.

"We best go back fore they lynch him!"

"Shit, he wanted to play, right?" said Son House, drawing nonchalantly on his pipe. "It'll toughen his ass."

"Damn, Son, you was a preacher before, ain't you got no mercy? You ain't gonna let them rowdies rip that boy's face off, is you?"

On the stage Bobby was as pitiful as a Christian in the arena. His voice was drowned by insults and whistling. Son House and Willie Brown rushed inside and created a barrier with their bodies. Willie put a firm hand on the young man's shoulder, and he had no choice but to surrender.

*

Bobby walks toward the highway. The blues don't want him this night, and maybe he would never again regain their favor. A glacial sweat soaks his shirt. In his belly, a nest of needles. He prepares to stay up until dawn, chewing on his humiliation like tobacco. A creature observes him through the smoke of a Lucky Strike. The moon casts his shadow on the asphalt. The creature stalks him like a patient hunter. Its prey is wounded, his blood doesn't yet flow, but his soul is in shreds. On the road, no lights, no sound. Bobby takes his harmonica out of his pocket, plays a requiem for the falling stars. The creature stops. Struck through the heart.

The night was ripe. Soon rotten. The boy was crouching in the hallway, his face striped by the light of a wall sconce. The wounded chords from a piano climbed up through the stairwell. Joshua had slept all afternoon, worried he would awaken his mother. He had eaten all he wanted, and then some; Joe, the owner of the saloon, had made him a chicken fricassee with beans. The memory of the greasy sauce remained on the boy's lips.

At the end of the hallway, a partially open door. The boy went up to it and heard water being poured into a basin, then the sound of his mother humming. A creaking behind his back. The stair steps. Joshua crouched down in the shadow cast by the lamp. A big-bellied man, a hat on his head, passed in front of him, leaving in his wake an aggressive male scent. The man took off his hat and went into the room. The child silently crept to the door. A few murmurs reached him, moaning without a source, and his mother's voice, crushed by a superhuman weight.

When he was younger, Joshua imagined that his mother was dying, that a man was killing her, then resuscitated her, so that another one could assassinate her anew. Today, he knew that behind the door his mother wasn't dying. Not completely. The lock emitted an alarm click. Joshua stuck his back to the wall and disappeared from everyone's view.

The boy stood up and walked to the other end of the hallway to the only window which opened onto a deserted alley. He leaned his head out and saw the devil who was watching under the pale glow of a lamp. The boy stopped breathing. The devil wasn't looking in his direction, he was looking at the dirt, as if to find the path that led back to his infernal den. He was tall, old but strong, his clothes were suspiciously clean. He had a little beard, pointed and carefully trimmed. Something pinned to his vest reflected the light. A cross. The cross of the devil. It wasn't the first time the boy had seen him in the alley, at an hour when even rats didn't dare defy the darkness. Was it his mother he was looking for, his wayward creature, or him, the lost child? Suddenly, the demon turned around and waved at him. He smiled. Joshua felt a pitiless hand twist his heart. He jumped backward and closed the window. A cold sweat ran down his neck. He lay down on the floor and the night crept over him.

Dora carefully wiped the bar of soap with a rag and put it in the armoire. She patted her tender stomach and the painful lips of her vagina. Her skin, captured by the ray of an electric lamp, was clean, but it would take several hours before the feeling of filth would fade. No longer tolerating her nakedness, she put on a robe. Stifling, sordid miasmas filled the room. She took a bottle of eau de cologne and sprayed. She picked up the basin, looked at the street below, and poured a colorless liquid into the night. Dorothy counted the bills she had slipped into the drawer of the nightstand. Twenty-five dollars. Once the rent for the room and the boss's share were deducted, she still had fifteen. She drew the curtains in front of the window, picked up a knife from the nightstand, crouched down, and with her shoulder pushed the bedframe. Using the blade, she lifted up a board from the floor. An iron box hidden under some straw. Dora touched her treasure, then replaced the wood board and put the bed back in place. The money she was holding, she was going to spend all of it. On her son. On Monday, she would go to the second-hand store and buy him some suitable clothes. No, on second thought, not to that dump, to the tailor's. When she had seen Joshua come in the day before, covered with bruises, his shirt torn, she almost started crying. Up to now, to avoid the other kids' jealousy, she had dressed him like one of them. Even so, they had beaten him. From then on, Joshua would be the best-dressed boy in the neighborhood. She would also buy him a switchblade, or even a small pistol, so he could defend himself.

Dora had devoted the past ten years of her life to building a kingdom that her son would be able to live in without shame. The treasure in the box was the fruit of the hours spent singing until her voice was broken, lying under the weight of men. That had lasted a long time, too long. Tomorrow, after the tailor, she would look into buying a used car. Before Christmas, she would take Joshua on the road heading north. Tennessee. No, farther north, Missouri or Illinois . . . There, she would open a grocery store or a flower shop. These weren't the fantasies of a dreamy girl, but the realistic plans of a woman who had toiled non-stop. The money was hers, so was the boy, and no one would ever take them from her.

Dora lit a cigarette, took several slow puffs. She was thirsty. She went into the hallway. The lamp was out. The stealthy moon had managed to slip through the baseboards and the frame of the only window. She heard a groaning, like an animal moaning in its sleep, and saw a shape lying on the floor. Her stomach clenched. She knelt down and passed her hand over the dry, thick hair. The barber. Monday, she would also take him to the barber. Dora raised up the little body, was surprised it was so light. She was ashamed when she remembered the meals she hadn't had the strength to prepare, the slaps she had given him so she would be left in peace. She put the child on her bed, took off his sweat-soaked shirt, and tucked him in. The miasmas of the room had dissipated. Dora watched her sleeping prince. She wanted to sing, but could only cry. Her tears made her mascara run and a peaceful sleep overtook her.

The Trinity Zion Church, built out of immaculate white-washed wooden planks, resembles a small celestial Jerusalem; standing erect atop a rectangular bell tower covered with slate tiles, an ironwork cross is drowned in the harsh morning light.

"It be Sunday, oh Lord, the most blessed day of all, when You chose to rest, after creatin the world in Yo image . . . "

Miss Rosetta Brown turns her back to the sun and begins walking around the building. She always begins by going right. She looks like an eighty-year-old girl, with her taffeta dress and a silk ribbon tied around her ash-colored hair. She will walk around seven times. It isn't a penance she has imposed on herself, rather the amount of time it takes to subdue the over-abundance of love that flows through her like an electrical current in the marrow of a condemned prisoner. Rosetta looks at the cross on top of the building. The sun has risen a bit more and forces her to shut her eyes.

"Lord, how You suffered up there . . . how You loved . . . "

Everyone still calls Rosetta "Miss," even though she has been married three times; Buster Brown, her last husband, died over fifteen years ago. Rosetta has long been a central figure in the congregation. When the great Reverend Powell died, and well before the young Augustus Lloyd arrived from Alabama, she had guided the community unofficially, organizing spiritual meetings on the banks of the river. The ambience in the shade of the willow trees invariably turned to ecstasy: froth rose to the lips of the believers, young virgins shrieked like debauched women, many began speaking in tongues, a jabbering filled with onomatopoeia which Miss Brown translated. Unfortunately, one evening an obese woman had a violent spike of holy fever—after shouting out high-pitched glossolalia—and she began rolling on the ground and ultimately died after choking on her tongue. Overnight Miss Brown's reputation had been ruined: from God's helper she had become a dangerous illuminati, almost a witch. Though she was still tolerated on the pews of the church given her advanced age, people pointed at her, and mothers forbade their children from approaching her. Rosetta had accepted this reversal of fate as divine will, and lived her disgrace stoically.

Rosetta opens her eyes and begins to walk around a third time. She passes the church apse. The magnolias that Reverend Lloyd had planted the year before need to be watered, their scent has evaporated, their whiteness resembles that of a cadaver—it doesn't matter, the old woman's heart is blooming, she skips on the gravel, her voice which up to then has only resounded in her head can be heard all around her: "My Lord, it be so hot! You must really love the world, Jesus, to hold it so tight against Yo ardent heart!"

Behind the magnolia grove there is a modest cemetery. A serene enclosure. The old woman takes care not to tear her dress as she goes through the gate. Rosetta says the names of the dead as she goes by the graves, getting their news from the shadows. None of those who are resting under the grass is forgotten. She knew them when they were robust and laughing, sad or angry, and meets them again every Sunday, at peace under the crust of time. Rosetta doesn't recall the exact year she came into the world; she knows she has reached a biblical age, because she has put into the earth dozens of women and men whom she had seen born. She is the last witness of the time before, that is, if you exclude that heretic Sapphira and that old goat Theodore. Miss Brown was born a slave, on a small plantation near Glendora. Her mother carried her on her back while she picked cotton with her bare hands. When she was a girl, Rosetta sang her first hymns among the interminable acres of fields, prayed in the woods, on an altar of stone, afraid she would be found and punished. Then the masters allowed the slaves to construct a cabin for services, on the condition that the preachers be chosen from among the foremen, docile and loyal Negroes. Nothing remained of that holy shack, except a simple wooden cross that Rosetta saved from the ruins and placed on the wall of her bedroom.

Following the Civil War, in which her father and uncles had been killed defending their White masters against the blood-thirsty Yankees, young Rosetta fled with her mother to Southaven, in DeSoto County. The town. A hard life. She performed a multitude of odd jobs: ironing and sewing clothes, as a shoe-shine girl, selling hair lotions door-to-door, hauling coal, and was even a barmaid once. She learned to read by taking classes at night. She followed her first husband to Louisiana and worked at an oyster farm, then when he died from malaria, she returned to the Delta, to Lyon, a stone's throw from Clarksdale. She was already preaching with some success when she met her second husband, Howard, an exceptionally upstanding man. Howard was a steward on the luxury Pullman trains that carried rich White folks in luxury sleeping cars all around the country. He was mistreated like a convict and despised like garbage. But Howard was a freedom fighter, he brought back copies of the *Chicago Defender* in his suitcase and passed them out clandestinely to the crowds thirsting for hope. A passionate reader of W. E. B. Du Bois, he insisted Rosetta read *The Souls of Black Folk*. The couple threw themselves body and soul into the struggle for equality; they recruited a few militants and even attempted to create a local branch of the Niagara Movement. One night when Rosetta was attending a secret meeting near Jonestown, the Klan struck. Rosetta found the bodies of Howard and his companions mutilated and hanging from streetlamps along the road. Rosetta again fled and settled definitively a few dozen miles farther north. She married Buster and took his name. Of the six children she brought into the world, not one survived past the age of forty. Rosetta Brown's existence reflected the shadows and the rare glimmers of light that was the lot of the people of the night. She knew more about it than any book and was tougher than a cedar tree.

Rosetta notices Reverend Lloyd's car parked on the road at the bottom of the hill. A white Plymouth, a bit too flashy for a man of God, is what she's always thought. The first of the faithful start climbing the path shaded by pine and cypress trees. Miss Brown watches that beautiful Christian crowd climbing the hill and her heart rejoices.

The incline is gentle, yet bodies suffer. Pearl is struggling in her white calico dress. She hardly had time to rinse off in a basin after she returned from the saloon; she has so many escapades to be pardoned for that she accepts this difficult ascent without complaint. In front of her, in a wheelchair, old Bartholomew Jones is wearing his coat with big copper buttons. His son and daughter-in-law are pushing him, their faces straining with the effort. The barber Presly Barnes has again forgotten to shave; a thick stubble covers his alcoholic's face. He is courteously holding the hand of Clarice Brooks, a seventy-something who looks like a schoolteacher, whose sophisticated hairstyle is admired by all the women in the town. To greet the mayor, Tyrell Jenkins, the grocer, is wearing his suit of a prosperous notable; his licorice-black face, which he lightens with powder, is as noble and respectable as he can make it. His wife, Dericia, a quadroon with severe eyes, is disgusted by the dust that is sticking to her pumps. A gaggle of children, their ears scrubbed by force, their hair shining with pomade, hold in their desire to climb the trees. Constance Reed holds little Cherry by her shoulder; her aunt, Kate Adams, is watching Buck, her boy, whose left eye is still swollen from a fight with friends or a paternal slap. Little Ada looks like a cherub with her ruffled dress and headband—if only that rascal Mooky would stop his dirty looks behind her back!

The crowd lingers in front of the church entrance and people ask each other: will the mayor come with his wife and children? Will he wear the blue flannel suit he was wearing last year for his Independence Day speech?

Betty walks faster and climbs the path. She notices Miss Brown standing apart from the crowd, staring at the cross on top of the bell tower. Pastor Lloyd assigned Betty the difficult task of preventing the old woman from entering the church. Betty is angry at the pastor for having asked her to do such a thing. She takes a step toward Rosetta, then, faced with her disarming smile, decides against it and goes into the church by a side door.

Two cars park below: a beige Lincoln and a simple Ford Model T which clashes next to the sedan. A Black chauffeur, dressed like a butler, opens the back door of the Lincoln and Richard Thompson gets out, accompanied by his wife. He is wearing his famous blue suit, and the faithful congratulate themselves for having guessed correctly. Mrs. Thompson takes her husband's arm and begins the climb. She has long chestnut hair, and her milky skin seems to suffer in the sun. A man who looks like a plainclothes policeman, a redhead with the build of a Dublin boxer, gets out of the Ford. The cop's eyes scan the crowd on the path which has parted, forming an honor guard to allow the mayor and his wife to pass. While his wife hides her distress marvelously, Richard Thompson shakes a multitude of calloused black hands, slaps robust shoulders, rubs the heads of a few little kids. His reelection campaign for the mayoral contest at the end of the following year is the Way of the Cross, and today' trial is one of the stations.

The mayor notices Bartholomew Jones slumped in his wheelchair. "What put you in that state, my good man? Are you a veteran by chance?"

"Oh, no suh, I weren't in the war," Bartholomew responds, spluttering his words around him. "I were too skinny accordin' to what those recruiters tole me . . . It were a mule knocked me on my ass! It stomped on me in the stable while I were cleanin' up its shit . . . Ah, talk about a bitch!"

The mayor avoided as best he could any more conversation with Bartholomew.

"Well, my good man, you know that we sympathize with your pain, and there is assistance for invalids like you. Come on down to city hall and find out more."

Finally, the heavy doors opened, a few notes from the organ escaped into the burning air. The Irish cop preceded the mayor inside the building and inspected the pews, looking for a potential assassin. Pastor Lloyd, standing in front of the altar which was decorated with a cascade of magnolias, his arms held out to the special guests, was wearing an off-white suit and the smile of an apostle. The organist, a mulatto with oily, slicked-back hair, struck the keys with chords of funereal gravity. The municipal delegation took their places in the front row. The crowd dispersed along the aisles, leaving several rows empty for safety's sake between them and the White folks. Pastor Lloyd noticed Miss Brown enter discreetly and gave Betty a reproachful look as she was busily lining up the children's choir on the stage. Rosetta Brown sat in the empty Amen Corner, curling up like a flower to better unfold when the time came.

Bobby drank his whiskey without ice or pleasure. He grimaced when the alcohol exploded inside him. At the end of the bar, Joe Hives was watching the young man in his fancy suit drinking like the last of the juiceheads. He wasn't a full-time drunk, just a guy who drowned his sorrows at the hour when others were washing their sins in church.

Joshua reached the bottom of the stairs, his face puffy with sleep, his feet bare. He went up to the bar and climbed onto a stool next to the owner.

"Yo mama still sleepin?" asked Joe softly. "An y'all be hungry, ain't ya?"

"I kin wait," said the child proudly.

"Then wait a minit . . . "

The owner went into the back room to the kitchen. Bobby turned to the boy and gave him a stiff smile in which tenderness was mixed with despair: "You a good li'l nigger, ain't ya . . . Y'all already know how to train yo stomach."

Joshua nodded and tried to look relaxed. Bobby finished his drink in one gulp. The owner returned with a bowl of steaming porridge and a bottle of syrup. Joshua poured a stream onto the mixture and started eating.

"If y'all have an empty stomach, too, they still some left." Joe said to Bobby.

"It here I be empty," Bobby answered, pointing to his head, "y'all can even see the bottom o Hell if ya start diggin!"

"Might be y'all should go on to church, then."

At that, Bobby stood up, as explosive as a keg of powder. "God—I piss on im, you heah?! If y'all see me in front of an altar one day, it be to burn it down!"

Joe didn't respond. He verified that his rifle was where it should be under the bar, sat down next to the boy and started reading the *Meridian Star* of the day before while watching Bobby out of the corner of his eye.

The bar's swinging doors opened and Joe frowned. Two White men came in without taking off their hats. Harry Bradford, the sheriff, ignored the bar's spittoon and put his cigarette out on the floor. He was a well-built man, still young. He was wearing jeans worn out at the knees, cowboy boots, and a denim shirt on which a tarnished copper star was pinned; a revolver with an ivory butt was in a leather holster strapped across his chest. His black eyes could have been soft if a violent light didn't constantly flash through them. He seemed intelligent, but of an intelligence that served his own interests. His deputy, Anthony Madden, had plump, clean-shaven cheeks; curly chestnut hair came out from under his hat, a revolver in its holster hung from his belt. Despite his weapon and his badge, he looked like an overfed kid. Madden kicked the spittoon which rolled on the floor.

"Shit! . . . I must still be blinded by that fuckin' sun!"

"It nothin," said Joe calmly. "I emptied it this mornin."

The sheriff looked at Bobby, his forehead bent over his glass. He recognized a sign of fear in his impassiveness and didn't insist. Harry Bradford's gaze passed over the boy and stopped at the bar's owner.

"Seems like y'all had a crowd this week, Joe. You done gilded your balls with gold, my man . . . Hey, good for y'all, I mean it."

Joe Hives took out a folded envelope from the back pocket of his pants and put it on the counter.

"Can I get y'all sompin' to drink, gents?"

"No, not today," said Harry, counting the bills. "Hey, Joe, what you give me is for the hooch and the gambling, but there's nothin' for the whorin' . . . They tell me that they was fuckin' up a storm upstairs with your singer."

Joe put his hand on the boy's shoulder: "Go on up to yo room, boy." Joshua got up and took his bowl with him.

"Just a minute there, boy, we ain't been introduced," said Anthony Madden. "Ah, wait a minute . . . It's your mama we talkin' about, ain't it? You the little son of the house ho?"

Joshua started trembling, anger soldered his jaws. His fists clenched, he took a step toward the deputy.

"Be careful, Anthony," said the sheriff, "the maggot's gonna knock y'all down!"

Bobby stood up. He was mentally calculating the distance between the bottle and the sheriff's skull, as well as his chances, minimal, of getting out alive.

Anthony Madden raised his hands up: "Please, child, don't kill me! I'm sorry. Just tell yo mama that she'll be havin' her regulation reaming soon, you hear?"

"That's enough, Madden!" said Harry Bradford. "Let's go, they're waitin' on us in town!"

The sheriff looked Joe in the eyes. "Don't you make me wait too long for the rest, y'all know I don't like that."

"Tomorrow, sheriff, tomorrow, it'll be right."

"You see reason, Joe, that's good. Tell yourself it's municipal taxes, that's all."

The sheriff and his deputy went out the swinging doors. Joshua took a few steps on the porch, blinded by the light. He shaded his eyes with his hand and through his fingers saw the sheriff's Dodge moving toward the White part of town. Under his breath the boy muttered an inarticulate promise of vengeance.

Everything had started out so well. Betty had sung above the organ notes, the children on the stage had taken up the chorus, and she had allowed her voice to ring out freely, until it had reached its fullness:

> *. . . God bent over me*
> *And I kissed His hands*
> *His hands burning with holiness . . .*

Betty was expressing all the conviction of her soul. The organist bending over the keyboard played a few delicate arpeggios; from atop his pulpit Pastor Lloyd was watching the reactions of his flock. The mayor's face remained indecipherable, but his wife appeared to be under the spell, marveling that the divine order had granted the gift of emotion to these inferior creatures. The Irish cop had a strange smile—Betty's voice transported him to a land sprinkled with clover, blessed by Saint Patrick, evoked in the lullabies of his grandmother.

> *. . . Oh, God bent over me*
> *And my poor heart began to beat*
> *Like that of an orphan . . .*

At the back of the church, the mass of faithful was mute, intimidated by the solemnness of the hymn. Pearl struggled to keep her eyelids, drooping with fatigue, open. Bartholomew Jones reflected on the pension that the mayor had promised him, converting it into gallons of whiskey and chicken legs.

Constance and little Cherry forgot the toxic vapors of the laundry. Presly Barnes devoured Betty with his eyes, trying to hide the beginnings of an erection that was distorting his pants.

Following an organ solo, Betty continued with a particularly moving number, a true wake-up call. She didn't like that hymn, its lugubrious melody, its harsh cadence. She would have preferred a hymn by Dr. Watts, but the reverend had changed the program at the last minute. The first note came out of her throat and Betty understood that she no longer had control over her voice:

> . . . *Oh, the blood burst forth*
> *And splashed me*
> *Your blood, oh Lord!* . . .

Clarice Brooks felt ants crawling on her ankles and breathed noisily. Presly Barnes had an erection like a horse, the blood in the song went through his being in delicious shudders. Miss Brown was crying, so overwhelmed was her soul.

> . . . *It's Your blood that saved me*
> *When I was abandoned by all*
> *And I was granted no light* . . .

Clarice Brooks trembled. The ants were now frolicking along her spine. "Hum . . . Humm! . . . Oh . . . Oh! . . . " The insects were now at her neck; she undid the ribbons on her bun and rubbed her scalp in rhythm while moaning even louder. From atop the pulpit the pastor saw her but couldn't intervene. The seventy-something woman got up from her seat, her refined hairdo had given way to a wild jumble.

> . . . *You died for us on the cross*
> *And Your blood flowed onto the earth*

Oh, Your blood covered everything
I say: Your blood poured over the world . . .

Betty's singing is sincere. She bears witness with her eyes closed. Christ is there, flogged on the marble slab, covered with spit and curses. Betty inhabits his wounds, his open wounds. He carries the wood on his shoulder. Nails, old rusty nails, perforate his flesh. Betty confirms it, yes, she has seen him, hoisted on the two crossed beams. The sun is also red. The spear has pierced his side and the blood pouring out is mixed with pure water.

. . . You died crucified
And the day began to bleed
And the night, too, oh Lord . . .

"Yes, oh, yes! . . . Hummm . . . Humm! . . . Yeesss! . . . "
Clarice Brooks' stridulations covered Betty's voice. The mayor's wife turned around, horrified. The pastor sensed that he was losing the match. Clarice, no longer able to contain herself, knocked into her neighbor and leapt into the aisle. Her cries were those of a lover on the edge of the firmament. Rosetta in turn stood up, her face flowing with tears: "My Lord, Your blood! . . . How sweet it is! . . . Oh, how sugared it is! . . . " Clarice staggered down the center aisle and knocked violently into Bartholomew's wheelchair, which began to roll and came to an abrupt stop against the altar, spilling the poor invalid onto the floor. The Irish cop stood up quickly. The mayor protected his wife with his arms. Clarice and Rosetta surrounded the invalid who was writhing on the floor like an overturned turtle.

"Jesus, raise him up!" cried Clarice.

"Raise up the oppressed, Lord!" pleaded Miss Brown.

Bartholomew, galvanized by the exhortations of the two women, was able to turn over; he leaned on his elbows and placed a leg on the floor. The entire assembly stood up to witness the miracle. Betty stopped singing, opened her eyes, and discovered Bartholomew up on his trembling legs, a few millimeters from being healed. For a fraction of a second, Pastor Lloyd believed in a good outcome, a finale in apotheosis. But the invalid fell victim to his big belly which pitched him forward; he tottered, spun around, and to soften his fall grabbed desperately onto Mrs. Thompson's dress, which tore, revealing a magnificent lacy slip. The mayor's wife let out a terrible shriek. The Irishman rushed over to poor Bartholomew and started kicking him in the side.

"That dirty pagan gone kill 'em!" shouted Clarice.

"Lord, protect us from the evil ones!" screamed Rosetta.

The cop continued to pummel Bartholomew who was muttering pitiably: "The blood . . . The blood it save me!"

The crowd was rumbling, the men were rolling up their sleeves; the clicking sound of a switchblade could be heard. Augustus Lloyd came down from the stage and gave the mayor a beseeching look. With a gesture Richard Thompson ordered the cop to stop the beating. The Thompson couple and the policeman left the church, escorted by the hate-filled eyes of the faithful. Bartholomew, with the help of his son and daughter-in-law, got back into his wheelchair, one of whose wheels had been damaged. Betty avoided the furious look of the pastor who was wondering if after such a debacle a sermon would still be necessary.

The oak tree spread its shadow over a grassy ground strewn with dead leaves and magnolia petals leading up to the steps of an imposing building encircled by a vast veranda. Built to resemble the Themerlaine Manor, the Conrad home was one of the most beautiful architectural achievements in the county, combining both Gothic and colonial influences with Southern refinement. The shade of the oak tree danced along the cornice, streamed down the carved panels of the façade. The chirping of the sparrows did not disturb the lofty serenity of the estate.

Just as at the laundry, Constance Reed felt no need to oversee the work of her hands. Sitting on the last of the front steps, she was contemplating the branches of the tree, glancing from time to time at Betty's dark golden neck. Her fingers spread apart the locks of hair, smoothed them with avocado oil, then braided them in regular plaits. Betty, her eyes closed, listened to the singing birds and chased away the bad thoughts that were assailing her.

A teenage girl wearing a poplin dress came out of the house holding a book. She took a few steps under the portico exhibiting the pride and assurance of her lineage. A shawl the color of wild honey covered her shoulders, a silver pendant in the shape of a clover hung from her neck. Ellen Conrad stood behind Constance, looking at her from the heights of her youth and her whiteness. "How many times do I have to tell you not to stay sittin' in front of the house? Go do your groomin' in your cabin, behind the stable."

The young woman's voice even when it wasn't contemptuous could hurt. Ellen lifted her pretty nose, pretended to sniff something unpleasant in the air, and went down the steps. Betty watched the old nanny struggling with her humiliation. The young girl who had just dressed her down, Constance had been at her birth, had changed her diapers, wiped her tears, and listened to her spoiled child's secrets. Without a word, Constance leaned over and finished braiding Betty's hair.

The reins were in the hollow of his palm, he scarcely held them, content to move his wrist slightly from time to time. The horse's headpiece had slipped, he adjusted the browband, moving aside the forelock drenched in sweat that was blinding the animal. She was a saddlebred mare, almost thirty years old, with a bay coat, a light nose. She moved in a slow gait, the typical gait of her breed; her breath was even, her enormous heart beat in her chest, a cloud of dust floated between her hocks, and her iron-shod hooves made imprints in the earth. James Conrad caressed the warm neck. He adjusted his hat. His face glowed, his blue eyes looked in the distance, beyond the rows of cypress and the pitiless blue of the sky. James slowed the animal down. The old mare snorted, not wanting to be restrained—she still wanted to serve, drown the bit with saliva, and run wildly through the plain. Mosquitoes buzzed in squadrons, horseflies planted their stingers into the animal's hide; the mount and her rider remained stoic, united as one: a centaur impervious to pain. James Conrad pulled on the reins and the mare stopped in front of the sycamore tree at the entrance to the grounds of the family estate. James looked upwards. Had he forgotten the tree? It was indeed before the war in Europe. An entirely different conflict, in which the victims were unarmed and the battles without glory. James Conrad couldn't remember the name of the man who had been strung up there. He only remembered his neck squeezed by the rope, his feet panicking when the air had abandoned his lungs, the urine dripping onto the grass, the crows announcing the sentence. Justice had been rendered. The predator had perished. James, a young boy wearing a linen shirt, had not looked away while the man died, encouraged by his father's hand on his shoulder and the calm dignity of the witnesses at the foot of the sycamore. His father's hand, the impassiveness of the crowd, said that it wasn't a murder, a lynching bungled by drunks, but calm retribution for a crime. The Negro with a wrung neck. The first man James Conrad had watched die. Dozens of others, friends and enemies, had fallen since then into the swamps of his memory, though he wasn't able to imprint their features on his mind. The little boy, despite his vain efforts to overcome his disgust, had vomited, splattering his father's shoes. An eternity later, in front of the unbending tree, the rider held back the bile in his throat.

James nudged the mare's sides with his heels and she went through the gate. He dismounted in front of the stables. An old man, his skin the color of soot, was cleaning a mule's hooves. The stables were a grouping of rectangular buildings with log walls covered with thatch roofs and windows without panes. A big sandy paddock opened up in front of a line of a half-dozen stalls. In the past, in the times of grandeur, the stalls were constantly smoky with the breath of donkeys and horses, carnal swirls that filled the heart of the young heir with joy. Then, the descendants of slaves became tenant farmers, itinerant workers, and the stables were emptied. James came closer, holding the mare by the reins. The old stableman stood up, gave a loud slap on the rump of the mule which whinnied and disappeared behind a barn. The old man nodded his head: "Y'all be insepr'able, you an Molly, ain't ya, Mist James? . . . An it be a long time that go on, oh Lord, yes!"

James smiled and handed the reins to the stableman.

"Let her drink as much as she wants, and spray her down a few times, alright Moses? She's been gallopin' in the blazin' sun for more than two hours."

"Yes, Mist James, then I gone throw myself into the river and paddle aroun like a duck!"

James went around the stables to take the path through the grounds. Behind a thicket of balsam firs he noticed his young sister, Ellen, reading a book. He took a few steps and could see the book's cover. *Evangeline* by Henry Longfellow. The type of elegiac poetry that well-educated young girls swooned over.

Ellen looked so much like his mother that James was taken aback. The same delicate opalescent face, the same green eyes, the same noble Gaelic forehead. James retained only his mother's scents and her glow—the vetiver in her wake, the moving folds of her dresses on the front steps, the singing paleness of her voice. Mary Eleanor Conrad, the rose of Cardiff, had died a few months before he enlisted in the army. Dead in childbirth, offering life to the one who would become her mirror image. Following the criteria of her caste, Mary had been an exemplary mother, an icon, destined for devotion more than effusive shows of love. James always addressed her formally, had obtained from her only scraps of affection, begging for a tender gesture, exorcising his frustration in interminable rides on the back of his mare.

James Conrad went up the wooden walkway that wound through the lawn toward the family manor. He had done everything he could to delay the inevitable, but could no longer keep himself from his obligations to his rank and his blood. He stopped under the shady cloak of the oak tree. Sitting on the front steps, Constance was fixing the hair of a young Negress whose name he didn't know, though he had seen her often on the property. James remembered the deep comfort he had felt as a child when his nanny cut his hair while humming hymns in which God seemed so close. Truly, Negroes had been the real interlocutors of his youth: Constance, Moses the stableman, Clarissa the cook . . . Hubs of the seasons, the Negroes were the guarantors of the balance of the world, that inner world which the war had destroyed. Their faithful presence, beyond time, reassured him and peopled his memory with marvelous daguerreotypes. Their dark figures scattered over the plain, the frieze of the pickers in the sunlight, celebrated the South, that great immutable dream. Just like the hills on the horizon, the white pods, blood-red suns, the furious floods of Ol' Man River, the Negroes were proof that the past had not been only an illusion.

James pulled himself out of his melancholy. He took off his hat when he went by Betty and smiled at Constance who gave him a strange look in return. In the space of an instant he had the impression she was contemplating her son. James patted his old nanny's cheek and crossed the threshold of his ancestors.

The family table where the dead took a seat, where the living feasted. A twenty-something Black woman took into the kitchen stemmed glasses in which a few drops of old wine still remained. She lowered her head when James walked by—a servile reflex which might have conveyed either fear or respect. The dining room adjoined a vast octagon with iron-handled windows; the daylight filtered through the linen curtains, stately leather armchairs surrounded a low table on which a carafe half-filled with a light, sweet liqueur had been placed.

Francis Conrad, the patriarch, was smoking his pipe; on his right, the mayor, Richard Thompson, was sipping a glass of sherry. Harry Bradford, the sheriff, was nervously crushing his cigarette in an ashtray. Anthony Madden, his deputy, ill-at-ease among this group of older and educated men, looked at the carafe, not daring to pour himself any more.

"Ah, here you are, son," said Francis Conrad. "You really missed something: Clarissa's cranberry turkey and potato flap-jacks were amazin.'"

James sat in the chair opposite his father and set his hat on the floor.

"May I pour you a glass, my dear James?" asked the mayor, in a cordial voice that masked a slight concern. James' virile and silent presence had introduced an indecipherable tension into the group, and everyone sensed they would now have to choose their words carefully. Francis Conrad was looking at his son, his dirty pants and his sweat-soaked shirt. The smoke from his pipe floated into the gray beard that rested on his powerful jawline. The resemblance between father and son was striking: a similar tension in their shoulders, an identical sky blue inhabited their gaze, though James' sadness was absent from that of the patriarch whose eyes shone with an unquenchable thirst to conquer. The sheriff watched James drink his liqueur as if it were a cup of water. Harry Bradford was the same age as he, just as muscled, probably just as tenacious. Yet in James' presence the sheriff felt a disagreeable sense of inferiority.

"Now I know you're not very curious about what is brewing outside this property," said Francis Conrad, "but our friend Richard here has just told us something real interestin."

The patriarch turned to the mayor with a conniving smile. "Richard, do you still have enough energy to tell my son about the events of this morning?"

The mayor lit a cigarette. Showing obvious pleasure, he started to describe the disaster he had witnessed earlier at the church. With a great deal of pantomiming, he described the ape-like hideousness of the faces, the obscene trances and the ridiculous posturing of Pastor Lloyd, as uncouth as an Alabama hick. James listened to him without reacting. He poured himself another glass, which he drank in one gulp.

"You don't seem all that amused, James," said the mayor, vaguely disappointed. "I can easily understand how the antics of nigras might bore you."

James looked at the politician with supreme indifference: "Please excuse me, Richard, but ever since I had a look at the cotton fields, not much can amuse me."

"Is it as serious as all that?"

"Well, if it doesn't start raining, we'll have to forget about the harvest and put off half the tenant farmers."

Richard Thompson put his still-smoking cigarette in the ashtray and his face regained the appropriate seriousness: "I understand. Y'all aren't the only ones, unfortunately. All the planters in the county are in the same boat."

The mayor patted the arms of the chair nervously.

"But there could be somethin' even worse, my friends . . . Imagine that in addition to this natural catastrophe, our dear town might in less than two years be led by a nigger! I know you find it as hard to believe as I do, but it is unfortunately within the realm of possibility."

The sheriff chewed on his lower lip. His deputy made a fist and said in an almost child-like voice: "But, Mayor, the niggers don't vote here!"

The mayor gave him a condescending look. "You're right, most of 'em don't, thank God. But some among the more influential have the possibility of casting their vote, and I fear they'll allow themselves to be seduced by the promises of that satanic Wallace. And it's even possible that some Whites, out of jealousy or ambition, might get behind him."

"Wallace is Longhorn's bastard, ain't he?" asked the sheriff.

"That's right," said Francis Conrad. "What shame for our friend Edward. He used to adore bridge parties and dinners, but we don't see him anywhere anymore."

James' capacity to endure such conversation was reaching its limits. His boots were tapping the floor.

"What do you want with me, Richard?" he asked dryly. "Do you want me to gather the Klan and you arrest this Wallace so you can string him up on a streetlight like in the good ol' days?"

The frankness of the proposal for a moment cooled the mayor who continued in a measured voice. "I don't think it'll be necessary to go to such extremes . . . at least for now. What I need is for you to have him watched and for you to give me a list of his main supporters."

Richard Thompson took a cigarette out of a silver case and lit it with the lighter the sheriff held out to him.

"Thank you, Harry . . . And, uh, shall we say that if necessary a cross or two was to be burned between now and the Fourth of July, that might make some of the black sheep who have wandered off come back home to reason."

James retrieved his hat and stood up in the light. An odor of hay and dung exuded from his clothes.

"I'll put one of my men on it right away," he said. "A Negro I have total confidence in, a veteran. Rest assured, Mister Mayor, Negroes are perhaps as untamed as you say, but they aren't crazy: they know when they must stay in their place."

James Conrad adjusted his hat and pulled up his belt.

"I must leave you, gentlemen," he said, "I must see to our irrigation system."

James Conrad shook the mayor's damp hand, the sheriff's rigid one, and the soft palm of Anthony Madden. He hugged his father and left. The sheriff watched him walk through the door to the dining room.

"What I like about your son, Mister Conrad," said Harry Bradford, "is he don't beat aroun the bush."

"Please excuse him, the war brought him back to us more ferocious than evah."

"Your son is a hero, my dear Francis!" said the mayor perhaps overly enthusiastically. "He's the young Titan we need to watch over our interests."

"You are no doubt right, sir," said the patriarch, and his gaze became filled with sadness. "But sometimes, I would just like for him to be happy."

A blanket with Navajo motifs swells and collapses like a tide of anguish. Asleep but vigilant, Sapphira is drifting in troubled waters. She has passed through the capes of hopelessness, fateful straights, never has she traveled so far. This night she has abandoned herself to the spirits that knead images and sleep has deposited her on the shores of the land of before.

She travels over a sandy expanse, then forges a passage through vegetation covered with dew and sap. A blond savannah, sleeping craters, smoky backwaters, irradiated canyons: a patchwork of textures and pigments. Squeaking and vague drooling rise out of the thickets. In the middle of a clearing a cailcedrat appears, its stature imperial, its branches cadaverous and its shadow spreading over the sand. Sapphira approaches the tree. Drums stun her with their syncopation. She searches the sky, studies the upper branches looking for the drummers. The old woman lies down at the foot of the cailcedrat, her body touching the trunk; the hours go by, then the years. The ground vibrates. She sits up. The spirits have come to meet her. Stateless divinities straddle the continents, bridging souls, fearsome orishas are incarnated for a moment soon to disintegrate. Despite their fantastic adornments and masks, Sapphira knows who they are. Right in front of her is Ogun, a saber in his iron fist; Ogun, ruler of the forge, born out of the alliance of blood and stars. Slightly behind him is a swaggering Shango, the assessor of storms; a double-edged hatchet rests on his shoulder. A scent of cinnamon and benzoin accompanies the beautiful Erzulie Dantor, the guardian of women; wrapped in a pale pink tunic, she is holding a newborn against her chest, and in her left hand a tapered dagger. Behind her, with her hair sprinkled with scales, is Yemaya, the guardian of salt and sea spray.

Sapphira kneels down, lowers her head, ready to receive the slicing of a blade or the anointing of a kiss. Shango raises his hatchet to the sky. Sapphira feels the iron graze her neck, then strike into the ground. An immense fissure henceforth separates her from the gods. Above her there is a burst of laughter. A figure without a face is perched on a branch of the cailcedrat. Suddenly, the branch breaks, the creature lands on its feet and, still laughing, begins to run through the underbrush. Sapphira recognizes Legba, the fantastic and unpredictable spirit. She cries out his name, but the figure has already dissipated in an avalanche of pollen and butterflies. The storm that Shango has summoned rises from the red depths of the earth. Clouds burst open, swollen with milt, rain-filled arrows riddle the sky, and water pours forth, bending the leafy branches, blurring all vision.

The death rattle of a drowning woman. Sapphira extracts herself from the blanket. She is in her home, between the familiar walls of her cabin. Rain is striking the thatched roof. A crushing downpour, announcing a dark monsoon. She pats her body, recovers her reflexes. She wants to be one with the storm, experience it against her skin. She goes through the door. The night is calm, warm, terribly dry. On her lips, in her chest, a name she has so much difficulty expelling. She mutters and her voice is amplified beyond reality: "Legba, Legba!"

The truck rolled along in the darkness. With every pothole from under the large tarp in the back there emerged a din of crates and clanking bottles. Jasper Mulligan had taken off his hat, his pomaded hair stuck to his forehead. He was holding the steering wheel with one hand; the other hand, sticking out the window, was taking the temperature of the night. With a nod he asked his brother for a cigarette. Wade took a Marlboro out of a soft package, lit it, and passed it to Jasper.

"Yer sure we got to go supervise the boys?" said Wade in a weary voice. "C'aint we jus go straight to Memphis?"

"No. We gotta look after the grain."

"Fer what we pay 'em, they might could do it theyselves."

Jasper took a deep draw on his cigarette and turned to Wade. "Don't y'all worry, brother, tomorrow fore noon you'll be on Beale Street in a real clean room with a lil white pussy on the end of yer stick!"

The two brothers burst out laughing, then went quiet. Enticing images were floating around in their heads. Eating on embroidered tablecloths, riding in sedans covered with shiny chrome, diving into the depths of a blue-eyed girl: that's why the Mulligan brothers were working so hard. These concrete rewards were spoils of war, scalps taken from destiny. It didn't matter that the restaurants they ate in were gangster dives, the cars they drove had been stolen the day before, and the women they screwed were drugged up to their eyeballs.

Money freed them more surely than the sermons of a pastor or the decrees of a big White House. Jasper and Wade were the spoiled fruit of Prohibition. They had begun modestly, distilling a few liters of "beer mash" in a hidden barn; then demand increased, and they had bought stills from a bankrupt factory. They had greased some palms, broken some jaws, ruined families; right now they were gloating, like cruel children or conquistadors.

The headlights illuminated a cornfield; stalks stood up gloomily behind a barbed-wire fence. The truck stopped at the edge of a dense forest from which the night seemed to have found its source. Wade and Jasper advanced among the sumacs and the ferns, trying to acclimate their senses to the darkness.

"You dint bring no flashlight?" asked Wade.

"Don't need one, look . . . "

Jasper pointed to a light coming from deep inside the forest that was moving toward them, wavering.

"Light up a cig'ret, so they kin see us." said Jasper.

Wade obeyed, and a thin light flickered at the end of his fingers. A hurricane lamp, held at arms' length, shone on a figure crowned with impure shadows. A young Black man stopped a few feet away, his face blinded by the flames of the lamp, holding the butt of a Winchester in his other hand.

"Who there?!"

"It's us, you fuckin' moron! If it was the sheriff, you'd already be full o' lead!"

"Sorry, Mist Jasper. I gone take you, it ain't very far."

"Git yer hand off the trigger, nigger! You clumsy enough to take out mah knee!"

The three men reached a moonlit spot that had been hastily cleared. Lamps filled with oil were placed in a circle around a cairn of flat stones. In the middle of the stones a fire crackled, exhaling an ashy smoke. On the mound rested the boiler, a conical copper vat connected to a zinc pipe ending in a water tube that plunged into a cylinder resembling a high-caliber shell. At the top of the cylinder a water source had been fixed, a long watering hose went along the grass up to a hand pump partially hidden by a thicket of brambles. A thin copper wire completed the works, standing ready to spit out its toxic nectar into a bucket.

Wade quickly approached the smoke to avoid the voracious mosquitoes. Two stocky men holding guns stepped aside and took off their hats. They were mulattoes from Alabama, experienced moonshiners whom the Mulligan brothers had brought up from the foothills of Appalachia. Wade became absorbed by the crackling of the flames and the shine of the copper. Distillation was beginning: the machinery came alive with fumaroles and gurgling. Each person got busy, feeding the fire, working the pump. The two mulattoes, masters of ethyl, supervised the still's reactions. The copper coil bled a pale liqueur that Jasper poured into a barrel, estimating the number of bottles, of glasses.

Rare stars shone like pennies on the zinc. The moon was a white whore. Before she went to bed, the bootleggers had filled three hundred-gallon casks to the brim and had loaded them into the truck. Then the moonshiners covered the tire tracks with dust, returning its innocence to the forest.

How can you sell something that is part of you? Bobby went over the smallest stitches of his only jacket. He had bought it two years earlier, in Itta Bena, when he had deigned to work a season of picking. Everything he earned was spent on it. Today, he was getting ready to sell his most precious possession. He could have gone to Mama or to any other woman "of a mature age" and scrounged enough to feed his body, but his pride prevented him from doing that.

The pawnshop, at the corner of Oak Street and Dixon Lane, was far enough from the main street to spare the down-and-outs who went there the shame of being recognized. Fuck shame; it was the very existence of all those pitiful souls that was being pawned, every day. A bell was fixed to the right of the door where an iron chain was hanging. Bobby didn't ring. Dust was stagnating in the room, it was dark and strangely cool. Metal objects, raggedy clothes all piled together. Among all this jumble Bobby made out a wooden horse that had escaped a phantom merry-go-round, and the neck of a guitar sticking out of a pile of books. He hesitated to approach the instrument but pulled himself together.

Bobby came out of the pawnshop looking defeated. In front of the bank he ran into Dorothy, the saloon whore, and her little boy, dressed like a dandy with his hair freshly groomed. Bobby told himself he was no better than she. His soul was also that of a slut—a bold and disillusioned soul. He walked in the sun. The rays punished him and strengthened his desire for desertion.

Bobby had been out of the town for more than an hour. Around him, the fields spread out pale and monotonous. He took his harmonica out of his pocket, placed it on his lips. Three cars went by. He held out his thumb and continued to blow on the instrument, emitting gritty and powerful sounds. A Terraplane stopped a few meters in front of him. A man, with droopy eyelids and greying temples, lowered his window.

"Hey, my man, y'all can really blow! I could hear ya at the bend back theah!" said the man, revealing a mouth in which a few nicotine-stained stubs were lined up.

"Gotta get yoself noticed."

"Where y'all headed?"

"Far from here. Goin' south."

The man looked at Bobby suspiciously.

"You ain't kilt nobody, didja? . . . Ain't got the marshall on yo ass, or sompin?"

"Nothin' like that. Just a few ladies who gonna curse mah name."

"Well, now, that don't bother me none!"

Bobby opened the car door and sat next to the man, on a seat dotted with cigarette holes. The Terraplane took off.

"I's Douglas, evryone call me Doug. I takin' the 49 West. Goin' to Parchman to see mah son. He doin' fifteen. Must be aroun' yer age . . . If'n y'all don' wanna see no cops or watch-towers, I kin set you down right befor."

"That be good," said Bobby. "I's got nothin' to hide, but jest aroun' the police, I feels guilty and they's got to know that from a long way away."

The man dug around in his pockets, slipped a chunk of tobacco against his cheek and began to chew slowly.

"I hear that, boy," he continued in a serious voice. "Me, too, when I goes to see mah son Abe in the pentent'ry, I feels guilty, just to be born and to have made him."

Dust flew around the inside of the car and covered Bobby's shirt. Wherever he went from then on he knew he would never escape filth, but at least his downfall would be chosen. He picked up his harmonica and played an improvised blues tune. A goodbye blues.

The ceiling-fan blades were spinning. The smell of hairspray and egg shampoo. In the hand of the barber Barnes, the razor became music; the blade, struck in rhythm against a sharpening belt stretched between two chairs, played nuances between the flat side and the edge. Casey, the barber's assistant, was moving a straw broom that scratched against the floor, like a jazz drummer caressing a snare drum.

Andrew Wallace was standing behind Presly Barnes, his chestnut eyes watching those around him. Only Pearl was fidgeting, the others looked serious, waiting for the meeting to start. Steve was sitting in a barber's chair with large armrests; on the seat next to him Rosetta Brown was looking in a mirror, smoothing her grey hair with her fingertips. The garage workers still had on their coveralls, Joe Hives had delayed opening his bar to attend the meeting. Aaron and Rachel Posner were standing near the door. They were the only Whites there and people regularly glanced over at them to verify they were in fact real. Sargent Elias, wearing his military overcoat, was watching the street through the shop window. Old Theodore came through the door into the room, escorted by the stench of bad bourbon which the fan spread around the entire room. Andrew Wallace signaled to the barber and Casey to stop their work. Presly greeted the crowd with a bow and received some applause.

Wallace cleared his throat. "My friends, you have come. You have endured the slander, the threats, and you are here. That means we have already won!"

The mulatto knew that reading a speech from a piece of paper would be considered lazy; he had to address the people right in their eyes and talk to them straight from his heart.

"You are here and that means Richard Thompson has already lost traction. You are showing him that he isn't the great lord he takes himself for and that the town he manages, so badly and so unjustly for so many years, doesn't belong to him. Because this town is above all yours!"

Wallace leaned forward like a preacher at the height of his sermon. Soon voices responded, the garage workers started shouting and stomping their feet, Miss Brown let out a "Hallelujah" from deep in her chair. The mulatto unveiled his plans for the town: a glorious dream, worthy of the Founding Fathers, in which this time the Negroes wouldn't be the black sheep. Everyone believed him, because Wallace spoke better than a teacher, because he was young and rich, and because the Negro blood in his veins had never prevented him from prospering. Pearl looked at him with loving eyes, forgetting that he was her boss, the very one who refused to increase her meager salary by even a penny.

Wallace opened his arms wide as if to embrace the audience. "I know that most of you, due to crooked and diabolical laws, cannot vote. But toiling blood and sweat—that you have a right to! Paying taxes for dirty water, that you must do! You must endure the fact that the lightbulbs on the front of City Hall stay lighted all night long, when you have only oil lamps to light your homes!"

When he heard mention of lightbulbs, Steve stood up, galvanized by hope. Wallace looked around at the Posner couple and gave them a big smile. "My sisters and brothers, know that many Whites support us. They, too, have had enough of the tyranny of Richard Thompson."

The audience turned to the Posners. Rachel felt deeply ill-at-ease. She, who had been persecuted on her native land, found herself a White woman here and forced to prove that she didn't belong to the caste of oppressors.

"My friends," Wallace continued, "announce it far and wide, spread the good news to every house: we have won!"

Thunderous applause. Andrew Wallace shook hands, endured a disturbing proximity with his employees, and managed to suppress a surge of disgust when old Theodore gave him a hug. The mulatto noted with satisfaction that a crowd had formed in front of the shop. He ordered Presly to open the doors so the clamor of happy days to come would reach the entire town.

The headlights passed by her and the sound of the motor was muffled by the thick darkness. Betty placed her hand on her chest to calm the beating of her heart. She had recognized Andrew Wallace's Cadillac. She had trembled, hoping he wouldn't stop, taking advantage of the night and the deserted road to force her to lie down, threatening her with a pistol. Because he was capable of doing that, like most men, and particularly those who were made all-powerful by money.

Betty wasn't lost, she could have gone the last mile to her aunt's cabin blindfolded. A warm breeze moved the hem of her dress. The wind came from the river and carried the scent of algae and mud. Clouds covered the moon. The lack of light in the sky worried her less than the presence on the road of a being as detestable as Wallace. Yes, she detested him. It was because of him, that damned mulatto, that she was walking on this path, this night, her clothes in a bundle on her shoulder. When Steve had returned from the meeting at the barber's, he wasn't the same. He spoke loudly, gesticulated, sang the praises of Wallace as if he were a saint. Steve couldn't stop talking about electricity; he had picked up the radio in a rage, holding it up like proof or a threat. When Betty objected, her beloved countered with terrible sarcasm and they fought. From both sides venomous darts had reached their targets. Betty had almost spilled everything: Wallace's scheming, the disgusting proposals he made her at the laundry. She held her tongue. But when Steve called her a coward, she had gone into the bedroom, taken a few random clothes, and slammed the door behind her. Her husband's remorseful pleading hadn't stopped her, the drunks on the main street and the stray dogs didn't either. She was afraid, that was true. Afraid Steve would become the puppet of a man without virtue, afraid of the Whites and of the brutality of their reactions, but she wasn't a coward.

Betty went through a curtain of branches and entered the clearing. The wind was picking up, rustling the leaves. Sapphira wasn't sleeping. A dim light came out of the open door. Several voices were overlapping, all coming out of the same throat. Sounds of shells clacking. The witch wasn't sleeping.

That night, Legba had assumed the appearance of a paralyzed old man, stricken with arthritis, shivering in a borrowed body. Inferior creatures had coalesced, teeming and quivering in the grasses: myriapods and Lepturians, roaches of the woods and latrines, dragon stalker Hagenia, sniper leafhoppers, seasoned jumping spiders, tarantulas and black widows . . . All God's damned creatures and insects gathered around the human rag and intoned the hymn of metamorphosis and rebirth:

> . . . *Iba l'Agbo é Agbo mujuba!*
> *Iba l'Orisha!*
> *Iba l'Agbo é Agbo mojuba O! . . .*

When a cohort of assassin bugs began to assemble on his spine, his carcass reacted and he moved one arm, then the other. A formidable sweat came out of his pores and drowned most of the insects. Leaning on his elbows, he crawled. His carnal envelope was only wrinkles and patches of skin. His vertebrae crackled and he managed to get onto his knees. His gaze attracted by the flame, he recovered his sight.

Legba was standing. His rags fluttered in the warm rising wind. The convalescing god recalled the catastrophes and misalliances that had led him from the throne of Abomey to this plain of desolation. He remembered his various names, the dialects that had baptized him. He was called Legba, others named him Eshu. He was "Avadra," the all-knowing, whom no one can ignore. The impregnable fortress and the near dead. Old, old Legba . . . Son of Mawu-Lissa, the firstborn or last offspring of the inaccessible essences. He also remembered the ridiculous names the Whites had given him: Satan, Belial, Azazel, Beelzebub, and so many others that had nothing to do with him, he, the gateway god spanning the abysses of sin. He wasn't the devil since he didn't tempt anyone—he accompanied, overlapped, opened up possibilities. Legba of barriers, Legba of enclosures. The master of crossroads.

He belched and began to grow. He went from shape to shape, his limbs grew longer and his veins throbbed. The old man transformed into a giant, ripping apart the black netting from his skin. He was a colossus who henceforth oversaw the fire. He was gigantic this evening, but tomorrow he could just as well be a filthy dog, a poisonous mushroom hiding under a tree stump, a blue bird, an echo.

The wind was howling. The clouds broke apart and the moon appeared. He took off his shirt, his pants. The wind rushed between his legs as under a porch. Naked among the gusts, offered up to the moon, he exposed his wounded flesh. A terrible scar ran from one side to the other. He remembered that wound. He had been assassinated so many times. The fact that he didn't die didn't change a thing. His body was a collection of wounds and ravages. He was the fruit of a great brawl. Surrounded by suffering, he was the elemental Negro. The custodian of the scream.

Far from tumult and close to murmurings, the communal cemetery spread out over a hill on the plain. Lichen and ivy covered the headstones. Clouds, emissaries of a terrible downpour, had taken complete possession of the sky. The trees and the dead desired that rain as much as they feared it.

James Conrad, leaning against an elm tree, was reading what he had written down in a notebook. Across from him, Sargent Elias was nervously scratching a flaky slab of stone. The two men were standing in the White section of the cemetery. Here, too, there reigned strict racial segregation. On the surface, at least, because when night fell, the dead ignored the prohibitions and blended the fragments of their voices.

"That's all? You're sure there were only twelve?"

"No, thirteen," Elias specified. "They was also that fella Steve."

"Steve who?"

"Don't know his last name. He work at the Frazier bakery. He married to a gal from the laundry, Betty Walker, the witch's niece."

James Conrad had never heard of the witch, much less her niece. He wrote a few things in his notebook. In front of him, the sergeant's face, with its wrinkles and second-rate boxer's nose, was deceptive. The man was teeming with forgotten stories, knew the details of minuscule lives not a trace of which could be found in the city hall archives. And James suspected that his genealogical knowledge didn't stop with just the Negroes of the county.

"Oh, yeah, they was also Theodore. He got there late, but was definitely there, that old monkey."

"Theodore?"

Elias's gaze wandered to the branches of the elm tree. His glass eye, badly adjusted, left a slight gap at the corner of its socket.

"Titus's little brother, Titus was the fella got hung in front of yo house long time ago."

For a few seconds James could see the rope and the suffocated face of the hanged man. A nasty bile rose from his esophagus. He took a flask of whiskey from his jacket pocket, let the liquid stay on his palate before swallowing. He held out the flask to the sergeant who, before drinking, poured a few drops onto the headstone at his feet.

"I remember a time durin' the war, in France," said Elias, sweeping the sky with his hand. "The clouds touched our shoulders, we couldn't see ten steps in front of us. We didn't want to shoot seein' as we couldn't make out the uniforms."

The painful churning in James's stomach calmed down as the sergeant's voice dissipated the fog.

"We put bayonets on the end of our rifles. When we stuck a fella he fell, and it was like he was disappearin' under a cover."

Elias wasn't bragging. He had gone to war under the flag bearing the sign of the bison, in the 366th Infantry Regiment, assigned to the famous 92nd Division, under the orders of Major General Ballou. Alongside Lieutenant Fisher and other

Negro heroes, he had fought in the villages of Lorraine and the forests of Argonne, during the great La Meuse offensive. The medals on his overcoat had been polished by an uninterrupted flow of blood.

James leaned over a headstone whose epitaph was almost illegible and set his empty bottle down on it.

"This one here will thank me," he said. "Mortimer Conrad: the worst drunk this earth ever received. He sullied our blood over at least three generations."

"Mortimer were in Gettysburg with General Lee, weren't he?"

James Conrad hadn't been mistaken; the sergeant knew his lineage better than he did. Elias stretched, his long arms grazed the clouds. Watching him, James Conrad remembered the giant he had come upon the other day in the middle of the cotton fields. He hadn't mentioned it to anyone and had ordered Jonathan Barrel, his partner, not to say a word. Whites were supposed to look down on that type of nonsense, leaving to the Negroes their fetishes and crocodile teeth as consolation prizes. James began to describe the creature, its incredible height, and the enigma of its face.

Sergeant Elias frowned: "It ain't *someone* you seen, it were *something*."

"One of your damned spirits, is that it?"

"I don't know, Mist Conrad, don't know nuthin' 'bout them thangs."

"Do you take me for an idiot? You and others in the regiment, you had pockets full of necklaces and amulets to protect you from bullets."

"Well, them necklaces must notta been very powerful, seein' all the fellas who got their skins shot up."

James didn't have a response. He took two bills out of his pocket and held them out to Elias, who shook his head no. "All I ask is that y'all warn me when yo friends plan to ride into town."

James Conrad shook the sergeant's hand which was colder than a tombstone. He zigzagged around the graves and went out the gate. "His friends . . . " Right . . . So brave when it came to burning a cross or cutting down an unarmed man, but complete cowards when it came to joining up to defend the country. No, thought James, not one of those men were worthy of his friendship.

Sergeant Elias watched the Buick drive off toward town. He walked up to the headstone on which the bottle of whiskey had been set down, slipped it into the pocket of his overcoat, and walked away.

Sergeant Elias walked with his head down following the dry dusty path. He who had never bent his neck in the face of danger submitted to the yoke of the clouds. He thought back to the money James Conrad had offered him. Sure, it would have improved his everyday life, but he was no Judas. He had made a deal with the Conrad heir; he informed him of the convulsions that agitated the Black community and, in return, James warned him when the Klan would show its force. This arrangement had held for almost ten years, and lynchings were rather rare in the county. The Negroes smoldered and the Whites suspended their fury. You just had to cross the Yazoo, to spend time near Greenwood or Bentonia where there were more Negroes than peaches hanging from branches to confirm that the agreement was working.

Elias stopped in front of the body of a toad crushed by the sun. He lifted the animal by the leg and the carcass peeled off the ground. The humidity was beginning to cover the flowers and grasses, a fragile dew shone over the surface of the landscape. When he entered the underbrush, Elias felt the toad's flesh soften between his fingers. He thought about what James had confided in him. James didn't drink enough to be in the throes of delirium, the creature he had come upon in the middle of the cotton fields was probably not born of his imagination. He had to act quickly, ward off what could still be avoided and not antagonize the parallel forces.

Elias pricked up his ears—a graceful, ethereal tinkling, like a dulcimer solo. He followed the melody to a clearing. A good tracker, he saw traces of steps that led to a mound. The moonshiners must have been working the day before; the still had been dismantled, but the ashes testified to their presence. He went around the water pump, forced his way through the thickets. He found the offering tree: a blue ash that the Chickasaw Indians honored long before Whites and slaves had landed. The base was covered with shreds of fabric, animal skulls and unidentifiable debris merging with the humus.

The bottom of the tree was the domain of the Indians, theirs the roots and the depths. Blacks had adopted the branches; dozens of soda or alcohol bottles were hanging from them, attached with cords or pushed in by the neck. Voices of spirit prisoners of the glass escaped in the wind; their groans were soft like those of women making love, but they should not be trusted. Elias, like many Blacks in the area, had Indian blood, distant ancestries that explained the clear nuances of his forehead. He started from the bottom of the trunk, pushed aside a sheep's skull, and set the toad down. The remains shuddered in contact with the tree. The offering was accepted. Elias mumbled a few words in a patois known to him alone, took the flask of whiskey out of his coat pocket, and stuck its neck onto the end of a branch at his height. He waited for a whistle that would have meant a spirit had been captured. The trap was too blatant. Elias waited amid the stench of rancid meat and moldy leaves. The monotonous sound of the branches rocked him and he fell asleep, standing, leaning against the bark.

Suddenly, a burn stabbed his eye socket, as if his false eye had been dipped in acid. He thought he had been stung by a hornet or a scorpion. Using his fingers, he pulled out the painted marble. A hiss arose from the cavity, a pulse of air. Elias collapsed on the ground. He trembled, out of his body flowed miasmas and liquids. He thought he could make out a burst of light through the filaments of his dead eye. Elias was no longer in pain. He stood up and saluted the tree, banging his fist against his chest, like a true Negro. He picked up the glass eye and inserted it into a fissure in the trunk.

Elias had reached the paved road. A new smile lit up his one-eyed face. He was free. The demons of war had left his soul. A young farmer woman carrying a log on her shoulder turned as he passed. Elias was beautiful.

In the intertwining of the river, people with tireless arms built mountains. The mounds they raised were larger than the pyramids of Egypt, they had the shape of the only masters they tolerated above their bravery: the cougar and the eagle, the wolf and the panther. Proud Chickasaws, Spartan in customs, who routed the conquistadors; Acolapissas from the banks of the Pearl, their chests covered in tattoos; Quapaws who painted their horses glorious colors; Koroas, ruthless collectors of scalps; elegant Biloxis with light moccasins; Choctaws, their language encrypted by the wind . . .

The ground you walk on is theirs and that of their heirs in broken lines: the eternal tribes, the untamed nations. Wherever you walk, you are in their footsteps. They gave their names to rivers and springs, to clouds and fruit. All that breathes and trembles, nourishes the soul and restores the blood, was named by them. They were never civilized; they were civilization itself. Attached to their rituals as they were to hot spikes, they grew corn, oats, and a love of every moment. They survived the unhealthy winds of typhus, diphtheria, and plague. They fought to the end, joining their sobs to those of the runaway slaves they sheltered in their tents. Even succumbing to coughing fits, their pride still resounded, when they went up the Trail of Tears alongside their Creek, Seminole, and Cherokee brothers. "Nunna daul Isunyi." As far as Oklahoma, to negation. Within the low works of history, the Indians wrote their legend in the future perfect.

The wooden mask was split from top to chin; Betty was sleeping on a mat in the middle of the room. The young woman was not initiated; she was vulnerable, and the mask watched over her. Betty had dozed off, her heart at peace. She had forgiven Steve and had no doubt that he had forgiven her, too. She saw their argument as a necessary step, a test to which couples had to submit to face the long haul. Spitefully, she had imagined her beloved forced to feed himself alone, angry at her, and in the end filling his stomach with breadcrumbs. Maybe he had drowned his sorrows in alcohol, had he walked through the doors of a saloon to be dazzled by the electric lights? After he got drunk, maybe he had been tempted to climb the big staircase to seek refuge in the arms of another . . . of Dora . . . No. Steve was not that kind of man. He was a Negro with no vice other than terrible stubbornness. Betty was convinced that this argument had strengthened their love. She had fallen asleep serenely in the cabin of her childhood, among the statuettes and cowrie shells.

*

The wind was plowing the plain, rushing between the plinths, shaking the attic. The horizon was gray and swollen, the wind had brought the clouds to heel, summoning them to the center of the sky. The transition between the vanquished day and the night was carried out in a stream of murderous shadows.

Behind the cabin, Sapphira was wearing a long, white tunic. Her bare feet trampled the ground strewn with old ashes. A scarf was wrapped around her head, no hair escaped. She had removed her jewelry, shaved her eyebrows. Sapphira hesitated for a long time before beginning the ceremony. She was so old . . . Would her bones continue to bear the weight of the mystery?

The fire crackled in the scullery. Flames with blue hearts, protected by the stone hearth, faced the squall. A few meters away stood the altar, the immovable rock, overhung by a human skull, glistening with resinous oil. Interlacing lines drawn with whitewash snaked around the jutting stone. A black rooster who had previously been drugged stood motionless, hypnotized by the dancing flames.

Sapphira stretched her hands out towards the heat. Her hands were crying out for the truth. She began to sway, left to right, her weight distributed on her toes.

It lasted a long time, it lasted long enough for the clouds to reap their harvest of volts and for the surrounding brushwood to bristle in violent waves. The old woman's eyes turned white. She spoke over the bushes and the branches, addressing the one who coiled in the darkness. She spoke in bastardized English, a low form of pidgin. The spirit came from the land of before, but it was at home everywhere, haunted each syllable.

"Legba, drink without thirst! Leader of goats under the blade! . . . Legba, belly of seeds, it be yo nails that sharpen the scythe! Legba, black postilion! . . . Legba, ancient hanged! . . . If you is under the bark, reveal yoself!

188

"Legba, open the floodgates, release yo birds! . . . Digest the night and regurgitate the dead! I got too much blood, it be for you, Legba! I have virgins in reserve, crush them under yo loins! Legba, snake lover, offspring of the swamp, show yoself!"

Sapphira went to the rooster and lifted it off the ground. The old woman smashed the bird's skull against the altar, spreading gritty blood over the stone. Her dress was soaked. Her soul was crystal clear. The old woman threw the remains of the bird into the maw of the brazier out of which arose a shivering of ash, of dread. A first flash of lightning streaked through the sky.

The iron rooster on the roof of the Abbot farm spins wildly. The pigs in the pen wallow in the cracks of the ground and groan. The first tiles come loose and dance in the turmoil. The storm lifts the pollen, strips the grasses of their treasures; filaments of cotton wool and tiny seeds flutter in the electrified air; the pines and cypresses creak with the groaning of an ossuary; acres of corn bend over in strange genuflections. The wind ravages, the wind takes no prisoners.

There's a gun pointed at the ground.
On the temple of the day the steel dictates its law

The stall is opaque. The mare panics, foam rolls on her chest, her gorgonian mane covers her eyes where madness dwells. The storm is under her skin. Lightning under her hooves. The door creaks open. Old Moses enters the stall with a hurricane lamp and a piece of sugar. The mare runs straight to the trembling light. The stableman narrowly dodges the first charge, bangs against the wall, and collapses. The lamp breaks, oil spills out. The smell scares the animal who rears up. "Molly, calm down! Oh, Molly! . . . " Hooves fly out wildly. "Don't do that, Molly, please, I begs you!" Dull stomping. The smell of blood covers that of oil. The animal goes through the door, forcing the hinges of the night . . .

There is an enigma and lamp debris.
A murderous horse gets drunk on thunder.

The branches bark with their glassy sarcasm. Shreds of fabric come off the tree. The wind that blows into the skull of a sheep begins whistling an ocarina tune. The spirits, taking refuge in the gaps, are not quiet. Prayers and amulets no longer protect people . . .

There is a rag on the edge of the precipice
A living nightmare on the other side of the Moon

· The sound of gunfire cuts through the thatch of the roof and explodes in the middle of the cabin. Betty wakes up with a start. She brushes the mat before daring to touch her skin. The shock wave disperses along her frame and is extinguished between her toes. She thinks it was an earthquake. At the second warning shot, when the mask falls off the wall, she understands. She walks in the dark, her hands protecting her head.

The walls vibrate. A shivering cloud engulfs the cabin. Beating wings on the ceiling. The bats lead her to the emergency exit . . .

There is a fetus whose heart no longer beats.
The rise of milk to quench death's thirst

An immense blindness, streaked with profane flashes. The stench of ground stone. Betty raises her voice against the wind. She calls out to her aunt, it is thunder that answers her. She walks around the cabin to the scullery. What she sees overturns language, makes all vision useless. A woman draped in red–white is standing, dazzled by the vertical brightness of a fire, a sacred fire on which the gusting of the wind has no hold. Betty stops a few meters away. She can hear the woman's chanting carried by the night. The woman in white suddenly turns around. Betty wishes she had never been born . . .

There is a mirror where reflections lie.
A brazier without witnesses that will die out
  tomorrow.

The sheets have drunk the sweat, the spurts of semen; they
are heavy and sticky. Andrew Wallace removes the cloth and
sits naked on the edge of the bed. He wonders how the girl
next to him manages to sleep through such an uproar. He sees
the almost empty bottle of Gordon's gin on the bedside table.
The little slut must have gotten up to drink. The lightning and
its roar are almost synchronous now. Through the window he
observes the macerations of the storm. The sleeping body is
covered with shimmers, pale stripes fleetingly shine on her
thighs and chest. Andrew drinks the last of the gin. He bends
over and slides the neck of the bottle against the girl's belly.
Pearl feels the coolness of the glass against her pubis. She hesitates to open her eyes . . .

There is a notch where time breathes.
Lovers damaged by cold caresses.

The bulb has gone out. Pastor Lloyd rummages in the
dresser drawer. His hands are annoyed at not finding anything.
He closes the drawer. An object breaks at his feet. The frame
containing the portrait of his wife. He knows there is a candle,
several, somewhere. He gives up searching and gropes for the
chair and the table. His fingers seize a pewter cup, bring it to
his lips. The rancid kiss of whiskey. Thunder rattles the windows. Lightning lights up the empty sky. On the whitewashed
walls, the light traces a rigid, dark cross. Augustus Lloyd has
trouble swallowing. He is afraid of dying. And, more seriously,
of betraying. His hands scrape the table and rest on the warm
leather of a book. A soothing warmth passes from the cover

up his arm. He will not die. A new explosion rocks the half-light. He has already betrayed . . .

There are eddies in the belly of the monster.
Forbidden psalms that skin the lips.

Shells fall, gunshots whistle. James Conrad returns to his element. Hands clinging to the lamp, he walks across the grounds. He is going to reassure the mare. He plans to ride out the storm in the stall by her side and even imagines riding her and traversing the plain like a horseman of the Apocalypse. A whinnying in between two flashes of lightning. It is the night that rears up, vituperates, tramples. James approaches the stables. He crosses the paddock and discovers the stall's open door. The light lingers on the trampled body of the stableman. The whinnying draws nearer. James touches the butt of his revolver.

There are sobs forever held back.
A flower thrown in the middle of the disaster.

The piano choked, the note was too high. The laughter died out and the bullets flew. The saloon is purged. The dominoes pile up on the tables, alcohol stagnates in glasses, all the cards are as black as spades. In the room, silence. Upstairs, Dora sings, sitting on the bed, leaning over her sleeping son. A villainous glow shines through the window. Dora strokes the child's head; his neck smells of shampoo. The lullaby against his cheek is louder than the thunder. Her voice filters anguish and her song is only love.

There is a crater where the shadows drink.
A tightrope walker awaits the sentence of the void.

The sleeping quarters are saturated with male effluvia. The lightning heats the iron bedframes white. On mattresses stuffed with sawdust, the tough are silent. Not one would admit fear. The hard ones settle their accounts. Between each strike of the gong, they recount their sins, list their crimes. The convicts know that the scales will be too heavy for them, so they smile in the dark, their hearts coated with suet. Abe sits up on his bunk. He thinks of his father, the sadness of his wrinkles, the kindness of his voice. Abraham looks up at the ceiling and his thoughts linger at the threshold of forgiveness.

There's a jukebox studded with diamonds.
A blue Cadillac to transport the ash.

His room is a shithole, but Anthony Madden, the sheriff's deputy, doesn't give a fuck. The penumbra suits him, it conceals the warped wallpaper and dirty dishes in the sink. A match, a candle. Anthony digs in the cabinet. He grabs his egro tunic and conical hood with holes at eye level. He contemplates his uniform, lying flat on the bed. The flame of the candle evokes other conflagrations. A flash of light through the window. The lightning must have hit a nigger's barn or shack somewhere. Anthony's smile accompanies the carnage.

There's a skeleton in the middle of the dancefloor.
The Boogie-man shakes his pathetic bells.

Rachel wants to scream but her lips are covered. She dreamed that a mob of men, clubs and black boots, had burned down the Semper synagogue. Aaron, at her side, snores peacefully. Her beloved's face is turned toward the window. She kisses him on his forehead. Every night Rachel returns in her dreams to the arches of the Auguste bridge, the deluge of daffodils and azaleas in the Palace Park. Every morning she wakes up, sad and resigned. The thunder outside her window doesn't frighten her. It is for her children that she trembles, for her people in distress and for old Europe.

There's a guitar with mangled strings.
A blind man leading his flock into the abyss.

Thunder seems to precede the light by a fraction of a second. This flash is not like the others. Steve is sprawled on the sofa in the sitting room. Two beer bottles are lying on the floor. The first drops sound on the sheet metal . . . Click, click, click . . . Steve spreads his arms out randomly into the darkness to embrace an absent body. His arms fall. The rain is falling.

Clock, clock, click . . . the rain scats . . .

The first drop is for the storm howler bird, the next for the spirit with phosphorescent feathers which goes downhill. Click, clock, clock . . .

The rain makes the earth cringe and the disdainful earth sends it spinning, sliding down a gentle slope. The sky spreads out like a pasha; the earth does not submit, it resists, clings to its hard clumps, its furrows, its flint.

*

The witch rain trickles, shovels the dust. The ruts vomit, the furrows are rice paddies. The wanderers of the night, opossums and foxes, have dripping coats. Is it night or day?

It's the rain, my man, it's the rain . . .

A furious xylophone resounds against sheet metal. Son House and Willie Brown, side by side under the veranda, watch the deluge. Willie Brown's cigarette burns in the corner of his mouth. Son House's eyes are washed by the monsoon.

*

"Oh Lord, oh, good wet-haired Jesus! Let Yo Word spread like a downpour!"

Miss Brown walks down the street, her drenched blouse sticking to her old skin, her face dripping with joy: "Let Your Word fall like dew! Like waves on greenery, like drops of water on the grass!"

Lightning strikes, a bluish streamer crosses the street, deadlier than a rattlesnake. Rosetta Brown stands still, her nostrils detecting sulfur and danger. She continues walking. She is already far away, her voice lost within the pounding of the storm.

*

The tombstones are slippery, the water runs between the graves, the lightning turns the granite into marble. The earth yields to the advancing sky, opens its pores and lets the gray water drown its depths.

*

Legba is there. You don't see him. For all those who speak of good, he is there. For all those who slander, he is there. He listens.

*

Little Ada is a catfish. On her shoulders, the splash, between her round cheeks, a laugh more powerful than the roar of the sky. Mooky and Buck have reconciled; braggarts, accomplices of the torrent, an unscrewed gutter floods them with joy. The downpour prances, the clouds turn in a tender carousel. Buck is a salamander, he rhythmically beats the wet drum of his belly. The children return to the original flood. They have challenged the authority of the old, the superstitious, the cautious. They are in their place, princes and princesses of wonder, in the street, in the rain.

*

The river swells, spills over its banks. The algae swirls, the pebbles collide like uncontrollable atoms. Pats' corpse suddenly detaches and surrenders to the current; the child moves between the black rocks and broken tree trunks, passes the locks and the dams, returns to the river with infinite banks. God willing—and God wills it—he will reach the waves, the troubled dream of Vespucci and Cortés, down there, south of the great Tropic, between the claws of the crab; Yucatan the red, the sargassum labyrinth; Pinar del Rio, the Isle of Youth, the gardens of the Queen, the bubbling foam, the undertow, fringing reefs and quiet atolls. Poor Pats' body will finally be heard. The child will be a griot of the abyss, a bard of silence and salt.

*

The drums take advantage of the storm to roar without restraint and to reign again. Shady balafons, sabers before dawn, djembes emerging from nothingness. To every tone corresponds a language, torn from the newborn mouth by deportation and terror. Fulani and Soninke drums, Ashanti and Yoruba drums, Fon and Bamileke drums, Fang drums, M'bochi and Kimbundu drums. Forbidden drums, confiscated by the masters; water drums, armpit and chest drums, outlaw drums, blackjack drums, death penalty, severed ears. Refractory drums that go up in spasms from the aorta, when anger cracks the skin, deafens hearts. Bayou St. John wizard drums, clairvoyant drums of Congo Square, brackish drums of Lake Pontchartrain, bloodthirsty drums of Bois-Caïman! Sudden and unalterable tom-toms, of never elucidated violence, they come back to haunt the plain, allying with the lightning, invoking the one who presides over tremors of fate. Atibon Legba, the trouble-maker, the lame emperor:

. . . B'omodé korin adjuba Agbo é
Agbo mojuba
F'èlègba eshu ona! . . .

*

"Legba! Your spurs are in my flesh! . . . I sweat the river! Oh, Legba, what are you waiting for to land on my shores?"

A curtain of rain. An unalterable fire. Betty is paralyzed with fear. The one who stands before her, her eyes bulging, her tunic drenched in blood, does not seem to see her. Sapphira, ridden by the spirits, is no longer her aunt, she belongs to the unbridled myriads, to the freefall.

Betty steps forward, puts her hands on Sapphira's shoulders. Icy, reptilian skin. With a push of immeasurable strength, Betty is projected onto the ground. The old woman stares at her with eyes of snow. She advances, her fingernails are sharp, her jaws ready for the hunt. A bolt of lightning strikes a tree a few meters away. Despite the rain, the fire is raging. Sapphira turns around and stretches her face toward the flames: "Legba, you have found the way! . . . Come, Legba, come!"

*

His huge body. The invisible imprint of his footsteps. He is called, wild poems are sung to him. He is called from the fragile ford, from the collapsed tower of dreams. He is called by voices twisted by want. Shango, his relative, is putting on a big show up there. That one has never known when to stop, and the world is stricken as one by his fury.

*

The lightning thinks he is a tree, the strike pierces him. Legba walks. He pushes away the darkness and the leaves. A woman is calling him by his name. Legba hurries. The smell of fire. The woman and the voice are in his line of sight. He has only one more step to take to consume the moment . . .

III

"Boy, it's sure hard to sleep
With a wolf at your door."

HOWLIN' WOLF
The Wolf Is at Your Door

There was only half a cigarette left in the pack of Camels. Bobby lit it. His guitar was in place, strapped across his shoulder. It was his first guitar, a second-hand Gibson Kalamazoo, which he had bought in Hazlehurst, on the advice of his pal Ike Zimmerman. A strange Negro, that one, violent and dreamy, a gifted musician but indifferent to success. Bobby had worked hard to pay for this guitar, accompanying Ike on the harmonica in the most purulent dives, railway taverns, and lumber camps. He had rehearsed entire nights with his partner in the little Beauregard cemetery; after reaping the silent approval of the dead, Bobby had persuaded himself that the living, too, would finally applaud him.

A whistle shakes the plain, a train whooshes by in a cloud of steam. Maybe the Yellow Dog or the Peavine. Bobby ignores it. Lately he has been jumping into any train car he could. He jumped onboard, gutted the mists, digested the landscapes. Not able to make out Vega, Deneb, and Altair through the dust-filled sky, he relied on the incline of a slope, the whim of the wind that carried him on uncertain paths. He discovered the great people, the conquered and the wanderers—heady darkness, hunter huts, shelters of prowlers and paroled spirits, putrid and silent pools, forgotten silver mines, bursts of greenery against the bare sides of a hill, industrious ants on its slope, a bucket of light pulling him toward the day, a pile of tires watched at midnight by an octogenarian Negress armed with a rifle, hoboes as flexible and thin as iron wires, sowing behind them the seeds of a new language, bums who no longer advanced, lost children, permanent hide-and-seek among the remnants of America.

It had been a while since he left that damn county and everything seemed new and powerful to him. The smell of the earth. Peppery and woody. Intoxicating. The scent of fallen magnolias, the sour and tangy odor of apples abandoned on the grass. Bobby rediscovered the perfumes that his memory had repressed: the dry hay and the breath of stables, the seminal and musky smell of plow animals, that of manure turned into compost again, the tawny exhalations of the sorghum thickets, the sharp fragrance of crushed pecans and the gloomy smell of rotting fescue grass. He approached the first buildings and detected the hints of sour milk and fricot, then a sudden puff loaded with hot grease awoke his hunger—it smelled like grilled pork cheeks, tripe marinated in spices, placed on embers. From an open barn there seeped miasmas of molasses and ethyl. He passed a worker drawing on his pipe, the smoke of his brown tobacco superimposed over the smell of bitumen on the partially resurfaced road. The cotton plants with fat, odorless pods surrounded him, odorless except for the tenacious smell of the sweating men and women he saw leaning over between the plants. The scent of fate suddenly permeated the air and Bobby rediscovered the pitiful aura he had never stopped running from. Then came the first machines and their diesel exhaust fumes.

Bobby left the white parcels and closed his nose to the desolation. He focused on the hum of the tractors, that of the still numerous flies in the sweetness of autumn. He heard the shouts of the mule drivers: "Hi! Ha! Gee!" and the echo of the braying donkeys. The elms, beeches, and maples were the color of clay, the sky blue-gray. He approached the river whose turbid waters carried branches and leaves. The pebbles at the bottom of the torrent knocked together. Bobby stroked the varnished wood of his guitar. He resisted the urge to sit on the shore and tune its sound to the metronome of the rushing water. He continued in the direction of the collapsed bridge which he saw at the edge of the forest. The sky was covered with black spots. He walked for miles without passing any building apart from an old meat smoker. The night would surprise him like a prowler. "Nigga, you gotta find shelter fore the moon be in the sky." Bobby knew the song, and in this type of place, songs were truth itself. If a patrol of hooded Klansmen picked him up in the middle of the fields, no one would hear him scream or struggle. A week earlier, near Leland, he had crossed a town where two corpses hanging from a lamppost served as public illumination. According to what a local guy told him, they were bootleggers, brothers who were filthy rich. The two brothers had fucked a red-headed whore and had paid her less than her regular fee; the girl had complained and the inhabitants of the town had lynched them. On the village square, there was jubilation, the kids ate ice cream at the foot of the dead bodies and a photographer captured the moment.

What frightened Bobby that evening, more than a pack of assassins, was the obscure and quivering magma forming on the side of the road. He bit his lips; a taste of iron against his gums. There was a presence beyond the shadows. The thing was coming back. That thing against which his clear mind had been struggling for months. It was in Clarksdale at the intersection of routes 49 and 61. Just like this evening, Bobby had been looking for shelter for the night. A dense, nitrous mist had covered the plain. It stank of moldy viscera from hell. The creature had approached him, its face indecipherable, wielding its tools of darkness. It reached out and Bobby gave it his guitar. Usually, he would have killed anyone who tried to take what was his, but in that moment he had complied. The creature had fiddled with the bridge of the guitar and returned it to Bobby with a carnivorous smile, before dissolving into the mist. Ever since that night, Bobby never slept until he had knocked himself out completely with bad gin. He felt the excruciating sensation that his cortex had been violated, that foreign and corrosive memories had been introduced under his skull.

Not the slightest gleam on the horizon. Bobby hugs his Gibson against his chest. If the creature returns, this time, he will fight and resist the bewitchment. The silence stretches across the countryside. The town is there, very close. With a lot of luck, Bobby will reach it safe and sound.

The plain vibrated with the roar of tractors, the steady breathing of the pickers. The sheds were overflowing with bales of cotton stacked to the ceiling; cast iron scales were completing their balancing tasks, always to the advantage of the planters and dealers, who pointed out to the workers, bitter when they felt in their palms just barely enough to fill a boiling pot, machines capable of harvesting an entire plot between dawn and noon. These were no longer the good old "cotton gins" invented by Father Whitney, but relentless separators, more durable than a thousand horses, more dexterous than children's fingers. These machines were expensive, but never complained, didn't risk sunstroke, nor snakebites. Workers grumbled pro forma, then submitted to the blackmail, hoping to earn enough before winter to afford a one-way ticket north. Hopes were quickly extinguished; the salary they earned at the scale was immediately spent in the landowner-owned supply stores; debts piled up and the workers found themselves bound to the plantations as securely as convicts in a chain gang.

Jonathan Barrel, seated next to a scale, scribbled nervously in his notebook—he was adding, subtracting, crossing out columns of figures and creating others. Nearly half a bale of cotton per acre. The situation could have been much worse. Despite the drought and the storms, the plants had held up, the abundance of the harvest compensated for the investment in the machines, they might even see some profit, provided they reduce the burden of wages as much as possible. Hidden behind the columns crossed out by Jonathan Barrel's pen, there were entire families evicted at dawn, the potentially unemployed and countless empty stomachs.

The last one. He would be the last man to pay her to spread her legs. She realized it when the body had collapsed on her chest and she had pushed it off unceremoniously. Alone in the room, Dora had washed with maniacal care, as one disinfects a wound. She had covered her skin with talcum powder and slipped in the fold of her bodice the money from her final trick. She had left by the service door, refusing to go through the main room, to face the lights and the voices.

Dora had abandoned the hiding place beneath the floorboards, and every week deposited her money in the bank. She planned to leave with Joshua and some luggage at the beginning of winter, her destination a small town in Tennessee, a peaceful town. She was going to buy her own business, a florist's shop. The banker had taken care of the paperwork. Dora walked down an alley, behind the saloon. A dirty alley, lighted by a flickering neon sign, it stank of the piss of drunks, but the stench was dissipated by the flowers Dora arranged in her mind.

In the shop there would be heaps of roses and magnolias, of every imaginable hue. Narcissus, too, and hyacinths . . . Maybe she would install a greenhouse and grow orchids. Joshua would go to school, and she would see to it that he was always wearing leather shoes and that his hair was freshly combed.

Dora walked to the old haberdashery. Shattered windows, loose boards, splinters. She lit a cigarette and sat down on the crumbling porch.

. . . There would be tulips and daffodils, camellias and irises . . . No funeral flowers, only those used for banquets, weddings, and christenings.

When Dora told Joe Hives she was leaving, he seemed deeply saddened, almost aggrieved. But her decision was irrevocable. Dora had already mourned her so-called career as a diva; she no longer wanted to rub shoulders with thugs or johns, didn't want to feel their filthy eyes on her flesh. Singing the blues and selling herself for a few dollars had become the same purgatory for her. She didn't want to lose any more of herself.

Dora exhaled a soothing puff of smoke. She thought lovingly of Joshua's first steps on Basin Street in Storyville. It was barely ten years ago but it seemed like an eternity to her. After a brief stay in Memphis, she had gone with her baby to New Orleans. Shitty, disillusioning jobs, she had failed at Mahogany Hall, once the most famous brothel in America; then a clandestine whorehouse, constantly threatened by police raids and the settling of accounts between gangsters. Lula, the madam, nicknamed Lulu White, more famous in New Orleans than the first lady of the United States, had become fond of Joshua and taken pity on Dora. Lulu watched the child while Dora, after satisfying the last customers, went to sing in the honky-tonks of Back'O Town and the Rampart Street joints. The young woman had left Louisiana before Joshua was old enough to understand what his mother's profession really was.

Dora stands up. She coughs and stubs out her cigarette under her bare foot. At the corner of the street, she sees the silhouette of Pastor Lloyd walking away. He can go fuck himself. She has nothing more to say to him. He has no hold over her, much less over her child. If he continues to prowl around in the evening in front of the saloon and terrorize Joshua at the window, she will take Joe's gun and make him leave.

Suddenly hands emerge from under the porch. Quick and carnivorous, they grab her ankles. An implacable vise, inhuman pressure. The hands pull her down. Tilting over. Knocked to the ground. Dora collapses, flat on her stomach. Dirt clogs her voice. The hands are winches locked onto her. Her nose is bleeding. Metallic liquid on her tongue. A force drags her under the boards of the porch. She is overcome by the speed, by dizziness. She has no time to be afraid, already the light is fading. Under the boards. The hands let go of her ankles, grab onto her hair. She manages to scream. Under her skull, inside. Vertebrae smashed. Neck broken. Hands indulge in a game of chance, nails tear lace, burrow in flesh.

Dorothy's final trick doesn't bother her. The bites, the clawing, the disgusting words can no longer offend her dead body. A steel blade slashes her neck. Bloody roses trickle onto the ground.

*

The boy wakes up; his fingers climb up the cord of the bedside lamp to the switch. He rubs his eyes. He dreamed of a field covered with sunflowers which he picked by the armful to place as an offering at his mother's feet. The window is open.

He can hear furious barking, very close; dogs fighting for a piece of meat. Joshua leans out, sees only the glare of the lampposts and the roofs of the shacks standing out in dark triangles. The barking settles down in the dark. The boy closes the window, drinks a glass of water. He hesitates to go out in the hallway to knock on Dora's door. It's better to let her sleep. Tomorrow morning he will bring her breakfast in bed and her kisses will taste sweet. The room becomes dark again. Peaceful breathing. Sunflowers fold their petals.

*

A dog is barking its head off in front of a shack with broken windows. A mutt with a coat worn by the brutality of the streets. Its misery is only apparent, an incredible power surrounds its carcass, a god dances under the filthiness of its skin. The dog's eyes reflect the night, reveal the smallest detail: a cigarette butt with its end circled in red, the imprint of a body in the dirt that disappears under the boards of a porch. The mutt sticks its muzzle under the boards. Among the opaque eddies, dozens of yellow eyes are moving. The animal backs away and barks even more wildly. He will bark until the light of day alerts the living.

The dog stayed at a safe distance from the crowd. Its sides retained the impact of the stones it had received. It had done its duty, its cry had disturbed the night, then the dawn.

Joe Hives approached the old haberdashery, his 9 mm Luger in his hand. When he was asked to use his gun to finish off the howling beast, he felt a flash of foreboding. He had locked Joshua in his room and rushed out into the street. Joe bent over to look under the porch. Thin streaks of light came through the boards, a shape was emerging, shadowy and unmoving. Joe was much too big to venture underneath. It was Mooky, the shoemaker's son, who was commissioned. The boy slid into the opening. A shriek of pure terror. Mooky came out into the open, trembling like a reed: "They sompin' in there! Sompin' dead!"

The crowd armed themselves with crowbars and clubs; the rotten wooden slats gave way. A cluster of rats fled into the dirt, the diligent mutt devoured one. Among bits of wood and cobwebs Dora's body appeared. Lying on her side, her robe torn to shreds, her toes and calves ripped apart. Under her chin, a blackish circle. Joe brandished his Parabellum to impose a perimeter of decency on the crowd. He took off his shirt and put it over the chest and face of the victim. He handed Mooky a dollar and ordered him to run and get a blanket, clean or dirty, it didn't matter, but quickly. The boy came back a few minutes later, out of breath, with a tarp covered with cement spots taken from a nearby construction site. Dora's shroud. The dog spat out a mouthful of rat fur and barked one last time, before returning to the haunted netherworld from which it had emerged.

*

Joshua had pounded on the door and the walls. His fists were sore. He had almost broken his neck leaning out the window. Now he was sitting on the bed, his brain filled with dark premonitions. He heard the key turn and jumped to his feet, ready to grapple with the devil. Joe entered the room, distraught, his eyes cast down. His pistol was hanging by his side, the barrel pointing down. He sat down on the bed and, without saying a word, started fiddling with the gun; he removed the bullets, a few rolled on the floor. Joe handed the unloaded gun to the boy. Joshua felt the heavy steel in his hand. "I'll give y'all the rest when yer a man . . . " Joe's voice faded out. The former roustabout was surprised by the lukewarm tears running down his cheeks, as if those tears couldn't be his. The boy, without letting go of the weapon, picked up the bullets between the grooves of the wooden floor. Joe walked over to the door. "I ain't gone let you down, Josh."

The key turned in the lock. The boy stuffed the last bullet deep in his pocket.

*

The coroner had come with two assistants in an old van disguised as a hearse. Part of the crowd had dispersed into the surrounding alleys to spread the news. The saloon whore was dead. Bled out. Fucked to death. Eaten by rats. The news had circulated to the houses on the edge of town and it made no one any sadder than if they had learned that a drowned goat had been found at the bottom of a well. The coroner had the body placed inside the van. He noted the most obvious wounds, the broken neck, the cut throat, the traces of semen and the multiple bites, then got rid of the tarp and replaced it with a sheet.

The sheriff got out of his Dodge which he had parked in front of the haberdashery. Harry Bradford was hungover and seemed in a foul mood. Anthony Madden adjusted the buckle of his belt where his revolver hung and followed the sheriff to the back of the van. The voices in the crowd became vague murmuring. The White folk had showed up, the matter was getting serious. The sheriff talked with the coroner for a few minutes, then returned to his car. The reporter from the local gazette who wanted to interview him was curtly rebuffed. The Dodge roared off in a cloud of dust, forcing the curious to scurry away.

"Why didn't y'all lift the sheet to look at the dead woman, sheriff?" asked Anthony Madden from the passenger seat.

"You askin' me why?"

"Well, I don't know, for the investigation . . . "

"The investigation is ovah," said Harry Bradford, his hands gripping the steering wheel. "I don't want to get my hands dirty lookin' at a nigger whore who may have a rat inside her pussy."

"Damn, sheriff, seems like y'all even more racist than me!"

"Than you? That ain't possible!"

Laughter broke out inside the car. The Dodge rumbled over a bumpy road, dazzling in the September sun.

It was a real roadhouse, oh yeah! That is, isolated, with no other buildings around, only the filigree trunks of trees at night. An authentic juke joint, yessir!—with its painted scrap-metal sign, its door open like a mouth filled with light. Electricity had reached it thanks to an act of piracy: a purloined pylon, cleverly extended wires, and spare fuses. At the back of the room strutted a Seeburg jukebox, a massive Audiophone with shiny wood paneling. In the belly of the machine, eight records played one after the other in a loop verging on overdose—eight black disks from Okeh Records, Vocalion, and Paramount, conveying the voices of local heroes: Leroy Carr, Blind Lemon Jefferson, Mississippi John Hurt. The same songs kept playing: "Black Snake Moan," "How Long Blues," "Nobody's Dirty Business." Sometimes the needle missed a groove and the record started to stutter; then Marvin, the owner, a Black man with straightened hair, shook the glass dome and the song resumed. Nobody else was allowed to touch the boss's little electric baby, unless they wanted a club to their knee. To play in this roadhouse a stone's throw from Banks, on the road to Tunica, was to defy modernity, affirm the superiority of man over this junkyard of fuses and blinking lights.

When Willie Brown and Son House entered the room that evening, Marvin immediately unplugged the machine and served them some of the best bootleg booze in the county. Son House glanced at the jukebox, smirking.

"With what yer 'piccolo' cost y'all, ya could have brought down a whole brass band from N' Orleans!"

"'Cept it don't drink a drop," replied Marvin, "not like those Louisiana trumpet players."

"Shit, yo beast consume a lot o juice," said Willie Brown. "We all don't needs a dynamo stuck up our asses for us to play all night long."

The boss nodded with a smile. Those two surely spared no effort working the audience into a frenzy. Son House and Willie Brown were some great blues machines.

Revelers were waiting outside in front of the entrance; guys were sizing up the girls' chests, the ladies were checking out the assets of their future escorts. Beautiful youth, fiery blood, shooting stars. Son House and Willie Brown began with an old Charley Patton classic: "Tom Rushen Blues," the story of the famous sheriff of Merigold who had thrown Charley in prison for public drunkenness.

> . . . *When you get in trouble, it's no use to screamin'*
> *and cryin', hmm,*
> *Tom Rushen will take you, back to the prison house*
> *flyin' . . .*

The crowd came through the door and began to sway to the rhythm of the guitars. No warm-up or observation period; the swaying and acrobatics imagined in front of the door were immediately unleashed on the dance floor in a mass of swirling bodies. To help out the less talented, Marvin had hired dance instructors. For ten cents you could go around the floor for one dance. But be careful not to confuse those teachers with the cheap whores—dime-a-dance girl was a serious and regulated profession: you dance, you pay, and hands off! Son House and Willie Brown played blues, ragtime, deep country, and even a kind of waltz, in which the muddy water of the Mississippi replaced the blue flow of the Danube. The jukebox in the back of the room could only observe the damage: everyone had forgotten it, and the ungrateful crowd treated it with less respect than they showed a set of pots and pans. Then Willie Brown played "Future Blues," his masterpiece, the only tune of which he was the undisputed creator. He upped the tempo, used his most lascivious voice to make it a real attack on modesty:

> . . . *I say, I got a woman*
> *Lord, and she's lightnin' when she smiles . . .*

After two hours of uninterrupted playing, Son House leaned his guitar against his chair and began to fill his pipe. The atmosphere had become stifling, and the crowd surged out into the warm night. Willie Brown had forgotten his pick, his bloody thumb demanded a break. He tore a handkerchief with his teeth and improvised a makeshift bandage. Son House's eyes suddenly lit up:

"Bill, look who comin'!" When his old pal called him "Bill" Willie Brown knew something extraordinary was happening. He looked around at the half-deserted room and smiled. "May the good Lord strike me down, if it ain't Little Robert come back!"

Bobby walked over the smoky dance floor, his dismissive gaze refusing to acknowledge objects or faces. He was dressed like a crooked bookmaker: a Barbour suit, a felt hat with a silk ribbon, a shirt with a starched collar, and a tie worthy of a Republican senator. Across his chest, over his shoulder, a brand new guitar. Bobby walked up to the stage. He took off his hat to greet the two musicians, as is done when you meet your elders in front of an old folk's home.

"So, boy, here y'all be at last," said Son House, shaking the young man's hand. "Where you been keepin' all this time?"

"I been gettin' along, Pop," Bobby said soberly.

"That one hell o' a guitar y'all got there," said Willie Brown, "it fo real, or just fo show?"

Bobby took the sarcasm without flinching and humbly asked his elders if he might play a tune before they resumed.

"Have y'all thought about it, boy?" said Son House. "The niggas 'round here ain't the tender type."

Bobby nodded, sat down on the chair and carefully adjusted the creases of his pants. He began strumming the strings of his guitar. He had tuned his guitar Sebastopol style and played a D minor, strong and clear. The kid's calm attitude was impressive but Willie Brown's smile was tinged with apprehension. Bobby played the first bars of "Memphis Blues." The little devil attacked the W. C. Handy tune, the cornerstone of the building! Son House's pipe almost dropped from his lips. Shit, how was he muffling the strings, rolling the bass?! And how could his hands move so fast on the neck?!

What happened next could have been included in the Pentateuch, between the plagues of Egypt and the crossing of the Red Sea. The guitar sent out notes like a swarm of locusts, the sounding board opening the floodgates to a deluge of harmonics. The revelers on the threshold dropped their cigarettes at their feet and rushed inside. Bobby started to sing. His voice had ripened like an ear of corn, a falsetto voice, high but virile, a voice that seemed born to lift skirts and crackle the light bulbs hanging from the ceiling.

> . . . I never will forget the tune that Handy called the
> Memphis Blues.
> Oh yes, them Blues! . . .

Nobody was dancing, though the rhythm was irresistible. Girls turned to jelly on the spot, some rubbed their chest through the fabric of their dress; the guys nervously scratching their arms, gripped by a phantom rash. Bobby cast lethal glances at the ladies in front of the stage; his long, slender fingers inventing improbable chords, bloodthirsty riffs, even his wrong notes were virtuosic.

Willie Brown turned to Son House, tears in his eyes. It was time for a coronation and never had a man seemed more worthy of sitting on the throne, ever since Charley Patton had decided to give up the wild blues life. Bobby dared a brief finale, awkward but full of daring, then stopped short and set his guitar on his knees. In the room, a heavy silence, interspersed with gasps. Bobby looked up at the two bluesmen and humbly smiled at them. Willie Brown touched the young man's guitar as if it were a holy relic.

"Where you learn to play like that, boy?"

"At the intersection of Routes 49 and 61," responded Bobby in a serious voice, "at an hour when you oughten' to hang around."

"Were it the devil gave y'all that guitar?" asked Son House.

"Maybe so," said Bobby. "Anyways, he were taller than a tree and stank like the bottom of a pot."

Son House's face wavered between terror and skepticism. Pleased with the effect he had had, Bobby stood up, shook the two musicians' hands and got down from the stage. The bar owner ran up to him, handed him a ten dollar bill, and begged him to get back on stage. The young prince declined and walked slowly to the door. In his wake three admirers elbowed each other to be the first to talk to him.

Bobby let them light his cigarette, loosen his tie, and even more. His hands worked more magic, he plunged into the damp of anonymous flesh and those violent eruptions were his only compensation that night.

The church door shut behind her. Betty turned away from the white building which hid a nest of vipers inside. Caught between anger and desperation, she sought an outlet for her rage. Pastor Lloyd's voice thundered behind her. He could always roar; from then on his biblical judgements and his patriarch strutting would no longer impress her.

Betty walked down the slope framed by pines and cypresses and reached Main Street. Everywhere, in the shade of verandas, in the dirt, they talked only of Dora, in terms so uncharitable that one might have forgotten that she had been murdered in the middle of the night, leaving a child of ten on the side of the road. Red ass, rattle bitch, dick garage, sewer hole, Jezebel, Babylonian: there was no shortage of words to brand her corpse. Betty wanted to strike every passerby, spit on the entire town. And to think that among these good people a fair number would come back next Sunday to wash their purulent souls at no cost in the aisles of the house of God. Betty's thoughts turned to arson. She imagined going back with a jerry can of gasoline and purifying this den of hypocrites in flames. She drowned her anger under the warm jet of a water pump near the garage where mechanics were smoking and chatting. While splashing her neck, she relived the scene. Reverend Lloyd quoting Isaiah, his index finger raised, taking refuge in obscure perorations so not to fulfill his duty as a Christian.

. . . But draw near hither, ye sons of the sorceress, the seed of the adulterer and the whore!

The poor man, stammering out his morals like a parrot, unable to let his heart speak! Pastor Lloyd had declined to preside over the service, to give the eulogy over Dora's body. He had even opposed her being buried in the cemetery next to the church or taking up a collection for her funeral. The pastor had refused everything, sending Dorothy's existence to rot and oblivion. Betty had cried, begged, she would have even kissed his feet to obtain his pity, but she had come up against a slab of cold virtue.

She drank greedily from the fountain and continued walking. Never again would she sing during services, and if the pastor refused to pronounce words of mercy over Dora's shroud, she, Betty, would speak.

The twilight was fulfilling its task of great disturbance; shadow and light were exchanged, tan streaks and ebonite highlights dripped in watercolor. The Cadillac, rolling on the paved road with its headlights off, turned onto a dirt road, skirted an islet forest and disappeared between two trees. Andrew Wallace exited the Caddy and approached a massive gate topped with tapered tips. A copper bell, as big as a head. He shook the bell, waited, then rang again. A hurricane lamp came up the driveway and stopped behind the gate.

"It's me, Booker, open up!"

The gate creaked open and Wallace entered the dark grounds. A face appeared through the glow of the lamp, that of a middle-aged Black man with large, almond-shaped eyes.

"Is my father in bed?" Wallace asked.

"No, Mist Andrew, but he not expectin' nobody."

The lamp lighted the gravel up to the entrance of a colonial-style house, less imposing than that of the Conrads, but just as old and venerable. Resin torches were burning under the overhang of the veranda, drunken moths swirling around the flames; sometimes a wing caught fire and the creature fell. The lamp-bearer stopped. He was dressed in a butler's uniform, as was worn in the previous century, the brass buttons on his jacket sparkled.

"Please, suh," Booker said, his eyes pleading, "Mist Longhorn gone punish me if I lets you in."

"Nothing will happen to you, Booker, unless you don't open the door . . . "

Andrew Wallace turned the front door handle and left the door ajar behind him. A grand staircase. A chandelier with flickering lights above. Wallace climbed the stairs to the landing dominated by a stained-glass window, its colors obliterated by the night. On the ground floor the butler was watching him, his eyes worried. Under a door, a thin ray of light. Wallace knocked twice and entered.

Edward Longhorn was sitting in an armchair, a blanket over his knees. His cheeks were clean-shaven and a sickly white, thin wisps of gray hair fell over his age-spotted forehead. When Edward Longhorn saw Wallace enter, the book he was holding fell onto the carpet.

"What are you doing here?! Booker let you in?"

"Leave your slave alone," said Wallace. "He was only doing his job."

"I've already told you to let me know when you wanted to see me, and to go through the servants' door!"

"The one by the chicken coop?"

Wallace walked over and picked up the book.

"What were you reading? *Titus Andronicus* . . . That suits you well, it's depressing and very old-fashioned."

"You came to my house to insult me?!"

"I came to talk to you."

The library was lighted by sconces attached to the wall paneling. In tall bookshelves around the room hundreds of books with leather covers were lined up. Wallace pulled out a chair and sat down in front of the patriarch. He looked silently at the worn-out face in front of him, trying to find in its faded features some traces of his own heredity.

"Are you going to stare at me like that all night? What the hell do you want to say to me?!"

Wallace didn't answer, and continued looking at the old man. Edward abruptly threw the blanket off his knees.

"Oh, no need to say it! I know you've launched a campaign against the mayor, against my friends, and I'm ashamed, you can't imagine how ashamed I am!"

"Your friends are corrupt, and the shame is that you insist on defending them."

Edward Longhorn did not have the strength to fight with a man as young and confident as Wallace. He leaned toward him and lowered his voice.

"I'm tired, Andrew. I have reached the age when human ambitions seem like miserable vanities. Maybe my friends have made mistakes, but you aren't obliged to stray, as well."

"Because I'm half-Black, I don't have the right to be ambitious?"

"Be careful, they won't let you try!"

"I'm not afraid. I've proved my worth and all the town niggers support me."

"You talk about support . . . The truth is, you aim to use my name to bamboozle honest people, and that I will not tolerate!"

"You didn't give me your name. I took my mother's. You didn't give me a penny, either. I raised myself up alone. And when I'm mayor . . . "

"You will never be mayor! Just be happy to be rich and alive!"

Edward Longhorn braced himself on the armrests of his chair and stood up painfully. He was wearing a gray suit in which his thin body floated. Andrew Wallace stood up as well. He towered over the old man by a foot and suddenly felt pity for him.

"Where is my mother?"

"How should I know? With the other servants, I imagine."

"You knew where to find her back then, when you felt alone in your bed."

The blood rushed to the old man's face, his legs began to tremble, he pointed to the door.

"Leave! Get out of here right now, you little bastard, you . . . "

"Dirty nigger?!"

Wallace kicked over the coffee table. A candlestick rolled and the flame immediately attacked the fibers of the carpet.

"You must be crazy!"

Wallace stomped on the flames. The library door opened with a bang. Wallace spun around. Christopher Longhorn entered the room. His eyes, clouded by bourbon, went from his father to Andrew, his face turning dark red.

"What the hell are you . . . what are you doing here?!"

As a reply, Wallace moved the tail of his coat aside and revealed his pistol, its butt sticking out of its holster. He headed for the door.

"I'm leaving, Father, we will see each other again next year at the town hall, if God allows you to live till then."

Wallace's retreating footsteps echoed on the stairs. Christopher Longhorn rushed out of the room.

In the foyer, an old Black woman, a scarf tied around her head, was waiting, her hands clenched together. Behind her, Booker was frozen in abject terror. Wallace went down the last steps and hugged the old woman, more delicate than a child in his arms, and she began to sob.

"Booker, you told her?!"

Edward Longhorn's voice rang out from atop the stairs. Immediately the old Negress released the embrace. Edward Longhorn was leaning against the railing. Next to him Christopher was holding a rifle.

"Booker dint call me, Mist Longhorn," said the old woman. "A mother always know when her son not far off."

The old woman put a trembling hand on Wallace's shoulder.

"Leave, chile. I gone come see you soon, I swear before our Lord on the cross, I gone come."

Andrew Wallace spoke to the two men upstairs.

"If you touch a single hair on the heads of my mother or Booker, you will pay dearly for it, you hear me?!"

*

Christopher Longhorn returned to his usual state: drunk, belligerent, and vulgar. He set down his gun on a chair and drank from a bottle of brandy. Edward, standing in front of him, was studying the burns on the carpet. Christopher put the bottle down on a side table.

"You never was able to stop stickin' your dick into any old hole, were you? You make me so sick I want to vomit!"

"Go right ahead," said Edward Longhorn, looking up. "You've been vomiting on my name for so long . . . "

"You prefer your little nigger with all that money, is that it? Is he the one you wanted as your son?!"

"I think I would have preferred not to have had any children at all."

Clouds from the distant ocean melted over the land. The Cadillac's headlights cut through the darkness on the shoulder of the road. Andrew Wallace smoked furiously, his delicate hands gripping the steering wheel. Through the windshield, he could see a deer, perhaps a fawn, hypnotized by the lights. The Cadillac accelerated. A splotch of red on the hood. In the rearview mirror Wallace saw a bloody mass, quickly swallowed by the darkness. He lit another cigarette. The animal sacrifice hadn't calmed his nerves. He started thinking about his mother and her damned slave mentality. For him, the woman was the symbol of a stuck race, he felt a distant affection towards her, one mixed with contempt.

Dragged around like a tool her entire childhood, throughout her young life his mother had slept in a shed next to the chicken coop. One evening, a man, White and lonely, had taken her on her way back from the fields. Sure of his rights, the man had shoved up her dress and stolen her virtue, as he had seen his uncle and father before him do. Edward Longhorn had turned the young Negress into a consolation prize, finding her whenever insomnia overtook him or when his legitimate wife refused to open her legs to him. When her belly was full of his efforts, Edward Longhorn brought the Negress in from the fields and had her tend to domestic chores. The young woman waxed each step of the staircase on her knees, thousands of times, draining her strength so that dirt would spare the masters' house. She gave birth, and blamed herself for not being able to wield a broom the next day. She gave birth to a baby boy with skin too dark to be absolved of the sin, too light to be confused with the tribe of cotton pickers and wielders of pickaxes. Edward Longhorn did not acknowledge the bastard, but tried to give him the semblance of an education. The little boy proved to be studious, eager to learn, much more so than Christopher, the official Longhorn heir, whose intellectual mediocrity destined him to degeneracy.

Young Andrew spent most of his youth in the large library that smelled of calfskin and cold tobacco, among the most glorious representatives of civilization. He met Seneca, Shakespeare, de Tocqueville, and Houston Chamberlain, whose two-volume *The Foundations of the Nineteenth Century* he devoured. The young mulatto thought he was White. Refusing to believe the evidence in the mirror, he began to speak to his mother as he would a vulgar chambermaid and to order around the other house Negroes. A certain intimacy had grown between Andrew and the one he didn't dare call his father. In the evening, as the wind howled in the trees on the grounds, he would read to the old man whose vision was declining. He read Horace and Pliny, Keats and Shelley. Edward Longhorn listened to him, a glass of scotch in his hand, an enigmatic smile at the corner of his mouth. The patriarch struggled with a terrible paradox. He was proud of this little savage who had opened himself to the light, attributing the boy's precociousness to the quality of his own blood. His friends and the other planters in the county had not held his misconduct against him; they believed that getting a Negress pregnant was at most a venial sin. But Edward was ashamed to have given in to his impulses, and above all to have dispensed his generosity to a child whom he would forever be forbidden to love.

Andrew Wallace exhaled and tossed his cigarette out the window. Along with the smoke, he chased away the ambiguous images of his childhood. The Cadillac sped along, taking no heed of the potholes in the road. Wallace clutched the steering wheel, the car turned onto a bumpy path, the jolts to the chassis went up to his empty stomach. Wallace was possessed by a crazy energy, he had an erection and was sweating, smiling in the dark. He was heading to his bachelor hideout, a discreet cabin on the edge of the woods, where a young laundress whose name he cared nothing about was waiting for him. The bitch had full hips, heavy breasts, with hard, brown nipples. Wallace wondered if he was going to have something to eat when he arrived or feast directly on her flesh.

He spat on the jumble of nettles and brambles around the squeezed-together graves. The elm leaves dripped to the monotonous rhythm of a seasonal rain shower. A buzzard turned in slow black spirals, field mice and lizards sought refuge between the slabs of granite. No one among the meager assembly had brought an umbrella and the drops on their faces took the place of tears. Not many people to accompany the whore to her bed of clay. The church faithful followed the pastor's irrevocable decision; husbands didn't want to be seen next to a horizontal woman, even one inside four plank walls; as for the town women, they would have gladly come to spit on the coffin, but had made do with rejoicing in the dry confines of their kitchens.

Joe Hives held Joshua's hand. The boy's gaze was frozen on the mound of dirt in front of the grave. Betty was shivering in her dress, a purple rose in her hair. Behind her, Constance Reed, in a mourning coat, let the rain glisten on her brow. Kate Adams had come, a bruise on her cheek showed that she had had to endure her husband's wrath beforehand. She was holding a pair of shoes by the laces and never let Joshua out of her sight. Sergeant Elias was sitting on a tree stump, a pirate's patch concealing his empty eye socket. Son House had taken off his coat to protect his guitar from the rain. He was uncomfortable with the idea of singing at a funeral, but at Joe's insistence he had agreed, unlike Willie Brown, who was superstitious, and refused to play for a dead woman he had slept with, even briefly, one drunken evening. Sapphira stood alone outside the gate, floating in her rainbow dress, a wool shawl over her shoulders. No one would have objected to her entering the enclosure, but the old sorceress wanted to maintain a boundary.

The rain stopped and a variegated ray of light, similar to the witch's dress, lighted the gravesite. The grave was located in the poor section, a wild corner where couch grass and weeds reigned. The last stop before the common grave. Steve came up the path, threading his way through the labyrinth of headstones, a soaked hat on his head. Traces of flour remained on his shoulders and temples. He took off his hat to greet the assembly, approached Betty, and hugged her gently.

Betty took a few steps toward the coffin. She had not prepared a speech. She spoke with a wounded voice, told the tale of two little girls, their crazy adventures, their tender friendship. She spoke of the mossy banks of the river, the song of branches and the serenade of blackbirds. Her words, like a long psalm woven with ivy and hornbeam, embraced the blurred contours of the past. Constance closed her eyes. She saw the amber soul of Dora flicker like a benzene flame and regretted having denied her affection all those years. When Betty had finished her open-air eulogy, Constance said "Hallelujah!" and everyone repeated in unison: "Hallelujah!" for the perpetual stranger, the betrothed of the stones, "Hallelujah!" for murderous time and childhood rediscovered! The echo of the blessing reached Sapphira behind the gate. The sorceress bent down, picked up some dirt, and whispered in the direction of the black bird flying over the graves: "Erzulie Freda, welcome her! Erzulie Dantor, avenge her!"

Son House strummed a few notes; his lips hesitated and his fingers on the strings were timid. An internal struggle was playing out within him, the extent of which no one perceived. It had been ages since he had sung a hymn. The contradictory facets of his personality clashed; the former preacher, the bluesman, the tireless worker, the Parchman convict, fought for his voice. Son House let the song flow, a sacred nursery rhyme, sweet as water deep in a jug.

> *. . . Now God walked down in the cool of the day,*
> *and called Adam by his name*
> *But he refused to answer, 'cause he was naked and*
> *ashamed . . .*

Betty gave the signal, clapping her hands to accompany the refrain. A dozen feet stomped the damp earth. Sergeant Elias stood up, waiting for the charge of the angels to sound. Son House pushed his voice to a no-man's-land where the notions of accuracy and balance no longer prevailed. His ecstatic face gazed at the crowd, he was enjoying crossing the gully between the shores, between blues and gospel. He looked like the devil disguised as an apostle, reconciling their contrasting souls.

Betty walked over to the grave and dropped in a handful of dirt. A dull sound against the wooden boards. A silent exchange on either side of the abyss: "Sorry, Dora, sorry . . . "

Constance came to lay her fragile contribution on the coffin, then Joshua let go of Joe's hand and walked to the edge. He took the shovel out of the pile of dirt and, bracing himself with his legs, threw in a shovelful, then another. Son House encouraged him by strumming harder, Betty began singing again. Sergeant Elias, standing at attention, admired the efforts of the young soldier. Joshua shoveled like his ancestors, swamp drainers, he toiled like a true Negro, like a worthy son of the Delta. When the grave was completely filled, he tamped it down with the back of the shovel, then collapsed sobbing, like a distraught puppy. Joe Hives picked him up and kissed his forehead. Kate Adams handed him the pair of shoes that had belonged to Eugene, her missing boy. As everyone was passing through the gate, Sapphira slipped a conjuring spell into the boy's pocket, wrapped in a piece of calico. Joshua became everyone's child, protected by magic and compassion.

The boy's bedroom had no window. Betty had hung a kerosene lamp on the wall, and she tended to its flame so the darkness would never be complete. Also on the walls, cotton batiks and a bunch of dried flowers. The bed came from the saloon, as did the sheets and blankets.

Joe Hives had thought long and hard before suggesting that Betty and Steve take the boy into their home. He loved Joshua, but could not reasonably take care of him. He didn't want him growing up in a saloon, amongst the slimy laughter and sordid hustling. He felt ready to crush the skull of any jerk who showed the boy a lack of respect, but how can you make wickedness disappear from the lips of a drunk man? Joe had felt that Steve and Betty would be exemplary role models: they adored each other, worked hard, and dreamed of having a baby. The joy that radiated from Betty's face when he made his proposal, and Steve's silent tacit approval convinced him he had made the right decision.

At the beginning of each month Joe gave the couple about fifteen dollars to provide for the boy's needs and to pay for his schooling. After tough negotiations with the banker—he had to place the sharp edge of a knife against the man's neck—Joe managed to have Dorothy's savings, nearly one thousand, three hundred dollars, transferred to Joshua, with interest, when he came of age. The boy did not protest when Joe brought him to his new home, suitcase in hand. In the false bottom of the case, hidden in a handkerchief, was the Parabellum pistol. Betty showed him to his room, and Joshua immediately fell asleep.

In the early days, the boy tried to follow the rhythm of the household. Betty spoiled him, almost force-feeding him, spending more time in the kitchen than ever before. Steve found him to be the perfect companion in silence. After the evening meal, the two sat side by side on the porch. Steve pointed out the stars to Joshua, following them with the tip of his index finger. He gave the constellations fanciful names: the Boat, the Heifer, the Two-Bladed Sickle . . . The boy listened, his face turned towards the sparkling immensity.

One morning, when Betty had to go to the laundry, she dropped the boy off with Sapphira. She was quite apprehensive, still traumatized by the memory of her aunt, her blind eyes, the thunder, and blood on her skirt. She worried about it all day long. When she returned to fetch him at dusk, the boy was splitting logs with an axe, smiling from ear to ear. The old enchantress seemed rejuvenated, and Betty rediscovered the woman she had always known.

With the frenzy of the harvest and the Great Depression, Dora's death was quickly forgotten. No one, not even Betty, who was obsessed with the boy's well-being and her new responsibilities, really dwelled on the assassin. The murderer of a whore, everyone knew who it was: it was the day and its spitting, the night and its knives . . . Those who raised their arms to the cross did not doubt that Satan had ultimately reclaimed his creature, and those who knelt in front of fetishes saw in Dora's tragic destiny a conspiracy of spirits. The Whites saw no need to carry out an investigation; the murder was just an inevitable fact, like hail or famine.

On sleepless nights, Joe went into Dora's old room. He had kept her clothes, her bottle of perfume and makeup implements, and in this empty mausoleum, through the light of a lampshade, he meditated on nothing. Joe, who had not been able to find the words to express his love, told her in a low voice, among the lacy garments and the evaporated music.

Cigarette butts in the dirt, like extinguished talismans. Theodore was carrying out his little harvest, his back bent. Like every Sunday morning, in less than fifteen minutes, he had gathered enough tobacco to fill his makeshift pouch. From the bottom of his coat pocket he pulled out a sheet ripped from a Bible, tore a thin rectangle and rolled a cigarette. The Good Book, even for a confirmed blasphemer like him, had its advantages. The old man smoked the last bit between his fingers, stroked his beard while waiting for the street to bring him his ration of curiosities.

Betty was heading for the church. Molded by habit, she got up early and put on her white dress and polished shoes. It had been almost a month since she had gone through the heavy door of the sanctuary. She felt a curious lack, comparable to a craving.

The cross appeared at the top of the hill. Betty stopped, paralyzed by the mental image of the pastor waiting for her in front of the altar, full of arrogance and reproach. A tiny shadow stood out in the middle of the magnolia grove. Miss Brown was conversing with her beloved departed. Betty said to herself that there in front of her was the only true Christian in the whole town, a tireless watchwoman, awaiting the return of the Master.

Betty turned away, her mystical thirst unquenched. The town was still reeling from the hubbub of the night before.

Seasonal pickers wandered around, groggy and dusty. Betty walked past the saloon and recognized Theodore, a cigarette between his lips. She greeted the old man. The smell of tobacco rose up and awakened her senses. She had never smoked, but suddenly had a terrible urge to ask the old man for a puff.

"Is that what botherin' y'all?" said Theodore, handing her the cigarette.

"Thank you, grandfather. Is the boss here?"

"No, Joe gone to fill his barrels somewheres. I's waitin' on him. Specially the barrels."

Betty left the old man and went to the Jenkins grocery store. The wide shelves behind the counter were almost empty, stripped by seasonal workers. She bought some flour, dried beans, and a box of Madam C. J. Walker hair lotion.

"I needs some coffee too, some White Swan."

"Don't got no mo White Swan," replied Dericia Jenkins dryly. "Jus a packet of Arbuckles left."

"That'll do. Do y'all have any cigarettes? They fo my husband." Betty asked in an unsteady voice.

"What brand yo husband smoke?"

"They white with an orange tip."

The grocer rummaged through the drawers, grumbling, and spread five packs of different brands on the counter.

"It this one, I believe," said Betty, grabbing a pack of Benson & Hedges. "I'll also take some matches, and toothpaste."

Betty felt a foreign presence in her mouth and lungs. A heady taste. She lit another cigarette with the glowing end of the previous one. She had already stopped coughing, the smoke escaped from her lips and clouded the bright morning light. She went through the gate to the house, drew a bucket of water, washed her hands and rubbed her teeth with the mint toothpaste.

*

She had climaxed without a sound so not to awaken the boy. Steve's breathing body was lying next to her. She got up and tiptoed into the kitchen. A box of matches and the pack of Benson's. She sat down on the front steps. The moon was three-quarters full and its light shone on the edge of the well. She drew on her cigarette with pleasure. The smoke had revived the music in her throat, and she hummed an old-fashioned corn song. Betty smiled as she stubbed out her cigarette in a flowerpot. A rustle of leaves, soft footsteps on the grass. Joshua was at the back of the yard, hidden behind a lilac bush. His torso naked, he was holding a pistol, the barrel aimed at the shadow of the trees. Betty left the child to his vengeance and went back inside, leaving the door ajar.

The mirror reflects a busty figure squeezed into a swirl of mauve muslin. The figure turns round and round, leans forward and reveals a bosom capable of feeding all the orphans of the Delta. Aaron Posner, scissors in hand, lets out a sigh. His customer finally seems satisfied. He has been adjusting the dress for almost three hours, fine-tuning the hem, letting out seams. The woman seems to enjoy this ritual at the mirror, and the tailor's annoyance; she has come from far away, and is about to pay a small fortune for this dress in the latest European fashion, and has no intention of cutting short the fitting session. The customer places a wad of bills on the counter, refuses to take off her dress, and goes out to her convertible sedan parked in front of the shop.

Aaron decides to take a well-deserved break on a bench in the square in front of the town hall; in his hand, rolled into a cylinder, is a copy of the newspaper *Der Tog*. It takes almost a month for the paper to arrive from New York, if it doesn't get lost on the way. Aaron is a busy man, and reading the newspaper, under the lime trees in the park, is one of his few distractions. Ever since he declared his support for Andrew Wallace, the mayor and his allies have been boycotting his services, but the excellence of his work, the sophistication of his cuts, attracted the elegant ladies and dandies from as far away as the state borders. His order book is full until Passover, and he is considering hiring an assistant to help Rachel with her accounting duties, which often carry on into the middle of the night.

Aaron sits on a bench and turns the pages of the gazette with relish. He can't help reading out loud, and the sounds of Yiddish tickle his lips like sparkling wine. The *mame losh*, the language of mama, the most precious keepsake Aaron brought from Europe. In the evening, Rachel asks him to read to her while she works at the sewing machine. *Der Tog* is a veritable gold mine—Edward Opatovsky, Yehoash, Avrom Reyzen—in it the best writers publish their short stories, poems, and jokes, too, which make the spouses laugh like two shtetl kids.

Aaron pauses, his index finger hanging at the bottom of the page. He turns pale and casts worried glances around him. No one seems to be paying attention to this man who is trembling alone on his bench. Aaron forces himself to return to the paper, to the anguish and shattering glass. In September, in Berlin, SA thugs looted Jewish shops and beat up passers-by to almost complete indifference. The Nazis promised not to stop there, and it was whispered that old Hindenburg was about to ask Hitler to join his government.

Aaron folds the newspaper and stands up. He runs to the Western Union office. On the way, he meets the mayor and his wife who eye him with deep contempt. Aaron ignores them, cares only about the children he left in the mouth of the wolf. He sends five telegrams one after the other, in German; the telegraph operator asks him to spell each word; Aaron stammers, has trouble breathing.

He leaves the telegraph office and tosses the newspaper in a trash can on the corner of the street. Back home, he brushes the mezuzah at the front door. A smell of cooked apples and cinnamon. A cup of tea, a pie, a festive cover on the table. Rachel greets him with a big smile.

"The newspaper has not arrived. It's getting worse and worse, that post office . . . "

The lie he has just uttered upsets him almost as much as the tragedy that is occurring thousands of kilometers away. Aaron kisses his wife on the forehead. Rachel looks into his eyes. She has guessed if not the details then at least the broad outlines of the crisis.

"Have you contacted the children?"

"Yes."

Aaron goes alone into the back room. He unfolds his tallit and bends over facing the wall. He addresses to the Eternal One, his God, his most urgent telegram.

A blazing sun accompanied her to the laundry doors. The wicker basket she carried on her hip had grown heavier with the weight of the boy's clothes and she walked slowly, economizing the effort of each step. In front of the barbershop, Betty spotted Andrew Wallace contemplating the size of the crowd of his future voters. To avoid passing by him, she turned off into an alley which brought her to the shantytown. Around her, shacks were on the verge of collapsing, everything seemed to be slowly decomposing. She heard the sound of a harmonica, a blood-pulsing blues tune, rolling off the roofs of the shacks. Her legs immediately felt lighter. The harmonica continued playing; Betty saw a man from behind, about thirty paces in front of her, a slender Black man dressed in an unusually elegant suit. The man turned the corner and Betty was sucked into his wake. She passed the old distillery; the building had been completely gutted by a swarm of greedy hands. The harmonica player stopped to retie his shoelace, still blowing into his instrument. The musician turned around. He was even younger than Betty, his face and his eyes seemed angelic.

Betty put her basket on the ground. Betty was no longer Betty: she was a dancing machine. The harmonica was wailing and cutting loose. Betty's body conveyed the nuances at the heart of the violent sounds. The blues, like warm marrow, strengthened her bones, restored her mislocated regions. A group of children approached, drawn by the music, and a few adults joined the circle. Betty was on her knees, the sun strong on her shoulders, in the dirt she traced a clear alphabet, the symbols that were language before the lie. The harmonica suddenly stopped. Betty was on the ground, dripping with sweat. When she raised her head, the musician had disappeared. The crowd stared at her as if she were a drunk on the road to ruin. A guy touched his fly with an obscene gesture, a kid kicked up a cloud of dust into her face. Betty stood up, as exhausted as if she had just given birth to that disrespectful child.

*

The moon in its fullness. Frogs croaking, gusts of wind between branches. Betty crushed out her last cigarette. Her throat was raw. The musician's radiant face continued to sparkle in her mind. She thought about praying. She had not turned her thoughts to God since her altercation with the pastor. Betty was teetering toward the unknown, sensing that the only truth was in her body, her impulses, the tension inside her, and nowhere else. She walked up to the well, pulled up the bucket which she placed on the grass, the moon was immediately reflected in the water. Betty took off her shirt and over her neck poured the comfort of a new baptism. She stood shivering for a long time in front of the well, then returned to her bed next to Steve, falling asleep only at the first light of dawn.

At the end of the following day as she was returning home from the laundry she ran into the musician on Dixon Lane. He was drinking a bottle of soda, not far from the pawnshop. She dreaded as much as she hoped that he would speak to her.

"Beg pardon, Miss, was you the one dancin' so good the othah day?"

Silence. The blood rising to her cheeks.

"We should put on a show, we'd be real successful, fo sho!"

The man walks up to Betty. She can smell his breath, warm with whiskey. She should have known that such a man would not be drinking orange soda. Betty instinctively backs away. The man raises his hat, gives her a smile the likes of which she has never seen. His teeth are perfectly aligned ivory. His hands, Lord, his hands . . .

His hands held her wrists, held them against the mattress. He wasn't looking at her, but was staring at a hole in the wall. He thrusted powerfully, into her depths. Her hands released, Betty stroked his smooth, warm back, following the shape of the muscles. She was hoping for a gesture in return, a hint of tenderness, something other than this endless pounding. He hadn't kissed her once. Her vagina, once wet with desire, now hurt. The body above her crushed her, negated her. She couldn't remember how she arrived in this shabby room, with the floor in ruins, whose only window overlooked an empty courtyard. The bedsprings creaked. The man was drunk, fucked without passion, with the pride of a male, the shocking vigor of youth. He was fucking her and seemed to be punishing her for opening her legs so easily. Betty thought of Steve, of his concern and compassion. She started to cry. The man above her took her tears as a sign of pleasure, and accelerated his rhythm. His penis, swollen with bad blood, sealed her opening, obstructed her vital space. Finally, he reared up and expelled his fury. He rolled over and took a cigarette from the bedside table. He smoked in silence. Betty didn't dare ask to share the cigarette. She got dressed near the window. The day was waning in shades of ocher and purple. Betty turned to the bed; the most beautiful man in Creation, in his primal nudity, was tuning his guitar. He looked at the instrument tenderly, whispering to the wood. Betty left the room so not to disturb the intimacy of the two lovers.

*

The grocery store had just lowered its metal door. She was out of tobacco. She was shaking and thought she wouldn't survive the night. The seed of the man flowed between her legs. Betty thought about joining her aunt in the depths of the forest. She was ready to be sprinkled with the blood of a rooster, to welcome in her depths the magic of a barbaric god. She returned home on the backroads, persuaded that her sin could be read on her face.

She walked through the front door. Steve and the boy were playing cards on the sitting-room table. Without a word, she locked herself in the washroom. Then, as she was preparing the meal, she allowed the saucepan to burn. Steve stood up and kissed her. That gesture induced a flood of tears; Joshua thought he was seeing his mother and her midnight sobbing again. The scents of charred fat and make-believe stagnated for a long time in the room.

The sheets were shaken out then plunged into the gray water, steam spiraling up a few seconds before vanishing in the surrounding vapor. Betty would have liked for her mind to be like that great washing machine, for all that remained of her remorse to have the vague odor of lye. Behind her, specters of mist; exhausted figures moving silently and no longer seeming to have thoughts, good or bad, to dilute in the undertows of the tank.

A scream brought her out of her thoughts. The cry of a trapped wolf. Betty turned around and saw a human torch staggering in front of the mouth of the furnace. She recognized little Cherry. Her hair and clothes had caught fire, she covered her face with her hands, her shrieking bouncing against the brick walls. Constance was the first to run up and tackled the girl to the ground. Pearl threw a bucket of water on her face. More buckets, a complete volley, put out the flames, but not the screams that continued unabated. Betty bent down and with all possible gentleness took the burnt hands away from the girl's face. Her fingers stuck to her flesh; Betty continued, but Cherry's shriek made her recoil. Her skull was raw, her face smoldering and scorched. The skin was curling, smeared with black varnish, horrible blisters covered her body and thighs. Cherry was a bombed city. The siren of her voice summoned a witness or a judge.

Pearl started running toward town and threw herself onto the bumper of the first car she met. The driver had no choice but to let her get in and take her back to the laundry. They placed Cherry on a sheet in the back of the car, and Pearl held her hand to the door of Doctor Howard, the only doctor in the county who indiscriminately treated both Blacks and Whites. The doctor observed Cherry begging for a trickle of air between her charred lips. He told Pearl to leave, then gave the girl a morphine injection in her arm, not worrying about finding a vein in the wrinkling of blackened flesh.

A ray of light splashed through the beveled panes of the window. The sky was absolute blue. Sparrows and swifts chirped above the shingles; Cherry moaned in a drug-induced sleep. The doctor rummaged in a cupboard, pulled out a vial without a label. He looked out the window; the syringe in his hand was shaking slightly. His eyes lost in the surreal blue, the doctor carried out his act of mercy.

The women awaited Pearl's return, they gathered together in a circle around the puddle where everyone kept seeing the child's writhing body. It was Alice, the discreet and placid Alice, who broke the group's stunned paralysis. She seized one of the large wooden paddles with which the laundresses stirred the laundry and threw it with all her strength against the wall. She grabbed another one and started hammering on the cast-iron body of the furnace, hitting the pipes, the covering, the bellows. She beat, beat, tears streaming down her face. The handle broke in front of her. Alice said:

"Cherry din't deserve that."

That was the signal: the workers' hands attacked anything they could destroy. Using pokers, they dismantled the planks of the vats; a soapy, steaming deluge spread over the ground. Betty, initially reluctant, joined in this uncontrollable release of pent-up rage. Only Constance Reed stayed in the background. When Alice wanted to set fire to a pile of laundry, the older woman intervened.

"Don't you do that! It be poor folks' laundry! We gotta stop ever'thin', the machines, the water, ever'thin' . . . "

She went up to a vat that had been spared, filled a bucket and threw it into the mouth of the furnace. A locomotive whistle, a volcanic hissing. The women took turns, buckets in hand, until the last embers were extinguished. Caustic smoke filled the space, the workers rushed groping to the exit, like survivors of a mine collapse.

They had to act quickly, not let their emotions die down. At dawn, the laundresses gathered in front of the door to the laundry. Iron barrels were glowing with a meager fire from which their hands drew the heat necessary to fight. On a carpet of embers, coffeepots hissed, ahead of the chirping of the birds. None of the laundresses had ever gone on strike. Strike: the word didn't belong to the vocabulary of the people here; it evoked the mythical North, the smokestacks, the foundries, the skyscrapers. None had ever voted in any election whatsoever, nor spoken outside their domestic circle. Constance was elected delegate in a vote of raised hands. Pearl found herself in charge of security: five workers armed with sticks and kitchen knives. Betty, who could read and write, supervised the making of placards and the writing up of their grievances on the blue lines of a school notebook. The slogans on the boards were extremely concise: "Freedom," "Work Is Not Death," and just a first name, written in a clumsy hand: "Cherry."

At first, the women were mocked, then threatened, some even beaten. They did not give in. They kept their legs closed to their husbands, proved deaf to calls for moderation, whether they came from Pastor Lloyd or messengers that Andrew Wallace sent regularly to the slaughter to start a dialogue. The women took turns dropping off provisions at the laundry gates, as well as blankets, bundles of wood. They collected the money needed for Cherry's burial and the coffin was constructed with their own hands, with debris from a vat. They could no longer imagine going backward. The men had to face empty pots, kids running between their legs. Tired of beating their fists against the walls cursing absent women, they began to think. Maybe those angry women were right after all, maybe on the edges of misery there existed a breach, a gap, a passage.

*

Augustus Lloyd was dozing on his bed in his shorts and undershirt, his wine-imbued breath filling the bedroom; in the necks of the bottles dropped on the floor, flies were becoming mildly drunk. There was a knock on the door. Augustus rose with great difficulty, stumbling to the vestibule. Constance Reed was standing straight in the doorway. She looked at him, assessing the extent of his ruin, and said in a pitiless tone:

"You ain't ready."

The laundress addressed him as Jesus might have spoken to his apostles sleeping at the foot of a fig tree. Constance turned her back on him, crossed the street and walked toward the church. The reverend quickly shaved. He cut one of his cheeks, his reflection in the mirror disgusted him. He returned to his room to get clean clothes, sat down on the bed, and sunk back into a swampy sleep.

*

The small cemetery next to the church had never been so crowded, even five years earlier for the burial of the victims of the great flood. The laundresses stood in the front row in front of the girl's coffin, their signs laying on the grass. They were united, their jaws firm. Behind, brothers and husbands, uncomfortable, rummaged through their pockets looking for chewing gum and bits of tobacco.

Rosetta Brown stepped forward and raised her arms up to the cross on top of the church.

"Them machines what killed that gal, they the work of demons! . . . I say, it no longer the time to gather stones, it time to throw 'em! It no longer time to sew, it time to tear apart! It a time to hate, it a time fo war!"

Rays of sun framed the old woman, her shadow covered the coffin. The women and men turned toward the force of her voice:

"Fools fold their hands and ruin themselves.
Better one handful with tranquillity
than two handfuls with toil
and chasing after the wind."

Biblical verses drawn from Rosetta's memory seemed to escape from a living book. Miss Brown knelt before the coffin.

"I saw the tears of the oppressed—
and they have no comforter;
. . .
And I declared that the dead, who had already died
are happier than the living, who are still alive."

*

The night through the window was dotted with fireflies. Augustus Lloyd opened his eyes, sniffed the gamy air in the room. He opened the window and chaos entered. He put on his pants and went to the front door. He saw the black street lighted by torches. The pastor closed the door, frightened by those people whose faces he no longer recognized.

*

She held the notebook to her chest. All the suffering, the frustrations of the workers blackened its pages. Because she had collected these complaints, had written them down in her childlike writing, Betty had become the scribe of misfortune. She had left Steve alone at home, Joshua in the care of her aunt. For a week she had been sleeping on a pallet in the middle of the laundry, returning home for a moment only to reassure those she loved, concealing the dark circles under her eyes, her monumental fatigue. She wandered like a sleepwalker into the shantytown. She could not forget the weight of her sin, the tenacious blues that vampirized her, the betrayal of everything she had believed she was: a loyal wife, a devout Christian, a trustworthy woman.

She was looking for Bobby. Without admitting it, she hoped for him in every night-painted face she passed. She walked miles and miles, exploring the darkest corners of the town and of her conscience. No trace of the man with the harmonica, just an exuberant crowd, exulting in its newfound freedom. She walked past the saloon. Joe Hives was standing on the porch, a rifle leaning by his hip. She questioned him, trying not to arouse his suspicion. No, Joe hadn't seen him. The man had disappeared the way he had come, between two moonbeams, without leaving an address. Betty didn't press him. Yes, she would be careful. Yes, Joshua was safe, in Sapphira's cabin, far from the fevers and the settling of accounts.

Betty mourned her one-night lover. She probably wouldn't have been able to find the words to express her remorse, and the man wouldn't have understood them. She had offered herself up to a solitary being, in search of an inaccessible riff. She alone had sinned. He had only passed by: on her body, her life, along the alleys of the town.

*

At the end of Pine Street, a crowd prevented a Dodge with its headlights on from passing. Fists pounded the chassis, shoes kicked the doors and wheels, gobs of spit and insults streamed down the windows. Old Theodore wielded rusty shears which he stuck into one of the Dodge's rear tires.

"Fuckin' whiteys! Now we gone deflate they bellies!"

The headlights shattered. The car rocked, while a Promethean force lifted the body off the ground.

"She-it! These motherfuckers gonna toss us like bales o hay!" Anthony Madden put his arm behind the sheriff's neck, the barrel of the revolver he was holding pointed at a black face with bulging eyes.

"Don't be stupid, Madden!" yelled the sheriff, and he pressed the accelerator while releasing the clutch. The wheels began to spin in the void, the hands let go and the Dodge slammed into the wall of muscles and bones in front of it. A dark mass struck the hood with a sound of splitting wood, the car sped forward blindly and mowed down another body standing in an intersection.

The sheriff grimaced, his hands welded to the steering wheel. The Dodge braked and then stopped. The beam of a flashlight lighted the interior and Madden's panicked face. The doors opened. The moon was a thin sliver, the stars, lye crystals, floating in an emulsion of dirty shadows. The light followed the stony grooves of the path. A stream gurgled behind a hedge of brambles. The sheriff and his deputy went by an old paddle mill whose paddles had disappeared; only the metal supports remained. They passed a collapsed barn out of which the sound of an owl flapping its wings emerged, then a stone trough overgrown with lichens, and endless barbed-wire fences supported at irregular intervals by rickety poles. The light lingered against the dented metal of a grain silo; the two men walked around it, trampling a puddle of coagulated slurry. They came out in the middle of a cornfield, passed the gate of the cemetery and arrived at the outskirts of the town. They slowed down as they approached the laundry. Flames were rising from metal barrels, workers armed with sticks stood guard, watching the darkness. The sheriff and his deputy slipped by at a good distance, their flashlight turned off. Passing by a row of cotton warehouses they went down the deserted main street. Sounds reached them from adjacent streets. Anthony Madden, on alert, held his revolver up in front of his face, his left hand steadying the butt. He saw a White man walking in the direction of the noise. Madden took aim. The man turned his back and passed the workshop of the mechanic whose half-closed iron curtain let out a streak of pale light.

"I think it's the tailor," Madden said. "That yid cocksucker gonna git hisself gutted!"

"It's his problem, not mine."

The sheriff and his deputy weaved their way through a maze of shacks, dead ends, bottlenecks so narrow that they had to advance in profile, bumping into tin cans, kicking away skinny chickens pecking the dirt. Finally, they reached the paved streets of the White part of town, the straight streets, the gutters, the multi-storied houses. The area seemed to be waiting for a tornado. Dogs tied to chains in their yards barked as they passed; neon lights swept the sidewalks where their shadows were cast, dancing as in the beam of a magic lantern. The square was like a forbidden sanctuary, filled with the scents of poisonous flowers. A crowd had formed outside the Spencer Armory. Heads of families loudly demanded that they be provided with the means to defend the virtue of their wives and daughters. Archibald Spencer appeared in a window above the shop, wearing pajamas and nightcap. He raised a rifle to the sky and fired twice. The good citizens dispersed like a flock of sparrows.

Armed police were stationed in front of the town hall steps. The sheriff took his badge off his shirt and waved it at the guards. He climbed the flight of stairs and entered the lighted lobby. Anthony Madden stayed in the street among the uniformed officers, ogling their guns, feeling the uproar of battle rise within him.

*

The man with the crushed legs dragged himself in the dirt, then fainted; the other, the one who had flown over the hood of the car, wasn't moving, his face turned towards the sky, his back broken. The angry crowd made an improvised stretcher using a simple tarp onto which they rolled the bodies. Chester Burnett, aka Howling Wolf, carried them to the door of Doctor Howard's office, escorted by torches. With a glance the doctor assessed the life expectancy of the two accident victims and allowed Chester Burnett to leave his burden on the entrance floor. He told the crowd to come back the next day, then locked the door, wondering why Colored people stubbornly confused his office with the cold room of a morgue.

*

Twists of gray smoke swirled above the roof tiles, in the air there floated the stench of burnt rubber and varnish. Steve approached the bonfire in the middle of the street. The looters had destroyed the barbershop, smashing through the storefront to grab seats, mirrors, and hair dryers. Theodore sat in a chair with wheels and was having fun rolling around the fire, his face transfigured by cruel joy. The crowd, which didn't dare to venture into White territory, turned its wrath against the owner of the shop and against half the stores on the street. Andrew Wallace, the mulatto, a traitor to his blood, was the perfect scapegoat. No one knew where he was hiding, rumor had it he had gone to city hall to demand the intervention of the police. The bastard was quick to change sides, revealing his true nature.

Steve was looking for Betty. He thought she was in danger and didn't want to stay cooped up at home waiting for her to come back. Chester Burnett stood guard in front of the alley leading to the saloon. Aaron Posner couldn't have arrived at a worse time. He got his bearings from the echo of voices and the light of torches; after wandering in the maze of the Black neighborhood, he found himself face to face with a burly man who towered over him by almost three feet. The little tailor from Dresden smiled affably and said:

"I say, that's a very nice shirt you're wearing. The fit is perfect and it looks very good on you."

Chester Burnett gaped in surprise at the man's accent and his incredible nerve. The man had appeared before him like a legendary gnome and addressed him in the language of a schoolteacher. He took the gnome by the shoulders and lifted him with his two enormous hands. Aaron was no longer smiling. He gathered his strength and cuffed Chester's sides weakly. Chester didn't flinch, stared at the tailor as if he were a naughty boy. A hand grabbed his shoulder, and Chester turned around without letting go of his prey. A skinny Black man, his legs trembling with fear, was threatening him with a half-burnt chair leg.

"Wait," said Steve, "you wrong. He not the mayor."

"I knows he not the mayor."

"Then let him go! Uh, please."

"Why? You knows him?" said Chester, pointing his chin at the tailor.

"Sho, he be Aaron, the tailor!"

"Oh yeah? What if I don't wanna let go o yo weavah?"

"Then too bad fo y'all!" said Steve, waving his poor piece of wood.

Chester guffawed like an ogre and dropped Aaron who landed on his behind.

"Ya'll make a funny pair, the two o y'all, a fuckin' pair o assholes!"

Attracted by Chester's laughter, the rioters came closer. The White man in front of them was the victim who would allow them to return home with their heads held high, with the satisfaction of having accomplished their task. If, to seize the little man with light eyes, they had to beat to death the skinny Negro who served as his bodyguard, that wouldn't be too difficult. Theodore, hateful and disheveled, cut through the crowd, maneuvering his barber's chair like a wheelchair. A bottle of whiskey was stuck between his legs, the neck standing erect like a glass penis. He began to shout:

"It him, it him! . . . don't let 'em 'scape!"

"Who him?" asked a childish voice.

"Fo God's sake, it the White man! It him, I tells y'all! Gotta hole him fore he get outta here!"

"No one gone touch a hair on this here man!" said Chester Burnett, his fists clenched. "This here my buddy Aaron."

The crowd returned to the flames, disappointed not to have seen some pale blood flow for the first time.

*

Betty looked up at the star-speckled sky which a cry had just pierced. Her chest contracted. Was it an animal or a man being slaughtered a few meters from her? She didn't know where to go. Fear was making its mark everywhere. She hid in a passage between two hovels; at the end of an alleyway, across from the haberdashery where Dora had been killed, she passed

Sergeant Elias, his pirate patch across his face. Neither of them greeted the other. This was not the time for niceties. Betty had one thought only: she had to find Steve and beg him not to join this demented carnival.

*

Andrew Wallace walked around a Pontiac whose open hood revealed a destroyed engine. He was puffing nervously on his cigarette. The harsh glow of the bulb lighted winches from which radiators, exhaust pipes, and heavy cylinders hung. At the back of the room, Pearl waited, staring worriedly at the metal-covered doorway to the street. The crowd had dispersed some time earlier and the only noticeable sound was the creak of the weathervane and the murmur of wind through the boards of neighboring houses. Wallace threw his cigarette butt on the cement. He was a prisoner. Of his garage, his fair skin, and his wealth. His political ambitions had crumbled in just a night. He who dreamed of himself as Moses the redeemer was now a hunted man.

Pearl walked to the metal door, determined to reach the open air. Wallace restrained her by roughly squeezing her wrist. He took a bill from his pocket and forced her to open her palm. The young woman closed her hand on the crumpled paper.

Andrew Wallace did not intend to be left alone this night. His fear and disappointment needed an outlet. Money still meant power: the power to corrupt. Before dawn he was going to fuck one of the leaders of the revolt and he would find a way to fuck them all, those ungrateful niggers: he would prevail over them, turn them inside out like a glove, until they carried him in triumph. Andrew lit a cigarette and blew the smoke in Pearl's disheveled hair. His Cadillac was parked in a shed a few hundred yards away. He was going to his hideout in the middle of the woods and prepare for the reconquest of bodies and souls.

*

The room was a perfect square. A massive desk on which reigned a Western Electric telephone, piles of folders, and a portable Remington typewriter.

The mayor, Richard Thompson, was sitting on a corner of the desk, his legs dangling, his tie loosened. Harry Bradford was stamping his feet sitting on a chair that was too comfortable to contain his nervousness. His shoes emitted a smell of manure. The sheriff took a pack of cigarettes out of his jacket pocket and gave a report in his image: precise and blunt. The situation, already perilous, was likely to worsen. A large-scale repression wasn't conceivable: the municipal police officers might empty their guns on the crowd, those bastards outnumbered them and essentially had nothing to lose. Following a bloodbath they would certainly see the federal government stick its nose in the town's affairs, and the National Guard would arrive. The grumbling of cotton pickers from neighboring counties could quickly turn into a general strike, trade unionists and all the communist mess would blow on the embers, while Andrew Wallace, beleaguered, would cash in at the next elections. No, they had to quell the flames of revolt, starting that night. Gather the Klan and unleash the furies.

Richard Thompson nodded his agreement. He picked up the telephone handset, turned the dial. He waited a long minute before speaking in an icy tone to the switchboard operator.

*

When the phone rang, Francis Conrad was absorbed in thought, facing the bay window of the sitting room. He looked for the phone. It was an old model, in the shape of a metal candlestick, the earpiece and mouthpiece were separate and Francis confused them every time.

On the first ring, James Conrad stopped reading the local paper and got up from his chair, his muscles tense. He had just returned from a secret meeting with Sergeant Elias in front of the cemetery gate. He was waiting for the call from the mayor, but still hoped it would take place the next day, in broad day-light, which would have possibly meant an outcome other than chaos. His father's face and his silence dispelled his illusions.

When Francis handed him the phone, James held up his hand to indicate it wasn't necessary. He knew his mission and wouldn't shirk his duties. Gather the Klan. Unleash the furies.

*

A demon that looked like his son stood in the middle of the library. Edward Longhorn couldn't endure Christopher's insane gaze, the sight of his soft, quivering mouth, his fingers with dirty nails gripping the phone. Christopher Longhorn slammed it down. Edward knew he would never have the strength to reason with him, unless he shot him. Christopher walked past the chair without a glance at the old man. He slammed the door and ran down the stairs to his room.

At the bottom of the steps, in the dark entryway, a Black woman with wrinkled cheeks listened to the echo of the approaching steps. Christopher Longhorn appeared on the landing. He was holding a long, white tunic folded against his chest. In his hand, a double-barreled shotgun. Christopher passed the old woman, giving her a grin on which the outlines of madness could be read. The old woman remained frozen. In the distance she heard the neighing of a horse being spurred and the pounding of hooves against the ground. She emerged from her torpor, took a handkerchief out of her pocket and began to wipe the stairs.

*

The torches in the distance rolled down the hill, red, moving dots. The ground vibrated, humming at her feet. It was not the men, their anger, and their claims that shook the ground; what she perceived was a fury that was terrifying in a different way. Sapphira placed her palm flat on the grass and took the pulse of the world. She stood up and hurried to the cabin. Through the doorway, she watched the sleeping boy breathe. Joshua was sleeping, perhaps dreaming, unaware of the vibrations which now were shaking the old boards of the porch and traveling along the retaining beams of the overhang. It had been a long time since the earth had trembled. Sapphira had her house built here on purpose, at the nerve center where the chthonic forces clashed and neutralized each other. It was a few years after the abolition decree, when the Yankees were handing out parcels to Blacks as compensation for years of slavery. Of course, just like all the others, Sapphira had not been given "forty acres and a mule," but at least her few acres of forest had never been taken away from her.

Sapphira leaned against the wall and the past washed over her. She thought of Theodore and the thought worried her more than the sounds of insurrection that reached her from town. It was Theodore who had built this cabin, following the plans she had drawn with a stick in the dirt. Forty years already. How time passes, how it wounds . . .

Sapphira took off the kerchief covering her head and passed her fingers through her white fleece. Theodore used to do the same thing, when her hair was still a beautiful jet black and she allowed his unholy hands to stroke her. She had liked his caresses, why lie to herself? She had felt his presence within her, this earthly pleasure, when she was not yet the exclusive companion of spirits. Theodore was already drinking, of course, but never enough to prevent him from fulfilling his duty. Alcohol did not keep him from getting up before daybreak and setting off, his axe on his shoulder, to clear the land, put up fences, bend the surroundings to his will. She remembered those long pauses when the two of them, on the porch, stared at the grandiose shadows of the trees. She would lean her head against the shoulder of that strong, silent man and still hope that the anger she sensed so often emerging through his muscles would not become a fiery hell. Sometimes Theodore broke the silence and opened up. He always returned to his initial wound: the hanging of his brother Titus in front of the Conrad house. Titus, the older and admired brother. Murdered. When he spoke of his brother, Theodore's eyes burned, a terrifying glow. Sapphira had tried everything in her power to soothe his soul, concocting calming potions for him, but it was in bad booze that Theodore had sought refuge, where no one could have helped him. Slowly, the worthy Negro had turned into an unspeakable drunk; always broke and boozy, capable of drinking rubbing alcohol, and consumed by an inextinguishable thirst for vengeance. When Sapphira had finally kicked him out, Theodore had made a gesture she would never forget. Then he had vanished into the woods without looking back, and Sapphira then only saw him from afar, witnessing his decline.

Surely Theodore, that night, was moving among the flames and violence, expressing his hatred of others and his disgust with himself. Sapphira wrapped her shawl around her and went into the cabin. She lay down on the mat next to the boy, his thin body standing in the way of madness.

*

One-eyed Elias walked through the darkness; he was going into town by a back road, protected by the dense darkness of the sky. A few stars floated, not managing to form a true constellation. The moon was just a sliver. Elias had taken off the patch covering his empty eye socket. He had walked so long that night trying to avoid the inevitable. He had spoken with the Conrad heir at the gates of the cemetery. The Grand Titan, the leader of the local Klan, had promised to warn him before ordering his horsemen to draw blood. As long as life flowed in his veins, Elias would fight so that the plain of his birth would not become a mass grave. Sergeant One-Eye went on the attack for the last time.

It was the smell that awakened him from sleep, a whiff of animal sweat seeping through the window. The nocturnal insects were silent, footsteps stirred the loose stones. Andrew Wallace looked for matches on the bedside table. His hand brushed against a camisole, knocked over a bottle, the crash on the floor wrung a sigh from the body at his side. The footsteps ceased, the smell of animals invaded the room and was superimposed on the vapors of spilled alcohol. He found the matches, scraped one against the nearest wall, removed the glass cover of the lamp and adjusted the flame. A naked girl was sleeping on the bed in a fetal position. Wallace quickly put on his pants, knelt down to close the window, and went into the kitchen, crouching. He stopped in front of a large, cold stove and distinguished the murmur of a voice on the other side of the door.

He went down to the cellar. The weapons cache. On the wall hung half a dozen Springfield and Winchester rifles. He opened a large trunk, grabbed a Colt Frontier and boxes of .44 caliber rounds of ammunition, which could also be used for the Winchester. He stuffed the pockets of his pants with bullets and went back to the kitchen. The silence was ominous. In his mind, there was no more room for doubt. He had been betrayed. This bitch, curled up in his bed, had given him away to the other niggers, telling them the location of his house in the woods. She had been a good actress while he was screwing her, and now she was pretending to be asleep, waiting for him to fall into the mob's murderous hands.

Wallace went into the bedroom and slapped the girl twice. Pearl woke up with a start. A burst of light struck her eyes, a shadow menaced her and pulled her by the legs. She struggled and cried out. A gunshot shattered the window and a shower of glass fell onto the bed. Pearl screamed louder. Wallace hit her with the butt of his revolver and emptied its bullets through the shattered window. His hand was shaking, the gunpowder stung his eyes. He lay down on the floor to protect himself from more shooting and reloaded his gun in the glow of the lamp. More silence. The night was panting beyond the shattered window. Pearl, her jaw broken, held her breath.

Wallace began to crawl. He scratched his chest on a piece of glass, a trickle of warm blood flowed down to his navel. He reached the cellar and barricaded himself, blocking the door with a wooden crossbar. He took down a Winchester, loaded it, and did the same with the other rifles. Let those cocksuckers come, he had what he needed to greet them. Even shooting blindly, he could kill a good twenty men. He sat on the ammunition trunk, removed the shard of glass from his chest and saw that the blood had soaked his cotton pants. Footsteps swept through the house, he heard crockery breaking, furniture being knocked over. The girl started screaming again . . . Shut her up, goddamn it!

Wallace was standing with the gun pointed in front of him. The light from the lamp flickered. A stream of smoke, gray and deadly, slipped under the cellar door. He gagged, searched his pockets for the ring of keys. He reached the hallway leading to the kitchen. The house, devoured by flames, was about to collapse, the wood crackled, the stove glowed red before him like an infernal totem. Wallace fired blindly through the smoke and the flames, the roar of the fire drowned the shots. Wallace staggered through the door. He felt a violent blow from the stock of a rifle come down on his head, and he fell face down.

A tight circle. A ring of figures draped and hooded in white, hieratic like a row of menhirs under the moon. There were six of them, about the same size, only crests and chevrons embroidered at chest level and on their sleeves differentiated them— otherworldly coats of arms, ranks and sub-ranks of an accursed army. The shiny spurs on their boots were communing with the fire, the tips of their hoods pointing upwards like gothic spires turned them into flagellants, ready to fend off the plague that they, themselves, had summoned. Their guns lay in front of them on the dry grass. The invisible Empire had gathered and would not disperse before dawn. They stood in front of the burning house, facing the red swirls and the crackling of the wood; their horses, tied to a tree, neighed and pulled futilely on their reins. The riders stood for a moment contemplating the funereal pyrotechnics, then one of them walked to the body of Andrew Wallace, his pants bloodstained, lying on the ground, his hands and feet bound together.

"I do believe he's dead," said one of the horsemen. "And the whore ain't doin' much better."

An initial kick to the prisoner's shoulder evoked no reaction, a second, near his liver, elicited a groan, proof of life.

A few meters away, on a carpet of leaves, lay the naked body of Pearl. From her lips flowed a thick drool, her chest was mottled with burn marks; on her thighs and stomach were streaks of semen and mud.

A man approached the prisoner. He wore a green crest on the sleeve of his tunic. His voice, authoritarian and hard, was that of the undisputed leader.

"Let's get this over with!"

The horsemen dragged the prisoner to the tree where the horses were tethered. As they approached, the beasts reared up, kicking into the air. The man with the green crest ordered them to be taken away. His order was carried out immediately and three horsemen took the panicking beasts into the depths of the forest. The men came back with a long rope with the noose already formed. Another burst of flames arose from the ruins of the house, illuminating the ghostly pallor of the surroundings.

It was long and painful. The tree was old, its branches groaned. Two men held the taut rope, their hands burned by the friction. The hanged man spoke through ignoble trembling. With his movement, his pants came down revealing his erect penis pointing in the direction of the fire. At the foot of the tree, the riders watched the jerking body. The man with the green crest looked away.

It was slow and excruciating. A spasmodic puppet, the body was human only in its pitiful will to live which made his mouth open for a bit of oxygen that his constricted throat would not allow. His teeth bit on leaves that brushed his lips, then spat them out sputtering.

"Is that a goat, or what?" said one of the horsemen.

No one spoke.

Then came the final reflexes, reptilian and pathetic: humanity leaving the flesh, sphincters, then the bladder releasing; the chest sagging, the legs stiffening, the eyes freezing and the twisted rope unwinding, spinning the body in slow motion. In the night arose the painful odor of the gallows.

Pearl suddenly felt cold and couldn't hold back a sneeze. She didn't move, looking stiffer than the hanged man. The hooded figures approached her. Their footsteps were coordinated as if they were a single creature, a saurian with countless legs.

One of the riders took off his hood and went back to the tree. Christopher Longhorn's face was as radiant as that of a child who has just had his wish come true. He stared at the body hanging above the ground, its soiled pants around its ankles. The horseman with the green crest slapped the back of Christopher's head sharply. Christopher turned around, held the icy gaze for a few seconds, then lowered his head.

"You must never show your face! Under no circumstance!"

"I thought we could in front of a dead man," sulked Christopher Longhorn, putting his hood back on.

"What 'bout her?!" said the man, pointing with the barrel of his rifle to where Pearl was lying.

A horseman walked up to Pearl and checked her pulse by squeezing her throat between his thumb and forefinger: "She still breathin'," he said, "but we only got the one rope."

The man with the green crest looked up at the black sky where fine white spots like mold were appearing.

"We have less than two hours before the sun comes up," he said. "Light the torches and take the horses. I'll see to the girl."

One after the other, the horsemen bent down to light their torches on the embers of the fire, then disappeared between the rows of trees and bramble groves.

Pearl was assessing her strength, gathering the few thoughts that had escaped her terror. She could get up and start running, without shoes and without hope of escaping the bullets. She could also wait, keep her eyes closed, wait for the blast to explode in her eardrums. She felt the ground vibrate under the horses' galloping hooves. A lone man approached. She sensed his all-powerful shadow above her. The sound of a gun being cocked. A blast. Reflexively, Pearl put her hands to her sides, seeking the impact, a hole to plug.

Another blast. Pearl sits up, sees a figure draped in white. Her feet defy the thorns and rocks. She runs blindly through the thickets, runs into tree trunks, falls down several times. She runs, the path uneven, a silver galloping form, a blue pepper mare, a cholera nursery rhyme, unbridled ebony! She doesn't bend, her neck is supple in the collar of midnight. Flee! . . . Her bones rear up, lilacs bleed at her temples . . . Flee! Belly like sheet metal, jaws shredded, a roasted moon, muscles, drool, tendons, sweat, dirt, clumps, drums, bells, drums! O Jesus, O Eshu, give her strength!

The last of the stars brush her chest. The milky dawn spreads over the plain and the outline of the town. Pearl leaves the forest, dives into a ditch, and breathes, breathes . . .

*

The horseman turned away from the woods into which the girl had fled. Even if she survived her wounds and her shame, she would not talk. He, himself, had not raped her, had not had fun stubbing out cigarettes on her breasts, but he had let the others do as they pleased. He turned toward the tree. The hanged man seemed to be an extension of the rope. Excrement dripped from his legs and formed a noxious puddle at the base of the tree. The horseman put down his rifle, took off his hood, leaned forward and vomited, then stood up, wiped his mouth on the back of his sleeve. James Conrad put on his hood and went into the forest where his mare was waiting for him.

Midnight riding. Dressed in snow, they carried fire. The torches fed on the wind and haloed them in a blinding mandorla. The furies spread out over the plain, spurring their beasts without restraint, affixing their fierce clarity on the world. They went past the old railyard, the ballast covered in nettles and the dilapidated train cars, crossed the river and reached the town from the north.

The riders communicated using gestures, sharp and unambiguous. In the absence of their leader, they submitted to the primal logic of black and white, living and dead. They didn't bother with any strategy, set fire to bases and summits.

The first witnesses came out on their doorsteps. The horsemen cocked their guns and fired first into the sky, then at windows and walls. The witnesses had to choose between bullets or fire. The horsemen did not linger. They came that night to frighten, not to exterminate. They galloped through the black section of town and gathered in front of the barbershop. Shards of glass glittered in the dirt where a wheeled chair was stuck. One of the riders threw his torch through the broken window. Fire quickly took over, soon the whole building was ablaze. From the second-floor window, enveloped in smoke, two arms stretched out into the void holding a tiny, wriggling package. The hands let go. A shadow passed through the window, jumped, and landed on its knees. The shadow crawled over to its baby, hugged it to its breast and blew on its forehead to dispel the dirt. Guns sounded again and hooves pounded the earth. The horde left in its wake a few persistent waves of light as well as indelible fear.

*

James Conrad let himself be guided by his mare. He hadn't lit his torch and moved among the shadows, his two hands crossed on the pommel of the saddle. His mind was freed from its burden of images. He had almost forgotten what had brought him to the woods. The mare entered an oak grove which emerged onto a rocky road. A falcon flew over the rider and his horse; the raptor engraved angular lines that cut through the sky. A ray of amaranth colored the flowing water and the heat rose swiftly.

Retracing the horsemen's route had not been difficult: Elias had only to note the ruins of a charred barn, terror on a mother's face. The dawn revealed the crime. Sergeant Elias had mastered the art of camouflage and was an expert in silence. Choctaw blood still flowed in his veins. He was a tracker for all eternity.

Elias crouched at the riverbank and saw the hoof marks, as deep as fossils, which came together and reappeared on the other side. He crossed the river by a hidden ford, about ten meters downstream from a collapsed stone bridge. The water came to his knees; his left hand balanced him, the other was gripping the stock of the rifle concealed under his shirt. He waded down the river, sheltered by the reeds. As he approached the forest, he climbed back up onto the bank, his trousers smeared with silt. His slime-filled boots sloshed on the grass. He was out of sight. He took out his gun, a shotgun whose barrel he had sawed off himself.

He sank into the darkness. On the broken branch of a poplar, a tuft of gray mane, which he smoothed between his fingers. The smell of fire, carried by the wind, indicated the way.

Andrew Wallace's little house had burned down. In the middle of the square of blackened foundation stones the stove stood, its cast-iron feet still red. The hanged man contemplated this destruction, his face covered with flies. The rope had been tied tightly to a branch and the weight of the body had made it even tighter. Elias didn't have a knife. He put the barrel of his gun on the rope and fired point blank. The explosion caused his arm to recoil and a swarm of partridges to fly upwards. The body hit the ground looking like a monstrous fetus strangled by its umbilical cord.

Elias couldn't untie the victim's neck. He was seized by a searing anger. He had been tricked, manipulated like a sheep in front of the doors of a slaughterhouse. He had sincerely believed in an unnatural alliance with the Conrad heir, he had believed in his word as a soldier. The sergeant reloaded his rifle and fired at the tree. His single eye watered from the gunpowder. The tree was disfigured. Elias bent down, wrapped the rope around the body, tying it as far as the chest. He lifted it up on his shoulders and took a few steps toward the woods. Like a god from a lower pantheon, hunchbacked and one-eyed, his rifle at his hip, he left the clearing.

He was upstairs in his childhood bedroom. Yes, the bed had been made, she had ironed the sheets, Monday or Tuesday. She always knew he would come back, a mother knows that. She had kept cleaning the room all these years, washing and folding his boyhood clothes. She was waiting for him. The front doorbell had rung at dawn. She was already awake, ready to greet him. Booker had forced her to stay inside. Booker had taken care of everything, and it was good that way. Now her child was up there, in his clean room. She had promised Booker she wouldn't go upstairs, not until he had prepared him. She had promised.

Her hands are shaking on the railing of the big staircase. She slept badly the night before. She didn't sleep at all. She climbs the stairs, one by one, the way she cleans them. The light shines through the stained-glass window on the landing, casting orange and mauve rays of light. She reaches the unlighted hallway. At the end of the corridor, an open door. Her heart quickens, beats so hard in her chest that she is afraid it will alert everyone. Her movements become very slow. She turns into a mouse on the floor, a whiff of air. She is in the doorway. At first, she can only make out a shining circle of light, then her eyes adjust. She sees the silhouette of a man, an old man sitting on a chair next to the bed. He is wearing a faded dressing gown. His head lowered, Edward Longhorn is crying. She doesn't approach him, stands motionless in the doorway, her eyes reduce the distance.

On the bed her child is asleep. The sheet is pulled up to his chin. Thin red spots ooze through the fabric. Her child's eyes are closed. His cheeks covered with bruises and wounds. But it is indeed he, Andrew, back in his bed. Her mother's eyes ignore the stigmata and see the traits she knows: the finely carved lips, the delicate dimples and that beautiful copper skin. Andrew is in his bed, at peace. She feels a terrible joy at seeing her son, even wounded, even dead, in his room again.

Edward Longhorn continues to sob. She has never seen him cry. She looks from her child's face to that of the old man. The dimples are the same, the strong chin, the broad and pensive forehead. Yes, they look alike. The old man leans over, his hand runs through his son's hair to remove a fragment of leaf.

He was expecting the worst. The night had exploded. Rachel was sleeping next to him, her fists clenched. Aaron got out of bed and realized that he had kept his shoes, shirt, and pants on. When the horses had come up the street and the first shots were heard, the husband and wife had gotten out of bed at the same time. Aaron had cradled Rachel in his arms until he led her to the gates of sleep.

Aaron went out of the bedroom. He had no weapon and regretted that fact. He would never really be an American if he couldn't wield steel in the face of fate. He decided to go to the Spencer Armory that very day. He heard voices at the front door. He turned the key in the lock, the sun struck him without making him recoil. There were men standing on his doorstep: five or six, white and scruffy. Aaron stepped forward to break the circle. The men gave him a dark look, as mean as an acid bath.

Aaron walked to his shop a few dozen meters from his house. The metal shutter that protected the window was riddled with the imprint of bullets. He said to himself that it was good he had invested in this shutter despite his wife's reluctance. Aaron smiled weakly; it was so rare that he won an argument with Rachel. He turned to the street and his smile dissolved. In the dirt was an inscription, scratched with the barrel of a rifle, in large letters. The men who had followed him to the shop saw his dismay and laughed. Aaron was devastated, on the verge of nausea. He turned away from the inscription and went back home. Here, too, in America, the land of the free, he was still a filthy Jew. A target. He would take a broom later and sweep away the insult, but something in him would never be erased.

IV

"I got a letter this morning, how do you reckon it read?
'Oh, hurry, hurry, gal you love is dead'"

SON HOUSE
"Death Letter Blues"

The children standing in a circle in front of the Boyd shoe repair shop wriggled like worms, and Theodore basked in the hold he exercised over his young audience.

"Here were Monkey ridin' on the back o the mule, but that bitch weren't gonna move, hell no! That monkey, tho he beat her rump raw with his stick, that donkey take one step fo'ward and two steps back. Dammit, say the monkey, at this rate I never gone leave the county! An if that hoofed bitch keep backin' up like that, I gone find mysef at the edge o the sea, instead o Boston!"

Theodore paused to spit out a stream of tobacco. Ten pairs of eyes were focused on his drunken face with nicotine-blackened lips.

"Then what happen?" asked little Ada.

"What what?!" growled the old man. "Ah, y'all talkin' bout Monkey . . . well, Monkey done decide to use drastic measures. He walk up to the blacksmith's, take a red-hot poker with pliers and shove it right up that mule's ass!"

The smaller ones let out a cry of horror, the older ones laughed.

"Yessuh! That beast she done set off at a triple time gallop, faster than any racehoss! She cross the plain, overtake the Green Diamond train rollin on them rails. White folks in the first class cars ain't never seen a monkey ridin' on a donkey goin' faster than a locomotive. But that damn mule, she weren't goin' north, west, nor east, she were gallopin' straight to Louisiana! Monkey cain't stop her no more, says to hisself he has to get her in water to put out the fire in her ass. So, when he approach a bayou, he pull on the reins, but that donkey stop so quick Monkey fly over it and find hisself in the middle of the bayou and sink like a stone."

"Were he dead?" asked Mooky.

"Deader than a piece o bacon, whachoo think?"

The old storyteller broke off again, stood up slowly and looked like he was about to leave. The kids begged him, Ada even shed a tear which didn't soften the old man.

"Y'all hurtin' me, brats. Ah ain't eat nothin' since Sunday and y'all want me to use up my last strength tellin' y'all nonsense. Go on an get me some corn beef an we talk some mo."

Thelonious Jenkins, the grocer's son, hurried off to his parents' shop and came back with a tin can concealed under his shirt; the old man opened it with the tip of his penknife and after two mouthfuls let out an odiferous burp, then resumed his story.

"Monkey stay there fo awhile at the bottom o the water. Then he feel the teeth of a 'gator chewin' on him, an he wake up. He go back to the surface. That po monkey, he all swollen and half rotten, but can think straight. He say to his exhausted self it no longer necessary to go to Boston, but to Glory."

"What Glory?" asked Dood.

"Y'all don't know? It the paradise of po niggas. Yonder you get as many hugs as you were whipped in yo lifetime. The fruit there be ripe all the time and y'all even have springs where bourbon with ice cubes flows. So Monkey ask the 'gator to lets him climb on his back and take him to Glory. But Gator were hongry and snap! He bite off po Monkey's leg. And . . . "

Theodore suddenly stood up. The grocer Jenkins was coming up the street looking furious, a leather belt in his hand. His son ran off first and the other kids dispersed in the surrounding alleys. Theodore took the rest of the corned beef and ate it hiding behind the old haberdashery. When he heard the sounds of the beating the grocer was giving his son, Theodore's face broke into a cruel grin.

Pearl faced the harsh weather and cast worried glances beyond the brush. A cold and vicious wind rushed in under her clothes. With every step she tried to contain the disaster of her body which was nothing more than a painful throbbing. Her joy and desires belonged to the past. Four months earlier, at the foot of the gallows tree, Pearl thought she was dead. The church bell rang at the top of the hill. Pearl had not returned to church since the tragedy; she couldn't bear to hear Pastor Lloyd's sermons, his pitiful pleas for forgiveness. Hate supported her better than a crutch. Staying alive was the first revenge she took on her torturers.

She went by a lumberjack's cabin, large oak logs were drying in the open air. Swallows sang a maternal and anxious song above her. She put her hand on her stomach. In her grew a poisonous thistle, more venomous every day. Pearl had gone into the woods to have its roots ripped out. She walked for a long time before she found the large moss-covered stone which served as a marker and pointed the way to the clearing. At the end of a span of brambles, she heard sounds, regular, rhythmic. A child of about ten was chopping wood; his arms lifted the axe and brought it down in the center of the log which split in two like an apple. The boy looked at Pearl warily, his axe held up, then he ran to the cabin without letting go of the tool: "Auntie! They be a woman here!"

Sapphira emerged from the cabin dressed in a gypsy dress and a woolen shawl. The sorceress stopped in the doorway. Without saying a word, she invited Pearl to come in.

She had taken off her clothes, revealing her scars. The muffled sound of the axe was heard through the walls. The room was illuminated by candles whose light flowed over her like honey. Lying on her stomach on a raffia mat on the ground, Pearl abandoned herself to the hands that rubbed her with a camphor balm. Hands suddenly grabbed her armpits, one knee landed in the small of her back, and a tremendous pull lifted her stomach off the mat. She cracked like a rammed ship; she screamed, then was quiet, to better feel the flow running through her vertebrae. Two thumbs sank in on either side of her spine, releasing ancient knots. Pearl moaned, suspended between two bodily states. Oily palms were placed on the back of her head, took her jaws in a vise, and forced them back onto their axis; then the hands left her and a voice invited her to stand up. Pearl abandoned her shedding on the floor. Sapphira watched her, her eyes lingering on her belly, and Pearl felt the thistle vibrating inside her.

"How long?" asked the old woman.

"What?" said Pearl, still refusing to admit it.

"How long it been there?"

"Since August, I thinks."

"Then I c'aint do nothin'. Would kilt y'all, too."

Sapphira's voice was definitive. She picked up Pearl's clothes and handed them to her.

"Chile, what happen ain't yo fault. But what you decide when y'all leave here, will be y'all's choice." said the old woman, leaving the room.

Pearl got dressed. She discovered her muscles were supple, her hips docile, her jaw without pain. Her body was now free to choose.

Nahum Abbot wielded a heavy club and brought it down on the pig's head; the animal sank down, its enormous belly raising dust. It was a three-hundred-pound male, as tough as a boar, with drooping ears and a muddy snout. The farmer straddled the animal and ran the blade of his knife along its neck.

His wife and his gaggle of children were waiting a few steps behind him. Ada was among her younger brothers and sisters. Only the sight of the knife prevented her from getting closer. The farmer picked up the rope and tied it to the pig's hind legs. He called his eldest son who helped him drag the animal under the sloping roof of the barn. Nahum thrust his blade into the trachea and split the animal to its bladder, releasing a tide of guts and urine. Ada came forward with a bucket of hot water and knelt down; the stench suffocated her when she grabbed a piece of intestine to empty it, but she knew that at the end of this disgusting chore her reward would be waiting for her.

*

Ada held back her tears. A burst balloon dangled from her hand; the balloon her father had made for her out of a piece of pork intestine, and which that rotten Mooky had burst on purpose, out of jealousy. The little girl cried, just long enough to soothe her resentment. She thought about how she had stood up to Mooky, how she had threatened to summon her father with his big knife, how he would gut him like the pig that he was and would make balloons with the skin of his balls. Mooky had trembled with fear. Ada stopped at the edge of the river, letting the flowing water wash her bare feet. She went up to a chinaberry tree, thought about picking a few berries, round and golden, but remembered that these were the fruit used by the witch of the forest to poison her enemies.

A path of ochre dirt bordered a large cornfield. Ada began to hum the tune she was singing with her friends earlier, before Mooky came to interrupt their game of blind man's buff and ruin their lives.

> . . . *Little Sally Water, sitting in a saucer*
> *Ride, Sally, ride!*
> *Wipe your weeping eyes!*
> *Turn to the east,*
> *Turn to the west,*
> *Turn to the one that you love the best . . .*

Her voice was delicate and scratchy. Mooky said it sounded like a scythe on a grinding wheel.

Pastor Lloyd hadn't wanted her for the choir, but Ada didn't care; nature was a much better sound chamber than church. A black sedan drove by throwing dust onto her face. The car came to a halt a few meters farther, and Ada was afraid. Two White men got out and walked toward her. They didn't look mean, at least not for White folks. The younger one, barely out of his teens, wearing a plaid shirt and dirty jeans, smiled at her. The older one had thin frame glasses, a suit and a tie; his face was serious, but did not seem particularly hostile. The younger one opened the trunk of the car where huge leather cases and a whole jumble of breaker boxes and rubber cables were stacked. Ada thought maybe they owned the field and had taken her for a corn thief. She didn't see any weapons on the two men's belts, but maybe the cases in the trunk hid a machine gun or a miniature cannon.

The younger White man came forward cautiously.

"Hello, Miss. Can you tell me the name of the tune you were singing? It sounded really nice, that's why we stopped."

Ada didn't answer, her panicked eyes searching for an escape route. The younger man understood her discomfort and turned to the older one.

"Dad, can you see if there are any cookies left in the car?"

The older White man rummaged in the glove box and handed Ada a packet of Hydrox cookies. There were about a dozen left in the pack, and for Ada it was like an early Christmas.

"My name is Alan Lomax," said the younger man. "That's my father, John. We travel around and record songs and people talking. Can you tell us your name?"

"My name Virginia," the little girl lied, scared. "But why you do this, 'cording' peoples?"

"It's to create a record, so that in a hundred years people will still be able to hear the musicians playing today."

"I ain't no musician," said Ada.

"You have a very lovely voice," said Alan, and the girl felt a sweet wave of pride wash over her. "And I'd love for you to sing us a little tune. Would that be okay?"

"Will my mama know 'bout this? Seein' as she don't like me talkin' to White folks and . . . "

"She won't know unless you tell her," interrupted the older White man. "Alright, let's not lose any more time. Alan, help me set up the equipment."

The father and son rolled up their sleeves and opened the different cases; one of them contained a strange machine, full of switches, buttons, wires and springs. Ada didn't move a millimeter. Alan took an aluminum disc out of a sleeve and gently placed it on the phonograph. He unpacked a tripod on which he fixed a microphone. He gestured for Ada to come closer and adjusted the microphone in front of her mouth.

The little girl sang with a full and pure voice. Both White men seemed satisfied. They packed up their gear, then the sedan drove off and Ada watched it merge with the line of the horizon. The girl turned back, munching on her cookies. She was proud and almost felt she had experienced a miracle. She had just spoken with White folks and had not been harmed. This made her a young girl with a bright future. She saved the rest of the cookies to share with her little brother. Drawn by the crumbs at her bare feet, a squadron of blackbirds flew up out of the corn and serenaded her.

His boss, that rotten Jerry, had waited for him to finish the last batch and clean the mixer before giving him the news. The coward, the lousy coward! Steve walked up the main street, filled with dark thoughts. The flour that covered his hair made him look like an anxious old man. He had just lost his job at the bakery. His boss had let him go, giving him the same excuses as cotton workers were given: the Depression, labor is too expensive, the price of wheat is climbing . . . Bullshit! Damn lies!

Steve wasn't fooled; he had been fired as punishment for attending Wallace's meeting at the barbershop. He didn't care who had denounced him; the terror distilled among the crowd made each person a potential traitor. From atop his pulpit, Pastor Lloyd had convinced the faithful of the danger of any rebellion. The White order was divine order, to oppose it was to see the furies and flames unfurl. It was the Devil who inspired those fierce urges for freedom. The good Lord loved calm, reason, damp furrows, ripe cotton, hungry and happy Negroes. Richard Thompson wasn't worried at all that he wouldn't be re-elected, nor was the sheriff. By decree, the mayor had prohibited Blacks from being in the streets after sunset and had set up checkpoints at sensitive intersections where the two communities came into contact. Only nurses and servants were allowed to cross the demarcation line. The few Blacks who were able to vote would make the right choice, that of keeping the peace, always preferring ugly scars to gaping wounds. As for the Whites, for nothing in the world did they want to relive that night when the wild animals had escaped their cages.

Steve felt terribly empty, deprived of his job, his livelihood. He passed old Theodore sitting on the steps in front of the shoe repair shop, dispensing his tainted wisdom to a few ne'er-do-wells. Steve thought of Joshua who every morning went to sit on the benches at school. Without his salary from the bakery and despite Joe's help, the ends of the months would be unsustainable. Steve wondered how he was going to break the news to Betty. It was useless to try to hide it, his wife read him like an open Bible.

The cup of coffee had cooled when Steve brought it to his lips. At the other end of the table, Joshua was immersed in a grammar textbook. Betty cleared his dish of oatmeal after making the child scrape the bowl. She looked at her husband. Her first instinct had been to reproach him for his support of that accursed Wallace, then she calmed down. She too, last summer, had held up signs and clenched her fists, she, too, had believed in the coming of a kingdom, accessible not through resigned patience but through courage and action. To blame Steve was to spit on the very idea of justice.

"Tomorrow we gone go see Joe," she said simply. "He know ev'rythin' what go on in town."

*

Joe looked at Joshua who smiled back at him. The saloon owner lifted the boy at arm's length, then put him down. The sun had just set and the room was empty. Joe gave Joshua a box of dominoes and had him sit down at one of the game tables whose felt cover was gray with dust. The saloon was quiet. There were very few who dared to defy the curfew. The drunks preferred to go to Fat Sam's or the surrounding juke joints, far from public lights and the sheriff's patrols. Steve realized he had no chance of being hired here. He told Joe he had been fired and told him of his desire to work again as soon as possible. Joe looked him up and down and sighed at his almost supernatural thinness.

"Have y'all evah carried heavy thangs?" Joe asked.

"I been luggin' hunnerd-pound sacks o flour and such by myself."

"Yeah . . . well listen now, I kin get the word out to my man Ambrose Mitchell. He the foreman on the Greenville docks. Might be he need some arms."

Steve was getting excited, but Joe immediately calmed him down.

"It be a dog's job, and I knows what I's talkin' about. Flour sacks gone seem like down quilts next to the thangs you gone lift."

"That fine with me." Steve said after detecting a gleam of approval in Betty's eyes.

The floor creaked. Joe turned around and pointed at the staircase.

"Now stop that, Josh! Go on, git down from there right now, boy!" The child froze on the first step.

"I done locked ev'rythin' up up there, there be nuthin' but bad mem'ries . . . ya'll understand me?"

The boy looked down and went back to sit at the game table.

"How 'bout a game o dominoes?" Betty proposed.

Steve lost interest in the game, lost round after round. He was trying to remember the one time his former boss had taken him to the docks in Memphis, at the bedside of Old Father Mississippi.

The locomotive scattered clouds of soot against the window. On a bench in the train car for poor Blacks, among jaded and complaining travelers, Steve observed the plain stretching out in a monotonous vista. He had left at dawn, lugging a heavy suitcase. Betty, unusually anxious, had accompanied him inside the car and had beaten him down with advice.

Night fell hard on the countryside. The train slowed down, the cylinders emitting a prolonged creak, and the valve released its triumphant song. Fleeting views of the river, factory smoke-stacks, slanting shadows pulled up by the incandescence of neon lights, brick sheds, intertwining rails and slag.

Steve followed the flow of people to the station lobby. The clock showed eight p.m. The street leading to the heart of the city was buzzing. The headlights of an armada of cars cut through the darkness. Carrying his suitcase, Steve looked like an electron ejected from a magnetic field. He saw mostly Black faces, a few mulattoes, a cluster of Indians emerging from an underground space, and a handful of Whites. Steve passed the courthouse, a huge stone building in the middle of a park where a column to the glory of Confederate troops stood tall, then skirted the First National Bank, a sort of capitalist temple, in front of whose entrance armed guards stood watch.

The docks spread out like a cement tongue covered with wooden warehouses, lined up side by side, as far as the eye could see. A city within the city. Street lamps cast shadows of cranes and winches onto the cement. The river, now invisible, exhaled its silty, acidic breath. Steve approached a pier overlooking the water where a barge filled to the brim with coal was anchored. A dozen Black men were working on the deck, shovels in their hands. They were filling sacks that other dockworkers carried on their backs to a lighted shed. A slow procession under a sky sprinkled with stars. The foreman, a stocky, bald Negro, walked up the column encouraging the workers. Steve took a few steps in his direction. The man was a bit shorter than Steve, a knotty musculature stuck out under his shirt, his jaw worked as if he were chewing tough meat. Steve asked him where he could find a certain Ambrose Mitchell who worked at the port. He added that Joe Hives had sent him. The foreman looked him over with a skeptical frown and pointed to a warehouse a little farther away.

"Wait over yonder, Ambrose be there soon."

"Thank you, suh," Steve said, holding out his hand.

The man ignored his gesture and headed for the pier.

Steve lugged his suitcase to the shed and waited in the semi-darkness, watching the ballet of the roustabouts.

The barge was empty. The workers, their brows smeared with coal dust, indulged in cigarettes. The foreman walked over to Steve, rolling his shoulders like a sailor at sea.

"Ambrose ain't comin'?" Steve asked, disappointed.

"He right in front of y'all," said the foreman.

"You Mist Mitchell?"

"Listen, boy," Ambrose said, lighting a cigarette, "out o respect fo Joe, I gone try y'all, but seein' how scrawny ya is, I gone give ya one week fore ya crack."

The man's accent was very different from the languid intonations of the backcountry; it was tense and sharp. The foreman took a bunch of keys out of his pocket, opened the shed's metal shutter. The warehouse, thirty feet high, was filled with bales of cotton, stacked on top of each other up to the ceiling.

"Y'all can sleep here. If ya need to shit, use that . . . " Ambrose said, pointing to a tin bucket left in a corner.

"I thanks y'all fo givin' me a chance, suh . . . "

"I gives y'all a week," Ambrose repeated, pulling down the metal door.

Nocturnal refuse stagnated on the river's surface—star pods and aluminum cans, vomit and angel hair. Crimson rays colored the water; shreds of mist carried by the breeze coiled around the pilings of the piers. A few double-crested cormorants crossed the new sky, their long necks twisting strangely, as if strangled by the spinning air.

Steve walked up the docks, shivering, dressed in just a shirt. A group of roustabouts bundled up in wool sweaters, hands protected by mittens, was waiting in front of a warehouse. Ambrose Mitchell showed up with a steaming pot. Steve and the men drank their coffee in silence. The whistle of an approaching boat drowned out the song of the cormorants. The men stubbed out their cigarettes and massaged their knees and elbows.

A tugboat came to the dock pulling a fifty-foot-long barge full of bales of cotton. Some of the dockworkers had long poles with metal hooks; they slipped the hook between the ropes of a bale, lifted it, and put it on the dock with disconcerting ease. Steve hoisted a bale on his back and carried it up to the open mouth of a shed. He laid his burden down at the feet of a worker who immediately hoisted it onto a first pile. Steve trotted back to the pier to get another load. His back burned, sweat covered his face. When his legs began to wobble and he was out of breath, he summoned images of his home.

He thought of Betty, toiling in the fumes of the laundry, then of Joshua carrying the weight of knowledge on his shoulders. His load lightened, his pain became bearable.

The barge was emptied in less than an hour. Steve wiped his forehead with the tail of his shirt and contemplated the river. He had known the Mississippi only through its meager tributaries and dead arms, and now was discovering its mighty course, its ghostly shores. The river divided into vast channels carrying the water toward other meandering offshoots, other estuaries. The Mississippi was like an interior sea, dotted with wooded islets out of which squadrons of birds emerged. Opposite the wharf, miles away, one could make out the plains of Arkansas still shrouded in fog; on the right, beyond the smoke of the shipyard, stretched the calm and fish-filled waters of Lake Ferguson.

Despite his indescribable fatigue, Steve endured the constant pain and aches. His reward was on the water. He saw all kinds of boats on the move: barges, coasters, tugboats, snag-boats, supply ships. If most were tubs with no hint of nobility, sometimes the legends of the Mississippi moored at the piers: the Tennessee Belle, with her ornate smokestack and copper railings; the Kate Adams, imperial and placid; old Quincy, still mighty. One Sunday he saw the American Queen speeding away, her huge paddle wheels striking the water like a thousand washerwomen.

Steve carried everything imaginable on his back: logs, sacks of sand, lime, coke, tractor wheels, cages full of poultry, tons of cotton, barrels of oil, animal carcasses . . . He learned the work songs and added his voice to the glorious roustabout choir:

> . . . *Oh-h-h-h!*
> *Po roustabout don't have no home,*
> *Makes his livin' on his shoulder bone.*
> *Oh-h-h-h! . . .*

Gradually, Steve received some signs from his co-workers that he belonged to the group, manly punching and fraternal mockery. They gave him advice on how to "swing" well: that famous roll of the hips that the downtown gals found so sexy. During breaks between two shipments, the roustabouts rolled dice and played Chuck-a-luck, a kind of poor man's roulette; Steve watched the dice slide on the cement, pass from hand to hand. His co-workers, making fun of how thin he was, had given him nicknames, the same ones he had had since childhood: "breadstick," "iron wire," "bag o bones;" he was given others, more original: "rolling paper;" "parrot mast;" or "hungry sardine." Steve never got offended. He received his first pay from Ambrose Mitchell.

"I's rarely wrong 'bout a guy," the foreman told him, "but I reckon I were wrong 'bout y'all." And Steve pocketed the largest salary he had ever earned in his life.

Now he had to find a room. His good luck appeared in Barnabas Thibodeaux, a roustabout he had hung around with a bit. Barnabas was quite the joker, he was nicknamed the Grinder due to his talent for grinding pleasure between female legs. He was born near Baton Rouge, had a Cajun mother and an unknown father; his mischievous black eyes lit up his face, beige, the color of a ripe pawpaw fruit. When Barnabas suggested Steve share his place on Nelson Street for three dollars a week, he gladly accepted.

Steve accompanied Barnabas by the light of the streetlamps along deserted streets, where mangy dogs made life hard for rats as big as beavers. The men left the area of inhabited buildings to venture into a large empty space, lighted by the halo of the moon.

"This Nelson Street?"

"No. First I gotta do somethin'," answered Barnabas in his Cajun accent.

Steve feared foul play, remembering the Barlow pocketknife Barnabas always carried and with which he had threatened another roustabout one evening after a heated game of craps. Steve, on his guard, followed like an acolyte along a murky expanse. Before them were acres of misery; hundreds of Red Cross tents had been set up in a row, secured to the clay with makeshift stakes. In a few words Barnabas explained the origin of the disaster. The river flood had been more violent in Greenville than anywhere else in the Delta. The flood had submerged the city center and the surrounding areas; for a week you had to travel by boat on the spreading water where bloated corpses, both human and animal, floated by. The standing houses had finally dried out, the port had been cleared, but the shacks of the Blacks in the shantytowns had never been rebuilt. The army had been requisitioned and a camp had been set up for the thousands of refugees on the site of the former municipal garbage dump. A battalion of workers, overseen by armed militiamen, had been forced to reinforce the dams. Then, the workers from the dams had come to swell the ranks of the castaways. The temporary shelter had become permanent, and the encampment continued to grow like a cancer, disfiguring the plain.

The moon was suddenly covered. Barnabas took out a lighter from his jacket pocket. Guided by the flickering flame of his Zippo, the two men came to a canvas hut identical to all the others. Barnabas gave Steve his lighter and his knife before going into the tent. Steve waited with his feet in the mud; around him, cats were fighting and their murderous cries froze his blood. Barnabas came out a few minutes later, wearing a broad smile.

"And now, bag o bones, onward on the road to hell!"

Plaster covered the floorboards, shreds of wallpaper hung from the walls where a colony of mushrooms was thriving. The single lightbulb hanging from the ceiling had burned out, light came from two kerosene lamps placed in opposite corners of the room. Steve was sitting on his new bed, a straw mattress that exuded miasmas of semen and stale beer. The room that he now shared with Barnabas was cramped and dirty but had running water, and the mere sight of it flowing from the faucet gave Steve the impression of living in luxury.

Barnabas brought over a bowl of rice and beans, two ears of corn and some dry biscuits. The two men ate on a sofa, accompanying each bite with mouthfuls of lukewarm beer. Barnabas took a small metal box out of his pocket. He crumbled something brown onto a sheet of cigarette paper, rolled it up, lit it, inhaled deeply, and blew the smoke up to the dark lightbulb. A sweet fragrance covered the smells of greasy food. Barnabas handed the joint to Steve, who was introduced to marijuana. He coughed and gagged while Barnabas laughed. Through the single half-open window could be heard the din of engines, horns, trumpets cut short, and scattered shouts.

"Come look at this, my man . . . " said Barnabas, leaning out the window. Nelson Street was an endless asphalt road lighted by kaleidoscopic neon lights, which started at the port and ended at the edge of Highway 82. Prestigious clubs, inglorious gambling dens, grocery stores, barbershops, eateries offering chicken skewers and catfish stews at any time of day or night. Scattered along the road, carcasses of blackened cars were being used as wedding beds by penniless lovers. Girls solicited on the corners, pimps paraded in their sedans.

"Goddam, what a city!" Barnabas exclaimed. His hand rubbed his fly. Despite the late hour, Barnabas obviously had plans. He brushed his teeth, tested his devastating smile on a piece of mirror, and left the room. "See ya later, 'gator!"

Steve lay down on the mattress, shrugged a cockroach off his shoulder, and slowly drifted off to sleep. He was startled awake by the slamming of a door and by laughter. Barnabas was in the arms of a woman in her fifties, completely drunk, wearing a muslin dress, her stockings torn.

"I present to y'all my little dumplin', Suzy! She from Arkansas," said Barnabas, squeezing the woman's bottom.

"Don't ya listen to this thug, I from Greenville," said the drunk woman, "it my ho mama be from Arkansas!"

Steve refused the offer of another beer, which didn't seem to bother the two revelers who were already getting down to business on the couch. Barnabas removed Suzy's camisole, tossed it on the mattress, and winked at Steve, inviting him to a little innocent threesome. Steve got up and left the room. He fell asleep on the front stoop leaning against the wall, through which he could hear the sounds of wild rutting.

Steve felt the door strike him on the back. Barnabas was standing in front of him, as fresh and clean as a salesman.

"You a funny nigga, mah man," he said. "Y'all pays three dollars a week and sleeps on the stairs . . . Get yo ass up, nigga, they's a tub waitin' for us!"

"What bout the lady?" Steve asked.

"What lady? Oh, Suzy! Don't y'all worry, she the landlady. I owes her two months' rent, but we in the process of workin' that out."

312

Barnabas headed down the stairs and Steve followed him like a lost soul. Nelson Street had finally calmed down, sated with noise, hooch, and sex. The sky was gray and bland, the color before dawn. They went up the street toward the port. An old Black man was sweeping the sidewalk in front of a general store, trying to preserve his little domain from the pervasive filth. Suddenly Steve stopped, frozen.

"What the matter now?!" Barnabas was getting angry, "Goddam, if we show up late, Ambrose will eat us without sauce!"

Steve pointed with a shaky finger at the entrance to an alley. A dark-skinned man was lying face down on the ground in his underpants and socks. A pool of clotted blood surrounded him, but it was unclear where he had been injured.

"You think he dead?"

"Oui, mon cher, poor man," Barnabas said calmly. "Musta eat a blow o Barlow."

"We gots to call the police!"

Barnabas' frowned: "Y'all want to end up like him? On Nelson Street we always hold our tongues."

Barnabas pulled Steve by his sleeve, dragging him from his macabre contemplation. They arrived at the docks just before the siren announcing the approach of a boat sounded. The mist covered the piers and the railings. The two men ran to the warehouse area. A dozen roustabouts were waiting, smoking cigarettes. Ambrose poured coffee. The boat began docking as the mist dissipated over the water.

Dawn arrived like a relief. Betty lit a cigarette, crushed it out after a few puffs. Her nausea during the night had exhausted her. Her belly was swollen, her nipples sore. Unable to sleep, she had rehashed her situation all night long, but had found no solution. She was pregnant and desperate. What she had wanted more than anything else now plunged her into the depths of guilt. All it took was a meaningless coupling for her life to change. She was fertile, full, no different from any other woman. Sapphira was right; it was Steve that nature had deprived of the gift of passing down his blood. Steve, the man she loved, the man she had betrayed, and who was returning tomorrow after a long absence. She couldn't keep it from him any longer. She would find the words. And if he dragged her by the hair down the stairs, soiled her name on the public square, she would accept it. But if he left her . . .

*

On the train station platform, she found him changed. He held his suitcase with his left hand, lifting it off the ground without the slightest effort. He walked toward her, his shoulders straight, his hips swaying in a strange way. She hugged him, soaking up his scent, so familiar and so unique. Steve suggested they walk along the river. His hand was firm and protective. Betty had the feeling she had said goodbye to a frail and indecisive being, and had now found a man. Her man.

314

At home, Steve hugged Joshua like a gift from heaven. In the warmth of his home, his tongue loosened. Betty was amused to hear his voice, slightly deeper, and the bizarre words: cool, anxious, bad, which he used all the time to emphasize what he was saying. They ate, Steve with the appetite of an ogre.

When the boy was asleep, the two lovers rushed to the bedroom. Steve insisted that she light the lantern on the bedside table. His eyes fell on her round belly, her heavy breasts. He did some things that surprised her at first, for a moment she dreaded that other women had introduced him to new pleasures, but she reassured herself, abandoned herself to his kisses, his intense caresses. They were two angels, sweating, exhausted, but still hungry for the crazy words they whispered to prolong the moment.

Steve took a metal box out of his trousers pocket. He rolled a cigarette of greenish tobacco and lit it with a Zippo. Betty watched him hold the smoke in his lungs for a long moment. His face opened up as the room filled with a floral scent. Steve handed her the joint and Betty smoked. She felt a gentle tingling against her temples, and then she slipped into a voluptuous lassitude.

"Yo tobacco be funny." she said.

Steve looked at her with his open smile. She snuggled up against his chest.

"Since y'all left, you learned lots o thangs . . . But I gots somethin' to tell you, somethin', yes . . . " she was going to say "terrible," but, carried away by the languorous wave, she said: "wonderful." She put Steve's hand on her stomach.

"I believe I's with chile."

Steve massaged her belly with the tips of his fingers, and stared at her for a long time, though she couldn't decipher what he was thinking.

"I guessed," he simply said. He kissed her passionately. His tongue tasted of sap, his hardened penis throbbed against her and her legs which opened to welcome him. Betty murmured, "Thanks you, God," with the certainty that among the thousands of prayers addressed to the Creator in that same second, hers was the most sincere and pure.

At daybreak, she hummed a lively song while she was washing in the tub. She walked quietly in the room so not to wake Steve, but he was already up, unable to take more than a few stolen hours from the night. Betty touched her stomach and rejoiced at the disappearance of the nausea. The partial confession, which she had imagined would be so painful, had only been a secret between them. Everything was so simple with her man, so cool, as he now said.

She stopped in the dining room doorway. Steve and the boy were sitting at the table. Joshua ran his finger over the pages of a notebook while Steve stuttered the letters of the alphabet. He stumbled over every syllable, but continued, eager to succeed. Betty went out the front door onto the porch where a cold sun sparkled in a cloudless sky.

Before returning to the train station a few days later, Steve put a small wad of money on the table.

"I just needs only twenty dollar to live there," he said, "ev'rythin' else be for y'all. You should stop goin' to work now, save yo strength fo what comin', right?"

Betty agreed. She didn't feel she was giving up the autonomy she had with her meager salary at the laundry. Steve wasn't trying to put her under his thumb, he was watching over the course of their life together with serene strength.

She accompanied him onto the platform. The train moved away in a cloud of smoke and Betty watched it leave without anxiety or tears.

The following months were the happiest of Betty's life. Steve sent her a telegram every Friday. One afternoon she received a letter he had written himself, in a childish script, which she found so moving that she pinned it to the wall. Betty took time for herself, strolling for long hours on the banks of the river. Time to forgive herself. She visited her coworkers at the laundry and told them the news. They all congratulated her, advised her on what she should eat, the talismans she should slip under her pillow so the pregnancy would go well. Only Pearl kept her distance and watched her with infinite sadness.

Steve came back for a few days every month, his arms laden with gifts: a fountain pen for Josh, perfume samples for Betty, and a beautiful coffee mill for Sapphira. Their reunions were occasions for an outpouring of tenderness, and despite the hundreds of miles that separated them, the lovers felt closer than ever before.

One Saturday night, Steve suggested they go to a movie in Helena. He had invited Aaron and Rachel Posner, whom he introduced to Betty during an impromptu meal. For the first time the young woman spoke and laughed with White folks without being uncomfortable. The five of them squeezed into the Posners' Nash, crossed the river, and arrived in Helena at dusk. They drove up Cherry Street, passed its saloons and general stores, and arrived at a theater that looked like a music hall. A crowd of Black people in their Sunday best waited on the sidewalk. The Posners were the only Whites. To put them at ease, Steve, Betty, and Joshua stood right next to them.

Sudden darkness. The hum of the projector could be heard, and a milky beam of light hit the screen. First came the news. Eleanor Roosevelt, the new first lady, was strolling through the aisles of the Chicago World's Fair, while her husband, the president, was signing a historic agreement with the USSR. The construction of the Golden Gate Bridge in San Francisco was advancing at a steady pace. A blizzard of black dust covered the arid lands of the Dakotas, forcing hundreds of families to leave their homes. At the sight of mothers with blue eyes pulling their children by the hands in a landscape that resembled the end of the world, Betty's heart clinched. Then she saw the face of the absolute ruler of Germany, a little man with a mustache who was reviewing fanatical troops carrying flags displaying a kind of cross. The violence suggested by his movements and his gaze exhilarated with domination made her think of some landowners from her childhood who watched over the cotton picking.

The film began, a low-budget Western with a rehashed script: the eternal convoy of wagons escorted by heroic cowboys playing with their six-shooters. Expressive pantomimes, outrageous make-up, grainy black-and-white. The film was silent, and it was the room that provided the soundtrack; comments rang out: "Hey, give that stupid sheriff a second asshole! Drop that bitch, man, she ain't worth a penny!" When the Indians attacked the wagon train, the crowd instinctively sided with the cowboys, and Betty, along with the rest of the room, cheered the defeat of the savages riddled with bullets.

As they were leaving, Steve suggested they have dinner at one of the eateries on the street, but Aaron and Rachel wanted to go back home right away. The Posners didn't say a word the whole way back, while Joshua and Steve, sitting behind in the Nash, were replaying the Indian attack. Aaron dropped the family off at the border between the White town and the Black section.

Joshua had a lot of trouble falling asleep and for the first time Betty had to raise her voice. Steve was packing his suitcase for his departure the next day. Betty hugged him.

"Yo friends be great fo White folks, I mean they great, really. But they seem so sad when we was goin' home."

"It be cause o Hitler, I reckon."

"Who?"

"The White man, back there, in the news, with the funny mustache. Aaron be 'fraid fo his fam'ly what stayed behind. The Jews there be treated worse than Coloreds heah."

"That Hitler, he be worse than Gov'nor Bilbo or the mayor?"

"Yeah, in any case, ain't any bettah."

The stone pestle struck the mortar, crushing the chicken bones roughly. Sapphira poured the contents into the coffee grinder; using tweezers, she carefully took about a dozen dry and poisonous berries out of a stoneware pot and mixed them with the bones. She turned the steel crank, then she opened the container and poured the powder into a calabash.

The coffee grinder worked beautifully. Steve had done well to buy it at a market in Greenville. Maybe she was wrong about him. He had changed since he started working on the docks. The way he had welcomed Betty's pregnancy had forced the old woman to revise her judgment. Steve had reacted like a true Black man. And her coffee grinder was saving her a lot of time. She now had a supply of gopher dust that would last several months. The black dust was the raw matter for most of the spells the enchantress cast—a restorative powder or a fatal poison, depending on the dose. Three tiny grains on the lip of a baby to stop colic, while a greater amount diluted in a beverage or sprinkled on a pillow could send an odious husband or an impudent rival over to the other side. Like all hoodoo doctors, Sapphira provided the antidote to her own spells; to protect oneself from the deadly dust, she made lucky charms, mojo-bags that she sold or gave away, depending on her mood. Now that Betty was pregnant, she would need her *gris-gris* more than ever. She would convince her to wear a braided anklet of viburnum roots, and a flannel pouch filled with Saint John's wort in her camisole next to her heart.

The old lady went out onto the porch. A rusty moon lingered in a corner of the sky. Sapphira lit a lantern, walked around the house to the scullery. On an iron grating placed above extinguished coals, there was an ear of corn she had grilled at noon. She wasn't hungry, but forced herself to eat, leaving the rest of the ear for the young rooster she had acquired and which prowled around the still-stained granite altar where his predecessor had been sacrificed. Sapphira suddenly felt weary and sat down on the grass. She had grown accustomed to these bouts of unexpected fatigue, not unusual at her advanced age; she accepted the turbulence of her body, not fearing pain or death, that big sister from Guinea. She fell asleep.

She came out of limbo a few moments later. The pain in her ankles, wrists, and neck was excruciating; she massaged her joints and gradually remembered. What she had experienced was not a dream, but a floating tomb. She had approached absolute anguish. The screams, the shackles, the hold.

The Middle Passage.

The great tribulation of bones and souls.

In the hold, bodies crushed by dysentery fought to breathe, the corpses thought they were alive and the living imitated corpses. Atrophied muscles, castrated males, unimaginable thirst and all-consuming hunger. Sapphira had experienced all this, chained among her sisters, brothers, children. At the bottom of this sarcophagus of wood and flesh, she had detected the presence of a foreign entity, an evil god, born out of the foam and fog: Baron, Baron Samedi! She had seen him crawling towards her, lugubrious and lascivious. He was wearing a festive white suit, glasses with smoky lenses; thick pieces of cotton wool blocked his nostrils. His breath smelled like sour ginger. Sapphira woke up just as the god was straddling her.

His right index finger was on the trigger. Just as he was about to pull it, one-eyed Elias could see his shattered face. Whoever came down to the cellar and found his body would never forget it. Surely it would be the girl, little Ada, the farmer's daughter, who came every week to drop off bottles of milk in front of his door and do some housework. She would knock timidly, then harder and harder; she would notice the filled bottles on the stoop and finally use her set of keys. She would enter, broom in hand, and . . . The little girl didn't deserve that. Elias sat up and left the room, leaving his rifle on the floor.

The sun distilled a chalky light, an icy breeze descended from the hills to the east. Elias stared at a point ahead of him; he was looking for a reason to live or, failing that, for a reason to die more valid than the atrocious melancholy that gnawed at him. He vomited his past, the patriotic impulses of his youth, hated himself for having believed in mirages of equality, of having imagined that a Negro in uniform could be something other than a pawn to be moved on a bloody chessboard. His attempts at reconciliation with his close enemy, the White man, had ended in resounding failure. Elias no longer had an ounce of self-esteem, his ego, zombified with shame, dragged itself as it moved along.

Elias felt the urge to give birth to a melody, to hammer the ivory of a keyboard. A flurry of notes, vibrant and playful, rose to his temples. He needed music but didn't want the devil to lean over his piano anymore. He still had the organ, the good old spirituals, the harmony that washes souls.

He stopped in front of the pastor's house. The shutters were closed. He knocked on the door. The one who opened it, dressed in haste, his eyes reddened by bourbon, only appeared to be awake. Pastor Lloyd was asleep standing up, was shamelessly scratching his crotch through the cloth of his trousers. When Elias asked if he could play the organ on Sunday at church, the preacher mumbled an incomprehensible response under his breath and shut the door.

Elias continued on to the church, defying the curfew. The moon shone on the façade and the cross on the steeple. He sat down on a rock at the bottom of the hill and put his hands between his knees. The night provided the right notes. He improvised blindly, his gaze riveted on the cross. At the top of the hill, a shriveled shadow trotting in front of the yard stopped to listen to him. Elias recognized the silhouette of Miss Brown. He smiled at her and let the wind sing through his fingers.

No one had seen her cross the water at the collapsed stone bridge and disappear into the woods. Pearl trudged doubled-over; in her hand, dressmaker's shears. She arrived in front of the offering tree. The bottles smashed by the storm had not been replaced. She took a few steps, bent to the point of breaking. The thistle in her had become a hedge of brambles, between her thighs trickled red waters. She lifted her dress up above her chest, undid the gauze bandages that compressed her stomach. She squatted, perched on her heels, turned her face towards the small square of sky revealed through the branches and surrendered to the pain.

Pearl went through the turbulence of childbirth without a thought for the creature which, little by little, after jerking and shaking, separated from her. She bit her cheeks, her tongue, the treetops. She felt a mass leaving her and falling to the ground, a crimson flood pouring down and soaking the leaves. Pearl accomplished the irreparable, as did so many women before her, in the eclipse of whips, at the twilight of the human. Female slaves, raped upon returning from the fields, inseminated like cattle, heroic and serious women, refusing to prolong their hell, to pass on their chains.

Pearl grabbed the creature and smothered it against her chest; she cut the cord with the scissors, dug a hole with her fingers and placed the cooled body in it. After quickly cutting her hair, she sprinkled it over the body. She filled the hole with dirt mixed with placenta and wiped her hands on the bark of a young pecan tree, lost among the hardwoods.

Pearl left the forest and went to the river. She sank in the icy water and let herself be carried without resisting the current. She had no intention of fighting, but when her head hit a log carried by the water, she decided to live. She clung to the reeds and hoisted herself onto the shore. Numb with cold, Pearl walked to town, not caring about her shaved head, her sodden dress. Of the myriad thoughts going through her head, not one of them expressed remorse.

Old Theodore kicked the pot over and rinsed his mouth from a barrel of rainwater. The old man was still angry. His hooch was undrinkable: fucked up, completely fucked up! It wasn't even white lightning or "tiger sweat"; there was no name for such abject booze. It was not for lack of trying, however; he had been working his ass off for years! He had distilled all kinds of berries, plants, had spied on the moonshiners employed by the Mulligan brothers, at night, in the forest, at the risk of being found and leaving his skin there.

Heavy drinking for Theodore was not a bitter hobby. Alcohol preserved him from himself. During rare moments of sobriety when he had run out of money, he never left the abandoned wagon that served as his shelter. Under a blanket, glassy-eyed, his mind atrociously clear, he felt an uncontrollable wave crushing him—he felt like biting, smashing stones with the blows of a hammer. He became an implacable warrior, a mercenary without a cause but thirsting for violence; the complete opposite of the tottering rag he looked like when he wandered around the narrow streets of the town.

Theodore again checked the padlock that protected the door of the storeroom next to the wagon: a sort of small shed, built of wooden crossbeams, the roof covered with tar paper and sheet metal. He looked at the sky. The sun was damned lazy, barely risen and it was already preparing to set at the other end of the plain. The old man mumbled terrible curses between his teeth. His aching arms felt as if he had wielded an axe for hours. A badly tended beast purred deep within him. He had no more tobacco left and chewed on a viburnum root to keep his mouth busy.

He walked along the old railway line; the ties had disappeared, he could barely detect the original rails that ran through the countryside, disappearing into the rushes in the distance. A crow pecked at the remains of a hare stuck in the slag. The bird did not fly away when he walked by. What Theodore felt deep down was worse than being whipped on a pole, it was a great dispossession, a forced molting.

He was running now, chin straight, shoulders stiff, his shadow on the pebbles was that of a young man in a hurry to meet his girl. Theodore stopped short and turned toward the forest. He had to see Sapphira. It didn't matter how that old witch with formidable eyes would receive him. She was the only one who could pierce the abscess of his soul, squeeze out the pus and soothe him.

Theodore crossed a shallow stream and sank into the underbrush. Without hesitation he found the clearing and the cabin he had built with his own hands. The door was wide open. He climbed the front stairs and entered the cabin, empty of any human presence. He looked at a collection of stones on the shelf and put his hand on a piece of basalt.

"Drop that stone, ya ol' fool!"

Theodore turned around. Sapphira was less than a meter from him, her eyes outraged. How could she have come up behind him without making a sound?

"You ain't nevah to come here evah agin, you heah?!"

"Wait now, listen to me . . . I ain't well, and y'all cain't imagine how . . . "

"Yeah, I kin imagine. But I 'specially know the evil what you done!"

Theodore wanted to leave, but his legs had deserted him. He leaned on a shelf that almost tipped over, then slumped to the ground.

"They ain't no alc'hol heah," Sapphira said, "jus vinegar."

"I don't wants booze. I wants y'all to get this sompin' outta me."

"Deep in y'all they ain't nothin' but darkness."

The sorceress rummaged through a jar on the shelf and handed Theodore something strange: two small bags, brown and wrinkled, which looked like the testicles of a newborn baby. Theodore sunk his teeth into the blackish flesh; he expected a rancid taste and was surprised by the aniseed freshness that flowed into his mouth. He chewed slowly. The old woman made him drink a lukewarm astringent decoction, then knelt in front of him, her chest upright, like a vestal virgin praying. Theodore suddenly began to shiver, his teeth chattered. Sapphira threw him a blanket, and he covered his shoulders. Finally the tremors subsided. The animal in his belly seemed overcome by the unknown sedative.

"I thinks I be better . . . thank ya."

"Don't thank me! I jus don't want y'all to die in my house."

"Now, why you bein' so harsh, darlin'?"

At that, the old woman gasped. She projected herself forty years earlier, when she shared a roof and a bed with this man, when she still forgave him for what he was, trying to convince herself that he was not solely responsible and that another being was acting through his hands.

"Don't ya evah call me that! If I'd knowed at the time I woulda made y'all drink a whole bowl of black powder and none o that woulda evah happened."

"What y'all sayin' were a long time ago," sighed Theodore.

"Liar! And I wants y'all to go find the Devil, yo only frien on this heah earth!"

Sapphira waved her arms in front of him, her gestures like great circles of light. Details came out with incredible clarity: the fibers of the mat, the age spots on the witch's hands. A thick liquid began to flow from his nostrils, Theodore passed his hand over his face and saw his shiny scarlet palm. He fumbled into his overcoat, found a scrap of crumpled-up newspaper, made two balls and plugged his nose.

"The blood tell the truth heah," Sapphira said. "I knows you done started agin."

"No! I swears it!"

His shoulders shook again, his stomach roiled. Sapphira stared at him, pitiless.

"Dora, Josh's po mama, you the one kilt her! I knowed it right away, just by throwing the cowries. Y'all kilt her, like the othahs! I shoulda gone fetch the sheriff so he could put the noose aroun' yo neck, oh yes, I truly shoulda."

Theodore threw off the blanket and stood up. He was panting, his mouth gaping, struggling against asphyxiation. The sorceress raised her arms to the ceiling.

"Legba! Shango! Fogive me fo takin' so long in gitten rid o this Devil!"

Theodore towered above the sorceress who remained motionless, sure of her magic.

"Ya ol bitch! What'chu make me drink?!"

"Sumpin' what gone soothe you fo'evah, and the whole world, too."

Theodore lunged at Sapphira, put his hands around her neck. The pressure was prodigious. From his nostrils dangled strings of bloody paper. The witch had a vision of the macabre god she had met in her dreams. In a final effort, she yanked on the fragments of paper and a rush of blood poured out, like the flooding of a wounded river. Theodore shrieked, let go, and left the room howling.

Sapphira gasped. She heard a crash of broken branches and growling in the distance. She would live. But how many others would perish that night in the claws of the beast . . .

What he touches is broken, what he embraces is doomed. His hands are shaking. The oil is dripping from the lamp reservoir and spills onto the ground. He brings the gas can to his lips, winces, and swings the jerry can over the wagon.

Theodore strikes a match. The fire rises, the flames shoot up, are reflected in his eyes. The old man contemplates his existence as it turns to smoke. He goes to the shed alongside the burning wagon. The key won't open the padlock. He unearths a mass hidden in a thicket, a railwayman's tool for driving rivets. He brandishes the hammer above his shoulders, brings it down and breaks the lock. He goes into the workshop. A doomsday jumble, a workbench overflowing with scraps: fermenting jars, fragments of cloth, rusty files and knives, a pile of cigarette butts. At the back of the room, on a hanger, a light dress stained with a brown ring, and a suit jacket, clean and ironed. He doesn't find what he's looking for. Smoke enters the room. The old man panics, his arms sweep the workbench, the filth spreads around. A wooden top rolls onto the ground. Theodore observes the toy at his feet and walks through the curtain of smoke.

The fire takes over the workshop. The old man moves away to admire his red work. He takes off his undershirt. The witch's poison evaporates in a stench of animal fat. The blood flows through his heart-still, its dark lands. His penis hardens like an old forged rod. Hideous and pyrolytic ectoplasm. He would like to fuck the fire, make it scream out his name.

Theodore sniffs the fumes of an imminent disaster. His eyes dissect the darkness, acidic flashing covers his cortex where his crimes march by. The child with the top. The kid by the river. The saloon whore, and other begging figures of whom he isn't even sure he was the assassin. Ghosts scratching on the screen of his soul.

His time had come. Lucifer himself couldn't stop him. There was nothing human about Theodore except his envelope of skin, the rest was only impulses. Not a monster, just an old nigger electrocuted by memory. A violence suffered for too long had reversed its course and had overflowed. Theodore had long ceased to justify his actions and no longer hoped for forgiveness. He did not believe in the spirits of Benin, much less that White god he had spent his life shitting on. He felt his forearms become covered with scales; on his legs grew a coat of coarse hair. The ultimate metamorphosis.

The moon covered the barn's roof tiles with a brilliant sheen. Theodore heard hungry yelps and saw dirty shapes moving in the darkness. He had arrived at the Abbot farm. He pressed his face against a window, watched the breathing of those who slept, watching every breath, every dream. He heard the cough of a child and the sound of a body turning over. The glass seemed as fragile as a dream. He was about to shatter it to pieces when he heard the sound of an animal through the planks of the adjoining building. A warm and spicy fragrance. He entered the barn on all fours, his nostrils alert, his hands touching the soiled straw.

A goat huddled against a trough was shaking with raw fear. Theodore jumped and tackled the animal to the ground. His fangs found the carotid. Hot liquid trickled down his throat. Theodore moaned with pleasure, the animal's spasms led him to a state of innocence which he thought he had lost. He drank until his stomach swelled and he wiped his lips on the animal's coat. The proximity to death caused black waves of desire to rise up in him. He lowered his pants, walked around the still-warm carcass and possessed it. He moaned, thrusting jerkily, caressing the animal's sides. In the back of the barn gleamed two gold jewels. A horned and hieratic form watched him commit himself to horror. Theodore did not scream when he was in turn penetrated. The horn punctured his side, turned around inside him, and Theodore smiled at the two eyes of fire.

The Abbot Farm rooster crows long before dawn. Nahum Abbot drinks his coffee, alone at the end of the table. He runs his hand over the oilcloth, then over his large belly. He puts on a jacket and goes out to watch the stars scatter. A wave of light covers the plain. The farmer notices the open barn door. He thinks of the slap he'll give his youngest son for his negligence. He goes into the barn and his face freezes. Horrified, he returns with a wheelbarrow, easily lifts the corpse of the old Negro and that of the bloodied goat. The farmer wheels the strange hearse into the yard and heads for the pig pen.

The wind blew a monotonous solo through the open window. Barnabas threw his cigarette butt outside and turned to Steve who was stoned, slumped on the sofa. On Nelson Street, as Christmas was approaching, the whores, pimps and dice players had left a piece of sidewalk to the Salvation Army bell ringers and gingerbread sellers. A brass band across from the general store played "Dixie."

Barnabas went over to the couch and inhaled the joint Steve handed to him. The day had been more difficult than usual. Tons of goods poured onto the docks: wooden toys, barrels of lard, fattened poultry, and fir trees from Wisconsin. The two roustabouts could no longer feel their joints, their legs were full of cramps that only the marijuana vapors could soothe. Steve kept looking gloomily at the ceiling.

"Tell me the truth: what goin' on in that head of y'all's, mon cher?" Barnabas asked in his swampy patois.

"I's thinkin' 'bout my wife who might be givin' birth. When I git back, it'll be too late, the baby gone already be there."

Barnabas punched his friend on the shoulder. "What kin y'all do?! . . . Me, when mah lil honey chile dropped mah peepsqueek, I were a sailor on the *Issaquena*, and when I see the baby, she were already jumpin' round on her lil legs. If y'all's cherie ain't a good-fo-nothin' she ain't gone kick up a fuss fo dat."

Barnabas found a fairly clean plate in the sink, filled it with some kind of polenta, and handed it to Steve. "Bon appetit podna! An stop makin' a face like dat, afterward I gone feel bad, I swearh!"

Steve understood one out of three words of his friend's Cajun gibberish. He ate the couche couche and set the plate down in front of him. Barnabas rummaged behind the sofa and picked up a dusty melodeon. He arranged the leather straps and sat on the window ledge. In the street, the marching band continued with a slow version of "Mount Rose."

"Oo ye yi! It not possible such a squeaking!" Barnabas complained. "Need to change that right now!"

He braced the accordion against his chest and squeezed the bellows. A shrill sound came out, dust rose from the worn out mechanism, then the music gained confidence until it drowned out the sound of the instruments on the street. Barnabas's voice was warm, languid:

> . . . If I evah return home,
> Will be to find my kids and then my wife
> Oh, baby gal, it been a long time
> Honey, do you remember me . . .

It was a zydeco waltz, slow and playful. While he was singing, Barnabas looked around him, as if the room was filled with swooning female admirers. Steve nodded his head, let himself be lulled by the notes. He rolled another joint and gradually purged himself of his accumulated fatigue. Betty's face, the setting sun, filled his head.

Tyrannical movements, unpredictable jumping, sudden flood-gates. Betty had ceased to own or want. She was no longer the mistress of the upheaval of her organs. Uterine movements, secret and violent. When the other you're expecting, the one you cherish blindly, assails you with kicks, sharp pummeling. There was rubble and tearing, rolling clots, freewheeling groans, all shades of suffering. No longer the mistress of herself, desperately free, Betty surrendered to the necessary obedience. Depending on the spasms and the wrenching, she found herself at once shrunken and enlarged, weak and all-powerful. Goddess and wreckage.

Betty on a bed. Doesn't speak. Barely cries out. Thinks about her man, far away, on the docks. Of the marvelous letter she received the day before yesterday, which expressed so simply, so passionately, his anticipation and affection. She thinks of the other, very close, below, in her belly; the other she knows nothing about: its sex, its face, its personality. She hopes that the baby will have the features of her beloved—a detail, a curve, whatever, as long as she can connect it to him. She fantasizes and is reassured. The face of the musician, floating in her daydreams, continues to haunt her. She is afraid she'll recognize his smile on the little crumpled face of the stranger who is arriving.

Sapphira is by her side. The old woman's hands press on her joints, regulate the opposing forces holding Betty hostage.

The young woman didn't hesitate before coming to give birth in the cabin of her childhood, the place seemed obvious to her. As soon as she felt the contractions getting closer, she had called out to Joshua. The child had shown exemplary calm; he had rented a cart, helped Betty get in, then took her to the forest. Her water broke the moment she started climbing the steps to the cabin. That had been this morning, she had been there for hours.

Sapphira was ready—scissors and needles had been sterilized, clean linen, the basin, which she reserved for the baby's first bath, polished and shiny. She had hung up a large fabric partition that cut the room in two. Behind the curtain, sitting on a mat, Joshua waited, worried and silent. A fire crackled in the stove, the room's temperature was ideal. Sapphira had helped more women give birth than she could count. She had always been there to help during the deliveries of girl-mothers, poor unbelieving women as well as penniless devotees. The closest maternity hospital for Colored women was in Memphis, that is, at the end of the world. She was ready. So why did she feel so anxious? Betty was too stoic. She needed to bring her screams to the surface. Sapphira wiped the sweat from her niece's brow and said in an authoritative voice: "Dammit, scream, gal! A baby gotta come with a ruckus! Y'all no diff'rent from othahs: you a woman, you is sufferin' worse'n death, so howl!"

Betty turned to the curtain that separated the room.

"I gone tell Josh to go out," Sapphira said.

"It too cold outside," Betty whispered.

"He not a lil boy no mo."

Vapor came out of his mouth each time his arm came down. The boy, who was no longer a boy, was enjoying splitting logs to perfection, striking at the heart of the wood—two halves flew above the block and fell onto the cold ground. Joshua, his forehead sweating, muscles warm, thought of the mystery that was unfolding behind the curtain, that tiny theater of suffering. He realized for the first time how young Betty really was. She was only ten years older than he was. Dorothy, his mother, was approximately the same age, since she had been baptized in the Yazoo River the same year. So Dora must have gotten pregnant at twelve, the age he would be next year. Joshua abandoned his calculations and wiped his brow. No more wood to split. The logs piled up on the side of the house, climbing to the roof's edge. Enough for two consecutive winters.

A shriek came from the cabin. Joshua thrust his axe into the chopping block and turned toward the sound. The cry was that of his mother when she was murdered. The cry that he had not heard at the time, shut in his hotel room, came back right in his face. Another moan could be heard. Joshua climbed the steps and stopped in front of the door. The cold had reached him and his teeth were chattering.

Betty held the infant on her chest. She breathed in her scent of overripe fruit. Her skin was deep black, lighter in places, on the shoulders and neck. It was a girl. A drop of night. Sapphira had cut the cord following the rules of the art, wiped the raw flesh with a damp, warm towel, then placed on the baby's lips the juice of a wild berry, praying to the parallel powers to watch over this new life. The old woman picked up her seamstress tools, diluted some alcohol in a basin of water, and bent between Betty's thighs. Despite her expert sutures, blood continued to soak through the cloths. She looked up and saw the baby suckling. The old woman rejoiced at still being able to cry.

"You choose a name fo her?"

"Dorothy. Her name Dorothy," Betty replied without hesitation.

Despite the dark circles and creases under her eyes, the face of the young mother beamed. The milk and blood coming out of her glorified her. The baby suckled greedily, eyelids closed. Above Betty's foot Sapphira put an anklet braided with honeysuckle root from which hung a coin with a hole in its center. She massaged her thighs and calves with mud extracted from a wasp's nest, mixed with avocado oil. The old woman washed her hands in the basin and went out. Joshua was on the porch, shivering.

"Y'all gots a lil sister," said Sapphira, in a voice that was more serious than she would have liked.

"What her name?"

When the old woman answered, Joshua's eyes lit up and Sapphira hugged him as if he were a teenage god.

*

Long streaks of blood on the white linen. Betty was asleep; she was breathing weakly, the infant on her chest. Sapphira had lit all the candles she had. It had been almost two hours since she had sent Joshua for Doctor Howard. The sorceress had finally admitted that her herbs, ointments, and incantations could not stop the hemorrhaging. She knew the gods of the land of before very well; they were not spirits of compassion, but of struggle and destiny. Even Erzulia Dantor, the armor of women, had remained deaf to her pleas.

The old woman whispered a few words in Betty's ear, but the new mother didn't react. Sapphira took the baby and made a diaper out of a piece of cloth. She noticed a diamond-shaped mark on the baby's left shoulder. The infant did indeed belong to her lineage. When the time came, she would pierce the invisible, would hear beyond the silence.

*

Sapphira stepped through the curtain to greet Doctor Howard. The doctor, satchel in hand, looked at the statuettes, fur and stones, trying not to show his contempt for these occult practices which offended both his morality and his scientific certainties. The doctor first examined the infant, who opened her eyelids when he put the stethoscope against her chest. The cord had been expertly cut, the baby was perfectly healthy.

"Did you sew up the mother?"

"Yes," Sapphira replied, "but she still bleedin'."

The doctor looked under the sheet. The sutures were precise, flawless. He couldn't have done better. He stood up and observed the needles and scissors lined up on a metal tray. Unable to meet the old woman's gaze, he said, looking at the floor: "Did you give her something for the pain?"

Sapphira showed the doctor a terracotta pot filled with dried leaves and bark shavings.

"What's that?"

"Blue verbena, California poppy, and willow bark. She drink it twice. If it go through the milk it don't matter, it make the baby sleep, that all."

The doctor suddenly had the impression he was talking with a medical colleague. "It's internal bleeding," he said, "probably in the uterus. She should be hospitalized and operated on right away. But she's already lost too much blood and the hospital is far away . . . "

He almost added that the nearest hospital didn't accept Coloreds, but was silent. He rummaged through his satchel and handed Sapphira an object she had never seen before, a glass container topped with a rubber bulb and suction cup.

"It's for expressing milk. You can feed the baby even if the mother is too weak. Do you have a baby bottle?" Sapphira nodded her head yes.

"Good. Don't forget to sterilize it. And, if necessary . . . "

The doctor stopped as if he were about to say something blasphemous.

"She asleep," Sapphira said, pointing at Betty. "An you kin tell me evr'thin."

"Well," said the doctor, lowering his voice, "you will still be able to express the milk a few hours after death. Then you'll have to find a wet nurse."

The doctor refused to be paid and just asked to be reimbursed for the milk pump. He finally accepted the embroidered quilt Sapphira offered him. "It the young gal what sewed it," she insisted. The doctor left the cabin, the quilt folded under his arm.

Sapphira told Joshua to lie down on the mat and go to sleep. The boy complied.

"Is Betty gone die?"

"Yes," said the old woman. "But the baby gone live."

Night train. Face glued to the window, Steve watches the faint lights on the plain: Shell and Texaco gas stations, piercing truck headlights, lit-up motel sign near Clarksdale . . . He still hopes to arrive before the birth, to hold Betty's hand during her labor, then cut the cord of the newborn baby and the next day go to the town hall to register the birth. Their child will not be one who doesn't belong, lost among all the Colored brats. It will have rights and expectations. Steve fidgets in his seat. Why is the night so impenetrable, interminable?

The train arrived at dawn. Steve found the house empty. He looked for a note, a letter. He started running along the banks of the river to the forest. The endurance required on the docks allowed him to reach the clearing without slowing down. He first saw Joshua sitting on the porch plucking a rooster, a basin of steaming water at his feet. When he looked up at him, the young boy's face was so desolate that Steve froze, as if hit by invisible lightning. Joshua left his task and disappeared behind the cabin.

Sapphira appeared on the porch. In her arms she held the infant swaddled in woolen blankets. Steve leaned over and felt the faint, lukewarm breath against his cheek.

"It a girl," said Sapphira, "her name Dorothy. She healthy."

"What 'bout Betty?" asked Steve in a tone that didn't really require an answer.

"She were brave all the way. I keep her eyes open. It fo y'all to close 'em."

Steve was a man of glass, ready to shatter. His face, a tragic mask. He walked through the door. Sapphira saw the half-plucked rooster abandoned on the ground. She looked for Joshua who had sought refuge near the woodpile and scolded him.

"Don't ya never leave nothin' fore it be finished, ya heah boy?"

The old woman thought of what the two lovers could be saying to each other inside, behind the curtain. She wanted to imagine Steve, who usually had so little to say, finding the words capable of moving death.

*

Never had the cabin in the middle of the woods greeted so many visitors. To pay their final respects to Betty, the poor people of the town had overcome a fear rooted in them since childhood; by entering the antechamber of the spirits, all had fought against a sense of imminent damnation.

Constance Reed went into the death chamber. Her first glance was at Steve who was standing, his eyes red from crying. Betty was lying on the bed, a peaceful expression on her face. Constance stroked her hair as she had done so often. Joshua, sitting on a chair, was rocking the baby; at his feet, a glass bottle in which a bit of milk remained. Constance put her hand on his shoulder.

"Chile, you an the baby gone come spend a few days wit me. I done made y'all a bed. Pearl and me gone take care o y'all's lil sister while you at school."

"But what we gone do 'bout milk?"

"Pearl got milk."

"But Pearl ain't got no chil'ren, whatchoo mean she got milk?"

Sapphira lifted the curtain.

"Boy, don't be askin' so many questions, an trust womens fo womens bidness."

The Posners' car was parked in front of the cabin. Aaron had given the keys to Steve without even asking if he knew how to drive. Steve carried his wife in his arms, Sapphira opened the door for him and he laid Betty in the back seat of the Nash. The old woman covered the body with a blanket, letting the face emerge out of the pastel colors. Sapphira kneeled down in the middle of the clearing, on the ground, getting ready to hold vigil until dawn.

"Auntie, y'all cain't stay like this all night," said Steve, "or ya ain't gone wake up no mo . . . "

"I knows what I's doin'!" snapped the old woman. "Go on an light me a fire, if y'all so worried bout my bones . . . "

The hurricane lamp flickered in the bushes. Pastor Augustus Lloyd had been wandering in the undergrowth for hours, too drunk to be really frightened. He saw a fire through an opening in the leaves. A ghostly car, an old woman sitting cross-legged by the fire, a rifle balanced on her lap. Pastor Lloyd took a few steps toward the fire. The old woman immediately stood up and aimed her gun at him.

"Whoever you be, if'n you come nearer, you gone be dead!"

"It's me, Reverend Lloyd! I come in the peace of our Lord Jesus Christ!"

"What peace?! An why you comin' in the middle o the night like a thief?!"

"I . . . I've been busy all afternoon preparing the funeral for our poor child, and . . . "

"Ain't nobody gone bury Betty over yonder, specially not y'all!" shouted the old woman, her finger on the trigger.

The pastor was taken aback and Sapphira took advantage of the pause.

"Betty, she weren't Christian no mo! She seen how y'all treated poor Dora, and how y'all become a dirty, selfish drunk! My niece gone rest at the bottom o the water with her ancestors, an it gone be no othah way!"

"You have no right! That . . . that would be a crime!"

"Don't y'all talk to me bout no crime, cause I knows ev'rythin' bout y'all," Sapphira responded with a sneer of deep disgust. "Joshua tole me evry'thin', an if y'all don't leave us be, I's gone tell evr'body!"

Augustus stood dumbfounded for a moment, then walked away, the lamp sputtering out in his hand. At another time, in other circumstances, he would have fought against the witch and would no doubt have emerged victorious. He was now just a shadow of himself. He was no longer worthy of taking part in the great battle between water and earth, fetishes and saints.

She sprinkled the body with a layer of sand, crimson and pure, like that which covers the canyons. The dead woman's skin sparkled with fine crystals. With a lime tree branch she swept off the sand, then rinsed the skin with spring water until the last grain had disappeared. She smoothed her hair with the rest of the avocado oil; as a foundation she used wax mixed with clay. Faithful to the tradition in Guinea, she lined her mouth and throat with raw cotton and closed the jaw with a strip of fabric which she tied on top of her head. Sapphira recited the consecrated words, which she never thought she would have to utter over the body of someone so young and so dear to her heart.

Mingus Whipple, the carpenter, brought the coffin a little after dawn. A simple rectangular box, without a lid. Sapphira was concerned about where the wood came from, she wanted to make sure it had not been treated, or varnished. Mingus assured her that he had just planed the wood and nailed it, nothing more. Former employees of the Mulligan brothers brought blocks of ice. Steve lined the bottom of the sarcophagus with ice and arranged Betty's body so it fit in the narrow coffin at the back of the car, then folded back the blanket. Betty seemed serene, lying in silence. Steve started to cry. To hide his pain, he went into the woods. Through the leaves he saw Constance Reed in a cart; she had come to pick up Joshua and the baby.

Sapphira went to the scullery. The rooster, plucked and preserved, was intact. The beasts of the forest hadn't dared cross the forbidden perimeter. The old woman held up the carcass to the misty sky. She called the birds, those that devour carrion and caw into infinity, she called out to them in the universal language that circulates between kingdoms and species. The birds answered the call. A dark cloud settled on top of a poplar that began to rustle with the flapping wings and cawing. The old woman placed the rooster on the altar. Two crows alighted and dug their beaks into the pale meat.

When he saw a black squadron of birds descend behind the cabin, Steve rushed to the scullery and found Sapphira, her arms outstretched, her face ecstatic; at her feet, the mass of birds was so compact that the ground could no longer be seen. The old sorceress cried out, the crows flew off into the forest. Sapphira turned to Steve.

"Y'all gotta prepare yo'self, boy, cause you gone see othahs . . . "

Steve hurried back to the car. A tiny little woman was leaning over the engine. She had opened the hood and was checking the oil level. Rosetta Brown was bundled up in a wool coat, a large cloud of vapor escaped from her mouth.

"Y'all here to see Betty, Miz Brown?"

"Oh, thank ya, son," Rosetta said, "I done seen her and alredy cried enough to fill a barrel. Tell me, what that scarf round her head?"

"Uh, that how it done," Steve replied.

"Well, I come to tell y'all that I gone with. I don't know where y'all takin' this po chile, but I's comin'."

"I's sorry, ma'am," Steve said, unsure of what to say, "they ain't no mo room in the car, given they already two of us with my aunt."

Miss Brown closed the hood and looked at Steve up and down as if she were going to make him a suit.

"You pretty tall, boy, but all due respect, you no thicker than a bean pole. Y'all can ride behind with yo gal. I'll drive an talk bout the good ol days with yo aunt. Do ya knows I's older than her?"

"Drive what?"

"Well, the car, ya big fool! I'm sure y'all have no idea how to start such a machine, right? Come on now, hand me the keys!"

Miss Brown listened to the engine purr. "Good engine, yes-suh. But I don't knows if'n it as solid as a Model T."

Sapphira came out of the cabin with a human skull, which she placed at the top of the steps to keep prowlers away. When she saw Miss Brown sitting behind the wheel of the Nash, she didn't seem surprised and greeted her cordially.

"My frien, is ya'll comin' with us?"

"Yes m'am," said Rosetta. "By the by, where we goin' to?"

"We gone to Jackson, then we gone keep goin'."

"I see. Well, if the Lord watch over us and the vehicle, we should reach there in two days' time."

"Only two days?" Steve asked, surprised.

"Absolutely, boy. The good Lord don't let me sleep no mo, so I kin drive without much stoppin'."

*

The Nash's tires slid on the cold asphalt. Sitting in the front, Sapphira watched the stretching road, the bare trees, and raw furrows pass by. In the back, Steve, his legs squeezed against the coffin, stared at Betty's face sticking out of the ice. The windows were open, the sticks of Maine incense that Sapphira was constantly burning scented the inside with the fragrance of woods.

"It were Buster, my last husban, rest his soul, taught me to drive his ol Tin Lizzy," said Miss Brown. "He were drunk all the time, so I's the one had to drive."

"I member Buster," said Sapphira, "drunk way too much, but he still look good . . . "

"Yes, real charmin'. Never had such a good lookin' man in my bed, and prob'ly never gone to agin!"

The two women laughed together. Steve was resigned to listening to the chattering of the two old women talking hungrily about a past that to him seemed more distant than the kingdom of Chaldea. They passed Stovall, then Tutwiller. Night fell on Highway 49. Approaching Greenwood, Miss Brown began to yawn.

"I needs to sleep fo a couple hours," she said. "Kin y'all take the wheel, my frien?" Sapphira hesitated.

"I kin do it," Steve said. "I watched how y'all do an I believe I kin do it."

"Quiet, boy, nobody akst y'all!" Sapphira snapped. "We jest gotta stop an make a fire. I put some logs under y'all's feet, you feel them?"

Yes, Steve felt those damn logs that had been tormenting his calves since the trip started.

The Nash stopped at the end of a dirt road. Miss Brown snoozed inside the car, while Steve and Sapphira warmed up by the fire.

"Y'all ain't a bad boy," said the old woman, nibbling on some cornbread. "You just too young to understand the why and how. Us old'uns, me and Rosetta, we done seen it all."

Through the window a dawn sprinkled in gold. The Nash continued without incident to Bentonia. Rosetta declared that she needed a coffee and pulled into the parking lot of a service station. Steve stayed in the car to watch over Betty, whose face was hidden by the blanket. Rosetta and Sapphira returned, each holding a steaming cup, lit cigarettes in the corner of their mouths. The Nash got on the road again heading to Jackson.

"Lord, that good!" Rosetta exclaimed, lighting another cigarette. "I were very stupid to stop some thirty year ago!"

In addition to the incessant chatter, Steve had to endure the cigarette smoke that stung his eyes.

"Watch y'all don't burn the seats . . . Uh, please . . . "

"Now, boy, you thinks we dirty?!"

Steve chose to keep his mouth shut. It was close to noon when they crossed the state line, after leaving McComb behind. The air was warm, the sun blazing. A few dozen miles after Kentwood, Miss Brown slowed down. A police car was parked on the side of the road. Two White cops were watching the cars go by.

"Lord!" exclaimed Rosetta, "do not let the impious impede us!"

"Legba," said Sapphira, "you who play with men, play with those yonder!"

The car passed in front of the police without arousing suspicion. After looking in the rear-view mirror to be sure danger had been averted, Miss Brown began to accelerate, pushing the engine to its limits. Sapphira sang at the top of her lungs: "Oh, Legba! Legba, oh!"

"Who yo Legba, girl?"

"He the one what watches the crossroads."

"What he look like?"

"He a tall nigger, got a beautiful smile."

"Like Jesus, then," said Miss Brown without taking her foot off the accelerator.

The Nash rolled on the roads of Louisiana. The winter sky was shades of honey and raw wool, the air full of Caribbean mist. The car traveled into a bleak and desolate landscape. Mist floated around the gum trees and naked oaks, moisture condensed on the windshield and dripped off the car's body. They entered the bayou before dusk. Sapphira leaned over the coffin; the ice had completely melted, the blanket was soaked. She took the dead woman's face in her hands.

"We there, dear gal."

Underbrush rustling, a heron skims the surface of the swamp and rises into the sky darkened by heavy clouds. Through the lianas the moon shines on the oily water . . . twisted moss-covered trees, asphyxiated by the darkness . . . cypress roots plunge under the black covering. Clandestine lapping. Rotten kingdom. Moving and spongy earth with sunken splendors. Bayou . . .

Steve woke up with a start. A crow was perched on the hood of the Nash and was hammering the metal with its beak. As big as an eagle, beady eyes, its feathers pitch black. Steve got out of the car, the bird turned its neck and challenged him with a look. Steve walked away to relieve himself against a tree, passing in front of Rosetta who was rekindling the embers of a fire.

"Shame on y'all defiling a sanctuary!"

A voice behind him. Steve hastily buttoned himself up and found himself face to face with three women.

"Y'all one o them bastards what piss where they please, that it?!" shouted one of them. Her frizzy hair was sprinkled with cowrie shells, and she had strange spiral tattoos on her forehead and forearms. The women stepped forward. Steve noticed one of them was holding a dagger with a curved blade.

He stepped back into a boxer's stance. Sapphira appeared behind the group.

"Peace mah sisters. He the husban o the gal I tole you 'bout."

The woman with the dagger glared at Steve with contempt.

"He comin' with us?"

"Yes," said Sapphira, "he gone row the boat. He don't look like it, but he strong."

Miss Brown walked up and smiled at the group.

"What 'bout her?" asked one of the women, a round felt hat on her head.

"She Rosetta, an ol frien," said Sapphira. "She represent Jesus."

The three women frowned, then seemed to calm down. After all, Jesus was a powerful spirit, and it was better to have him on their side.

"Leave us be now," Sapphira said to Steve and Rosetta. "We needs to discuss how we gone do the ceremony."

The three sorceresses didn't know each other, nor did they know Sapphira. They had simply answered the call of the birds and deciphered their cawing. They were powerful women, seasoned conjuring women. The oldest, the one wearing a hat, was one of the sisters of the Pleiades Constellation, a New Orleans mambo society of women. She had left her house on stilts in the Algiers district and in her bags had brought the famous oil that was reputed throughout the South. The second, the one with a dagger, had come from the French Vieux Carré and claimed to be a distant descendant of

Delphine Lalaurie, the damned soul of the fearsome Marie "Snake" Laveau. And the youngest had come from Saint Francisville, near Baton Rouge, her cabin was located not far from the haunted Myrtles plantation. All three had coupled with devious spirits, all knew the price of internal exile, when the gods whisper explosions of syllables in your ears. They were preparing to transship the soul of the young woman the next day, to immerse her body in the original swampland. They had already carried out this ritual, in their dreams and while awake. They were going to have to barter for the passage and see the dirty face of Baron, the henchman of the ashes, whose mood was swayed by massacre as much as by irony.

The sorceresses crouched in a circle on the damp ground. Each tried to approach the tessitura of the others, and succeeded. Only one voice could be heard which sounded on all their lips.

"She must be completely naked to join the water . . ."

"I will rub her ankles with spirit oil . . ."

"I will put a silver coin in her mouth to pay the *guédés* . . ."

"She must return home before the moon is in the sky . . ."

"So no mo time to waste, mah sistahs . . ."

The sorceresses broke the circle. Sapphira offered each a cigarette and they smoked, their faces lifted toward the top of the gum trees, humming somber hymns.

The canoe, forty feet long, cut out of a single tree trunk, was moored at the edge of the greenish water. The four enchantresses had undressed Betty and rubbed her ankles with fragrant oil. The dead woman waited naked on the mossy shore, her jaw still held tight by the strip of fabric. Seeing her, Steve recoiled. He overcame his shock, lifted the body and placed it in the middle of the canoe, then helped Miss Brown on board. Sapphira and the three women sat down on either side of the dead woman. Sapphira untied the mooring. Steve propelled the canoe with a long pole; when they reached deeper waters, he traded his pole for a paddle and started paddling vigorously. Rosetta prayed under her breath, her hands clasped, her eyes closed, while the other women sang ancestral hymns at the top of their voices. Steve saw a couple of alligators on one of the banks. He stopped paddling and dared interrupt the women's song.

"I don't want Betty to be ate by them beasts!" he said in a loud voice, pointing with his paddle at the two animals. "I not gone let you do such a thang!"

The woman in the felt hat looked at him gravely. Her voice was that of a child, incapable of lying.

"Nobody, no man, no animal, gone approach her, my brothah, I swears it. She under the protection of Erzulie, of Legba, even of Jesus," she added, with a glance at Miss Brown who was still praying.

Steve continued paddling in the meandering dark water where the light of day was but a pale inconsistent ray. The canoe approached a gigantic tree, its roots submerged in the mud. The woman with the dagger suddenly stood up and motioned to Steve to slow down. She pressed the blade of her dagger into her palm and drew blood. She uttered an incantation whose refrain was picked up by the other three enchantresses, then wiped her bloody palm in Betty's hair.

Steve couldn't move. The sorceress's voices turned into obscure yelping. They waved their arms, hips, and the boat rocked dangerously. The song stopped abruptly and the four women froze like ebony statues. Sapphira turned to Steve.

"If y'all want to kiss her one last time, go 'head."

Steve moved to the center of the canoe. The woman with the dagger cut the strip that was holding the dead woman's jaws. She handed Steve a silver coin, as shiny as if it had just been minted.

"Slide it into her mouth."

Steve looked away and put the coin on the damp wadding inside Betty's mouth. The four women lifted the body and immersed it starting with the feet. The dead woman floated for a moment on the murky water as if on an unreal mooring, then gently sank down. Steve's eyes met those of Rosetta. The old woman embraced him. "You brave, mah boy. God always gone love y'all." Steve felt the old woman's heart beating against his and burst into tears. Betty's hair was still floating on the surface when Sapphira began reciting:

"You come from water and water welcome you back. Greet our dead and tell them they welcome in our dreams and in our voices. The dead be not dead!"

The three sorceresses repeated:

"The dead be not dead!"

And Rosetta whispered a definitive "Amen."

The swamp made a pact with the darkness. One of the women lit candles which she stuck with wax on the edge of the canoe. The sorceresses emptied their pouches and threw into the water dozens of amulets and shells. Steve picked up his wooden pole and turned the boat around. Careful not to disturb the flames of the candles, he paddled slowly into the deep night.

Pastor Lloyd opened the Good Book on the pulpit. His mouth was pasty and he had a terrible headache despite the quinine pills he had taken when he woke up. Every thought he had seemed to have been delivered by forceps. No sooner had he ascended the platform overlooking the faithful, than he felt threatened. The faces in front of him no longer seemed compassionate. Rosetta Brown and the deacons had gathered in the Amen Corner and the faithful were turning toward them, as if waiting for a signal. It had been months since Augustus Lloyd had let down his flock; he had tried the patience of the most charitable and opened a breach into which those who had sworn to his downfall would soon rush. The pastor cleared his throat in absolute silence. The platform was dirty, the organ covered with a gray film. In the first row, in front of the pulpit, Sergeant Elias was looking at the keyboard and his one eye was burning with reproaches.

Augustus Lloyd searched his pocket for the draft of the sermon he had scribbled the day before, before the alcohol had made his hand shake. On the crumpled page there spread illegible scribbles and ink stains. Augustus would have to improvise, take every risk. He breathed noisily and went headlong into battle.

"Traitors! Yes, traitors, those who rejoice in the misfortunes of the sinner and no longer have either compassion or pity for him, and who rub their hands together at the thought of seeing him fall."

His voice echoed in the silent room. Not a heartbeat in the holy enclosure, not a "Hallelujah" for support. The pastor continued, his forehead sweating: "So speaks our brother Ezekiel: those who are for pestilence, to pestilence, and those who are for the sword, to the sword; those who are for famine, to famine, and those who are for captivity, to captivity!"

The words knocked around in his skull. He had confused Jeremiah and Ezekiel, and this lapse hadn't escaped Miss Brown or the deacons. A murmur moved toward the platform. The pastor bent over the Bible, anxiously turning the pages and made a final attempt to recover.

"He who spreads slander reveals secrets! Don't meddle with the one who opens his lips and . . . My brothers and sisters, you must believe me, you must believe what I tell you because . . . because . . . "

He went no further. The Word had dried up. There was a moment of hesitation, then Augustus saw Miss Brown approach the pulpit. Everything happened as in a dream, without unnecessary violence. Rosetta put a hand on his shoulder and led him to the wooden stairs. Augustus felt a strange relief. The masquerade had finally ended. Soon he could go back to his room, to his familiar demons and to his shame, his new companion.

It was winter, biting and drab, but Sapphira continued to cook outside. The flames licked the edges of the pot. On a board sitting on two stones were bowls full of meat, vegetables and spices. The old woman warmed her hands above the fire. Across from her, Steve was sitting on a log, shivering. Sapphira opened a bucket of lard and put some into the bottom of the pot. She added quarters of red onions, okra, and a beautiful pork hock.

"That a damn fine slice o meat, Auntie. Y'all expectin' guests today?" asked Steve, just to make conversation.

"I's the one invited. Rosetta askt me to do the chitterlings with black eye peas, like in the good ol times."

Steve knew not to depend on the old woman to help him formulate the request he was eager to make. Up to then he had been careful not to ask her anything, but he no longer had a choice. The telegram he had received from Greenville was clear: if he didn't return to the docks by next week, his job would be gone. The old woman's hands held the pig tripe; in contact with the burning grease, the chitlins sizzled and gave off a strong odor. Steve moved his seat closer to the fire.

"I gots to go back to work Monday."

"Uh huh . . . shorely work be important," said Sapphira, stirring the intestines with a wooden spoon.

"I's doin' fine with the baby," Steve said. "Baby bottles an all that hardly be compl'cated."

Sapphira tossed a dozen small turnips into the pot along with a few leaves of fodder kale. The old woman cooked without a recipe, used what she had on hand. Soul food. That of former slaves who made do with scraps, beechnuts and peelings. She dipped the spoon into the stew, brought it to her lips. She waited a few minutes then added two handfuls of white beans.

"I wants to earn my keep like a true Negro," Steve added. "Cept Joshua cain't stay there alone like that a whole month."

The old lady poured the contents of a water pitcher into the pot. She skimmed off the foam and watched the steam rise for some time, her face serious.

"Y'all wants me to move in with the chil'ren, right?" she asked, as if she were talking to the pot. Steve couldn't go backwards.

"Auntie," he said, "I knows we two ain't never been well tuned, but I always have, how you say, shown respect fo y'all."

"Fore I come, I wants to be sure of one thang," said Sapphira, looking into Steve's eyes.

"What?"

"I wants to be sure y'all knows bout that baby."

The old woman was cooking him on the flames of truth.

"I knows," Steve said without hesitation.

"Y'all knows she ain't yours?" she insisted. There was no cruelty in her voice, only the will to set everything out straight.

"Yes. But that baby, I loves her like she my own. She were in Betty's belly and that all that matter."

The old woman's face lit up.

"I gone come tomorrow," she said. "Y'all send Josh round with a cart to help me carry my thangs."

Miss Brown had kept the Bible open, like a beacon. She signaled to Sergeant Elias who played a painful chord on the organ keys. Rosetta Brown turned to the crowd and rejoiced in not feeling pride. She had not defeated Pastor Lloyd, had not risen by bringing another down. Her only enemies were hatred and misplaced pride—Satan's two crutches. She had planned to organize a great collection among the faithful so that the pastor could go heal his sick soul and body in a hospice near Helena.

The church was full. Many parishioners who had deserted the place, no longer able to bear the reverend's cold discipline, had returned to the fold. The deacons had donned their ceremonial tunics again. Children were present in large numbers, curious to see the adults abandon their reserve and indulge in dancing and ecstasy. Something was in the air, crackling and bright. The link with the invisible, which had been broken for years, was in the process of being restored. The Amen Corner would regain its greatness, the echoes of Africa would once again find their legitimate place. A frizzy-headed and glorious Christ would come to uplift humbled hearts.

Rosetta turned her face to the front door that she had left ajar so that a potential sinner might dare take the decisive step.

"Turn to me," she said, "and you be saved! You who is at the end of the Earth! Because I am God and there is no other!"

The women in the front row held out their arms to the ceiling and the children were children, noisy and alert.

Pearl didn't want to take anything with her. She put her suitcase down on the bed and took out whatever she didn't need. She counted out a wad of bills, put her hand under her blouse; her breasts were deflated, the milk no longer flowed. She hid her money under her camisole. Pearl walked out, her shoulders covered in a woolen coat. The sight of the streets of her childhood, the laundry, the shops, the crowd of Negroes, moved her to tears. Dry tears. She went to the bus station. She saw some White folks waiting on the sidewalk, smoking cigarettes, their noses in their coffee cups. Instinctively, she bit her lip. The rare times when she encountered White men she couldn't help but think maybe they were the ones who had left her for dead in the woods. She walked quicker.

A man was sprawled against a fence near the toilets reserved for Coloreds. He looked like a living garbage dump, with his crumpled shirt sticking out of his pants, his purple eyelids and his eyes struggling to distinguish some bits of reality.

It took Pearl a moment to recognize Pastor Lloyd. She stopped, shocked, and had to fight herself not to feel pity, that repugnant feeling she refused to indulge for herself. She placed a quarter at the drunk's foot and he thanked her with a grunt. Pearl crossed the lobby of the station, a simple wooden shed, and boarded the Greyhound bus for Memphis. She would first make a quick stop in Nashville, then go on to Indianapolis where a distant cousin was waiting for her. Pearl had refrained from sleeping the night before so she would be sure to doze as soon as the bus rolled out. She sat in the back, behind an elderly woman who looked like her mother, or rather like the fuzzy memory she had of her mother. The Greyhound started moving. A pale sun streamed over the dark earth. The bus skirted the forest to reach the highway. Pearl's eyelids closed when she saw the tall trees.

Sapphira got up, walked like an automaton toward the kitchen, and prepared the bottle. She measured the water and powdered milk with the same care she put into her spells. She came back to the bedroom and little Dorothy drank greedily.

Dawn seeped in through the blinds. She heard Joshua cutting bread in the kitchen. Sapphira placed the little one in her bassinet and took her to her cabin in the middle of the woods. When she returned in the evening, a letter had arrived. Joshua read it while the old woman prepared dinner. Steve was working hard on the docks. On New Year's Eve he had seen a fireworks display. The letter spoke of the shimmering colors in the sky and the reflections on the surface of the river.

The old woman needed to feel the hard ground under her bones, and lay down on the floor next to the bed. She thought back to the Christmas meal at Rosetta Brown's house. Zucchini fritters, cornbread, fried chicken; everything was perfect. Between the servant of spirits and the new preacher at the church, an unbreakable bond had been forged. She had had to wait more than eighty years before finding a true friend on this earth. Sapphira fell asleep and dreamed of the bayou. Betty emerged from the dark water. She held in her hands a phosphorescent fish and used it as a lamp to illuminate the riverbank. The dead girl smiled, her face showed no suffering. The old woman woke up with the certainty she was on the path marked by the gods.

*

Steve returned at the beginning of March. He had gotten a bit heavier and his voice was deeper. The next day he disappeared, returning only in the evening. He reappeared at the front door on a wagon filled with wooden poles. The poles were twenty feet long and their ends had been sharpened. Sapphira surprised Steve at dawn going through the gate, a shovel on his shoulder. He returned in the early afternoon accompanied by Aaron Posner. Sapphira offered them coffee and Aaron filled her in.

"That's it! We have dug twenty holes and tomorrow we can plant the first post."

"What y'all doin' with those dang wood poles?" Sapphira asked.

"Auntie," said Steve, "I promised Betty we gone have 'lectricity so she could listen to the radio. If the mayor ain't doin' his job, then we the ones gone take care of it."

The old woman watched the two men, the White tailor and the Black roustabout. Nothing would stop those two.

"If it fo Betty, make sure it done right," she said.

*

At first, the locals paid no attention to the holes along the pavement, dumbstruck at the sight of the White man wielding a shovel and pickaxe. In less than one week the street was lined with poles, planted at regular intervals, and the locals began to get excited. Aaron called an electrician to check the accuracy of the installation; large wires snaked from one end of the street to the other, going under doors and walls.

371

The mayor, Richard Thompson, was eager to take ownership of the project, which hadn't cost the municipality a penny. He appeared one evening, surrounded by policemen, and inaugurated the new power line. He gave a brief speech which no one really listened to, and left. Night fell, the first bulbs came on, light could be seen through the windows of the shacks.

Steve had invited Aaron and Rachel to celebrate the end of the work. The radio was on the kitchen table. Steve turned the knob, searching for a station, and fell upon a song by Charley Patton. A rich and gritty blues. At the end of the piece a voice announced that the singer had died the day before, near Indianola. In her cradle little Dorothy cried out, as if moved by the news.

V

"You may bury my body, ooh
Down by the highway side
So my old evil spirit
Can get a Greyhound bus and ride."

ROBERT JOHNSON
"Me and the Devil Blues"

Mississippi, February 1946

The snowflakes graze the asphalt and die. A military convoy rolls toward the border. The wipers sweep away the powdery snow. Under tarps, uniforms, stainless steel canteens, boots and helmets will no longer be used. The snow has sounded the armistice. The war is over. Flat, white areas muffle the furrows, silence rolls over the plain as on the felt of a billiards table. The Delta greets the frost with open arms.

Abraham's cheek is glued to the glass. His striped jacket is filled with lice and bedbugs—the vermin are everywhere, like the flakes falling on the other side of the bars. The guards have confined the convicts to their dormitories, lest they take advantage of the blizzard to escape. Inmates in striped uniforms watch the falling snow. Abe has no intention of escaping. He is going to be released next week. He thinks of the grave of his father, old Doug, covered by crystals from the sky.

A cry runs up his back, dull shocks, supplications. Surely a poor convict whose pants have been pulled down and who's about to be taken. Abe doesn't turn around. The tall watchtower in the courtyard is invisible under the frozen padding. It could snow like this for months, nothing would cover the horror he has experienced within these walls. The cries behind him have ceased, only sighs, hissing, like a body being dragged, remain.

*

The Trinity Church of Zion has never seemed so close to the clouds. The roof, the overhang, the front are covered with a miraculous carpet. Rosetta struggles to move forward, her head emerges from a thick wool coat. Each step is a trial. With her chisel-carved forehead, she looks like a statue trying to reach the forest from which it came. Miss Brown is alive. She herself might doubt it, when her eyes can no longer distinguish the shining of the lamp from the darkness of night. She's alive and she and Sapphira are the only ones left to attest to the snows of the past. The snowflakes take refuge in her open palm. Her voice resounds, hoarse from the centuries:

"You will no longer be named abandoned, your earth will no longer be named desolation. Your land will be called wife, yes, my God, the earth will have a husband!"

Hands are placed on her shoulders, familiar and respectful.

"Grandma, you should go inside."

The old woman turns around. Elias looks at her with the tenderness of a son, rather a great-grandson.

"I still gots to go round one mo time."

"Y'all can finish later. Come on now, I put a log in the stove."

Rosetta allows herself to be guided toward the wooden door.

"I's happy to go in, but I wants y'all to play me a tune on the organ."

"What sorta tune?"

"Well, you know, the music y'all play when you thinks you alone."

"Jazz?! But will the good Lord like it?"

"Course He gone like it, He got good taste!"

The copper filaments carry the incandescence to the four corners of the room. Steve keeps his hand on the switch for a moment. Through the window the snow is falling in all its majesty. His temples are white, too, his reward for the years that have passed. His face is serene, he slept enough to dispel the fatigue he accumulated on the docks. Steve goes into the sitting room and steps on bones and a pile of rags. That silly old woman Sapphira continues to confuse the house with a witch's lair. She must have gotten up in the middle of the night again to prepare spells that no longer interest anyone.

Steve goes up to the radio placed on a side table. The wooden case polished with beeswax shines under the glow of the lightbulb. Listening to the news on the evening radio shows with Dorothy and Sapphira are the best moments of his short visits home. And in the past three years the Hertzian airwaves have been his only link to Joshua. The little family listens religiously to the news of the war, the advance of the troops, into Sicily, then France and now the ruins of Germany. Since he joined up, Josh has written only three letters that took months to arrive. The last one, in the fall, announced his likely return before Thanksgiving. The Thanksgiving holiday had passed, then Christmas and the New Year, and Joshua was still away from his family.

Steve stopped fiddling with the airwaves when he heard the scratchy voice of Robert Lockwood Jr., his favorite bluesman. The King Biscuit Show was an unmissable event; Sonny Boy Williamson II, Pinetop Perkins, and the most eminent offspring of the Delta appeared on this show sponsored by the famous flour maker. Steve did a dance spin and poured himself a cup of coffee. Pinetop launched into a virtuoso solo on a battered piano. Steve sat down to sip his coffee and passed his hand over his belly which peeked out from under his shirt. He had put on more weight and Dorothy, who had inherited her mother's tender irony, had not failed to point it out. The girl was at school, and Sapphira was probably cutting the throat of a rooster at her cabin in the middle of the woods, where she would still go, whether it was raining, windy or snowing.

The radio continued with "After You've Gone." Bessie Smith's voice rose up, almost cracking:

. . . You know I've loved you true for many years
Loved you night and day
How can you leave me, can't you see my tears?

Within seconds, Steve found himself back in the shabby room he shared with Barnabas Thibodeaux on Nelson Street. Barnabas truly worshipped Bessie. He spoke of her like a saint, and when he learned of her fatal accident on the road to Clarksdale, he had wailed like a baby. In hindsight, Steve had concluded that it was the death of the singer that had hastened the decline of his old friend. Barnabas, the poor guy . . .

Steve stood up. His brain rewound the tragedy with pitiless clarity: the gigantic winch, the belt unwinding at full speed, and Barnabas's arm trapped. Steve, helpless before his friend's shrieking, his blood covering his shirt, his pain-stricken face and eyes that understood that everything was lost. The inevitable amputation. The painful weeks of convalescence. Barnabas's silence and his desolation at no longer being able to stroll around. The girls who turned away and the days of waiting among the cockroaches. Often Barnabas woke up with a start, turned on the light and looked for his phantom arm on the floor. One evening, Steve had found the room empty. No note, just the box of marijuana, like a final wink. He had searched for his friend on the streets of Greenville for a long time. He ran into him one afternoon begging on the corner of Nelson and Shelby, filthy and stoned out of his mind. Steve hadn't dared to approach him, and said a mute farewell.

Steve turned off the radio and went into the bedroom. The box of weed in the nightstand drawer was the only thing he kept from those days, which he thought of fondly, because he was young and spirited and Betty was still alive.

The snow had stopped sprinkling the landscape, and the sun had pierced through the fog. A beautiful winter sky. He went out on the porch, in an undershirt and without shoes. His co-workers on the docks, no longer able to make fun of his thinness, now nicknamed him "buffalo skin." He rolled a joint with fingers that had been damaged by constant contact with ropes and metal. He looked at the white coating that covered the yard. And to think that Betty died before she could see the miracle of stubborn snow on this damned earth. Steve lit the joint and took a puff which he held in his lungs for a long time before releasing it into the freezing air.

Dorothy was running down the path. Her joy kept the wind and frost at bay. As soon as Miss Baldwin, her English teacher, had announced the soldiers would soon be returning home, the girl had ceased to be interested in anything else. She had climbed over the school's brick wall not worrying about the whistles behind her. Next week Joshua would be back, he and all the heroes who had gone to fight the swastika monster. The warriors would all be there, in the middle of the streets, and they could see them, touch them, hug them . . .

Dorothy stumbled on a root concealed by the snow; the pain didn't break her smile and she kept running, like a dove ahead of spring. She tried to remember as clearly as possible the facial features of her big brother. She was scarcely eight years old when Josh had gone through the front door, his backpack on his shoulder, headed for the recruiting center. The last time she had seen him, in front of the town hall, he was in uniform, among the other Black volunteers. She remembered the band playing "The Star-Spangled Banner." She had not taken her eyes off her brother, admiring the defiant way he looked up at the starry flag.

Dorothy slowed down at the edge of the woods. A fine mist covered the leaves. A deep silence. She walked to the clearing. Her grandmother's cabin was deserted. She turned back to the road along the river. The sun was shining and the snow was beginning to melt on the pavement. Passing through the gate to her house, Dorothy remembered she had left school without permission. She was convinced that the news she was about to tell her father would absolve her. A grassy and heady fragrance, carried by the wind, wrinkled her nostrils. Steve stubbed out his cigarette and came to greet her with open arms.

How to tell her? How to explain the abyss, the very impossi-
bility of thinking? Aaron hung up the phone. He didn't know
any more than he did yesterday and, to tell the truth, no more
than the year before. He didn't know anything about the fate
of his children. He prayed that they were alive, but when
lucidity prevailed over hope, he begged that they didn't suffer
too greatly before dying. How to tell Rachel that this latest
phone call to France had brought nothing new?

Aaron wished he could go out without going through the
sitting room where Rachel was waiting for him, not him, her
husband, but the messenger, the one who was finally going to
tell her what she wanted to hear: Myriam and Karl are fine,
they are in Paris, they have obtained a visa and are about to
board an ocean liner headed for Long Island, they should be
here just before Purim. Aaron felt even less useful than a raven
of ill omen: he spread only emptiness, uncertainty. No one had
had word of their children since they had fled Belgium. The
almost daily calls to Europe were costing them all the profits
from their shop; they had had to sell the Nash and, while the
snow was piling up in front of the door, they were economizing
as much wood for heat as possible. Aaron, who cut dresses
out of gorgeous pieces of raw silk, had only a patched jacket
to wear. This poverty was the only way to endure the wait.

Aaron resolved to face his beloved, her eyes had turned
gray from crying. Rachel was sitting in the chair, wrapped in

a blanket, her dull hair cascading over her shoulders. Aaron told her he had spoken with the head of an aid society that organized the return of deportees to Paris. Hundreds of people were still arriving, and the Lutetia couldn't hold any more, but survivors were housed elsewhere, in Red Cross barracks or with individuals. They shouldn't lose hope, absolutely not.

The bus is full. In the back, in the section reserved for Coloreds, they are squeezed together, sharing their smells, their weariness. Joshua is back in good ol' "Miss'ippi." He has just spent three years under the stars and stripes, every second risking his beautiful black skin, but just a few dozen miles from home he still can't set his buttocks down where he wants. He remembers the Metro and trams, in Clichy and Montmartre, the smiles of Parisians, and especially Parisian women. He would never have believed it possible that so many Whites could be so friendly. He rummages in his military bag and pulls out a crumpled magazine. Between two advertisements for cigarettes and toothpaste there is a pin-up with shapely legs. Joshua concentrates on snippets from his happy days. He experienced his first sexual encounters in the arms of girls with milky skin; with them it was not just a question of money, their caresses didn't lie, nor did their tears when he left.

Joshua looks out at the plain and the wooden shacks along the roadside; apart from a few modern cars and more tractors, nothing much has changed. If he dared talk to a blond woman here, war hero or not, there was no doubt they would hang him from one of the trees along the road.

The bus stopped a short distance after Tutwiler. A guy in his thirties—cast-iron shoulders, square jaw, carrying a canvas rucksack—climbed aboard. The guy took his time buying his ticket and counted his change again. It looked like he was discovering the world, that he was simple or that he had taken a Benzedrine pill. The passengers on the bus looked at him distrustfully, the guy didn't seem to notice, and eyes passed over his smooth, hard face. He went down the center aisle and stopped at Joshua. With a nod, he sat down.

"Thanks, my man."

"No problem, bro', long as you Black, you still have the right to sit here."

"You bet I Black! Mo than all these others, actin' like fuckin' plantation owners!"

The guy had spoken as loud as possible, ready to confront anyone. He stuck out a hand cooled by a long stay in the wind, firm and roughened by handling a pickaxe.

"Name's Abraham. Abe, for the right guys."

"Joshua. My pals call me Josh."

"Josh, that fine . . . "

Abe gestured to the magazine sitting on Joshua's lap.

"That Elizabeth Grable on the cover, right?"

"Yeah, luckily she were there at the front, at night, helping us sleep . . . You comin' back from the war, too, bro'?"

Abe hesitated. His neighbor's face expressed no preconceived notions and his gaze was frank.

"Nope. I done a stretch. At Parchman. I done fifteen yeahs."

"I see," said Josh. "Y'all musta fought hard, too, then."

The two men fell silent. The snow covered the hills, the embankments, and the fields. The fences sectioned off a land owned only by the ice.

"I's gettin' off at the next stop," Joshua said. "Where you stayin'?"

"I gone stay with an aunt who have a house down by Lake Cormorant. But first, I gone to town to the cemet'ry."

"Who you gone see down there?"

"My daddy."

"I gone see my mama. If y'all want we can go there together then go our own way after."

"That fine . . . "

A few miles further on, the snow had melted. The bus braked at the roundabout, just before the bus station. Joshua walked up the aisle behind Abe and put a sure foot on the land of his birth.

*

Protected by the bulges of the plain, saved from the flow of people, the cemetery preserved intact the treasure that had fallen from the sky. Joshua and Abe walked through the gate in silence. They skirted the graves in the section reserved for Whites, passed the great elm whose branches creaked under its snowy burden. Joshua recognized the location of his mother's grave. He stopped and Abe passed behind him.

Joshua knelt down and brushed the powder off the cross, until a last name and a first name appeared. On the ground was a wreath of holly, studded with artificial roses. So someone was still honoring the memory of Dorothy Payne. Joshua was about to speak to the deceased, as he had done since he was a boy, but he only had stories of shells, stretchers, mutilated friends and annihilated enemies to tell. The dead don't want to hear that.

Josh stood up and watched Abe brushing off the crosses with his palm, one after the other, bending over and standing up, looking dejected. He joined him in the middle of the graves.

"What yo daddy's name?" Josh asked.

"Doug. Douglas Brown Jr. But I don't see his name anywheres . . . "

"Did yo daddy have any cash saved?"

"Nothin' at all. He had a Terraplane, but he had to sell it. The last few years he come see me by bus. Why you askin' me that?"

Joshua gestured to the common grave, whose boundaries were marked by simple upturned stones like a checkerboard on the snow.

"If he had no dough, he prob'ly buried there."

Abe ventured into the territory of the penniless dead. He stomped on the snow and turned back to Josh.

"I reckon you right, man. Old Doug must be down there. Anyways, he were too humble to want a grave all to hisself and he loved company . . . Oh, and then shit!"

Abe was breathing through his mouth, his fists clenched, his voice tearful, but his eyelids remained dry.

"Okay, I gotta get goin'. I gone go downtown Sat'day night, seems there be a new club at the end o Main Street. If y'all wants to join me."

His combat boots stomped on the thick snow. Joshua warmed his hands against the cloth of his parka. A group of young people were joking and smoking cigarettes in front of the Jenkins grocery store. A lady dressed in an elegant coat smiled at him. He recognized Ada, little Ada. The girl had become a young woman sure of her charm, a real "baby doll." The boys at her side, as frumpy as peasants, stared at him jealously and with some fear. Josh, the whore's son, the witch's protégé, was now a bona fide war hero.

Crossing the boundary marking the town's White enclave turned out to be almost as frightening as crossing no-man's-land under gunfire. Joshua adjusted his beret and walked trying not to look weak or arrogant. He would have to forget the war and relearn how to be a resourceful young Negro; it was a question of survival. The grocer had given him Joe Hives's new address. Joe had sold the saloon to an idiot who went bankrupt the following year. Joshua stopped in front of a wooden house wedged between tall stone buildings. He knocked on the door. A deep voice told him to come in.

Joe Hives took a step back when he saw the young man on his doorstep. He didn't say a word and showed him into the sitting room. The room was as quiet as a wax museum whose figurines had vanished—no trace of dust, no ripped curtains, no wrinkle in one's memory. Joshua immediately recognized his mother's rosewood mirrored chest against the back wall, and on the marble top her perfume bottle with the vaporizer; through the half-open door of a wardrobe some dresses were hanging.

Joe gazed at the young soldier with a pained smile. He rummaged in the wardrobe, pulled out the Parabellum cartridge, and handed it to Josh.

"I don't reckon you in a rush to use it," he said.

"Maybe one day," Josh replied, thrusting the cartridge into his pocket. "They ain't no shortage o bastards."

The former roustabout passed his hand over the young fighter's cheek. "It hard to see you agin, son. I is happier than y'all can imagine, but . . . "

"I understand. I come back later."

"Y'all ain't stayin'? I kin offer you a beer, I got a fridge now."

"Nother time . . . "

Joshua, standing in the doorway, turned to Joe.

"You the one put the wreath on her grave, ain't you?"

"I go see yo mama ever'y day. If you arrived two hours earlier, that where we woulda met."

Night had fallen, barely overtaken by the streetlights. Joshua walked past the Posner's shop, which was still lighted. He thought of knocking on the door but told himself he needed to follow a certain reunion hierarchy. At the corner of the street he passed a White man, about fifty years old, pasty face, who looked him up and down. The man stood at attention. Josh returned his salute and hastened to find the narrow streets of the shantytown.

James Conrad stood in the middle of the sidewalk, his chest sticking out, his hand at his temple. The sight of the young Black man in uniform gave him a contradictory feeling of joy and despondency. James walked to his car. A growl came from under the hood; he forced the ignition key and pressed the accelerator. The engine seemed to be flooded with a greasy, icy reflux that had crippled the Buick's valves. James persisted until a sickly gurgling made him understand that all was in vain. The cold inside the car brought vapor out of his mouth. He lit a cigarette. In the passenger seat was the empty leather halter of his old mare. To save Molly, last summer, he had attempted the impossible, bringing in veterinarians from neighboring counties at the price of gold. In the end, he had decided to let her go with a bullet in her heart. Molly was over forty but James thought she was eternal. He had burned her on a pyre in the middle of the paddock, like a sacred mount of the Ulster legends, sobbing and keeping vigil all night until her ashes had scattered in the dirt.

James Conrad rummaged through the rack in the door and took out an envelope tied with a ribbon. He opened it with numb fingers and reread the announcement of the birth of his nephew, Matthew, Ellen's son. His sister had married a fellow from Austin, the heir of a family of bull-breeders, a boastful and self-confident Texan. Throughout the wedding banquet James had refrained from punching him in the face, while the pissant allowed himself to criticize the strategy of the troops in Europe, and to mock the planters of the old country who persisted in cultivating cotton when prices were plummeting. At least Francis Conrad, the patriarch, had had the satisfaction of seeing his daughter married before succumbing to a heart attack. When he had buried his father a few months after the wedding, James had not shed a tear.

He got out of the Buick and slammed the door. He would call the mechanic tomorrow and have the car towed to the junkyard or he wouldn't call. If bums sought shelter from the snow inside the car or if niggers used the back seat for a fuck-fest, he didn't care. He didn't really know where his self-esteem was anymore, but certainly not in this pile of scrap metal.

James Conrad went across the town, on the White avenues, the Black back alleys, rediscovering the pace of military marches, opposing darkness only with the glow of the cigarettes he lit one after the other. He reached the entrance to his property. The gate was permanently ajar since he had misplaced the keys. No cat burglar would have wanted to enter this abandoned estate filled with brambles. His father rested under the sprawling oak. Old Clarissa was now the only servant remaining in the house; she had left a hurricane lamp burning under the porch awning. On the threshold, the accumulated dust caught in his throat. Clarissa was over eighty years old and no longer had the energy to clean the big house, making do with preparing meals and doing laundry. James went into the sitting room and dropped down into a big leather armchair.

James was slumped over, in the middle of the deserted room where shadows captured by the glow of the lantern glided by. He was the last of the Conrads. Jonathan Barrel, his partner, had retired somewhere in Florida. The estate would go to Ellen and his nephew, people who didn't know the smell of rich earth.

James Conrad heard noises upstairs. Clarissa was awake. He heard her muttering in a dreamy and choppy language. Often the old servant, an insomniac, would join him in the sitting room. She sat down on a stool in front of him, sipping a glass of brandy, and watched him without speaking. In their exchange of glances passed ardent reproaches, age-old incomprehension, aborted revenge.

Joshua was the center of attention. He may have taken off his uniform, stuck it in the back of a closet, he still remained the one who had crossed the ocean and fought for the glory of America. Joshua helped himself to another piece of fried chicken which he drizzled with hot sauce. His stomach was getting used to the pungent flavors of the South again. On his left, Dorothy gazed at him as if he were John the Conqueror himself, a Negro lord, able to ward off danger with a frown. Across from him, Steve beamed with the pride of a father, happy to see his son surpass him in strength and experience. Sapphira, seated on his right, wrinkled and almost blind, had to bend over her plate to see its contents. Josh put his hand on the old woman's; she began to smile, her face turned to the lightbulb. At the end of the table, the Posners looked uncomfortable. They had brought their own food and their own dishes. The strict observance of the Law had become indispensable, insurance so that they wouldn't founder.

Rachel watched Joshua's every move, waiting for the right moment to ask him. Finally she caught the young man's eye.

"Excuse me," she said, "did you stay long in Paris?"

"Not that long, a few weeks," replied Josh, who expected to have to talk about the city of lights and their reflections on the Seine.

"Did you see any deportees returning from the camps?"

The sound of people chewing around the table ceased.

"I walked past the Lutetia one day," said Joshua, unable to look Rachel in the face. "They was plenty o trucks with blankets for those comin' back. But I was just passin' by and don't know much mo . . . "

"You haven't heard about what happened to the Jews?" Rachel asked more harshly. "You don't know anything, is that it?"

Aaron squeezed his wife's hand and felt her pulse racing. Joshua wondered if he should answer. Yes, he knew what he had been told. But how could he tell a mother looking for a glimmer of hope?

Aaron peered at the cloudy sky through the window. He would have to learn to cherish evanescent beings, to honor the unburied dead. Steve joined him. It had been a long time since he, too, had prayed through the clouds and his love of a ghost had warmed his heart. He would teach that to his tailor friend and that lesson, once again, would pass through silence.

Sapphira had fallen asleep without finishing her sentence. Dorothy put a log on the hearth and went out. She was used to the sudden fading-out of the one she called her grandmother.

The shade of the forest had preserved the snow's perfection. The young girl ventured into the middle of the snowdrifts. The air was dry and invigorating. Crows animated the sky with their cawing, the woods were brightened by tiny beings. Everywhere the footprints of hares, sparrows, weasels. No trace of humans. The forest enjoyed a blessed respite.

Dorothy had never been afraid to step into this land of shade and silence. Sapphira had taught her the art of being accepted by the trees and animals. She passed by the ravine, a uniform layer of snow covered the trash, letting a few bits of scrap metal emerge. A little further on a stream flowed. She plunged her hands into the icy water. It tasted like bitter licorice and copper. She raised her head and nearly screamed when she saw standing before her a being of supernatural size. The shock prevented her from bolting. The giant smiled. His lips were thick and his eyelids slanted like the cartoons of Japanese in the newspapers. He was wearing a dark shirt and faded jeans; in his belt, a hunting knife whose handle protruded from its sheath. Dorothy was unable to move. She searched in the bi-colored eyes of the being in front of her for a clue to his intentions and detected no cruelty, nor that voracious desire which sometimes gleamed in the eyes of males. More than anything, the creature seemed afraid of frightening her.

"You should go home, Dorothy, Sapphira is waiting for you."

The voice was slow and warm.

"How come y'all know my name and my grandmother's?"

The giant walked away without answering. Dorothy decided to follow it along the snowy trail. Its steps did not make an imprint on the white surface. Dorothy understood that she was with a spirit and was reassured. It was probably Legba, the Master of Crossroads, the divinity from Africa her grandmother had spoken about so often.

Legba and the young girl stopped at the edge of the river, beyond the collapsed bridge. Legba sat on a pile of stones which had once served to support the bridge. Dorothy did the same, keeping a respectful distance. She was afraid when the giant took out his knife to sharpen its edge against a stone. The scraping of steel on rock became rhythmic and the young girl understood that the blade's song was the prelude to a marvelous tale.

"What do you want to do later, Dorothy?"

"I gone leave heah and nevah come back."

"And where will you go?"

"Oh, far, over yonder, to the North, where Coloreds are respected and there be work to spare . . . " said the girl, repeating what she had heard a hundred times, in the middle of streets and fields.

Legba began to stomp on the earth, the pale grass and rotten leaves.

"It's not just mud you have under your feet, it's meat. It's the flesh of us others."

He scraped the bottom of his boots with the knife, wiped it on his jeans and pointed the blade at the landscape.

"It's suffering that made all this grow. Even the stones, it's the poor fellows who carried them on their backs. You will see, when you're in the North, your spirit will escape through the window and come right back here, alongside the river."

"My spirit, that fine," said Dorothy with a bit of impertinence, "as long as the rest, it stay far away."

Legba smiled and sheathed his blade.

"I knew a guy like that," he said, "he spent his life trying to escape. His name was Bobby."

"Bobby? The guy at the gas station with pimples on his nose who think only of fiddling with gals?"

"No, another one. He passed through here a long time ago, before you were born. He was a musician. A handsome guy, oh yes."

"The Bobby you talkin' bout ain't the one sold his soul to the devil?" asked Dorothy, suddenly intrigued.

"That's what they say, yes. But the devil, he doesn't buy just anything. Bobby had something more to offer than just his soul."

"What?"

"It's a long story. And it will soon be night."

"I ain't afraid of the night," said the young girl with some swagger.

"You're not afraid of much, are you?"

Legba got up and walked through the gray water. The current was fed by the melting snow, ephemeral eddies swirled around the pebbles of the ford. Dorothy followed him, rocking from one foot to the other, following the rhythm of an imaginary jump rope.

Holy shit, this burg was ugly! Stuck in the dark glue of the past, swollen with remorse and unpunished crimes. Even the expanses of cotton had lost their brilliance; half the acres were abandoned to crabgrass, the shacks of former sharecroppers were taken over by stray dogs and bums. The Delta had suffered the great bleeding. Its lifeblood—the authentic Negroes and the tireless Negresses—had gone to inseminate the cities of the North with their courage, leaving the plain bloodless.

Joshua passed in front of the Abbot farm; the pigsty was riddled with hoof prints. Joshua continued on his way, he wanted to get shitfaced tonight, to drown his roaring memories in alcohol. He almost regretted leaving Europe, not signing up for a few more years. He thought longingly of the clandestine bars of Palermo, the cabarets of Montparnasse, the caresses of White women, and of that exhilarating sensation of finally belonging to the race of conquerors.

He walked along the river and saw Dorothy sitting on the ruins of the bridge, chatting with an invisible friend. The girl laughed, waved her arms, then froze with a skeptical frown. He couldn't hear what was being said on the other side. Night was falling. Joshua hesitated to let his little sister wander at dusk, with no other compass than her child's heart. He convinced himself that she was safer in the darkness woven with moss and ferns than in the unhealthy alleys where he was about to lose himself.

Joshua turned off onto a frost-cracked road, tried to ignore the defeated faces and the crumbling shacks of the shantytown. He found the bar Abraham had mentioned. He lit a cigarette and watched the crowd waiting for the doors to open. This night, bad bourbon and good sweat would flow, maybe blood, too.

The double door opened, emitting a surge of Chicago-style electric blues. Joshua stubbed out his cigarette and went into the bar. He had neither past nor memory. He was no longer a soldier, no longer the illegitimate son of an alcoholic pastor and a whore with a broken voice. Just a young Black man balancing on a tightrope.

The smokestacks of the steelworks were cold, the smoke no longer rose to mock the clouds. The factory had closed without notice. The end of the war sounded like an ultimate call for exile and the town seemed like cardboard décor.

Dorothy had found Legba, the accomplice spirit, near the factory. With his felt hat pulled down on his head he looked like an austere and serious Quaker. Legba scrutinized the smokestacks, as if he wanted to rekindle the flames of the foundry.

"I'm going to leave," he said. "If I come back here one day, I hope you won't be here anymore."

"Already? You never tole me how that musician died."

The Master of the crossroads allowed himself to be weakened by the child's tricks.

"Who told you he died?"

"Well, when ya make a deal with Satan, yo bones don't get old."

Legba and Dorothy passed an irrigation canal clogged with stones. Legba pointed his finger at the horizon, indicating a land beyond the plain.

"That's where Bobby's story ended, near Morgan City."

Legba sat down on a fallen tree trunk.

Dorothy sat down next to him and put her little hand on the bark.

"Bobby was playing in a juke joint in Three Forks. He was paid peanuts. I believe he was never interested in the money. He couldn't stay in one place, he had to change scenes every day and have a new bed every night."

"And who was in those beds, huh, little darlins?" Dorothy asked boldly.

"Women, yes. Good for the most part. But that night he had sweet-talked the wrong pretty lady. Her man was in the room and he knew Bobby's reputation as a player. So the guy ordered a bottle of bourbon and put poison powder in it. The guy had the bottle taken to Bobby who began drinking from the bottle like a parched man. He felt worse and worse and then collapsed, dead."

"And where he buried?" asked the girl.

"There are three graves with his name. One in Morgan City, one in Greenwood, and the other on the road to Quito. But Bobby's not in any of them."

Dorothy turned to Legba but couldn't see him anymore. She was alone, sitting on the tree trunk, in a familiar, sinister landscape. But someone was breathing a few inches from her face, she could feel the warm breath against her cheek. Dorothy waved her arms in the air but encountered no obstacle. She thought she was going crazy and started to cry.

And Legba's voice was heard one last time:

"Little sister, here is the evening and its extinguished torch. Here is the wind in your hair, here is the night searching for resemblance. Go home, little sister, before the leaves do what they promise, before the trees tell their lies.

"I wanted to tell you about the train cars leaving, the North drowned in red steel, the sunlights of Harlem, the sparkling Apollo, the beauty that tumbles out without warning between Fifth and Lenox Avenue, the dawn that covers the Bronx with sequins and tears.

"And I, older than mud, creakier than an axle, I'm talking to you about here, about the furrows of exhaustion, about the bloody sweat and the songs of convicts.

"I wanted to tell you so many more things, but there is too much weight, laws, drizzle, spit against my mouth.

"I can no longer breathe. *I cain't breathe, sister, I cain't breathe no mo . . .*

"Little sister, it is through your voice that I want to be reborn. But first, I have to inject you with the blues. The disease of living. The blues is a man who collapses and doesn't get up.

"That's how it is, little sister. That's the way it is.

"And if I'm lying, it's because the truth is even sadder, and I don't want to see you cry anymore."

Song Credits

Bessie Smith (1894–1937)

"After You've Gone," lyrics by Henry Creamer, Columbia Records, 1927.

"Nobody Knows You When You're Down and Out," lyrics by Jimmy Cox, Columbia Records, 1929.

"Careless Love," traditional song, Columbia Records, 1925.

Charley Patton (1891–1934)

"A Spoonful Blues," lyrics by Charley Patton, Paramount Records, 1929.

"Shake It and Break It (But Don't Let It Fall, Mama)," lyrics by Charley Patton, Paramount Records, 1929.

"34 Blues," lyrics by Charley Patton, Vocalion Records, 1934.

"Down the Dirt Road Blues," lyrics by Charley Patton, Paramount Records, 1929.

"Tom Rushen Blues," lyrics by Charley Patton, Paramount Records, 1929.

Willie Brown (1900–1952)

"Future Blues," lyrics by Willie Brown, Paramount Records, 1930.

William Christopher Handy (1873–1958)

"The Memphis Blues," lyrics by W. C. Handy and George A. Norton, Victor Recording Company and Columbia Records, 1914.

Gertrude "Ma" Rainey (1886–1939)

"Don't Fish in My Sea," lyrics by Ma Rainey and Bessie Smith, Paramount Records, 1927.

Ida Cox (1896–1967)

"Wild Women Don't Have the Blues," lyrics by Ida Cox, Paramount Records, 1924.

Son House (1902–1988)

"Preachin' the Blues," lyrics by Son House, Paramount Records, 1930.

"Grinning in Your Face," lyrics by Son House, Columbia Records, 1967.

"John the Revelator," lyrics by Son House, based on the original version by Blind Willie Johnson, Columbia Records, 1967.

"Death Letter Blues," lyrics by Son House, Columbia Records, 1967.

Howlin' Wolf (1910–1976)

"The Wolf Is at Your Door," lyrics by Howlin' Wolf, Chess Records, 1951.

Robert Johnson (1911–1938)

"Me and the Devil Blues," lyrics by Robert Johnson, Vocalion Records, 1927.

Additional Song Credits

"I'm choppin in the bottom . . ." Parchman prisoner song. Cited in: Alan Lomax, *The Land Where the Blues Began* (New York: The New Press, 1993).

"I ain't been in Georgia . . ." Parchman prisoner song. Cited in: Lomax, *The Land*.

"O Rosie, stick the promise you made me . . ." Parchman prisoner song. Cited in: Lomax, *The Land*.

"I seen little Rosie in my midnight dreams . . ." Parchman prisoner song. Cited in: Lomax, *The Land*.

"I'm going to Memphis . . ." Parchman prisoner song. Cited in: Lomax, *The Land*.

"Berta, Berta . . ." Parchman prisoner song by Thomas Vent. Found on YouTube.com.

"Po Rostabout don't have no home . . ." Song of roustabouts working on the Mississippi River. Cited in: Lomax, *The Land*.

"Little Sally Water." Traditional nursery rhyme. Cited in: Lomax, *The Land*.

Select Discography

BROONZY, Big Bill. *Trouble in Mind*, Smithsonian Folkways, 2000.

BROWN, Willie, with Son House and Louise Johnson. *Legendary Sessions Delta Style*, Paramount Records, 1973.

BURNSIDE, R. L. *Mississippi Hill Country Blues*, Fat Possum Records, 2000.

CARR, Leroy. *Prison Bound Blues*, Snapper Music, 2004.

COX, Ida. *Blues for Rampart Street*, Riverside Records, 1990.

HANDY, William Christopher. *Father of the Blues*, Saar Srl, 2012.

HOOKER, John Lee. *It Serves You Right To Suffer*, MCA Records, 1999.

HOUSE, Son. *Death Letter*, Columbia Records, 1998.

HURT, Mississippi John. *Spike Driver Blues*, Dark Was the Night Records, 2016.

JAMES, Skip. *Devil Got My Woman*, Vanguard Records, 1968.

JEFFERSON, Blind Lemon. *The Rough Guide to Blues Legend*, World Music Network, 2013.

JOHNSON, Lil. *Press my Button*, Suncoast Music, 2015.

JOHNSON, Robert. *The Complete Recordings*, Columbia Records, 1996.

LEADBELLY. *Sings and Plays*, Roots, 2000.

LOCKWOOD JR., Robert. *The Complete Trix Recordings*, Night and Day, 2003.

LOMAX, Alan. *Negro Prison Blues and Songs*, Legacy International, 2006.

PATTON, Charley. *Screamin' and Hollerin' the Blues*, Revenant Records, 2001.

PERKINS, Pinetop. *Born in the Delta*, Telarc Blues, 1997.

RAINEY, Ma. *The Mother of the Blues*, Documents, 2008.

REPAC, Nicolas. *Black Box*, No Format!, 2012.

SHINES, Johnny. *Standing at the Crossroads*, Testament Records, 1970.

SMITH, Bessie. *Classic Recordings*, Firefly Entertainment, 2008.

WATERS, Muddy. *Hard Again*, Blue Sky Records, 1977.

WILLIAMSON II, Sonny Boy. *King Biscuit Time*, Arhoolie Records, 1989.

WOLF, Howlin'. *Moanin' in the Moonlight*, Chess Records, 1959.

Bibliography

BALDWIN, James. *Harlem Quartet* (Christiane Besse trans.). Paris: Stock, 2012. [*Harlem Quartet*, originally published in France, is based on Baldwin's *Just above My Head* (1979)]

DUPONT, Jean-Michel, and Mezzo (illus.). *Love in Vain: Robert Johnson, 1911–1938*. Grenoble: Glénat, 2014.

FERRIS, William. *Give My Poor Heart Ease: Voices of the Mississippi Blues*. Chapel Hill: University of North Carolina Press, 2009.

GURALNICK, Peter. *Searching for Robert Johnson: The Life and Legend of the "King of the Delta Blues Singers."* New York: Plume, 1998.

JONES, LeRoi [Amiri Baraka]. *Blues People: Negro Music in White America*. New York: Quill, 1963.

KOECHLIN, Stephane. *Le Blues, les musiciens du diable* [Blues, the devil's musicians]. Paris: Le Castor Astral, 2016.

LAFERRIERE, Dany. *Pays sans chapeau* [Country without a hat]. Paris: Zulma, 2018.

LEVET, Jean-Paul. *Talkin' That Talk*. Paris: Outre Mesure, 2010.

LOMAX, Alan, *The Land Where the Blues Began*. New York: The New Press, 1993.

MARCELIN, Emile. "Les grands dieux du Vodou haitien" [The great gods of Haitian Vodou]. *Journal de la Société des américanistes* 36 (1947): 51–135.